NATION OF THE BEASTS

The Lord of the Sabbath

Mariana Palova

NATION OF THE BEASTS

The Lord of the Sabbath

translated and edited by M.L. Anderson

Nation of the Beasts: The Lord of the Sabbath

Cover design and artwork by Mariana Palova

Translated and edited by M.L. Anderson

The Mage's Lantern, LLC
P.O. Box 361012
Los Angeles, CA 90036

www.themageslantern.com

Library of Congress Control Number: 2019901271

ISBN 978-0-9992809-8-0 (Hardcover)
ISBN 978-0-9992809-3-5 (Paperback)
ISBN 978-0-9992809-4-2 (eBook)

Paperback Edition: March 2020

Printed in the United States of America

0 9 8 7 6 5 4 3 2 1

To my family.

Because family's not important.

It's everything.

Prologue

OF ALL THE STRANGE THINGS about me, there are only three I can share without the fear of being locked in an asylum: the most miraculous, I was born premature at just seven months in my mother's womb; the most worrisome, I didn't walk until the age of four; and the most peculiar, I never dream.

When I close my eyes, I just come back to life hours later, frantically escaping that trance called sleep. I convinced myself that if my nightmares were going to assault me while I was awake, at least my brain, out of sheer exhaustion, would let me sleep as soon as I fell into bed.

But I might have dreamed once. I remember something red in front of me with dark cracks forming a sea of scars. And then suddenly, I was awakened.

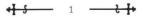

Only three years old at the time, I hadn't taken my first steps. My tutor pulled me from my straw bed and embraced me. He slipped the envelope I kept under my pillow into his pocket and rushed me out of the room. The lamps on the walls had been extinguished, and whispers filled the blackness of the hallways.

The old man raced out of the monastery and secured me in a wicker basket hitched to the only horse in the place. He blanketed me with scrolls and books that only hours before had rested on the altars. Weighted down, and with the cold penetrating my bones, I began to cry. My tutor covered my mouth with his icy hand and whispered sweet words, but when he couldn't calm me, he gave up.

He mounted the horse and struck the animal with fury. We charged forward, and I cried, struggling to understand what was happening. Screams echoed behind us, and I turned to see a thick cloud of smoke rising above the monastery.

Over time, I understood that we had fled for our lives.

The Chinese government's scourge of Tibetan culture had reached our sanctuary. The old stone structure, nestled in the desolate mountains of the Himalayas, fell in the span of a heartbeat.

That night, we embarked on a journey of more than forty days in which we experienced horrors that would drive anyone mad. But my tutor, an old and experienced monk, a perfect example of calm and patience, helped me face the hardships with encouragement and prayers.

After we crossed the rugged Tibetan border and arrived at a refugee camp in India, we were safe from the Maoists, but life became so hard that I wondered if it wouldn't have been better to die the night of the escape. We went from living in the tranquility of a humble but peaceful place to being crammed in a tiny camp with more than two thousand people in brutal conditions.

The only clue left of my life before the cold mountains and the cruelty of the refugee camp was that worn-out envelope because, just a year after we arrived in India, my tutor and any chance to discover the truth about my past lay buried in a mass grave.

I would never know why, of all the disciples, my tutor decided to save me. People said he chose me because I was a white child, a Westerner with an unusual appearance, and he feared the bloody future that would come to me if I fell into the hands of the communists. But I've always preferred to believe he chose me because he loved me like a son. After his death, another monk raised me with a much colder and more distant affection, and I felt as though I had lost a father once more.

Clinging to a blurred past I long to discover, I know this life, this desolate world of which I've been a part of for so long, has to end.

Today, fifteen years after my escape to India, it's time to flee again.

PART ONE
A MONSTER AMONG US

Chapter I
The Abyss Flashes

"Hey, Elisse."

I feel my shoulder rocking and fight exhaustion to focus on the blurred silhouette of Carlton pointing out of the truck's window. "We're here."

I peer through the fogged glass, and a strike of admiration straightens my back.

The light rain has left a layer of mist, and a damp glow paints a typical and charming American neighborhood in shades of gray.

Just like in the movies I watched on community television, a beautiful collection of elevated houses parades both sides of the street, each with their respective porches and separated by green lawns. Trees and gardens cut to perfection adorn the front of each home, and some have the flag of Stars and Stripes planted in the ground. The street is empty except for a dog roaming down the block.

A pang of skepticism invades me. I can't believe I've reached New Orleans, the other side of the world.

"What do you think?" Carlton asks and smiles so forcefully that his face might split in two.

"It's—"

"We're in one of the most desired family neighborhoods since Audubon Park is a few blocks away." Carlton gets out of the truck and gestures toward the end of the street where there's nothing but fog.

Before I can pull the door handle, Carlton circles the vehicle and stops at my window. The pink man fiddles with his keys. He shifts his eyes from the ground, to my eyes, and down again, and then he clicks his tongue like a nervous squirrel.

He and I had a bad start. When he picked me up from the airport, there was a small incident concerning my appearance. I didn't care much, but it embarrassed him a great deal. Now he's acting so awkwardly, I don't know whether he's trying to be nice to make up for his mistake, or he just can't help making things worse. For his sake, I hope he doesn't open the door for me like a gentleman, because I swear, by the most sacred thing, I'll go back to India even if I have to swim across the sea.

Thankfully, he just backs away and shakes his bald head.

I hike my mustard-colored robe and get out of the truck with my travel bag pressed against my chest. As we splash through icy puddles, I study each and every thing, less out of curiosity and more out of fear of what might be watching me from every damp shadow.

"Here it is," he says and stops in front of a house.

I form an "o" with my mouth to fake surprise. It's not that I'm disappointed. It's just different from what I imagined.

I'm used to the extravagant religious buildings of India, so the New Orleans Buddhist Center is simple enough. It's a one-story house with large windows and a blue sign glowing at the entrance with the name of the place in both English and Tibetan.

Carlton hurries to the entrance and fights with the lock as if it insulted him.

Down the street, the dog paces side to side and transforms into an amorphous spot as it drifts away. My stomach sinks when I imagine it as some kind of spirit lost in the fog.

"Got it!" Carlton's shrill voice startles me.

Inside the center, a pleasant warmth and a creaky wooden floor welcome us. Two rooms open along a red hallway with a curtain at the back. One side opens to a kitchen, and the other side opens to a shop perfumed with the sweet and familiar scent of sandalwood. The shelves display traditional wood-carved ornaments, Tibetan prayer flags, incense, Buddha statues, meditation books, and oriental music records.

I remove my thrashed sandals and recall the faint memories of my first years in Tibet. In India, we didn't even have the resources for a decent altar in the tent, so this feels bittersweet.

Carlton steps toward me and scrunches his nose. "I'll call everyone to come meet you, but if you want, there's a bathroom over there," he says and points to the door at the back of the shop.

I don't know which makes me more anxious, *everyone* or Carlton's not so subtle attempt to ask me to clean up.

"Yes … of course. Thank … you," I say so slowly that I soon realize it came off as sarcasm.

Carlton frowns and turns his back on me before bouncing down the hall in his rain boots.

I'm not trying to be rude. I have to enunciate through my accent so people will understand me, and that still causes problems. Even the flight attendant, tired of my trembling English, ignored me almost the entire trip.

As I cross the shop, light pours through the window. Peaceful Buddhas watch me from thangkas and bronze statues displayed along the red and gold walls. I close the bathroom door and face my deplorable appearance in the mirror.

I didn't have a chance to bathe before I left India. In fact, a shower is a luxury rarely afforded in a refugee camp, so along with that and a sixteen-hour flight, I probably stink like a dead cat.

It's never been easy for me to deal with people. I've never been able to fit in anywhere, even though I've tried so hard my whole life. I can never be Tibetan or Indian, and I'm not a very good Westerner either.

I grew up surrounded by Buddhist monks and apprentices who practiced one of the sweetest religions on earth, but still, I've never felt a part of that world. I admired their habits and their philosophy, but I was never a model of patience and contemplation. I'm somewhat disobedient and swear more than I should—not to mention I keep a repertoire of sarcasm on my tongue.

Either my heart or my logic never let me adopt a faith. Something about me, and about religion, keeps me from finding comfort in the invisible and pious beings watching and taking care of us. None of the invisible creatures I know are merciful at all.

After enough soap and water to become a mixture of clean face and matted blond hair, I step out of the bathroom, rubbing a paper towel over one of the lovely stains on my robe.

I stop short.

The only thing welcoming me in the shop is absolute silence. I blink a couple of times.

The shop window has darkened and become something like a black screen. On the ceiling, the faint yellow glow of a single light illuminates the statues and thangkas along the walls. The heads of the Buddhas, now faceless, are frightfully twisted in my direction. And even though they don't have eyes, I know they can see me.

I hold the air in my chest and try to keep calm, keep silent, until everything ends. But when the light flickers, my blood freezes.

Whispers in strange tongues swell around me, and the blackness of the window deepens with every passing second. I widen my eyes until they ache. The abyss is watching me.

A sickening smell emanates around me as if I were sitting on a pile of rotting corpses. I stagger against the doorframe, dizzy with disgust, and the whispers grow into a chorus of screams. I whip the door closed and back against the wall with my eardrums ringing. I close my eyes and wish with all my soul that this would end and whatever crawls out there, with who knows how many eyes, teeth, and tongues, doesn't reach me. But the abyss speaks to me. Its gurgling crosses that mouth of darkness.

Elisse.

Elisse.

"Elisse?"

When I realize it's Carlton calling me, I open my eyes. I recover the air in my lungs and inch the door open. The blood returns to my veins when I see the shop has returned to normal.

"By the gods," I say under my breath. I can't believe crossing the globe wasn't enough to escape my nightmares.

I take a moment to pace my breath and quickly wipe away the tear forming in my eye. I finally leave the bathroom in a frantic pace and eye the statues whose necks have untwisted and enlightened faces have returned.

The sounds of footsteps and doors echo down the hallway, and I watch the curtain at the back with my fists clenched and await a horde of shadows. But to my relief, two perfectly human people come out with Carlton.

"Welcome. We were waiting for you," says a man who wears the serene and bright expression of the sun. He speaks in perfect English as if Tibetan was not his mother tongue. He's almost as short as I am, though he's older by fifty years or so. His head is shaved, and he wears an impeccable crimson robe with mala beads that hang from the pocket.

I take his right hand between mine and bow to touch my forehead to his fingers.

"Tashi delek, Geshe-La," I say in a soft voice.

He must be Geshe Osel, a good friend of my first tutor and the director of this center.

Over Geshe's shoulder, a plump woman with black hair streaked with gray, beams at me with bright enthusiasm.

"Hello, hello, welcome," she says with a smile and extends a ceremonial scarf before me.

I lean over for her to drape the khata over my shoulders, and I offer a shy smile.

She steps in front of Geshe and encloses me in a powerful hug that leaves my arms dangling and my heart racing.

She finally lets me go.

"My name is Louisa," she says and taps her chest gently with both hands as if she were standing before a small child. "I'm very happy to meet you, Elisse. Look how tiny you are! I hope you're hungry. Today we're having a dinner in your honor."

Her smile grows like the waxing moon on the face of the night. Not a single display of disgust or pity. A sudden tenderness rises in me along with a slight regret for not returning her embrace.

"Many thanks," I say. "You've been so kind. Forgive me if I am a burden on you."

"Don't apologize," Geshe says. "It's a pleasure to do a favor in memory of Geshe Palden. So, please make yourself at home."

Louisa takes my arm and leads me to the other side of the curtain to show me the interior of the house full of Buddhist images. An emergency exit at the end of the hall leads to the garden, and the room next to the exit fills the entire house with light.

But it's the "library" that steals my breath. In the room, a bookcase occupies an entire wall, and there's a bed, a bureau, and a small lamp, everything to turn this place into a bedroom.

My own bedroom.

Smiles climb up my back, and either the room heats up, or the reality of my new home warms me enough to burn my cheeks.

Chapter 2
Hungry Creatures

It seems Elisse has brought a hurricane in tow. Since he set foot here, the icy breath of the sea has begun to blow over the great sorceress New Orleans. Spits of rain threaten to conjure a storm as if the boy, more than a human, were a dark omen of what awaits this land blessed by spirits.

I whip my spine and strike one of the many clouds swirling in the sky to fix my eyes on the earth. For centuries, I have remained vigilant over the inhabitants of these swampy lands and know almost what they think and feel. And for the first time in a long while, I focus on something peculiar: a pickup truck swerves from the road to enter the open field. Damp earth drags beneath its tires and splashes mud over its polished red skin.

The vehicle enters a wooded area, and I slip into drops of rain to descend to the earth and move closer to the powerful vehicle. The massive cargo in back of the truck rebounds at each pothole and spills a little more of its contents over the metal floor. By the way in which Johanna wrinkles her nose, the light rain does nothing to alleviate the smell.

My young Johanna, my little girl with the violent heart and gentle eyes, you growl each time you hit your head against the window, though you dare not complain about it. You know perfectly well that even if your skull shatters the glass, nothing will persuade Nashua to take his foot off the pedal. The work must be done.

After forty minutes of driving along the ambiguous paths of the swamp, you and your companion stop at the edge of a lake surrounded by thick hair-like weeds, far enough not to sink into the ground.

The wind shakes the treetops and invites me to nest, but I have no need to hide from you or the man who accompanies you. My presence for most mortals is just the echo of a whisper.

"We can throw the bastard here," Nashua says and jumps down into the mud.

That young man couldn't go unnoticed even if his life depended on it. His muscled physique nearly overwhelms his six-foot-two frame, and he's inherited traits from the old blood I've been watching since the first settlers came to this swamp—a severe face, square jaw, and dark skin.

"Next time let me drive," you say.

"And not get here till Mardi Gras? Stop complaining and help me."

Although you step down carefully, you can't avoid sinking deeper into the mud. You take a long knife full of teeth from the glove compartment along with a plastic bag—the sad, ghostly kind that swim in my rivers. You walk to the rear of the truck and tie back your dark hair in preparation for the long and unpleasant job that awaits you.

"God, it didn't stink this much when we threw it back here," you say and eye the black canvas.

When Nashua throws the tarp aside, your face decomposes in a hilarious mix of disgust and astonishment. The body has only been dead a few hours, but it's in such an advanced state of putrefaction that a small white worm crawls out of one of its nostrils.

Uneasy before the corpse that barely resembles anything born of nature, you swallow. Great antlers stand out from a pile of flesh, and the creature's elongated face is petrified in a humanlike grimace.

"Don't get sentimental. You know he wasn't with us." Nashua points to your forearm wrapped in a bloodstained bandage.

You shrug and pass the jagged knife to Nashua. He saws off the corpse's horns as if they were branches of a tree and lifts them before his eyes. "We can't sell them. They're already porous," he says and tosses the antlers.

He examines the carcass more closely, and a faint smile crosses his face. He grasps the creature by its severed stumps and, in a single pull, throws it into the mud as if it were a simple sack of flour. Organs spill from a tear in its bloated stomach, and you leap out of the way to avoid a bath of rotting fluids.

Nashua chuckles as he drags the body by its underarms into the swamp, leaving a trail of blackened blood. As impressed as I am proud, I smile. That creature must weigh nearly a half ton.

You trace the muddy organs back to the truck bed and squeeze your eyes until spiders crawl from the corners. My poor girl. No matter how many corpses parade in front of your foggy eyes, you'll never get used to the blood and guts.

"Bring those guts here," Nashua shouts, amused by your expression. "If we leave this shit in Tared's truck, he'll make us clean it with our tongues."

You know this is more of a warning than a joke and gather the bloody organs in the plastic bag. Your face twists each time a fleshy mass slides between your hands. When you discover a severed finger, a new retch rises, but you contain the vomit at the back of your throat. You know to whom the finger belongs and place it in the plastic bag.

Nashua raises the massive carcass to his shoulders, indifferent to the mess ruining his leather jacket. He advances as far as the ground allows and heaves the corpse into the muddy waters. The surface stirs with swaying spines, and he smiles as a pair of alligators swim in the direction of the corpse.

With the bag of guts sloshing behind you, you reach your companion and then empty the filth into the water. Afterward, you compress the bag and stick it in your jacket pocket. Nashua pats your head, sending sludge sliding down your forehead.

"Pig!" you shout.

Nashua laughs and endures the sharp blows you give to his arm.

Tired and covered in filth, you are both satisfied with the job and certain there will be no trace of the body. But just as you climb in the truck, you look at each other. That horrid mess is still fresh in the metal bed.

I feel for you. Despite your attempts, you'll end up cleaning that precious metal monster in the most unpleasant of ways.

✦ ✦ ✦ ✦

THE NATURE RESERVE near New Orleans is one of those mystical sites where the simple croak of a frog grants enlightenment. For good reason, the people who oversee and protect the land don't allow visitors to camp within its boundaries. They take meticulous care of the swamp as it has suffered many scars from irresponsible visitors and insatiable hunters.

There are also quiet places in which no person may enter except the park rangers and select individuals. So, the refuge of the swamp, built in a leafy area north of one of the reserve's large lakes, remains private and inaccessible to curious tourists. And it's right there where you and Nashua go.

I follow you through the steeper trails of the marsh and into the dense forest where you land at a clearing.

The village consists of five old but well-preserved cabins, armored by a wall of trees, with a stone fire pit at its center. On the lake behind the cabins, a moored fishing boat rocks against the pier.

The truck's tires rolling over the gravel announce your arrival. A man with autumn-colored hair and a bushy beard approaches. He's a few inches shorter than Nashua, but his stature is just as intimidating.

"How'd it go?" he asks with a smile in display of his usual good humor.

"Dropping that son of a bitch took longer than we expected," Nashua answers with a sharp tongue as he brushes the dried mud from his clothes. "Luckily, we didn't run into anyone."

"Things have been quiet here," Julien says. "I guess no one heard what happened."

"And Grandfather Muata?"

Julien's face grows somber. "He went completely blind at dawn shortly after you left."

Nashua releases a thunderous blow to the vehicle that only hours before he treated with so much care. He stares at the dent left by his fist in the metal. "Fuck. Just what I need."

Julien laughs at the misfortune of your companion but instantly clears his throat after receiving a threatening glance.

"What are we going to do? If Grandfather dies—" You bite your lip when you realize the gravity of your words.

The respectable Old Muata, despite living through his ninth decade with astonishing tranquility, leans out each day, little by little, to a diffuse threshold for the living. And that's become as painful as it is inconvenient for everyone on the reserve.

"I'm going to check on him," you say.

Nashua closes his hand around your wrist like a shackle. "No, Johanna. Go to Mama Tallulah and see if she needs anything."

Your throat burns to reply, but you don't have the guts to challenge him, so you nod and obey the order like a tame pup.

Nashua locks his eyes on your back until you enter the cabin of the woman who, even without bearing children, everyone calls *Mama*.

After you slam the door, I stay close to Nashua. A perceptible sadness rises in him when he sees where Julien's ring finger should be, there's now a ball of bandages and healing herbs.

"Aww, don't look so worried. It'll grow back," Julien says.

Concern washes from your face. "You're an idiot. That thing bites off your finger, and you act like it's done you a fucking favor."

Anger overcomes you once more, Nashua. A pity. I like your stern face crumbling to calm—a privilege reserved for those who know how to soften you.

You shake your head and walk toward the cabin where Old Muata rests. I follow closely. You gently knock on the door of the oldest cabin and compose yourself before entering. The door closes in my face, so I slip through the cracks.

Your great-grandfather sits in a wheelchair and faces the wide window of his room, surrendering to the dim light slipping through the clouds. He wears his long white hair tied in a tail.

I slide up the wall and sink into the window glass to see his face. Tiny blue crystals now cover his pupils. I extend before him, but to my disappointment, he doesn't sense my presence.

Despite his body being thin and fragile like the stem of a flower, his face possesses an intimidating dignity that bends your thick back. Like a small child, you sit on the floor next to Old Muata and feel for a moment the tenuous cold surrounding him.

"How are you, Grandfather?"

"Disoriented," Muata replies. "I never imagined that by going blind I'd lose so many of my abilities. I must be a burden for the tribe now that I'm of no use."

"Don't say that!"

The old man reaches out and gropes for your shoulder. When he finds it, he gives it a subduing squeeze rather than a caress, and you shake your head in embarrassment.

"Forgive me. I didn't mean to speak to you like that."

"You've always been my most trusted boy. And that has nothing to do with you being my blood family."

"Grandfather, I have no words—"

"Then, do not speak. Words spoken without purpose do not deserve to be heard."

You lower your head. Unable to look into your great-grandfather's eyes, you grapple with how much has changed since you and Johanna disposed of the body.

"They say when you lose your sense of sight, the others become more acute. But I've discovered that's not always the case. I've lost something more than my magic, boy. I'm also losing my ability to hear, to feel. At this rate, in a few months, I'll be as useful as a fallen log." The old man fingers a small crow skull hanging at his chest.

"Ridiculous. We need you more than ever," you say.

"I know, son. But when the earth calls, one must return to it. There's no choice."

"What will we do without you, Grandfather?"

"What our blood has done for thousands of years when they lose a part of the *Dreamcatcher*. Sew the holes."

You start to speak, but the old man raises his palm to silence you, and then he moves that same hand to the window and presses on the glass right over me. I stare with fascination at Old Muata, whose muted gaze bores a hole through me.

"Before darkness surrounded me, I had one last vision," he says.

"Another invader?"

"It might be. But now I'm so doubtful of my abilities, I hope for our own sake that I misread the message."

"Should Tared organize a search?"

"No, do not spread the words I tell you, much less to him. He already has enough things to worry about."

To your amazement, your great-grandfather stands up. He staggers and feels through space to orient himself in his own darkness. You don't dare move a finger to help, as it would only offend him.

"Nashua," Muata says and finally settles on the edge of the bed. "The hurricane may have brought with it something other than rain and fog. At dawn, before losing my sight, I was awakened by the smell of bones."

"Bones?"

"Yes. I've never sensed something like this in my life, but I am certain. And that's not all," he says. "I felt the shadow of a very old tree dying. Then, I saw an eye, huge and white, peering through glass. And the moon falling into a mouth, an opening into the infinite bowels of the earth."

"Have you figured out what it means, Grandfather?"

"I could not investigate further since I was blinded after having such a horrible vision," Old Muata says. "Nashua, I don't know what is hanging over our land, but be alert. There may be a monster among us."

Chapter 3
A Family of Two

DEVOURING THREE BOWLS OF GUMBO without taking a breath isn't the best way to make a good impression, but it's been a long time since I could eat until I felt satisfied. Now my belly feels as inflated as Carlton's face.

As I wash dishes, I smile at the thought of Louisa scolding me for eating rice with my fingers instead of using silverware. I'm sure she did it more to help me adapt to Western customs than because she found it unpleasant. Although she has a strong personality, she is sweet, which is why I like her—maybe too much.

Geshe, on the other hand, is calm and attentive, so I'm relaxed in his presence. But I can't say the same about Carlton. Despite saying only two or three words to me, he grew increasingly uncomfortable during dinner and looked at me as if I were a circus animal.

After I finish my chores, I practically skip across the kitchen at the thought of returning to the library before Louisa and Carlton come out of the office. I've had enough of that pink man for a whole day.

But all my thoughts vanish when I enter the hall and face the darkness of the Buddhist shop. I crawl my fingers along the wall and turn on the light. The yellowish glow bounces off the inside of the room. To my relief, each Buddha has its respective face as if that terrifying experience never happened. In my twisted world, things going back to normal is typical. So far, my nightmares haven't appeared in the same place twice.

I shake my head and enter the room. I can't believe this space is for me alone. It's small, but compared to the tiny tent where I shared a bed with five other boys, it's more than I expected.

A stack of clothes sits on the bed, and new boots stand on the floor. All my life I've worn monastic robes, so these gifts take me far away from that mustard ghost in the trash. My whole world has changed in a blink, and in a way, it's too good to be true.

My Indian tutor and Geshe Osel agreed that in exchange for living here and the amount of fifteen dollars a week, I have to take care of this place. When I learned of the arrangement, the long process of paperwork to move to this country as a refugee and the stacks of books and movies I binged to improve my English became pure entertainment. Not only did I have a chance at a new life, to flee my past and perhaps my nightmares, but I also had the opportunity to embark on the quest I've longed for since I was a child.

I take out the only valuable item I have in my bag—an old photograph wrapped in a yellowish envelope. In the picture, a tall, blond, coarse-looking man poses in a meadow sprinkled with flowers at the foot of a mountain. His penetrating eyes, half hidden under a prominent brow, stare directly into the camera as if they were watching me from the paper.

At first glance, my father looks like a tough guy, but when I see myself as a baby wrapped in a blanket, I imagine he was just a man uncomfortable showing his feelings.

Written on the back of the photo is the date I was delivered to the monastery in Tibet. I was only a couple of months old. My father had sent this to me some weeks before our monastery fell, so I have no idea if he sent letters after our escape.

Despite more than one person trying to convince me otherwise, I'm sure my father never intended to leave me. When I'd contemplate this picture to the point of staining my cheeks with tears, my tutor would tell me repeatedly that my father was in great danger. I guess he fled the communists, as did everyone else at that time, and that's why he had to leave the monastery, to save himself from whatever was pursuing him.

People often ask what a white man was doing crossing the Tibetan Himalayas, so far from the nearest Western country, but I haven't the slightest idea. The only person who knew was my tutor. I just hope my father is still somewhere in this country. The envelope has a faded United States postmark and nothing more.

It may seem like an absurd odyssey, but my only wish has been to meet my father again, so as soon as I learned that my new tutor in India had a friend in the United States, I did what I could to gain enough sympathy and to collect enough money for a one-way ticket. For a child that had been orphaned in a refugee camp, getting that much money involved years of effort, luck, and vigilance so no one would steal what I earned. I put in a lifetime of work in the hope of reuniting with the person I've loved since I can remember.

There are many things men of my age want, things that can be found in stores, on the streets, and even from people's bodies, although, call it loneliness or despair, sometimes the world has to treat you the worst to make you crave the best. That's why, even if it's made of just me and my father, I've always wanted a family. I've crossed half the planet to look for one.

I just hope whatever awaits me here is no worse than the demons I've brought.

Chapter 4
An Unusual Appearance

A TREMOR SHAKES MY OLD BONES, and I raise my head. I slide along the wall of the Buddhist shop, over cold portraits and peculiar objects, until I reach the crown of a statue, the best place in the lair of karmic teachings. The first thing that delights my eyes is the sweet and motherly Louisa, a woman with an Atlantean smile who carries the weight of the world behind her old, cracked lips.

"Incredible, Elisse's story, right?" you say to Carlton as you slip on your coat. "Seventeen years old, and he's already managed to cross the world on his own. And the way he speaks, he sounds so grown-up. He's very intelligent."

"I guess so," Carlton says.

"I still can't believe a white boy was lost over there. I wonder what his pa was doing in Tibet?"

"No idea."

The next words die in your mouth, replaced by a tight line between your lips.

"Is something the matter?" you ask.

The old man drops his chin. The tactic to cover the lie eating his face is useless since even his bald head turns red.

"Carlton?"

"It's Elisse— No, I mean, it's me," he says.

You raise an eyebrow and scrutinize him with deep severity. "What nonsense have you done?"

"You know me, Lou. I swear, this time I didn't mean to make him uncomfortable."

"And exactly what did you do?"

"You can't blame me." Carlton flaps his arms like a pair of wings. "Geshe never told us who was coming, and at the airport, I barely recognized the kid because of the monk's robe, and … that is … when have you seen a boy with such a pretty face and not a single hair of beard or mustache? How would I know that—?"

"What the hell are you saying?"

"Well, I … " Carlton takes a deep breath. The words finally align on his tongue. "I thought Elisse was a girl."

Your eyes expand like a pair of broken eggs, and I laugh.

"What?"

"Yes, yes. In the car after I picked him up at the airport, I asked him if he'd left all the boys in India heartbroken. You know. I wanted to be funny, but he looked at me like I was crazy and laughed. He told me he was … well, a he."

"Oh," you respond in a low voice. You don't know what to say. When you first saw the boy, you were also a bit surprised by his appearance, but your highly developed intuition told you almost immediately he was not a girl.

Even though Carlton is the kind of creature who should only open his mouth to eat, I don't blame the old man. Elisse is blessed with interesting features. Between his legs lies a male sex, but his body, small and narrow like a bird, and green eyes that soften his face, present otherwise. Yes, Elisse's androgyny is a mental challenge for beings as unperceptive as Carlton, who could never imagine the boy's appearance is much more than incomprehensible beauty.

"Yes, I know, I've screwed up," the old man says, resigned to endure his own stupidity.

"Elisse didn't look angry with you or anything like that. I'm sure he wasn't offended." You try to contain a laugh at the clumsiness of your friend, whose nervousness sweats all over his face.

"I beg you, please, don't tell Geshe," he says.

"Don't tell him? That's what I'm dying to do right now, you fool." You release a melodious laugh as you walk toward Geshe's office.

Carlton's disappointed that there isn't enough traffic on the road, because when he hears the thunderous laughter of the Tibetan master, he longs to run in the street, lay on the asphalt, and see if someone does him the favor of crushing his head.

Chapter 5
Not Everything Opens from the Outside

I SLIP THROUGH THE SHADOWS of the city to a place crying out for my attention today—the old St. Louis Cemetery No. 1. I climb to the top of the wall that delimits the small square tombs, which sit like concrete chests of drawers.

New Orleans is a constant victim of both hungry hurricanes and the raging Mississippi, so burying the dead underground is never convenient. Floods might send bodies floating like logs, so the tombs are sheltered in large funerary walls or concrete chapels placed above ground.

But today, someone unsheltered is the young and inexperienced Ronald Clarks, who shivers under the drizzle and appears quite frustrated by the mud smeared across his freshly polished shoes.

Boy, who told you to be so neat in a city where even the dead have to lift their skirts to keep from getting wet?

"Holy shit, right?" a colleague says and takes pictures of the crime that's brought you here.

"How long has it been like this?" you ask and blow warm air over your hands.

"After the hurricane warning a couple of days ago, the cemetery was left unattended, so maybe that's when they broke in." The man takes another picture of the tomb.

"You've got to be kidding."

"Did your boss say if he found anything?" he asks.

"Yeah, right. The jerk acts like I don't exist."

"Officer Clarks," a voice says behind you.

You widen your eyes at your colleague, but he hides behind his camera and pretends to find something interesting to photograph in the distance. You stifle a sigh in your chest and gesture to the man approaching you.

The man locks his eyes on the ground and follows an imaginary line.

"Good morning, detective," you say.

Detective Salvador Hoffman responds with a snarl. He slips on his raincoat and looks around at the police caps floating like little blue ghosts among the chapels. Yellow tape cordons off the area, and he scoffs at such a curious scene. It's as if his colleagues marked the perimeter of a murder scene bursting with corpses.

"Sir, what do you think of this? That is, we haven't found any footprints. The water washed everything away," you say with a thick voice.

To your annoyance, your boss is more interested in the cigarette he pulls from his pocket than by your remarks. When he lights up, the nicotine enters the detective's lungs and gives him the necessary motivation to investigate the vault in front of him. His brown irises constrict as he focuses inside the open belly of the tomb stripped of its vital organs.

Old custom dictates that once the bodies become ashes, they are placed inside urns and stacked in vaults to save space. Tourists often take flowers, stones, and even dirt from the St. Louis Cemetery because it houses the remains of many well-known figures, including the renowned Marie Laveau. But no one can explain why someone would desecrate one of the vaults to take a dozen urns and leave behind only a sheet of shattered concrete—all without a witness to the act.

This morning, Hoffman checked files and death records and discovered that the remains didn't belong to anyone famous, and with the exception of four brothers, the other dead had no relation—neither in life nor after it. The ashes were almost two centuries old, and the deceased no longer had living descendants who might be interested in taking them.

It's clear to Hoffman who might want something as useless as a pile of ashes, but something tells me his mood is influenced by the fact that you're unable to see it.

"Sir?" You wait for your boss to tell you something, anything to help you figure out what happened.

Hoffman's dark eyes stare at the ground of the cemetery.

"Did they take anything from the scene?" he asks.

"No, nothing. Everything here is as we found it. What do you think, sir?"

Hoffman sighs.

"Rack your brain, Clarks." His neck boils with redness at your ignorance. He finishes his cigarette and throws the butt into the vault. "Crazies or drug addicts do this kind of thing. The city is full of people who'd sell their mother's hair.

Investigate the neighborhoods on the other side of the river. Search the French Quarter. There are twelve goddamned urns. Think of who the hell needs something like this. It's not that difficult." Hoffman turns his back and lumbers away.

You babble and turn red with embarrassment at the dressing-down you received in front of your colleagues. I shake my head and slide along the wall to follow the detective. You wake up and run after us.

"Sir, where are you going?" you ask.

"To the office. To have you sent back to elementary school. I haven't worked more than twenty years in the police department to tell you how things should be done."

By heavens, Hoffman. You didn't even give poor Ronald a chance to be offended since you left him behind in a blink with his mouth wide open like one of those tombs.

Unable to remedy the poor condition in which you left the young man, I follow your punishing steps until we exit the cemetery and climb into your car.

You sit quietly for a few minutes and then turn on the radio. An old song by Johnny Cash plays. The man's music isn't your favorite, but when the rain worsens, anyone would take a liking to it. Even me. Because I feel quite at ease in the back seat of your car.

You sigh for the tenth time and finally accept that you're being too hard on the guy. Ronald has only been working in New Orleans for a few months, after being ripped from his home in Utah. He's a rookie and still has many things to learn about the profession and the city.

But that's not what worries you. There's a detail, something evident about the crime scene that makes you doubt your own sanity. Yet, it's better to be blind than to be insane.

You play with the steering wheel and tear pieces of plastic from the worn cover as the rain crashes on your windshield. The city's streets slowly turn into raging rivers that aspire to be extensions of the Mississippi.

Chapter 6
There Are Always Witches Here

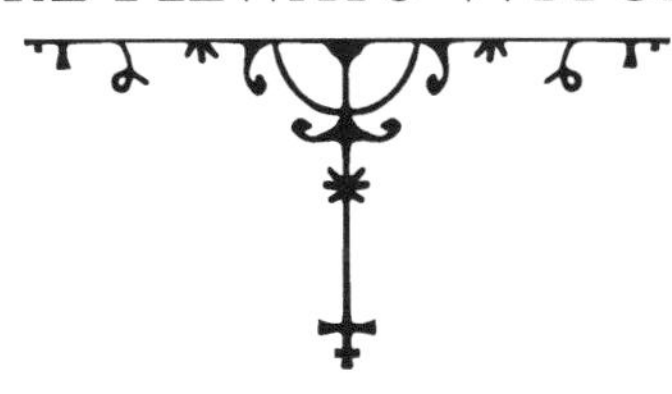

As soon as I entered the tent, the bustle that characterized the refugee camp at night was severed. Something outside moved in the grass, and my heart became a violent drum. I dropped the bowl of rice in my hands, slid under my cot to curl up in the darkness, and prayed the light of the oil lamp caught no part of my body.

At six years old, my innocence made me believe that hiding would be enough to protect me from whatever crawled outside. It circled the tent, rubbing against the tarp at my back and along the sides as if its only purpose were to torment me.

I covered my mouth with both hands and watched the fragile barrier that separated me from it. A hand with long fingers began to pull at the canvas. And then more hands began to claw at the tent, and I asked the most divine of the world to make me invisible.

The hands withdrew.

The scattered white grains mocked me. I bit my lip and sobbed quietly. I knew I would eat what was left on the floor because that was my only meal of the day. My stomach roared, but I didn't have the courage to move for several long minutes.

Finally, I crawled to the edge of the cot, far enough to stretch out my arm and reach for the bowl. I at least wanted to eat what little was left, under the protection of the cot, a place which at that moment felt the safest on earth.

Suddenly, an amorphous shadow ripped out the stakes and tore away the entrance of the tent, and I jerked my arm back to my chest and screamed.

The oil lamp rocked from the table and fell to the ground without breaking. As the dimmed flame projected dancing shadows onto the fabric walls, a stinking smell began to fill the tent, and bile burned in my throat. I wasn't alone anymore.

Wobbling from side to side, a mass of bloody flesh driven by protruding arms palmed the ground with a wet slapping sound as if it sensed by touch what lay in front of it. It had neither head nor eyes but knew where I hid. I held back a whimper as it passed over the bowl of rice and bathed it with clots of rotted blood. My heart stopped when its hands gripped the edge of my cot and climbed to stand on its limbs.

In the abdomen of that bloody creature, a face stared at me with bulging bloodshot eyes and smiled with a mouth full of yellow teeth.

I screamed and bolted out of the tent, only to be caught by my tutor. I cried and thrashed like a feral animal with that monstrous smile inside my head. The man pressed me to his chest until my energy calmed. He tried to comfort me by reciting a mantra while curious people leaned over us and watched the horrible spectacle I had become.

Despite his efforts to soothe me, to insist everything was fine, I'll never forget the sour smell of my urine-soaked robes.

It's not clear to me when I started to hear voices, to see eyes in the dark, to spy little tails that became crawling bits of flesh, but it wasn't long after I learned to walk. Sometimes I think when I stood to take my first steps and removed my hands from the earth, the abominable creatures that chase me came out of the shadows.

Often I wonder if I really see things or if these monsters are a product of my imagination, and if the place to where I'm transported in my nightmares is just an illusion that creates my madness. On my worst days, I convince myself that I'm just crazy. If those things never touch me, and they limit their presence to scaring me, they aren't real.

At least today, the supernatural beings *are* real. The city is full of monsters, or rather people disguised as them, so the streets are haunted for tonight.

I've been here for more than a month, but it's the first time I've had the opportunity to go out and explore. The storm had everyone on a mandatory curfew for several weeks, so just a few days ago, the police cancelled the alert in time for Halloween. Despite being alone with my paranoia in the rain and continual blackouts, my nightmares haven't visited me.

Thankfully, the hurricane warning has finally ended, so the city fills with life. I can see why. New Orleans's charm attracts people from all over the world. I've been told it's a permanently enchanted city.

Bourbon Street, the most famous street in the French Quarter, is a beautiful road flanked by old mansions converted into hotels, shops, and bars. Elaborate iron balconies filled with orange lights and pumpkins that have infected the city's skin, form a catwalk for creatures to go from place to place asking for sweets in exchange for forgiving tricks.

I lean against a cold lamp post to study the street buzzing with people. A neon sign with the words "Bar Louis Armstrong" shines brightly overhead.

I like this city. It's a place lost between the old of its houses and the extravagance of its people. It has a dark mysticism, different from that of India, that attracts me. Growing up surrounded by superstitions and myths from Indian and Tibetan cultures, I learned to fear the shadows, but in this place, the shadows are a part of everyday life and comfort me in an unsettling way.

Down the street, Louisa speaks with the other volunteers from the center. I've barely been able to meet them because of the storm. After a good Cajun meal and many uncomfortable, personal questions, we came to Bourbon Street, where everyone's dispersed to greet neighbors and acquaintances.

Geshe said I could explore the area on my own as long as I don't go beyond the block. And truthfully, I'm already bored of standing around doing nothing, and curiosity taps at the heels of my boots.

I pass crowded bars and souvenir shops full of masks, obscene t-shirts, hats, and straw dolls dressed in purple, green, and gold—colors that dress every shop window in the city.

I enter one of the adjacent streets, which is rather lonely, gawking at the beautiful old houses, each of a different color and design. The concrete walls are molded to look like wood and give the structures a charming, aged appearance.

A pull at my senses stops me in front of a two-story house that's been converted into a shop. On the wall, stooped in a prominent arch, some sort of doll dressed in a ragged black tunic wears an animal skull for a head and towers up to the roof.

I haven't seen a Halloween decoration on the street as creepy as this one, so I approach the doll and stand on my toes to examine it up close. The irregular texture of the bone makes me think it's a real skull, one as big as my torso. Its empty sockets look like a pair of dark chasms. Long pointed fangs, maybe from a wolf or a bear, jut out from its jaws. Above my head, "Voodoo Shop" flashes in red neon.

Voodoo. The word on my tongue tastes like wood, but smoky like when it burns.

In the shop window, a row of tiny blackened heads hooked on a wire like Christmas lights hang before my eyes. Some of the heads have their eyes and mouth stitched closed. Jars of powders, bags of herbs, and things that only could have come from my nightmares surround animal skulls that watch me from behind the glass.

Strange enough, these oddities offered as harmless toys comfort me. Apparently, it's common here to trade with bones, pincushion dolls, and deformed creatures. It's as if the shop sold my demons, and people can buy them like they buy their vegetables.

"You like them?"

I jump when a voice next to me echoes down the lonely street. An attractive woman leans against the frame of the shop entrance and pins me with her dark eyes.

She must be in her late thirties and has a youthful beauty. She wears a head wrap and a long purple skirt with a loose blouse. An extravagant number of necklaces and colorful bracelets stand out against her dark complexion.

"I asked you if you like them," she says, deepening her voice.

"Ah, I suppose."

"You suppose? Dear, you stand before the offerings of the gods. You should watch your words if you don't want their blessings withdrawn." She laughs, surely because of the ridiculous look on my face, and goes back into the shop.

There's something familiar about this woman, so I follow her with my eyes. She sways her hips, sending glances over her shoulder in a way that makes me uncomfortable, and then disappears into a back room.

I turn around to head back to Bourbon Street, but I freeze in my step.

The doll with the animal skull has vanished. Where the thing was hanging, a thick, dark stain drips down the wall. I try to remain calm, convince myself someone moved it, but when my intuition drags my eyes to the end of the block, all the sun of India drains from my skin.

The doll stares at me from under a streetlight, bathed in an orange, spectral glow. A couple of people pass behind the creature but don't notice its presence.

The thing advances toward me with shadows dragging behind it, and I close my eyes. I clench my fist and wait for the blow of putrid air and the screams of a thousand tongues.

But nothing happens.

I open my eyes.

The bone monster is gone. I scan every blackish corner. Cold sweat soaks my neck, and my stomach tightens in anticipation of that thing leaning out from the darkness.

I quake with rage. No matter how many times these demons appear to me, either in broad daylight or in the depths of the night, I'll never get used to their presence. My nightmares always take some grotesque form, torture me with stench and screams, and disappear as quickly as they arrived. There's only one consolation. They never hurt me. It's as if they just feed on my fear.

After so many years, I long for the day when I can finally get used to these beings. But how do I live with the torment of seeing things that no one else can see, and even worse, from which no one can protect me?

Once I arrive at Bourbon Street, I take a few minutes to compose myself and realize something unusual happened this time. Whenever I have a nightmare, everything becomes silent as if I entered a dimension split from what is around me. But this time, it seems the nightmare entered my world.

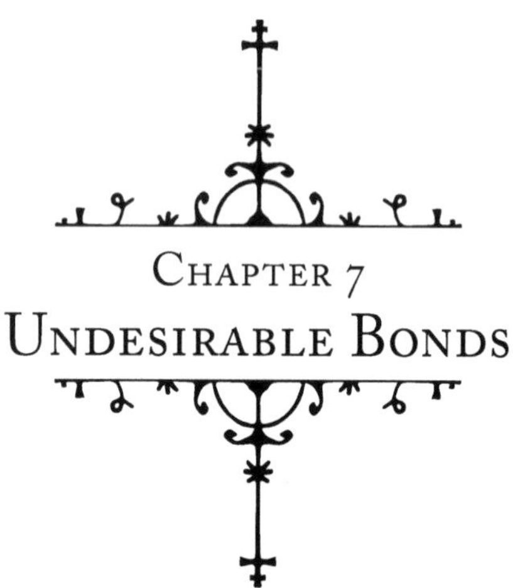

Chapter 7
Undesirable Bonds

I SPEND FIVE MINUTES pressing random buttons until the cash register pops open and crashes into my stomach. I take out a few coins, count them carefully, and pass them to the man in front of me.

"Sorry," I say without looking up, ashamed that I can't deal with an old cash register.

The man scowls. He takes the box of incense he purchased and slams the door as he leaves.

Geez. What a good Buddhist.

Thankfully, it's time to close. I switch off the entrance sign so people won't get a chance to see another display of my brilliant idiocy. I grab the newspaper from the doorstep. I can't believe I left it there all damn day. The headline across the front page reads:

STILL NO TRACE OF THE REMAINS

It's becoming clear to me that New Orleans is a city of madmen. Over a month ago, someone dug up twelve bodies, or what was left of them, from the St. Louis Cemetery, but the hurricane interrupted the investigation. Now they've resumed the case, but in my opinion, they should focus on the damage caused by the storm, not on things where there's nothing to do. The remains were so old that no one has claimed kinship with the dead.

After this news and the incident I had in the French Quarter, I have no desire to walk the mystical places of New Orleans. I'll have to stay as ignorant of this city as when I arrived.

Someone knocks on the door, and I curse out loud. When a woman's voice calls from the other side, I'm relieved I only swore in Hindi.

When I open the door, Medusa could have been standing there because I turn to stone when I see the woman from the voodoo shop.

"What a surprise. Or fate, maybe?" she says with a smirk.

She passes by me and crosses the hallway as if she were in her own house. She slithers along one of the shop chairs and casts a wide smile.

"Excuse me—"

"Did you have fun the other day in the French Quarter?" she asks.

"What? Oh, yeah. I think so." Goosebumps creep along my flesh at the thought of that night. "Can I help you with something?"

"I doubt it," she says and looks at her fingernails. "I came to see my sister, Louisa."

I thought she looked familiar.

"She's not here, but if you want, I can call her to come," I say more to get rid of the woman than to do her a favor.

"Don't bother. Just tell her I stopped by."

"Are you sure, ma'am?"

"Call me Laurele, child," she says.

I nod my head and keep my eyes on her. I usually trust women, but there's something about Laurele I don't like. I don't know if it's the way she flaunts her chest or the constant way she looks me up and down.

"You have a peculiar accent, child. Are you European?"

"Indian, ma'am."

"You're kidding. A blond Hindu?" She arranges her hair under her head wrap.

"I wasn't born there. I only grew up in that country. And Hindus are just those who practice Hinduism. Indians are the people of India in general."

Laurele laughs. "I suppose you came to New Orleans to see breasts at the carnival like all young men?"

"Women aren't circus animals," I say sharply.

To my satisfaction, her smile dies. She rolls her eyes, and I do my best not to imitate her. She gets up from her seat, and we both walk toward the entrance.

"What's your name, boy?"

"Elisse."

"Beautiful. I like you, Elisse. You should come visit my shop. I think you'd have a better time there."

"Goodnight, ma'am."

She lets out a roaring laugh and finally leaves.

I lean on the wall and direct quick glances over the whole shop. I don't mean to be suspicious, but I need to make sure everything is in place. Louisa's sister or not, I don't trust that woman.

I walk to the chair where she sat and find a small red book. Immediately, I run to the shop's entrance and call from the door, "Miss Laurele!"

The woman is nowhere in sight.

I pass my fingertips over the hard cover. The word "Voodoo" vibrates from my lips. My damn curiosity gnaws at me, but after that frightening experience in front of Laurele's shop, I don't open the book. I don't want to get mixed-up with Voodoo or Laurele, so it's best to give the book to Louisa.

✦✦✦✦

"Elisse, may I come in?" Louisa asks from the other side of the door.

"Yes, come in."

My attention diverts from the computer to Louisa, who enters the office with a smile and pats the crown of my head. She lifts her glasses from around her neck and stares at the computer screen.

I'm sure she's wondering why I can't open a cash register, but I can manage a computer fairly well.

"Immigration records?"

I smile and shake my head from side to side. It takes a minute for Louisa to understand I'm saying "yes" the way we do in India and another minute for me to realize I have to stop doing that.

"Oh, your dad, right?"

"Yeah. A few days ago, I went to the post office to see if they could identify the postmark on the envelope he sent, tell me which state he mailed it from, but it was impossible. And then it dawned on me. If I can find a list of foreigners who moved here around the time I was born or a couple of years later, maybe I can locate him."

"Heavens, it never would have crossed my mind to do something like that."

"I'm sure there are better ways to do it."

If she didn't have the idea, it's because only I can think of something so pointless. I don't know my father's last name or the exact year in which he arrived in the United States, but I want to believe that there's a photograph of him somewhere in the border records accessible to the public. It's an impossible task, but I have to start somewhere.

Louisa glares at me over her beaded frames. "You've been practicing your English. Your accent is improving."

"Thanks," I reply and make myself small in the chair.

"Geshe Osel told us that you only finished primary school, but you express yourself very well for a boy with little education," she says and glances at the pile of books beside the desk.

A slight paleness replaces the warmth of my cheeks. "English is one of the official languages of India, so I've practiced it almost my whole life."

"I don't mean that. The things you talk about. You seem less like a boy who turned eighteen yesterday."

I don't tell Louisa that if I appear mature, it's just that. Appearance. I'm well aware that inside I'm just a boy forced to grow up too soon. When you learn about the world on your own as a child, you stop appreciating it with an innocence that only a family can protect. And if you're lucky enough to see things with more detachment than anger, you set out to learn everything you can, so nothing takes you by surprise, keeps you from surviving. But that hasn't made me an adult. Not at all.

"I brought something for you," Louisa says.

"Oh, ma'am, you really didn't have to—"

"Not another word, young man. It's a birthday gift. I made it myself. And it's been much cooler with this weather, so you'll need it."

Louisa rummages through her bag and pulls out a button-down, wine-colored sweater made of wool. She extends it in front of me with an illuminated face.

A knitted sweater from an old woman feels like the most cliché gift on earth, but Louisa's gift, presented with such excitement, melts my heart.

"You don't like it?"

"It's very nice, but I'm embarrassed that you've wasted it on me."

"Oh, come on, it was no bother. You are a small thing, so I used very little yarn. Promise to wear it. The weather has been off these months. We've never had a fog last so long."

I sit blinking in disbelief. In just a few weeks, Louisa has taken on a particular role in my life. She's as gentle as she is strict. She's always attentive to me and treats me as if she's known me my whole life. In a short time, these kind gestures are as close to the love of a mother I have ever had.

"Go ahead, try it on," she says.

I take the sweater and caress the fabric. It feels kind, like her, and I turn red. The sleeves cover my fingers a bit, but even if it had six more feet of fabric, I would still love it.

Louisa's eyes grow glassy, and unable to bear an outpouring of emotion, I turn my eyes to the pile of books and the red book Laurele left in the shop. "Is it true, you have a sister? Laurele?" I ask. "She came here a while ago looking for you."

Louisa's face hardens like a rock. She arranges her glasses with trembling fingers. "That woman doesn't have a shred of shame," she says. "I'm sorry you had to deal with her. I'm sure she said something to make you uncomfortable."

"No, not at all."

"Goodness," she says and clutches her chest. "Do not get involved with Laurele. She's not the kind of company a nice boy like you needs." She squeezes my shoulder and transmits a heat that could leave a mark.

She leaves, and I go back to my room to rest. For now, I just want to close my eyes and pretend nothing bad can ever happen to me.

Chapter 8
A Landscape in the Skin

E*LISSE.*

I awaken to a chill in my bones. On the bookshelf, the red light of the clock glows four o'clock in the morning like eyes in the dark. The blanket has slipped to the foot of the bed, so I cover myself again. My heavy eyelids drag me back into semi-consciousness.

The door murmurs, and I open my eyes. I rise on my elbows and see the dim bluish light from the hallway sneaking through the half-open door. My breathing grows heavy. I'm certain that I locked the door before going to sleep.

Suddenly, the door swings open as if an invisible hand pushed it, and something crawls across the floor. I dart my eyes around the room, but the shadows remain still. I fight the impulse to turn on the lamp.

A cold breath brushes my crown, and I close my eyes. That thing's not on the floor, it's on the ceiling. I lie back as quietly as possible, holding in a terrified moan, and cover myself completely under the blanket. Every squeak of the mattress becomes torture, and I pray to whomever can hear me, may it all end soon.

The blanket rises—one edge lifts, and then another—and falls to the floor. I push a scream to the back of my throat and hold my breath.

Elisse!

Something sticks my side like a fork and tears my flesh. I cry out and leap from the bed. In a single stride, I flee the room and slam the door shut on the thousands of voices rumbling behind me. I barrel through the emergency exit and into the backyard with a scream trapped in my throat.

At the edge of the garden, I stop and look back at the darkness inside the Buddhist center. The cold wind whips my face, and warm blood runs down my side, but my eyes lock onto the swirling blackness and the giant animal skull with fangs like knives.

The bone monster emerges from the abyss.

I hop over the wood fence and run into the street. The creature cries for me, its tongue possessed by my name.

"Help! Help!" I cry, but only my voice returns in echo.

I reach a neighbor's house and beat my fist against the door. "Help, please open!" I scream. My knuckles stain the wood red as if I were punching concrete. My heart drops to my feet when I realize no one will open this door. I'm in that awful place of my nightmares.

I take-off down the street. My feet burn against the asphalt, but a fear greater than the pain propels me. The bone monster follows and quakes the ground beneath me. Through the shrubbery of Audubon Park, a fog-covered path appears like the entrance to the underworld.

This is suicide.

I cross the street and enter the undergrowth to a path flanked by giant trees. The mist thickens, and I can hardly see where I'm going or what's beyond the nearest trunk. I pass under an old rock bridge, and my body reaches its limit. The pain in my side makes it difficult to breathe, and I stumble to the ground.

"Damn, damn." I look around.

The only sounds are my labored gasps and the rustle of leaves beneath me, so I dig my hands into the earth to—Wait… soft damp soil? I've returned to the real world. But I don't let the relief comfort me, since the demon might still be out here. My senses heighten. At any moment, that creature could appear in the fog.

The wound on my side stings and pulls a moan out of me. Five claw marks slashed across my ribs prevent me from taking deep breaths. Even if I wanted to rest, nothing assures me that the demon won't come back, so I try to stand up. I have to get to the center and call an ambulance before—

"Help!" a man yells from the other side of the park. "Please, someone help me!"

Did the monster catch someone else? Impossible. I'm the only one able to see it.

My mind tells me not to be an idiot and get out of here, but my bloody knuckles remind me of the terror I felt when no one helped me.

"Shit." I clutch my side and walk toward the screams with the hope that something inside my weak body grows strong enough to make a goddamn difference for once.

The cries grow louder as I enter the park. I try to find something to defend myself against the creature, but there are only thin branches and small rocks in my path. It's clear to me. I'm going to die.

A rotten smell moves through me. My stomach turns when I stumble upon a trail of mud and bloody leaves that extends into the fog. I shuffle along the trail toward a small lake until I find who's pleading for help. I blink several times in confusion. It's not a man.

"Please, please help me." A deer the size of a cow flops around in the grass. Its belly is sliced open, and its white eyes point to nothing.

"What the fuck?" A twinge of pain throbs in my skull, and I touch my head with bloody fingers. I'm about to explode in panic. I must be asleep on my bed at the center or even on my cot in India because this couldn't be more ridiculous.

My eyes scan the area to make sure there aren't any creatures in sight besides the one begging for help in front of me.

"I'm hurt," the creature says. It moans and writhes on the ground, further opening the tear in its abdomen.

By the gods. Are those guts? I'm surprised it's still alive.

Something in the grass moves behind my back. When I look over my shoulder, fear rises over me like a shadow because all possible worlds have lined up today to drive me insane.

Out of the fog, a colossal wolf emerges and growls from deep in its throat. Delicate branches crack beneath its legs, and its heavy breath steals mine.

Its coat, neither white nor gray but a resplendent silver, darkens and takes on the color of a storm—a landscape in the skin of the beast—as beautiful as it is terrifying. Its volcanic snout with black lips issues steam, and its long bleeding fangs form rivers of lava.

"Can you speak?" I ask the wolf in a voice so calm that even I'm surprised. They say when someone's on the verge of death, they go without a care, or they go insane. I think I'm staggering between the two.

"Are you going to devour me?" I ask. I'm not sure if it can understand me.

Its blue eyes flash as if the wolf were watching lightning break through the clouds. We observe each other for so long that I feel the creature is lost in my eyes too.

"No, no, please no!" the deer screams behind me.

The silver beast raises its head, and the fur on its back bristles like sharp needles. The wolf charges and rams my wounded side, which I can barely cover with my arm, and my body is launched into the air like a doll and rolls several feet before landing near the edge of a lake.

I try to move, but when the treetops blur, I stop fighting. I'm conscious enough to watch the wolf launch at the deer and tear apart its legs, skin, and guts, but the thick fog covers the scene like a curtain closing at the height of a show.

The blood loss, the cold, and the terror overcome me like a shroud. Everything grows opaque and merges into darkness.

Chapter 9
People Who Know Too Much

When Salvador Hoffman catches the lascivious look of a young woman from across the street, he suffers a sudden but usual outburst of irritation and walks at a faster and more agile pace between two passersby.

Whether by luck or misfortune, you stop in front of a local shop in the French Quarter and fix your eyes on the brown concrete. A wave of anger boils beneath your skin. You close your eyes, take a deep breath, and vow not to kill anyone today.

You enter the shop without stopping to look at the cruel oddities. In your line of work, you've seen so many dead bodies that a pile of bones is nothing. Besides, you've spent so much time surveying this witchcraft business, I wouldn't be surprised if you've memorized the inventory.

To have a full view of the shop, I wind around an alligator skull mounted on the wall.

Poor beast. Its spirit cries for release from this cursed place.

You beat the service bell.

Footsteps clack through the back room. A woman appears from behind the curtain, and her naturally slick expression dissolves.

"How can I help you this time, Detective Hoffman?" the witch Laurele asks.

"You know what I'm looking for." You toss several snapshots on the counter. The pictures show various angles of an old human skull lying in a basin of the river. "Yesterday, a boy found this in the swamps."

Laurele casts her eyes toward me. I flick my tongue, and she looks to you again.

"And you've come to show me this because . . . ?"

"Because it was stolen from one of the tombs of St. Louis."

"You're kidding," she replies. "Aren't you looking for urns or ashes? This is a skull."

"Just tell me, ma'am." You lean over the counter. "Has anyone been selling you bizarre things lately, Ms. Fiquette?" You look around at the irony of your question.

"There are dozens of voodoo shops in New Orleans, not to mention healers and fortune-tellers. I hope, for your sake, my business isn't the only one you've come to visit."

"Things are being done according to protocol—"

"To hell with protocol, detective. I'm tired of being the first person you come to whenever a madman believes he's a Voodoo priest after a few drinks on Bourbon Street."

With a deep breath, you hold off the urge to throw Laurele on the counter and wrap your hands around her neck. "Fine. Call if you see anything suspicious," you say soberly and consider the matter settled.

It's probably for the best. If the conversation continues, I'm afraid you won't be able to control yourself.

"Go to hell, detective."

You laugh and Laurele grows more rabid. You leave the shop without giving the woman the opportunity to curse you.

She turns her angry eyes toward me, reaches into her pocket, and throws a fistful of salt into the air.

I flick my tongue and slip through the wall, but not before taking the poor spirit of the alligator with me to grant its precious freedom.

Chapter 10
The Crazy Boy

I STAND ON A BOAT floating in the Mississippi River. On the horizon, a thick, silent fog covers the city of New Orleans. The gray cloak expands upward to swallow the sky and cover the stars, which begin falling to earth in a rain of fire.

In a blink, I step barefoot on cold grass moistened with dew. The river and the boat vanish, leaving me in an extraordinary place. Shades of dark blue and jade bathe an open field as if the night fell upon the earth but not the sky. Thousands of eyes, white and bright, watch me from among the trees surrounding the land.

Graves dot the landscape. Not the graves with tombstones, but those cold cement boxes that rise above the earth like small chapels. Their wide-open bellies spill gold coins, jewels, and pearls that, despite their glistening beauty, stink of the dead. Whispers rise from the tombs and echo off the precious treasures as fog rolls like sea foam over the grass and washes over my feet. The sweet scent of tobacco fills my nose.

A crypt calls my attention. Unlike the others, it's empty, and in its open mouth, the vast darkness has no end.

I move closer.

The concrete walls are carved with the symbol X in various sizes. The symbol awakens a strange feeling in me. I want to turn around and run, but a force more powerful than my own will draws me toward the crypt.

"Where do you think you're going, boy?"

A whiplash of chills races across my flesh at the sound of the smoky voice. Slowly, I turn around. A man wearing a top hat sits atop the treasure of a tomb.

For a moment, it looks like he's dressed in black, but then I realize he has skins hanging from his waist, legs, and wrists. His flesh, as dark as oil, makes it appear as if he were dressed in a suit. Sunglasses cover his eyes, and the torn flesh of his cheeks and nose expose the white of his skull. It is here, the smoke from his cigar, from which all the fog blanketing the cemetery floor emanates.

"Have you lost your tongue?" he asks.

I look again at the grave behind my back, and now a concrete wall seals it.

I hear laughter.

The man stands up and sashays toward me while swirling a bottle of liquor he was not holding seconds ago. The smell of alcohol and rotted flesh intensifies with each step he takes.

"Believe me. You don't want to go in there. At least not yet." He passes by me and takes a deep puff of his cigar. Along his back, the bones of his rib cage peek out from torn flesh. He turns around and smiles with crooked teeth. "I'm eager to meet you, Elisse. We're going to have lots of fun." And with a snap of his fingers, flames engulf my body.

I scream as tongues of fire lick my flesh and melt my skin. The pain breaks me. I want to drop to the floor and roll, but I can't move. It's as if something's restraining me from head to toe.

"Let them burn, let the witches burn!" he shouts, dancing wildly and obscenely in front of me.

Tiny men in top hats and rotting skins rise from the treasures of the tombs and approach the bonfire I have become. They dance around me in some macabre ritual. Through the fire, I see the monstrous man remove his sunglasses. He has no eyes, just empty sockets that delight in my pain.

Smoke rises from my body, and in an instant, the glow of the fog blinds me and an incandescent light bathes me in icy coolness.

When the glare clears, a ceiling fan spins into focus, and the softness of a pillow cushions my head.

"Damn." A twinge of pain knocks my temple.

"Nurse! Nurse!"

I recognize the voice of Louisa and hear the tapping of her heels moving farther away.

A montage of images flashes in my head as a sequence of violent colors. Did I … dream? I try to catch something, a nuance of these diffuse images, but I can't remember a thing.

"Shit, where the hell am I?"

"Boy, take care of that tongue."

I turn my head toward the door and meet Geshe who enters the room with a nurse and an anguished Louisa.

"Geshe! Louisa!"

"We're glad you're finally awake."

"How'd I get here?" I ask and try to press up on my elbows. "I was in the park and—"

"Easy, son." Geshe gently pushes me back to the pillow.

The nurse checks the IV bag attached to my wrist. "I'm going to give you something for the pain," the woman says and draws fluid into a needle.

She finishes her work and leaves, but not a second goes by before Louisa stands in front of the bed with her hands on her hips.

"By God, Elisse," she shouts to the ceiling as if all this time she held her breath. "What happened to you?"

Instantly, I remember the frightening experience in the park, down to the smallest detail—the bone monster, the deer, the wolf. My blood drains to my feet, so I squeeze my eyes tight and try not to pass out.

"And the deer?"

"What deer, Elisse?" Louisa asks.

After such a massacre, something has to be left, something to prove I'm not crazy, but when I see their puzzled expressions, I know there's no trace of the animal.

"H-how did I get here?" I ask.

They give each other a troubled look.

"A couple of joggers found you on a trail in the park this morning. They thought you were dead, so they called the police," Louisa says. "Your sleep pants had the center's logo, and they contacted us."

Now I want to throw myself out of the window. How the hell did I get to a park trail? I was on the shore of a lake.

"Luckily, nothing serious happened to you, child. Just an ugly bruise and some scratches, surely because you weren't wearing a shirt."

I lift my hospital gown to examine my side and gasp. Where five deep claw marks should be, there are only faint white scars so clean, they could have been there for years. The only proof of that awful scene is a large bruise on my arm where the wolf struck me.

"Elisse, the police want to know if someone attacked you," Geshe says. "So, Officer Clarks is here to ask you a few questions."

"Officer?"

"Good Morning." A young man with carrot-red hair stands at the entrance of the room and smiles. "Hi, Elisse. I'm Officer Ronald Clarks. How are you feeling?"

"I'm fine, okay, thank you," I answer and once again show my unsteady English as if all these weeks of practice went to trash.

"I came to take your statement about what happened. Is that okay?" He pulls a small black notebook and a pen from his jacket pocket.

I sit up slowly and bite my lower lip. I know I'm going to tell him everything but the truth. I've had to lie my entire life about the terrible things I see, and if there's no evidence of the hellish creature that chased me into the park or the wolf that devoured a talking deer, then no, this won't be any different.

"Can you give me your full name, please?"

"It's ... Yes. Elisse N. N."

"N. N.?"

"No name, officer. Elisse is an orphan, so he doesn't have a surname," Louisa says.

The officer apologizes, and I just nod without giving much importance to the matter.

"Age?"

"He's just turned eighteen," Louisa replies again.

"Ah, the perfect age for the carnival coming in February. You're lucky, but I better not catch you drinking," he says jokingly.

I force a smile.

"Where are you from, Elisse?"

"India, sir."

"India?"

"Elisse was not born in India, but he was there most of his life," Louisa says and now sounds like an overprotective mother.

"Yeah, it's clear to me, but please, Miss Fiquette, let the boy answer."

"Oh, I'm sorry."

"Elisse, can you tell us what happened? Did someone break into the center while you were asleep?"

I wring the sheets between my fingers.

"Nothing happened, officer," I say calmly. "Nobody attacked me. I just had a night terror."

"A night terror?"

"They're like nightmares but worse, and they make me sleepwalk. I've had them since I was a little boy."

The officer looks at Geshe, who nods calmly, but I grow more nervous.

Night terrors. My perfect lie. When you see things nobody else can see, hear voices in the dark, and run like a madman in the middle of the night, pretending to be normal isn't easy. Saying that I suffer from night terrors is just a screen, something to explain my panic attacks and avoid a trip to the asylum.

I want to believe that my night terrors are just nightmares and like any other dream they will end someday. But in the end, I have found they are a reality that is increasingly difficult to escape.

I hate to lie, but I hate the idea of being thrown in a psychiatric hospital even more.

"Do you remember how you bruised your arm?"

"Don't know. Could've fallen." I answer in short to make clear I don't have the strength to talk.

The officer asks me a couple of additional questions and leaves with the promise of staying informed of my recovery. When Louisa and Geshe leave me to rest, I finally relax. I couldn't bear the pressure of her questions and the scrutiny of the tutor any longer.

I look at the dark bruise on my skin and think about the wound on my side. I can't explain how I healed so quickly, almost without a trace, and how so many terrible things have happened to me in such a short period.

The blue eyes of the wolf appear in my mind, and terror and excitement awaken in me, like the feeling of vertigo at a great height and that strange desire to plummet.

Maybe I should have let the bone monster get me. After all, who says it won't come back to tear me to pieces? Who says it's not better to die than to feel like prey for the rest of my life?

Chapter 11
Lie in Wait

Thankfully, I haven't had another mishap like the incident in the park several weeks ago. And I haven't seen any more creatures in broad daylight or heard any voices call to me from the darkness. But I still haven't recovered from that frightening experience. Since that day, I've never felt alone.

It's as if the blue eyes of that wolf were watching me, accompanied by something that has changed in me, like something has ... awakened. I feel it in the breath of the night, in the grass beneath my feet, and in the mist among the trees.

My senses feel more alert, or maybe the things around me have a stronger, more alive presence. I don't know if it's the fear created by my desire to survive or the delirium of my disturbed mind. Perhaps the horrors I witnessed as a child have served as a buffer for this moment; otherwise, I don't understand how I can endure all this insanity.

Louisa insisted I move into her house so she could take care of me if I had another night terror, but I refused flat out. Now that I know my nightmares not only can hurt me but also can seep into reality, what will happen if they can hurt her too? I'd rather have my ribs ripped out completely before I place her in danger.

I press harder on the accelerator and carefully handle Louisa's old purple Cadillac through the streets near the French Quarter.

Driving has always brought mixed feelings. When I turned twelve, I decided to work repairing the roads to the city of New Delhi, as did almost all refugees from Tibet, but being so young and thin, I couldn't perform heavy labor. Instead, they taught me to handle all types of vehicles, so at least I could transport materials from one place to another.

I was happy to earn my own money, but in exchange, I had to leave school, which left me with a bitter feeling and a latent hunger to read and learn about everything within reach to fill the void in my heart. I earned enough money to travel to the United States, but in return, I could never aspire to be someone in life—not a teacher, not a doctor, not an engineer. Nothing.

But for now, I'll have to set aside my misery. I have more important things to take care of. Laurele's red book sits in the passenger seat like a corpse I'm dying to get rid of.

I park the car and throw my bag over my shoulder. I walk toward the voodoo shop but stop a few yards from the building. I loathe this place, not only because of the eccentric owner but also because of the bone monster. When I think of that thick, bloody stain sliding down the wall, I'm tempted to turn around, but the weight of the book in my hand makes me want to get rid of it once and for all.

When the service bell chimes, Laurele saunters from the back room with that chilling, jagged smile. "Look who's come to visit me. I've missed that pretty face," she purrs and leans her elbows on the counter.

"You left something at the Buddhist center the other day."

The smile wanes from her face when I show her the red book.

"Ah, how nice," she says with her voice rising a couple of octaves. "You shouldn't have bothered."

"I'm sorry I didn't bring it before. I was busy." I don't want to tell her I was in the hospital. With everything that happened, the damn book was the last thing on my mind.

"I see. But if by chance it comes back to you, don't forget to bring it back, okay?"

My forehead wrinkles. "Are you implying that I stole it?"

"Oh no, not at all. This book has little legs."

"And why would I want something like this?"

"Why?" She laughs. "Let me explain something about Voodoo, child." She circles the counter, stretching out her long arm, and captures my chin with three icy fingers. "It is the most powerful force on earth to get what you desire. Don't you want riches, fortune, or even to catch the love of your life?"

I pull her fingers away from my face. Her words sound like swindles, cheap gadgets like those sold on television. "No thank you, I'm not interested in those things, much less after you called me a thief."

I drop the book on the counter and turn around to leave.

"Were you not as a young boy? A thief?"

As if her words were poison, Laurele's tongue paralyzes me at the entrance.

I turn slowly to her.

Her dark eyes shine as they dig into me like a pair of fangs. She opens her mouth to speak, but her gaze drifts beyond me. "Who are your friends?" she asks.

I look toward the street, but no one is there.

"A few seconds ago, there was a girl and a man there. He looked rough, but she looked at you like you were the last glass of water in the desert." She laughs and winks an eye. "Apparently someone is becoming quite popular, huh?"

I spin around and hold back the urge to slam the door as I leave the shop.

Back in the car, I'm about to toss my bag in the passenger seat when I see the red book sitting there wide open. I look around to see if, somehow, that crazy Laurele reached into the car to place it here, but there are no signs of her.

"How in the hell . . . ?"

Maybe I took it unconsciously, or perhaps I never left it on the counter in the shop. My hair stands on end. I pinch the book by its edge in case at any moment it jumps on top of me.

The open page reveals a pair of snakes drawn in dark red ink. More than a book, it's a journal of notes with almost half of the pages blank. Several paragraphs are written in a language so small that the words read like whispers.

"Invoking the Loas," I read aloud.

I slam the book closed, ready to get out of the car and throw the thing as far as possible, but my hand remains tense on the car door.

Were you not as a young boy? A thief?

How does Laurele know about me? Does Voodoo help her find out things about people? It can't be possible. She must have learned another way, but I'd never share that with anyone, not even Louisa.

The longer I stare at the book, the more I get a feeling that there are ways to get information about people or maybe even find them. The picture of my father flashes in my head, and I decide to keep the book a while longer.

✦✦✦✦

THE SIGN ABOVE the Buddhist center entrance is turned off. Although the end of the year approaches, I'm sure we didn't plan to close today. A bad feeling turns my feet into blocks of lead.

Inside, Carlton and two other volunteers from the center stand in the middle of the shop and speak in such low voices that I can barely hear them. They didn't notice my arrival, so I clear my throat.

"Oh, Elisse, hello," Carlton says with an awkward smile. "Louisa's inside. Why don't you go see her?"

In response to his poorly disguised nervousness, I limit myself to obeying. When I cross the hallway, everyone's eyes needle my back.

In the living room, Louisa contemplates a point in the middle of nowhere.

"Louisa?" I say without using the formal and distant "Miss."

She strains to stand up, but unlike the others, she is calm in my presence.

"Honey, you just arrived?"

I nod and don't bother to hide the dismay in my face. "Is everything all right? Mr. Lone looks somewhat worried."

"My child," she says with a sigh. "Have you seen anyone suspicious near the center these past few days? Anyone unusual hanging around?"

I'm tempted to say the only weird person who stepped into the shop was her sister, but I bite my tongue. "No. Actually, no."

"I see. That's what I was afraid of." She unravels imaginary threads in her fingers and twists her mouth. "It's best that we call the police."

"Police?" An alarm sounds inside me. "Why? What happened?"

She looks at me with weighted eyes and takes off her glasses.

"Elisse … Someone has stolen money from the shop."

Chapter 12
Blind Trust

It's nearly six in the morning, so the sky is just beginning to clear. Fog covers both ends of the street, causing the asphalt to disappear behind dense grey curtains. It's as if the first day I came to this city never ended, because the landscape struggles to repeat itself over and over.

The shop is closed for the holidays, but here I am sweeping the steps, making piles of dust, and fighting a drowsiness that even a strong cup of coffee couldn't shake.

I wasn't able to sleep last night. I fixated on the sounds of the building and worried that, at any moment, the door of my room would open with a crash. I don't know what to fear anymore. Animals, demons, or people.

Crazy. Freak. Thief.

I sigh and think of the litany of awkward questions the police asked me yesterday. I'm not an idiot. I know when money disappears, the first suspect is the newcomer. The

only thing that saved me from being blamed is the fact that several members of the center have access to the cash register and the safe.

I'm not proud to admit, but if in the past I had to steal, it was out of need. Almost every hungry or barefoot child in India does it, but only a fool would throw roof and hot food in the trash for a few dollars.

Well, it wasn't a few. According to Louisa, almost a thousand dollars is missing, but I wouldn't take twenty. The only thing keeping me somewhat calm is that she and Geshe are convinced I didn't take the money. With both of them backing me up, I have nothing to fear, right? I hope doing extra work at the center will help me gain the trust of the other members, who certainly will never see me the same way, at least not until I prove my innocence.

An exhaust pipe roars at the end of the street, and a vehicle illuminates the fog with its headlights. A red pickup truck stops in front of the center, and a bad feeling grows in my nerves. The window lowers to reveal a man with blond hair.

"Good morning," he says in a deep voice and lifts his thick beard. He looks me up and down and laughs.

My concern turns into anger. "Can I help you?" I ask.

Without answering, he turns off the vehicle and gets out.

By the gods! This guy's a giant. He pounds the ground with his heavy boots as he approaches. He towers above me, and his fitted shirt accentuates his build. If he wanted, I'm sure he could snap me like a twig.

"You're even less impressive up close," he says.

"What do you want?" I grip the broom in my hands.

"You really want to try your luck with that stick?" he says.

"Are you suggesting I'll need it?"

The smile on his face evaporates. "Look, I didn't come to hurt you." He takes a couple of steps backward with his palms raised. "I just want to talk. You're Elisse, right?"

Something familiar about him strikes me. I let the stick breathe again and take a step forward. He smells like smoke, and his gaze is as heavy as a boulder. Something about his presence stirs me, draws me in, like the feeling of vertigo at the edge of a cliff.

"Do I know you?"

"No, Elisse. This is the first we've met."

"Then, what the hell do you want?" I ask, afraid of the emotions this man ignites in me.

"The only person who wants something here is you, and I've come to offer it."

I get it now. This guy's a crackpot. My first impulse is to run inside and dial the police, but when he sees my frightened expression, he places his hands on his waist and stares at the ground as if he were checking an armament of motives to persuade me not to run.

"Aren't you sick of being afraid?" he asks and looks up again.

"What are you talking about?"

"Don't you want to be certain, for the first time in your life, that you're not crazy? That everything you see and everything happening to you is real?"

A monstrous void opens inside me. "Who are you?" I ask.

"Elisse ... " He takes a step toward me.

I stamp my boot against the broomstick and point the splintered tip at him. "Leave, or I'll beat the shit out of you!"

He raises his hands again and looks at me with expanding eyes. He blinks several times. "Elisse, listen to me," he says slowly as if he were choosing his words carefully. "If you come with me, I'll tell you everything. I assure you that all your questions about who you are and what you see will be answered. But if you refuse, I can't do anything for you."

"How do you know about me?" My voice trembles.

"I warn you. This is my only offer."

More than a warning, this sounds like a threat. It's clear to me this guy isn't your average person. The story of my life can't be guessed by looking at my face. How do I know this isn't a trap? If I refuse, is he going to take me anyway?

I keep the building entrance in the corner of my eye. I fear something dangerous might happen if I agree, but my instincts tell me to go, to take a step toward discovering the truth.

The man remains silent and waits for my response without pressing me as if he empathized with the dilemma swirling in my head.

If I don't get in that truck, I'll never discover what this man knows about me, so...

"I'll go," I say. "On the condition that I'll be back here by eight."

"I give you my word." A smile paints his face. "We won't go far. I promise."

His promise means nothing to me. I'm not even certain he won't kill me. I toss what's left of the broomstick next to the broken brush and follow this guy to his truck. But something stops me.

A hand slides out from the truck bed and grasps the chrome-plated rail. A naked man rises slowly with his body convulsing violently. His stomach is split open and spills blood like a waterfall. He holds a piece of flesh in his hand

and reaches toward me as if he desperately wanted me to close his gaping wound.

"What have you done to him?" I whisper.

"Did you say something?"

"What have you done to that man?" I shout, and my voice echoes down the lonely street. Everything begins spinning.

The giant follows the path of my gaze and throws himself at me. "Are you seeing something, Elisse? Tell me." He shakes me by my shoulders.

"Let go of me, you maniac!"

I pull away from his grip and race toward the house. Before I can reach the doorknob, a beastly force yanks me back. The guy covers my mouth and nose with his wide hand and nearly suffocates me. He lifts me up as if I weighed less than a feather and drags me back toward the truck. I kick and fight, but I can't get away.

"Elisse. Elisse, look again. No one's there," he says in my ear, but I don't stop writhing. He holds me with one arm and catches my chin with his free hand, forcing me to look at the truck.

I lose my breath when I see that whoever was in the truck bed is gone. "But there was a-a … " My heart nearly stops, and my hands dance incessantly.

As if his instincts shouted at him, he squeezes me tighter to calm my tremors with a firm but gentle pressure. I turn my head to look at him, but I can't focus.

"Elisse … " His voice grows soft. "I know what you're going through. You think those beings have only come to torment you, to feed on your fear, but it's not like that, Elisse." He repeats my name as if he were trying to create familiarity between us. "We fear because we don't understand what we fear. If you come with me, you'll understand, and you'll stop being afraid."

Finally, he lets me go, and on the verge of tears, I nearly collapse to my knees. The man stands in front of me and catches my shoulders. He moves closer, and his warm breath comforts me.

"I want you to trust me," he says.

I press the bridge of my nose with my forefinger and thumb. Whatever he wants to show me can't be worse than my demons, worse than the anguish of not knowing what's happening to me, so I nod slowly.

He smiles and walks toward the truck, and I follow.

I scan the truck bed one last time with my stomach knotting and my heart racing. The mutilated man isn't there, but I can still smell his blood.

More than understanding what's happening to me, I want to end this horror. I want to know what it feels like to sleep at night and live in peace during the day. But I have to be realistic. Maybe things won't get better. Maybe they'll get a lot worse.

"By the way," the man says and looks at me over his shoulder, "I'm Tared."

Chapter 13
Eyes of the Caiman

The scent of tobacco and wood fills Tared's truck, and a dreamcatcher hangs from the rearview mirror, swaying as we drive down the road. The stereo clock shows seven in the morning. We left the Buddhist center nearly a half hour ago and crossed the bridge over the Mississippi, so we won't get back to the center by eight. At this rate, they're going to kick me out.

A sign welcomes our arrival to the famous marsh reserve outside New Orleans. We pass several miles of vegetation and houses mounted on thick pillars along the riverbank. After another ten minutes of driving, we pass an abandoned house rotted with mold and dampness. We must be entering a private area. There aren't any signs or roads for buses.

When the paved road becomes mud, the white trees grow denser. The fog here is thicker than in the city, and the croaking of frogs surpasses the singing of birds. It's an authentic swamp.

From time to time, I shift my eyes from the landscape to Tared, who has become a human chimney smoking one cigarette after another.

"Still a ways to go?" I ask in the interest of staying awake rather than the desire to talk. I already peppered this man with questions, but he was so reluctant to answer them that I gave up.

"We should be there in about twenty minutes."

"You said you'd have me back by eight."

Tared chuckles. "I never said by eight in the morning."

"How clever."

I lean my head against the glass, growing drowsier and nearly drifting to sleep, but when I spot something on the side of the road, I shoot up.

"By the gods! Was that an alligator?" I say and look behind us. "It was huge!"

Tared slams on the brakes, and had it not been for the safety belt, I would have broken my teeth against the dashboard.

"What the hell's wrong with you?" I say.

Tared doesn't answer. He looks over his shoulder through the rear window of the truck. He scans the grass, and to my surprise, the whites of his eyes flood with red.

"Fuck." He takes off his seat belt and gets out of the vehicle.

"What's going on? Where are you going?"

He doesn't answer.

My jaw drops to the floor when he opens my door and reaches behind my seat to draw a long, heavy shotgun.

"Stay here," he orders with a scowl and closes my door.

He stands in front of the truck bed, raising his chin and turning his head to ... sniff the air?

I'm about to ask him what the hell he's doing, but the grass shakes violently. Tared faces forward and remains still as if his head were plastered in place. Then, in a blink, he turns and throws himself against my window.

"You know how to drive?" he asks with his voice choked in agitation.

"A-ah, yes, I—"

"Get behind the wheel," he shouts and jumps into the truck bed with the shotgun pointing into the fog.

"Tared? Where am I supposed to go?"

"Follow the path."

I slide into the driver's seat. In front of me, a faint path marked by tire tracks disappears into the thick swamp. Sure, the easiest task in the world.

A deep roar echoes behind me, and I look back. The safety of Tared's shotgun clicks. The birds, the frogs, and the grass go quiet.

Bam!

Something with a long greenish body slams into the truck with such force that the entire vehicle rocks, and then the figure retreats into the fog.

"What the hell was that?" I yell and cling to the wheel.

Tared fires the shotgun and another cry echoes through the trees.

"Fuck! Let's go!" he shouts.

I slam the accelerator to the floor. The tires spit mud and the truck goes off. Another roar rises behind us as I drive through the thick forest and follow the trail as best I can.

"What the hell is going on?" I yell through the back window. Instead of an answer, Tared fires the gun again behind my back.

In the rearview mirror, about ten yards from the truck, an alligator with slimy skin covering its muscled limbs and humanlike torso runs on its hind legs. Ivory claws protrude from its palms, and rows of thick teeth fill its snout.

The animal cries again, but its voice, more than a bestial roar, sounds like a human scream. Fear twists my insides, but I can't take my eyes off the creature.

"Watch out!" Tared shouts.

I crank the wheel to avoid crashing against a tree and swerve back onto the road. Through the rearview mirror, I see Tared point the shotgun at the head of the alligator. A powerful shot blasts off its fangs and a block of flesh, but the creature doesn't fall back.

"Faster! Faster!"

The animal charges again. Tared holds the rails as the creature rams the vehicle. The truck rocks and almost overturns.

"Fuck! My truck!" Tared uses the opportunity to take a close shot at the creature, but it dodges and regains speed.

It advances to the side of the vehicle, just a few steps from my window.

"Shit!" The animal stinks like a corpse, and I struggle to control my urge to vomit.

Another blast of the shotgun strikes the creature's back but doesn't slow its chase. Tared curses as the thing stays close to the truck.

Several yards ahead, a thicket of trees forms a wall.

"Hold on!" I cry without checking whether Tared heard me.

When the creature lines up perfectly, I twist the steering wheel, and the side of the truck slams against the wall of trees and crushes the monster in between. The metal screams as I accelerate, and the alligator squishes along the trunks. Parts of its flesh shred off, smearing a bloody trail along the timbers. The creature's arm lodges between two trees, and the animal smacks to the ground and rolls like a barrel behind us.

In the rearview mirror, Tared clings to the side of the truck in horror while the shotgun slides from side to side in the metal bed.

He looks at me and explodes in laughter. "You're fucking nuts!"

My blood freezes when the creature rises behind us. Torn flesh hangs from its body.

"It's alive! It's still alive!"

Without dropping his smile, Tared looks back at the alligator and picks up the shotgun. The road widens and forms a clearer path. Ahead, a group of cabins appears.

"It won't last much longer," he shouts as the alligator begins its pursuit again.

I look over my shoulder and see Tared aim the gun, but when I return my eyes to the road, a fire pit is in my path. I crank the wheel, and the vehicle flips and catapults into the air. The truck squeals with crushing metal as it rolls, and my body bounces like a rag doll. The windows shatter, the windshield breaks, and finally, the truck lands upside down.

My whole body hurts like hell, and a sharp pain knifes me on the side of my head. Growing dizzy, I touch my temple. Something sharp pricks my fingers. Glass? Blood enters one of my eyes, and everything becomes red.

"Elisse!" Tared screams.

Through the busted rear window, I watch him crawl on the ground for the shotgun a few feet away from him. A horrible gash crosses his forehead. I want to tell him I'm still alive, but I'm so disoriented that I can't get more than a moan out of my mouth.

I can make out the head of the alligator, who cries in an otherworldly, human voice. The creature passes Tared's side without looking at him and heads straight toward me. I clench my fist. We have done the impossible and still haven't been able to kill it.

Out of nowhere, a huge shadow whips against the face of the alligator and tears the mandible from its upper jaw. I wince and lean back when the being with abominable strength begins tearing the alligator's body apart.

A beast with fur as black as an abyss rips out the creature's entrails, and each time I blink, the body of the alligator transforms. As if by magic, the rotted corpse of a jawless, gray-haired man mutates back into the ghastly alligator. As he dies, a symbol glows brighter on his forehead as if the image were absorbing his life little by little.

I can't make out the symbol, and I don't have the strength to complain when my body is dragged from the truck.

Chapter 14
And the Storm Returns

"How many hours has he been missing, ma'am?"

"It's Louisa. And I don't know, officer" you say. "We haven't seen him since we closed the center yesterday. He was supposed to be here when we arrived at eight."

You try to take a sip of tea, but your hand trembles, so I tighten around your wrist to help you raise the cup. Carlton's complaints all day about the boy's irresponsibility haven't helped your nerves one bit.

The officer reviews papers he believes to be important and stacks them next to your written statement. While the cop relays information about Elisse's appearance into the radio on his shoulder, Carlton plays with his own cup of tea.

The door swings open and gives way to a man who's left his manners under a rock.

"Mr. Lone, Ms. Fiquette," he says with a grimace. I imagine it's a nuisance serving twenty years as a homicide detective and finding yourself in search of a missing child.

He sits in the only free chair and presents a piece of shiny gilded metal from his pocket. He throws the badge on the table as if it gave him the authority to move at ease. You roll your eyes looking for patience. Everyone in the city knows Detective Hoffman's poor social skills, and, likewise, they know he's the one to call when things go sour.

"I want to believe this gentleman's already taken the essential information," he says without looking to the other officer who sweats at the statement. "So, I'll just do my part. Do you have a picture of the boy?"

"Yes, I've even made a copy." You offer a black and white photocopy of Elisse's passport.

The detective takes the paper, stuffs it in his pocket, and takes the real passport from you. His brow gathers. "Isn't this the boy found unconscious in Audubon Park?"

Detective Hoffman had never seen Elisse, but after the peculiar description provided by Ronald Clarks, he immediately identified the boy in the picture.

"Do you understand my concern now?" you say. "I'm afraid he's hurt, and we found the broken broom on the steps. Someone may have kidnapped him."

"It… could be an attack of night terrors," Carlton says.

"Again? He's not medicated or something?"

"No, sir," you reply. "The doctor assured us that what happened in the park was from the stress of moving to a new country, and we shouldn't worry. But it may have happened again."

Hoffman snorts and takes the notes from the officer without asking. After reading a few pages, he stops and casts his cold eyes on you. "You reported a robbery yesterday?"

You turn pale.

Carlton nods vigorously. "Yes, yes, detective," the old man says. "Someone's been taking money from the center, so we reported the incident."

"And you don't think it's funny that the boy disappeared the next day?"

You harden your look in a way I've rarely had the misfortune to see. I draw myself into my body and point my head toward the detective, yielding to the threatening instincts of my blood.

"One doesn't have a damn thing to do with the other. Elisse is a good boy, and Geshe and both of us are willing to vouch for him." You glare at Carlton as if you wanted to tear out his tongue, and the idiot looks down.

Hoffman drops the papers on the table. He stands up and tucks his badge into his raincoat.

"Whether it was him, Ms. Fiquette, given that he hasn't been in the city long, I'll pass his profile to my colleagues, tell them to be on alert in case they spot him."

"Thank you, detective."

"Anything else, contact Officer Clarks, who took Elisse's statement at the hospital. I'm sure you already have his information."

I wrap myself around the detective's ankle and refrain from twisting it. The last I see of your face veiled with worry touches me. The officer apologizes to you and Carlton for the behavior of his superior, and I leave the building cleaved to Hoffman's bones.

Outside, the detective's old car waits on the street with its hooves covered by thick fog. When you sigh with weariness, I wonder if you'll ever find peace in your soul, Hoffman, because you have years of making enemies of those who cross your path.

You dig your hand inside your pocket to retrieve your keys, but the copy of Elisse's passport is the first thing your fingers touch. You unfold the paper, and I climb up your back to peek over your shoulder.

The poor kid has an uneasy expression. His dark-circled eyes suggest he hasn't slept in days, but there's a brightness that reveals he's more alert than the rest of his face shows.

"So, you're a troublesome boy, huh?" you say.

Fine drops of water fall on the paper and send black ink running down the cheek of the young man. You ball the document and throw it into the river that's forming in the gutter. As you drive away, your tires squeal, and the water washes away the portrait of Elisse in a raging current.

Chapter 15
Something Familiar

I DON'T FEEL THE NEEDLE pierce my skin and enter another piece of flesh, but I do feel the drop of hot blood running down my temple, which I clean with a swipe of my hand.

"You're very lucky, little one," a woman's voice says beside me. "The glass didn't embed too deeply."

I try to respond, but words don't come out of my mouth. I'm so shocked and exhausted by everything that's happened that the mere act of speaking is too much effort.

She runs another stitch, and this time I wince.

"I'm sorry my boy. That was the last one," the woman says. "The good news is that the wound won't show under that nest you have for hair. It's clear from miles away that you cut it yourself, but I admit, you look adorable with those raggedy bangs."

It's surreal for her to talk about my hair right now, so I don't respond.

I must have spent hours convalescing, slipping between consciousness and delirium. I was barely able to grasp what was happening around me. My body felt so hot at times that I thought my blood might evaporate. Voices spoke to me from all sides, but I couldn't understand what they were saying. Silhouettes of people moved back and forth over the bed like hungry vultures circling my corpse, and I wondered if I hadn't already died. It wasn't until the penetrating herbs brought me back to reality that the dark figures dispersed like clouds of smoke.

The first thing I saw when I awoke was the old woman next to me whose eyes, to my surprise, were as light as fog. She cradled a steaming bowl in her hand and plucked one of her long white hairs to use as thread. At that point, few things could have surprised me. I no longer knew in which part of the universe the idea of normalcy had been hidden.

"What time is it?" I ask.

"Later than you would like, I'm sure," she answers in a melody like the song of a bird.

"And Tared? What happened to him?"

"He's fine, boy, and much less injured than you are, if you ask me," she says with a smile and clasps my wrist. My nervousness vanishes with her sweet touch.

Another pang shoots through my head, and I squeeze my eyes. She passes the herbal bowl under my nose, and I inhale the camphorous scent of its waters. The pain subsides almost instantly, but the thought of Tared still lingers in my head.

"He ... he said if I came here, the answers he would give me," I say without caring that my accent shines. "But I don't think I understand anything about this world anymore, not after everything I've seen today."

"At least you're still alive, son." The old woman caresses the back of my hand with her feathery fingertips. I sense a maternal aura around her, similar to Louisa.

She takes a cloth, moistens it in the herbal water, and passes it over the wounds on my face and arms while I look over the room with more clarity.

The aged wood of the cabin exhales an air of the old past. In front of the bed, the sweater Louisa knitted, now blood splattered and in shreds, wilts upon the back of an old rocking chair. I cast my eyes to the large mirror on the dresser to keep from bursting into tears. For some reason, the sight of the ruined sweater makes me feel like I've kicked Louisa.

My heart expands when I see my reflection and that of the old woman.

Feathers peek out from under her clothes and around her bronzed face. She has large eyes as black as a pair of onyx stones. White wings with ivory fingers at the tips heal my wounds with incredible precision. Her nose is normal, but her features are enough for me to recognize the animal in the reflection.

"An owl," I say under my breath.

She looks at our reflection and smiles. "So, you can see my ancestor."

"Ancestor?"

"That you see there is my soul, Elisse."

Her enigmatic response evokes something I have never felt in my life when face to face with the supernatural. Fascination.

Unable to behold the amazing creature any longer, I turn my eyes to the necklaces of feathers and fangs that hang on the corner of the mirror. On the dresser, several candles burn on top of old books that have a thick layer of dust. Antlers and dreamcatchers of different colors decorate the walls. Frames with mounted butterflies adorn the open spaces. There are no windows, so the room feels more like a cellar of extravagant souvenirs than a person's bedroom.

"I'm done with you." The old woman stands up from the bed with the steaming bowl in her hand and pats my arm. "I'll leave you, my boy. Someone else wants to see you."

She opens the door and smiles when she meets Tared in the frame. He returns the gesture as the old woman leaves.

"Finally, you're awake," he says calmly. He sits in the chair and takes out a cigarette from his leather jacket. "You had a good thrashing. We were surprised you didn't completely lose consciousness all this time."

"Things still aren't very clear," I say softly.

"How are you feeling?"

"Like a giant alligator rolled me over."

The man roars with laughter and dances the cigarette between his fingers.

"How about you?" I ask.

"Bah, it didn't make a scratch," he says.

I look for the wound on his forehead from when he was thrown from the truck. My heart quickens. There's only a thin white scar, just like the claw marks on my side. I search his eyes for several long minutes until I finally find what I'm looking for.

Deflecting my eyes to my hands, I play with the strands of the bedspread. I feel Tared's curious gaze on me. He scratches his thick beard and clears his throat as if he were trying to cut the tension born between us.

"Is something wrong?" he finally asks.

"You're the wolf from that time in the park, right?"

His face briefly shows surprise, and he stamps out his cigarette.

"They're not alike," I say. "The color of your hair and the wolf's fur, but... you have the same look."

Tared's blue eyes, bright like a flash of lightning, get lost somewhere in the room.

"I'm sorry for the hit I gave you," he says. "What I was doing that morning was necessary. It's enough for you to know that."

"Am I here because I saw you?"

"No. But at that moment, I knew you were different from everyone else."

"I thought I was just crazy."

"Maybe you're not far from it," he says without looking at me. He leans forward and gives my shoulder a squeeze before standing from the chair and stretching.

"Tared? You promised me answers."

"And I'll give them to you. I promise. But rest for now. Mama Tallulah will bring you something to eat, and then you can meet everyone at the fire pit. Or what's left of it."

"Tallulah is the old woman who sewed my wounds?" Even her name sounds like poetry.

"Yes, but don't joke and call her old woman or just Tallulah. You'll offend her."

"Uh ... okay, I suppose."

"Elisse?

"Yeah."

"Welcome."

Tared leaves the room. I stare at the door for a few seconds and fall back into the pillow. A slight pain throbs in my right leg and in both arms, but even so, I'm not as battered as I should be.

In the cracks and spots of the ceiling, I imagine infinite figures crawling out to pounce on me and crush me.

Welcome.

The strangest feeling overcomes me. I'm in a foreign world with things I've never seen before but feel terribly familiar. The smell of herbs, smoke, and blood in such an old and wild environment induces great nostalgia. It's as if I've finally reached a place where my fears and visions, and everything I've always been, fit.

Now, I just need to find out who I really am.

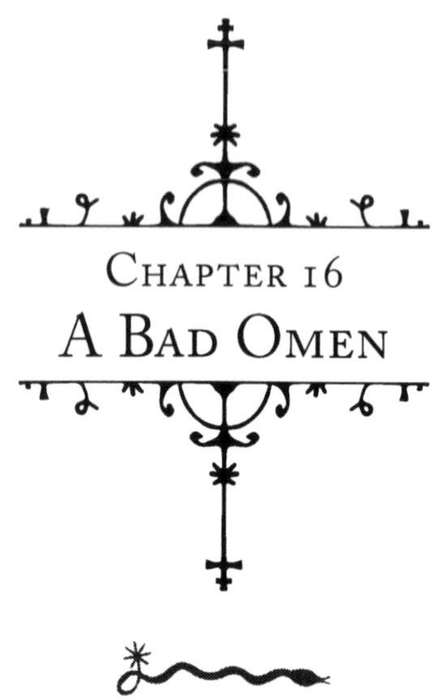

Chapter 16
A Bad Omen

MIDNIGHT PEEKS ITS FACE over the reserve, and flames burn with delight in a makeshift bonfire. It's so exquisite, I can't help but embrace a burning log and imagine warming myself in the flames. Around a freshly dug hole, fragments of rock destroyed by Tared's truck form a semicircle. The seats are gone, so everyone sits on the dirt. In my eyes, it's much better that way—closer to the earth and farther from the dark sky cloaked in clouds. I raise my head from the fire to contemplate the people around me.

A man from the old land, the only man standing, leans on a wooden staff. A wolf pelt draped over his shoulders radiates blue tones against his dark skin, and the animal's upper jaw crowns the old man's head with black fangs.

It's not hard to believe that you're just as powerful as you were in your youth. I've known you since you were a child, and I've watched you grow with such strength that your own people call you Father Thunder. Even now, at sixty-eight, your straight back refuses to bow.

My beautiful Tallulah, a sweet and delicate canary of a woman, sits at your side. And Johanna, a noble creature unable to understand the extent of her powers, wraps herself in a blue shawl and embraces a thick leather-bound book in her arms. Julien and Nashua tighten their lips. One tries not to tell a silly joke, and the other holds back a sigh.

Everyone sits silently and watches the embers rise through the fire. The atmosphere is tense as if everyone were balancing the celestial vault on their heads.

"So, did you get rid of everything?" Johanna asks to break the silence.

"We threw the body into the river and ditched the truck in the junkyard," Julien says in relief at the opportunity to open his mouth again.

"Tared didn't say anything about his truck? He's not angry?"

"No. And that pisses me off," Nashua says with a spit. "Remember the blow I gave that piece of junk? I had to pay every penny of the damn repairs. But that stupid little brat totals it, and that asshole Tared doesn't say a thing."

"Nashua. Don't speak like that of your brother," Mama Tallulah says.

Nashua drops his head. "I'm just saying, Tared should have transformed in front of the boy and handled it without turning the reserve to shit."

"He used his head before acting, unlike others," Julien says. "Think about it. What if the boy lost his cool when he saw Tared that way? He might have believed it was all a trap and tried to run him down along with that lizard."

Nashua frowns and demonstrates with his silence that Julien, in the vast wisdom hidden below his good humor, is right.

"After all this, how is he?" Johanna asks.

"Definitely like Grandfather Muata. But not as ugly."

"Not funny, Julien," the girl says. "I mean, how is he on a personal level? And it's disrespectful to speak like that about Grandfather."

"And you're a kiss-ass," he says with a laugh and makes the young woman snort.

"Children!" Mama Tallulah shouts, sensing what you yourself yearned to do. The old woman's voice echoes through the trees and silences everyone. "Elisse is a fine example of his lineage, but that doesn't mean we should consider his appearance as important. I'm sure he'll earn our respect with his abilities."

"We'll see if he stays," you say finally. "Nothing is decided."

Mama Tallulah looks at you in bewilderment at such a cold response. A new member for the tribe is a rare blessing, but in this case, something inside tells you not to let your guard down. The arrival of the boy is too good to be true.

"Will they also bring Grandfather Muata?" Nashua asks through his teeth.

Poor creature. He has spent so much time by your side that he's beginning to look more like you every day. In both good and bad ways.

"I gave the order to Tared that no one is to be missing," you say and establish silence like a code among your tribe. The clouds in the sky break away to reveal the full moon. You and I raise our heads, almost at the same time, and ask for its blessing.

The door of the nearest cabin opens. Tared carefully pushes Grandfather Muata's wheelchair, and immediately, everyone around the campfire stands up to welcome him.

"And the boy?" Julien asks Tared.

"I'm going for him now. First, I want Grandfather to be comfortable." He arranges the sack of feathers behind the old man's hunched back, and Muata palms Tared's wrist in gratitude.

A faint smile crosses your lips when you see your boy. The pride shining in your eyes almost dims the flames of the fire.

Tared heads toward the cabin where Elisse rests, and disappears into the darkness of the night.

"Do you think Muata approves of him?" Johanna asks Julien under her breath.

"Speak up, girl. I'm not deaf yet," Muata says.

"I wanted to know if you think the boy is a good candidate—?"

"I don't know, child. The important thing is to know if he considers himself worthy," the old man says, but he holds in his throat the words he really wants to speak.

The great-grandfather squeezes the crow skull that hangs from his neck. You, on the other hand, harden your steely gaze even more because only you can read something unusual in Muata's neutral expression.

Chapter 17
Stories by the Fire

We leave the cabin, and I pull over the woven poncho Tared lent me. I have to settle for this because my shirt's as useless as Louisa's sweater. I walk with a slight limp but try to match the long stride of the man next to me. We form a curious scene—Tared, so tall and stocky, by the side of a boy who barely weighs a hundred and ten pounds. To see us together must be comical for those around the bonfire.

The extraordinary heat of the flames radiates through the fabric and warms my skin. Another familiar feeling. As we get closer, I scan the audience of new faces.

At the center sits the harshest looking man I've ever seen. He wears a wolf skin that shines by the firelight. For a moment, my heart jumps when I see the fur, but when I look more carefully, I know the pelt is from a wolf different from … Tared.

To the right of the old man is the gentle Tallulah. And to his left, an old woman with long hair sits motionless in a wheelchair, perhaps lost in thought. By the pale and crystalline tone of her pupils, she appears to be blind.

A man with red hair and a beard greets me with a hand missing a finger. At his side, a girl with dark brown hair and light eyes presses a thick book against her chest. The last man, with a dark, rough face, stares at me as if my mere presence insulted him. He and the elders look alike, with similar skin tones and sharp features.

"Come, boy, get close to the fire," Tallulah says to me in a voice as soft as a chick. "It's been years since we've had a child so young. I'm so happy." She opens space for me to sit between her and the girl.

"Tallulah ... " the man in the wolf skin says, tempering her enthusiasm.

She looks at him and folds her arms.

He stares at me and narrows his eyes as if something about me displeased him.

Truthfully, I don't think anyone could ask this man for the time without receiving daggers; regardless, I sense he commands respect, either that or the dog outfit made more of an impression than it should have.

Tared squeezes my shoulder, placing my feet back on the ground with inexplicable ease, and takes a seat next to the old woman. I feel vulnerable out of his reach.

The girl next to me opens the book resting on her lap and, with a simple pen, begins writing.

A chill lashes my spine when her eyes turn white and the ink disappears into the paper.

"The Book of Generations is open," she announces loudly.

The old man with the wolf skin casts a solemn gaze over us.

"I, Father Thunder, head of the Comus Bayou tribe, invoke the stories by the fire tonight," he says in a thick, authoritative voice. "I cry out for the voices of my people to narrate what their eyes have seen, what their ears have heard, and what their hearts have told them. Everything revealed will be written and narrated to our children across the sky of generations to preserve the voice of the earth. Open your jaws and feed us legends, make us immortal with word, and honor the land inherited from our gods. Be then, heard."

The man sits before our expectant faces.

Tallulah is the first to break the silence. "You've come for answers tonight, Elisse," she says and smiles. "Even though we are all here to answer them, we know you have a lot to share. So, tell us about you."

I rub the poncho fabric between my fingers, not knowing where to start, so I resort to the first thing that comes to mind. My nightmares.

"Ever since I was very young," I say with my voice trembling more than I'd like, "I've seen things no one else can see. Creatures. Demons. Monstrous things. Everything started when I was about four years old, but it feels like they've been there my whole life, watching me."

The girl writes at superhuman speed and notes everything I say without looking at the book. She gazes at me through her white eyes as if she could read on my lips what my voice has not yet spoken.

"They appear one at a time, and I rarely see the same creature twice. And they always stink like the dead. But what frightens me most is that everything around me becomes silent. I enter a place where only those monsters and I exist. The objects around me stop being what they are. Like they're part of a stage set made of concrete in an empty dimension. The creatures had never touched me until—"

"The day I found you in the park," Tared says.

I dart my eyes to him. I think of the bone monster and swallow.

"Yes. That had never happened to me, I . . . " A lump rises in my throat. It's so difficult, for the first time in my life, to tell the truth about what I see. The only time I tried was when I was a child, and the person I told slapped me. He told me they were hallucinations, and if I said those things, people would believe I was possessed.

In the superstitious society in which I lived, it wasn't difficult to believe that sort of thing, so I kept silent for years. They wouldn't believe I saw demons, but they believed I could be possessed by one. Since then, I knew the world was the crazy one, and lying would be the only way to fit into an absurd reality.

"Do you see them often?" Tallulah asks.

"Sometimes I see two or three a week. Sometimes months pass without seeing one."

"Where were you born?" Father Thunder asks abruptly.

"I don't know. I spent my first three years of life in Tibet, but I had to escape to India along with my tutor at that time. I lost the little contact I had with my father, and I don't know anything about my past or my origins."

Metal squeaks. The old woman in the wheelchair leans forward a couple of times as if she were uncomfortable. Everyone focuses on her. She remains silent, so Father Thunder continues his interrogation.

"Why did your father leave you there?"

"I don't know."

"Why did you come here?"

"Because the last letter I received from my father had a postmark from this country."

"So, did you come looking for him?"

"I also wanted a new life."

"Why? Did you do something? Did something make you want to escape?"

"That's none of your business," I reply with the same severity in which I was being questioned.

I cross my arms to protect myself from a new wave of questioning. More than one person stirs in their seat, surely in disapproval of the way I responded to this man, but I don't give a damn. I came here and risked my life for the answers offered to me. It isn't right that this has turned into an interrogation, and it isn't fair if I have to reveal the things I did to survive.

"Father Thunder." Tared's voice rises above the flames. "Elisse knows nothing about our hierarchy, and I think that's why he spoke to you like that. I beg you, in his name, forgive him."

My teeth catch my reckless tongue.

"I think the boy is eager to ask questions," he says. "And after everything that's happened today, it's his right. He'll tell us about his past later."

The old man glares at Tared. There's a duel of looks as if each expected the other to burst into anger. Is Tared … challenging him?

"So be it." Father Thunder gives in first, to my surprise.

Tared nods at me to continue. With a little more restraint, I clear my throat.

"Who—or what are you?" I ask.

The redhead laughs, and the girl with the book sighs and continues writing.

Father Thunder doesn't respond, so Tallulah takes the question and gives my hand a gentle squeeze.

"The last time we heard that question was three years ago when Johanna came to our tribe," she says and looks tenderly at the girl writing with a slight smile. "We, and this includes you, my child, are *wanderers*."

A spell breaks. The word ignites something in me as if the flames of the fire whispered in my ear.

"Wanderers?" A warm taste permeates my tongue.

The old man with the wolf skin releases a deep sigh. "Have you ever heard a parrot speak?" he asks. "That is, have you seen how it can perfectly imitate the voice of a human being?"

I nod, unsure of his point.

"For thousands of years, there were certain kinds of animals who could do much more than that," he says.

"According to the legends of our nation," Tared says, "when those creatures saw humanity advancing, tearing itself from the roots of the earth to form civilizations, they decided to approach man to establish an unbreakable bond with them, so they would never forget where they came from."

"They became humans," the redhead shouts from the other side of the fire. "They took on their appearance and began to walk and move like them."

"Our ancestors," the old man says, "named these beings, in their primitive understanding, *manmimickers*."

"Despite appearing human," Tallulah continues, "the manmimickers only looked like them and nothing more. They roared, bellowed, and howled, but they couldn't speak. There was no way to understand them."

Father Thunder explains: "Through the mystical arts, the first shamans, men and women connected to nature and its mysteries, wore the skins and bones of different animals to transform themselves, and with the help of magic, to establish a language, a bond with these beings that took human form. In this way, the first *skinwalkers* were born.

"Centuries passed, and over time, manmimickers and skinwalkers mated, formed families, and created us. The wanderers. Neither human nor animal, but something in the middle of both, something that dwells between the two species. Our human side dominates, allows us to walk unnoticed among man, but our animal side gives us the ability to transform into beasts, into authentic children of nature."

My face must look like the most emotional poem in the history of humankind. Never in my life, not even in Hindu legends, have I heard anything like this.

"There's more you need to know, honey," Tallulah says. "With the rise of civilization, the manmimickers disappeared like the skinwalkers and left the legacy of both in our blood. That's why we wanderers can't transform without the help of beings we call *ancestors*—a mystical being, a spiritual product of the magic of the shamans and the souls of the manmimickers. They watch over wanderers and give us the opportunity to take their form and benefit from their power."

"So, you can all turn into wolves like Tared? Are you werewolves?" I ask.

Tallulah laughs. "No, boy. In Tared's case, his ancestor is a brave and powerful spirit he's named *Wolf Lightningskin*. But we are not all wolves. Each wanderer has an ancestor as unique as a personality. You saw mine, didn't you?"

"I suppose so," I reply softly and recall the owl who looked at me in the mirror.

"Elisse, mythology exists because of the wanderers," she says and smiles once more. "Werewolves, Egyptian gods, Greek monsters. It's always been us."

I think of the Hindu deities of my country. The idea of a man with an elephant head had to come from somewhere.

"What about the alligator that chased us? Was he a wanderer?"

The old woman's eyes dim, and the men's eyes flush with blood.

"Just as there are creatures who choose to keep our species a secret for our sake, hidden in the shadows are others who have little or nothing to do with us," Tallulah says. "There are monsters you hear named only in the most sinister and oldest myths of humanity. Unnatural creatures. And in the case of the alligator, wanderers who have lost their sanity."

"Elisse," Tared calls me. "We keep at bay the beings who dare make havoc in the human world, and we protect ourselves by not allowing humans to discover what lives in the darkness. That is our mystical nature."

I try to digest all the information thrown at me, so I appreciate Tared's pause to allow me to understand the extraordinary world in which I have just become a part of.

"For generations," Father Thunder says, "we've made an effort to keep our species anonymous. Can you imagine if humans knew of our existence? Just look at what they do to nature and animals. Look at what they do to one another! Our race has fed the folklore of cultures for millennia because of the carelessness of our people, those who have been seen by humans or have allowed humans to see other creatures. But we've done everything possible to remain only as legends, and to this day, it's worked for us."

"Are there many like us?" I ask in an attempt to get all the pieces of the puzzle to fit, finally.

"We don't know. Wanderers are creatures who transmit our legacy through the blood. So reproducing is the way we survive as a species. But I hope it won't be necessary to clarify. It isn't as simple as that."

"And the deer from the park? Was it one of the creatures the wanderers want to get rid of?"

"No. That too was a wanderer but completely transformed," Father Thunder replies.

I look at him as if another head grew from his neck. He narrows his eyes.

"When a wanderer takes the form of his ancestor, he can transform in parts, in a gradual manner. We can transform a single part of our body, then transition through a perfect hybrid of human and beast until we become equal to an animal of great size. Just like that deer or this boy," he says and points to Tared with his cane, "when they met in the park. From there are born legends of mermaids, fauns, angels, and any other creature you can think of."

Even with this twisted logic, it makes sense. Still, there's something I don't understand. How the hell do I fit in all this? I've never barked or howled in my life. I've never felt like an animal in any way. And something tells me that I don't carry anything like an ancestor inside me.

"So, if you have blood from ... a skinwalker, from the shaman, does that mean all of you can see the same things I do?" I ask and try to keep my voice from sounding too excited.

"No, Elisse," Tallulah says. "Each wanderer has a specific function, a task that makes them fit within the tribe and makes them useful in their own way. We have three bloodlines in our nation. The *skineaters*, like these boys you see here. Father Thunder, Tared, Nashua, and Julien were born under the star of battle. They are here to defend our tribe, fight with claws and fangs, and crush our enemies. That is why, in their human condition, skineaters are men and women of impressive strength and size."

She glides her hand through the air and points to the girl next to me. "We are also the *bloodkeepers*, like me and my little girl Johanna, who dedicate ourselves to transmit the legacy of the wanderers through the Book of the Generations to preserve our traditions. Also, we're born with the special gift of healing."

"You can thank Johanna for fixing your side," Tared says and points to my ribs. "She always does great work."

I look at the girl, but she hides under her sharp bangs.

"Our clouded eyes are our most distinctive trait," Tallulah says and points to her grayish irises. "Here among us, the bloodkeepers are the brains behind so much muscle."

The men burst into laughter, and Johanna sinks into her seat as if any kind of attention caused her pain.

Tallulah touches my wrist. "Well, boy, we finally reach what concerns you most," she says, and my heart wakes up.

"There's the third and last lineage of the wanderers. The rarest and most unusual creature of our extraordinary species. But let the man in the wheelchair tell you," she says and points to the person I thought was an old woman.

She notices the surprise in my eyes. "Oh, you thought he was a woman, right? I bet you've heard that."

I thought with everything that happened to me today, my capacity for amazement was destroyed. But I was completely wrong.

"How... ?"

"Do you want to explain it, Grandfather Muata?" Father Thunder asks.

The old man finally lifts his head. "My task is to give voice to what cannot be heard in our world," he answers in a thick whisper like an echo bouncing off the walls of a deep well. "I translate the language of those who are no longer here in the flesh and those who have never had it. I can interpret the heavens to offer omens to my people, read the soul of fire, and whisper the words of the wind. I am the oracle of the spirits, a link that moves between light and shadow, between real and legend, between the living and the dead. I am a *shadowgazer*."

The truth rolls over me like an avalanche. Each cell of my body rushes toward infinity along with my soul. I feel weightless as if a heavy burden on my shoulders vanished. My narrow world finally widens.

"I'm a shadowgazer?"

"That's right, boy. You've finally awakened," Tallulah says, and a shower of smiles falls on me.

"So, the silence and the emptiness ... ?"

"The void you perceive when you are called by a spirit is what our ancestor shamans called the middle plane," Muata says. "The middle plane is the limbo of spirits, a place where the souls of men and animals who haven't yet passed into the world of the dead, roam. A place different from the world of the living but shares the same space. Above all, it's the womb that births those creatures the wanderers must control."

"How come I can enter that place?" I ask. "Why are some of them so deformed? And that horrible smell? How is that—?"

"These mysteries will be revealed to you once you begin your training as an oracle," the old man says.

"What? But—"

"Do you have an ancestor? A spirit that supports your bloodline as a shadowgazer?"

The question takes me by surprise. I open and close my mouth like an idiot.

"Son," Tallulah says. "Have confidence in Grandfather Muata. He only does what he thinks is best for everyone."

I purse my lips.

She smiles, patient before my obvious despair. "Do you want to know how Tared knew you were one of us?"

I turn to Tared, but he refuses to look at me.

"Shadowgazers also have a physical characteristic that distinguishes them from the other bloodlines," Muata continues. "The beings that inhabit the middle plane, as well as ancestors, are not bound to the laws that govern our world. They no longer have age or sex. So, to become their oracles, shadowgazers must be as ambiguous as they are. Neither men nor women but a little of both. At least in appearance."

"You got lucky!" the redhead says. "According to the legends, those of your bloodline are incredibly beautiful creatures."

"Oh God, Julien." Tared turns deep red and buries his face in his hands.

The groans of everyone around don't phase the comedian, who just laughs to himself.

"Johanna, do not write that," Father Thunder orders.

The girl nods and can barely hold back a smile at the corners of her lips.

"But most important of all, Elisse," Tallulah says and squeezes my hand, "we must always be together no matter what our lineage. We are a family, and among the wanderers, there is nothing more important than that."

Family.

The word pierces my chest like an arrow, and the memory of my father stings my heart. Did he know I was a wanderer? Was that why he abandoned me?

Gasps of wonder snatch up my thoughts as Old Muata carefully rises from his wheelchair.

"Grandfather Muata, please, don't try," Johanna says.

The old man circles the fire and walks toward me as if he were perfectly able to see.

He stands in front of me, and although his blind gaze does not rest on mine, somehow those white eyes study me through the darkness.

"I have been the shadowgazer of the Comus Bayou tribe for more years than I can remember. Now, nature calls me back to her bosom. Our eyes, bound to contemplating the place of two worlds, end up blind over the years, so I can no longer see anything of the human world or the spirit world. When that happens to a shadowgazer, his ancestor abandons him," he says and caresses the tiny crow skull that dangles at his chest. "So, in the face of the horrors we have witnessed in these months, now more than ever, we need someone to take my place.

"You, boy," he says and lifts his long finger to point at me, "are the first oracle-blooded creature to step foot in Louisiana for over ninety years. If you prove to be worthy, it will be your responsibility to replace me."

I blink until my eyes ache.

Replace him? I can't even pass a shadow without jumping. What the hell am I supposed to do? Have tea with a thousand-armed monster? Rather than finding the answers of my past, I have run into a future of nightmares.

"Elisse," Tallulah calls me. Her voice sounds distant. "Now you must decide whether to take your oath and stand beside your brothers or choose to forget your roots and lose the blood of your ancestry to the history of humanity.

"If you accept our path, you'll belong to this land, to this tribe, and to these beings who now accompany you in the heat of the flames. You must stop fleeing from those spirits that have tormented you and communicate with them. Your life will never be as it was. You will become a true shadowgazer."

The firelight dances on the faces of everyone around the campfire, teetering between warm and spectral. It feels like I've known these faces for many years, and behind them are hidden memories that have accompanied me since before my own. I feel nostalgic, melancholy, and also … afraid.

"And if I don't accept?" I ask cautiously.

"I told you he was a coward." Nashua finally opens his mouth and spits on the ground. "After Johanna and I followed him through the French Quarter, I knew he was a coward."

"Coward? I'd like to see you endure the relentless torment of demons."

"Who do you think you are to talk to me like that?" He jumps to his feet, and his eyes pool with blood.

"Sit down, Nashua!" Tared's voice booms in my ears, and his face flushes. He points at Nashua. The intensity of his eyes restrains me—with even greater force when Nashua reluctantly obeys without looking up.

Father Thunder sighs. "If you do not accept, you'll be returned to the humans, and you'll never hear from us again. Your gifts as a shadowgazer will isolate you for the rest of your life, and you will never obtain the knowledge required to make the spirits your allies. Your only consolation will be that you will never have to endanger your life for anything or anyone. So, consider carefully."

I crash my eyes against the fire, and my chest rises and falls. All my life I have looked for the answer to my fears, and now that I have it, I feel I have returned to the same point of departure. I don't know how to avoid spirits, but maybe I could get used to them, even learn to ignore them. But then what? Who says there's no purpose for me beyond being a loner who can see the dead?

If I agree to become a part of this tribe, I may not find anything other than a world that costs what's left of my sanity. But isn't this why I traveled to the other side of the world? Isn't this the reason I abandoned everything I knew and had? Didn't I want, from the depths of my being, a family?

I empty my lungs and look at Mama Tallulah. My eyes water, but I swallow the sentimentality and push it deep into my throat.

"All right," I whisper.

Mama Tallulah smiles and throws herself around my neck. The red-haired man claps loudly in celebration along with a silent and smiling Johanna, whereas Nashua's expression makes it clear he isn't happy.

"There's nothing more to speak of. The tribe has chosen, as well, its new member," Father Thunder says as he stands up. "Tared, the boy will stay in the reserve cabin until we give him a permanent bed, so bring his belongings tomorrow."

"Wait a minute. I never said I was going to move here," I say. "I can't vanish like that out of nowhere. Those who welcomed me in the city must be looking for me."

"I suppose the prince will want us to take him home now, right?" Nashua's voice rises.

"What the hell is your problem?" I send my common sense to the devil and stand up to charge at Nashua. I'm ready to tackle the idiot, who's also risen to his feet, but Tared intervenes between us. He plants his powerful hand on my chest while his other hand twists the collar of the giant's jacket.

"You," he says to me between his teeth. "Learn to control your impulses now, or you'll learn the hard way later. And you," he says several shades louder to Nashua. "Stop messing with him, or you'll have a problem with me."

Nashua, a couple of inches taller than Tared, would appear to have the advantage, but the ferocity of Tared's eyes shows otherwise. After a brief exchange of looks between each of us, Nashua sits down again.

I try to calm myself. To fight this man wouldn't have been the smartest thing in the world, but I'm sure I wouldn't have regretted at least trying to defend my dignity.

Father Thunder presses the bridge of his nose with his middle and index finger in a gesture oddly similar to the one I make.

"We have a phone, Elisse. Use it to call whom you need, and tell them you'll spend the night here. If you think it wise, Tared will return you to the city tomorrow."

"What if he speaks of us?" Nashua asks.

"If he does, I assure you we'll be the first to know," the old man says. "Do not get too comfortable there, boy. Soon your responsibilities will be to this tribe, and you'll have to prepare for what's coming. Do you understand?"

I don't even get a chance to nod before he strikes the ground with his cane.

"With this, I conclude the stories by the fire."

At that moment, everyone stands as if they followed a strict protocol.

Father Thunder leaves with the wolf skin dragging behind him like a tail. Mama Tallulah follows, but not before giving me one last smile.

"Have a nice night, son," she says.

Nashua throws me a crooked glance and takes the handles of Old Muata's chair to wheel him away.

Julien passes by me and slaps my back. Johanna follows with the leather book pressed against her chest and looks at me with those clouded eyes that finally return to normal.

In a blink, Tared and I are alone. He gazes into my eyes, but I can't sustain for long. I look up to contemplate the vast sky above us and soak in the light of the moon.

One thing is clear to me. Everything that has tormented me in my life is real, and I've never been crazy. But after everything I've heard today, maybe I'd rather be.

PART TWO
A MONSTER LIKE US

Chapter 18
Corpse in a Bottle

I PASSED THROUGH the window glass and sought refuge on the washing machine that had finally stopped spinning like a wild dancer. Even though I couldn't feel the heat suffocating the inanimate creatures in the laundry room, I writhed in anguish at the sight of a very young Louisa panting and drenched in sweat.

Outside, the gravel road radiated waves of heat. Its blackish flesh roasted in the 104-degree sun that scorched the state of Louisiana and turned each home into a small oven that baked its poor inhabitants.

The machine next to me churned furiously, frothing hot bubbles that elevated the temperature of the room and turned your white uniform into a cotton sauna.

Powerful nausea lashed you to your knees. In the seven years that you've labored as a domestic worker, the smell of bleach had never caused such discomfort. So you were certain that what you had smelled when you opened the bottle was not at all the same substance to clean clothes.

You pressed your bulging belly and gnashed your teeth until your gums nearly bled. You were more afraid of your employer hearing you than of the pain twisting your insides.

It was bad enough that a few days ago, that aggressive white woman had caught you listening to messages of racial desegregation on the radio. So, naturally, you didn't want to risk being fired for having an incident in her home and embarrassing her in front of her neighbors.

Despite your brave efforts, your lips broke, and you moaned like a wounded animal before that dreadful sensation that was sadly all too familiar. You turned your watery eyes to the edge of your skirt and watched with anguish as a dark spot devoured the white fabric.

You knew you were having another miscarriage, the third since you were married. First, the doctor had said your loss was from lack of nutrition, then it was stress, then you had worked too much. At that point, you didn't know why you couldn't carry a child, and that monster of a husband who had beat you and blamed you for your inability to have children didn't help the matter.

But what you couldn't understand was why that container of bleach had exhaled the deep and abominable smell of a corpse.

Chapter 19
Family Doesn't Mix

THE SWOLLEN WOOD of the old dock grinds when I sit on the edge. I dip my bare feet into the murky water, and instantly, fine icy needles dig into my skin. I let the cramps worsen because the pain, almost medical, brings me back to earth and reminds me how alive I am.

I sweep away a water lily floating near me to peer below the surface. The spine of a small alligator sways in the darkness at the bottom, so I raise my feet, more disgusted than terrified, at the thought of yesterday's monster. Wrapping myself tighter with the poncho, I contemplate the soft mist hovering over the surface of the lake.

It's after six in the morning, and I've slept less than I would have liked. I've always seen things some might consider extraordinary, but now, all that falls short compared to what I experienced yesterday.

The dock creaks behind me, accompanied by light steps. Johanna approaches with the hood of her sweatshirt over her head. Her bangs draw a sharp line across her forehead. I want to greet her with a smile, but I can only make a funny face. She sits next to me and hides her hands in the pouch of her sweatshirt.

"An animal will rip your feet off if you put them back in there," she says.

"Things are so weird now, I wouldn't be surprised if they grew back," I say lightly.

She laughs, although I wasn't joking.

"How are you feeling?" she asks.

I look around and stop at Johanna's face, which I can see better now that daylight breaks. She's probably several years older than me, but I could be wrong. The wanderers—we—are never what we appear to be. I thought Tared was in his thirties, but Julien said he's just twenty-eight. Perhaps everyone here has aged because of the things they've experienced.

"I feel a little older," I say.

She nods as if she understood me. "When Nashua brought me here, I felt so disoriented."

"I guess that's normal. It's not every day you wake up knowing you can turn into an animal."

"I know what you mean. But even when I was little, I knew something wasn't right with me. I was always wilder than my parents could handle."

"From here you are?" I ask.

"Pardon?"

"I mean, are you from New Orleans," I say, correcting my accent.

"Oh, no. I'm from Texas."

"You're really pale for being from the desert."

"Look who's talking, child of India," she says, and now it's me who laughs.

Suddenly, Johanna seems a little younger. I rub my nose against my sleeve and return to stare at the water.

"Do they know what you are?" I ask.

Johanna doesn't respond immediately, so I turn my eyes to her. She's pensive with a half-born smile on her lips.

"The truth is ... I didn't get along with them. They said I was a problem child," she says and softens her voice. "So, when I moved here for a job, I stopped talking to them. After a few months I had my first awakening, so they don't know anything about this. I'm not sure if I want them to know someday."

A mixture of emotions floods me. I feel bad for her, but the temptation to judge digs at me. Her story makes me think of someone who throws away food while another person starves.

"What's your ancestor? What did you name it?" I change the subject so things don't get complicated.

She shrugs and stares at the water lilies. "I'm not supposed to tell you."

"Why?"

"Father Thunder says we have to get to know the family from our human side first, that talking about our animal part might cause snap judgments."

"You think I'm going to judge you by your appearance? Believe me, I've been judged so many times for the same reason."

Johanna smiles. I'm sure because I don't need to explain what I mean.

"I don't know... " she says.

"Go on. I promise not to tell anyone you told me." I give her a slight nudge.

To my surprise, her face turns red. She looks briefly at the lake before looking into my eyes, and finally…

"*Coyote Garrasrojas.*"

"What?"

She blushes even more.

"It's Spanish. It means Coyote Redclaws."

A smile creeps across my lips, and she draws her hood tighter.

"Don't look at me like that," she says.

"Why are you embarrassed?"

"It's like a stereotype. A girl from the desert with a coyote for an ancestor."

"Oh, come on, it's not that bad. It could be a cactus."

Johanna kicks me and arches forward laughing. I look over the lake and endure the painful urge to laugh, too.

Although I've only known Johanna for a few hours, she awakens something pleasantly familiar, as most women do. I've always had an enormous respect for women, especially after seeing how some of them in India were treated like animals or punching bags to release tension.

When my tutor died, the woman who took care of the smallest orphaned children in the country was the first person to comfort me and tell me everything would be fine. When I arrived in New Orleans, Louisa welcomed me as any mother would and showed me affection as if I were her own child. Here, Mama Tallulah took care of me, held my hand so I wouldn't fall into despair, and called me "my son" even without knowing anything about me.

My whole life I've had the appearance of a girl. That has provoked prejudice, hatred, and rejection from many people, something that has greatly fueled my loneliness. But I'll never be ashamed for being mistaken as a woman. There's nothing demeaning about being one.

I've learned to embrace my emotions, admit feeling fear and pain, and accept that longing to give and receive affection doesn't make me weaker. I don't have to fit into any model of manhood to be, precisely, a man.

The tires of a vehicle grumble behind us. Tared drives a sand-colored jeep and stops before reaching the dock. His face is as flat as a wall. He sticks his arm out of the window to signal Johanna. She shoots up like lightning and runs toward him, and I take the opportunity to put on my boots.

Out of the corner of my eye, I catch Tared gesturing with his fingers while Johanna nods, crosses her arms, and shrugs her shoulders from time to time. I think he's scolding her, so I entertain myself with the laces of my boots and pretend I'm not paying attention to the scene.

"Elisse. It's time to go." Tared's authoritative voice vibrates through the air, so I stand up and walk over.

Johanna smiles and waves as she leaves without even looking at me.

"Is everything all right?" I ask.

"Get in. We have to talk." He lights a cigarette and brings it to his lips.

"Should I say goodbye to the rest of the ... tribe?"

He doesn't reply at all, so I take that as a "no."

Julien comes out of a cabin, eating a piece of sausage, and waves with his mutilated hand.

As we drive, silence drowns us, and each second becomes more uncomfortable. I divert my eyes to the dreamcatcher, which is now singed and missing feathers. After we pass the reserve booth, there's still no hint of this talk.

"Um, did you want to tell me something?"

Tared releases a puff of smoke and crushes the butt in the ashtray.

"Do you like Johanna?"

A needle of discomfort digs into my palm, so I rub it against my pants to relieve the itching.

"Should I not?"

He pulls another cigarette from his pack. I'm beginning to think his real ancestor isn't a wolf but a chimney.

"She's pretty, huh?" he says.

I roll my eyes, trying to look inside my skull.

"We were only talking, clearly." I say. "Hey, look, if she's your girlfriend or something—"

Tared breaks into laughter, and my face unravels in confusion. He steers the jeep off the road to park on the shoulder. He crushes the cigarette against the ashtray, even though the tip isn't even lit, and sits back in the seat to face me.

"Johanna isn't my girlfriend, she's my sister. Not of blood but of family, just like you," he says.

"Can we speak the same language, please?"

He scratches the back of his neck, and for a moment, I think his cheeks redden beneath his tanned skin.

"Elisse, from the moment a wanderer agrees to become part of the tribe, he also becomes part of our family. And as you should know, family doesn't mix," he says. "Father Thunder said it last night. It's not that simple. There are rules regarding the perpetuation of our species that we should always consider. I mean, have you ever seen a lynx mate with a fox? Or a rabbit with a cat?"

"What?" Now I turn red.

Tared sighs and moves close to me so the distance between us becomes a few centimeters of confidentiality.

"Look, our species is maintained by reproducing, there's nothing magical about it. But our ancestors are an essential part of each one of us. They are as unique as people. We carry them in our blood. We have their roots and the burden of their ancestors. Everything inherited is mixed and transformed just like genes are. So, unless you want to have deformed children or have your wife burst because she can't give birth to a moose, you should never sleep with another wanderer. Understand?"

I don't remember how I'm supposed to nod, so I just open and close my mouth in surprise and embarrassment. I blink to remove my idiot's face.

"So, we can only... mate with humans?" I ask. The question sounds so outrageous. Just a few hours ago, I considered myself a human.

"Yes. Your children or grandchildren will have almost no chance of being born as wanderers even though your great-grandchildren might, as in the case of Grandfather Muata and Nashua, who are blood relatives. Our species is reduced each passing century, but that's much better than to risk losing your entire family, right?"

"What about wanderers of the same... kind?" I ask. "Say that both have a type of wolf as an ancestor, for example."

"The danger is the same. Grandfather Muata and Nashua are direct relatives, but they have different ancestors, so you don't know if the blood of your ancestors is going to mix, even if your partner has the same species of ancestor."

I agree almost mechanically. Everything he's telling me is logical, and maybe that's why it's not difficult for me to understand.

Tared combs his hair back, a gesture I interpret as discomfort, so I smile, almost certain I understand why he's telling me all these things.

"That doesn't stop someone from falling in love with another wanderer, right?" I ask.

The question seems to burn Tared. He moves away from me and starts the jeep. He doesn't seem annoyed but upset.

"You have nothing to worry about. At least not from me," I say with absolute sincerity.

I won't deny that I'm flesh and blood, but sex or romance has never been a priority. The kind of affection I've always wanted is in the deep bosom of a family. Besides, with my nightmares, being in a relationship was the last thing I was worried about finding in India. And I don't think things are different here. At least for now.

When Tared doesn't respond, I move closer to him to break the distance he imposed between us, stubbornly trying to bother him. I think he owes it to me after everything I went through yesterday.

He looks at me with an expression of defeat and digs into his pocket for his cigarette box. When he finds the pack empty, he crushes it and throws it to the floor of the jeep.

"Well?" I say.

Tared snorts. "When Johanna first reached the tribe, she confused the brotherhood I offered her with something else, and the truth is, she had a bad experience. I don't want something like that to happen again."

"I don't think she'll pay attention to me if I just—"

"I'm not saying to her. I'm saying to you. I don't want us to have problems. Do you understand?"

"I swear, Tared." I shoot his name from my tongue like an arrow. "Don't worry about me."

"We'll see, Elisse." He wields my name from his mouth like a shield.

I move away and lean against the car door.

Discomfort grows in the back of my neck. Not for Tared. But because we're already entering the city, and I'm thinking about the tremendous scolding that awaits me when I get back to the center.

✦ ✦ ✦ ✦

WE PARK IN FRONT of the Buddhist center. Louisa stands next to the shop window with her back toward us. I don't look at her for long, fearing she may turn around, so I turn to Tared.

"Thank you," I say and take off my seatbelt.

"Don't thank me yet." He gets out of the jeep, to my confusion. "After the scolding they gave you over the phone last night, I don't think facing them alone is wise."

I look at him with indecision for a few seconds, but considering the convenience of his offer, I nod. I don't know how brave it is for me to feel grateful for his gesture, but the truth is, Tared has just become my lifeline once again.

I walk behind him. Louisa has disappeared from the window.

She's probably still angry, and I can't blame her. When I called last night, she yelled so loudly that she almost burst my eardrums. I alleged that Tared had accidentally hit me with his truck the day before because he couldn't see me in the street through the fog. That helped explain why I left the broom on the ground. But nothing seemed to calm her.

I also told her that I refused to go to a hospital because I didn't want the center to end up paying the expenses, so Tared offered to take me to his home and tend to me. Because it turns out, he also knows first aid.

The lie was weak, but it was the best we could think of, and I think Louisa was more interested in telling me how irresponsible and inconsiderate I was than in questioning my story. I wish I had hurt my leg to make the lie more credible, but the cures of Mama Tallulah and Johanna have been so effective that I no longer have traces of yesterday's accident.

The thought of their cloudy eyes twists a scream of impatience in my veins.

There's so much I don't understand about us and about myself that I'm about to go crazy. But I don't get a chance to throw up questions before Tared rings the doorbell. He gives me a firm look that grounds me.

The door opens. Arms sprout from within and constrict the breath out of me like a pair of anacondas. "Elisse, thank heavens!" Louisa says. "I'm so glad you're okay."

I'm baffled to infinity. No scolding or shouting, just a hug. I stretch my neck to look at Tared, who just shrugs. Louisa lets go and looks me up and down as if she were checking for missing body parts.

"You must be Tared," she says to the giant. "Thank you so much for taking care of him."

"Don't thank me, ma'am. I was the one who hit him."

"I'm sure it was Elisse's fault. He's as careless as a child." Her scolding returns to the charge but now in a much less hostile way. I can't help blushing, especially in front of Tared, who has a great time in front of my shame.

"Sorry," I growl, and my face grows hot. Tared messes up my hair and makes me feel even more like a little boy.

I find it most surreal that this guy is a creature of mythology unfolding as a totally normal person, but still, it's difficult to imagine him becoming a wolf as he talks to Louisa.

"Now that I've delivered him in one piece, I'll be on my way," he says with gallantry and descends the front steps.

"Won't you stay for breakfast?" Louisa asks.

"I'd love to, ma'am, but I'm running late," Tared replies. "Maybe another day."

"I see. Another day then. And again, thank you."

Jeez, he wasn't that nice when we met.

He nods goodbye and leaves for the jeep. I stare at his back, and once again, his imposing stature astounds me. *Skineater* ...

As soon as he sticks a foot inside the vehicle, I dart toward him. "Tared!" I shout.

Far from looking surprised, he smiles as if he knew I was forgetting something.

"What's next?" I ask.

"Grandfather Muata will start training you when he considers it wise, but until then, you'll have to deal with us, so come up with a good excuse to be away," he says and glances at Louisa.

Geshe Osel appears in the doorway with a smile and waves at us.

"Thanks, for everything," I say with a twisted voice.

He offers a handshake. My hand feels like it shrinks in his wide palm as if suddenly I became the smallest person in the world. The feeling isn't intimidating. Rather, it conveys great protection over me and encourages me to yearn for that strength, to equal it.

"I wouldn't feel so grateful," he says. "You still owe me a truck."

The smile fades from my lips, and he roars with laughter. He starts the jeep, raises his hand to the air, and then disappears into the light morning fog.

Who would have thought I'd end up owing a werewolf?

Chapter 20
Comus Bayou

It's the eve of the New Year, and a few days have passed since I discovered that I'm a wanderer and what it's like to be part of a group of extraordinary and diverse creatures. I still haven't recovered from the emotional shock of knowing that I'm some sort of mixture of human, animal, and witch. I feel like I've entered a different reality, or I've inhabited the body of a totally different person. And something tells me today won't feel any different.

Losar, the Tibetan New Year, doesn't coincide with the Western New Year, so the Buddhist center doesn't celebrate tonight. Even so, I found it strange that Geshe and Louisa immediately agreed, at the request of Tared, to let me spend the night at the reserve. In fact, Louisa looked thrilled that I was making "new friends," despite Carlton, who never ceased to repeat how strange it is that I'm suddenly friends with a man ten years older than me.

But encouraged by Louisa's growing fondness for the wolf, and Geshe Osel's usual nonchalance, I get in Tared's jeep at four in the damn morning. On the way to the reserve, the wolf gives me my first lesson on being a wanderer.

"You see," he says and lights a cigarette, "the priority of our species is to keep total and absolute secrecy. The loyalty we form with other wanderers and the humans who enter our world are vital to our survival. To fortify bonds and strengthen the instinct of protection toward our own is something we carry in our blood, something innate. So it's important to introduce you to the tribe, not as a new member, but as a lost brother who's finally returned home. One way to do this is to have you participate in the simplest of our customs."

The warmth of his words is so pleasant that I can't keep from blushing.

The cabins appear up ahead, and Nashua and Mama Tallulah welcome us at the entrance. She gives me a hug and the news that today we'll be hunting a deer for New Year's dinner—with our bare hands.

The idea produces mixed feelings. On one hand, I'm excited, especially if I get to see these people transform, but on the other hand, what an unsettling way to spend the end of the year with family.

Nashua laughs through his nose at my shocked face.

"We're wanderers," he says with pride. "Instinct is alive inside us, and we encourage it with our traditions. This isn't a hunt, boy, it's a ritual."

With those words, I wait for everything from drums and loincloths to feasts of blood, but the reality is different. After a colossal breakfast, Tared, Nashua, Johanna, and I venture out dressed in simple mountain boots and raincoats to an area of the reserve where hunting is permitted. The light fog grants us easy passage to a stretch of land surrounded by moss and cypress trees that spread like an opaque, grayish hair over the forest.

We—or rather, they—track prey in a hopelessly human way. I'm dying to know everything about how wanderers hunt, but at the moment, we're nothing more than overgrown children taunting the shrubs and feeling for tracks in the soil.

After walking a few hours, we encounter a good-sized dinner drinking from a lagoon before the bulging eyes of a pair of small alligators.

"We're not going to transform to catch it," Johanna says.

I'm disappointed at first, but when the three ambush the deer, my astonishment grows to absurd levels. Tared breaks the animal's neck with his bare hands, showing that even in their most human form, wanderers can become exceedingly strong. And then Johanna, who barely weighs a hundred and twenty pounds, throws the deer over her shoulder and begins carrying it without breaking a sweat.

After a few minutes of walking in silence, still in awe of the wanderers' strength, I ask if I have an ancestor inside me. No one says a word, so I stop in my tracks and look at them to show that I really want an answer.

"No," Tared says and steps over a fallen tree. "In your case, that matter is somewhat complicated."

"In my case?" I start walking again to keep up.

"Skineaters and bloodkeepers are born with an ancestor," he says. "We carry them already in our blood, and they're such an innate part of us that we even give them a proper name. So, these spirits are usually animals that exist in our region of birth or that of our ancestors."

"What the hell are you doing?" Nashua shouts at Tared. "You know well that—"

"Don't worry. Elisse has already proven to be quite persuasive at getting information."

Under my squinted gaze, Johanna accelerates her pace and leaves us.

"Tattletale," I say under my breath.

"As I was saying," Tared continues, "skineaters and bloodkeepers are close descendants of beasts, while shadowgazers are close descendants of shamans. That's why we acquire our ancestors in different ways. The ancestors of shadowgazers are existing spirits that may have belonged to another wanderer in the past. So, a shadowgazer must be accepted by an ancestor."

"So, how do you awaken them, so to speak?" I ask.

"In our case, an ancestor can manifest at any time in our lives, but it usually happens in adulthood during dangerous situations. Although, there are cases in which a person dies without ever knowing that they're a wanderer. Some will never be in imminent danger or around other wanderers where they can reveal their nature, you know?"

"Are there more like us in New Orleans?"

"Not that we've found," he says. "We detect other wanderers by means of smell. Because we carry an ancestor inside, we have a more distinctive scent than that of humans, who usually have a smell of little significance to our noses. But for years, we haven't sensed a lost wanderer or another family member, and because of that, we comb the city regularly."

"Well, then, how did you find me if I don't have an ancestor?" I ask cautiously.

"Androgynous people are not that common, and much less those who see spirits. If you think about it, it's a simple pattern to track."

We finally catch up to Johanna. Tared takes the deer from her and throws it over his shoulder as if it weighed nothing. The girl massages her back in relief, and I keep bombarding them with more questions.

"Is there some kind of wanderer mafia?" I don't know if I used the right word, but when Nashua bursts out laughing, I realize that I screwed up.

"You mean if wanderers have organizations or things like that?" Tared asks.

"That's what I meant."

"You could say that. Families of wanderers generally model their structure based on blood relationships. That is, parents, children, grandchildren, and the humans with whom they've become close to. Unfortunately, the only humans who've lived here in recent decades were the women of Grandfather Muata's family, a succession of single mothers who died of old age or uterine cancer. Those factors have considerably reduced the size of Comus Bayou over the years.

"When a tribe is as small as ours, it's normal to want other wanderers who haven't awakened or don't belong to a family, in order to increase our numbers. Blood doesn't matter. Anyone who joins a family of wanderers is considered a brother or a sister. They're our fathers, our mothers, and our children. We're not werewolves or coyote men or anything like that. We're wanderers. A nation, without a doubt, but with creatures so unique and complex, relating to other tribes is not always easy."

"There's much more history behind all the legends and myths of our race," Nashua says. "But Grandfather Muata is supposed to instruct you in this, just as Father Thunder did with us, and Mama Tallulah with Johanna. In this family, we follow the tradition of the Comus Bayou lineages. We have done so for hundreds of years, and we're no one to change things now."

A light finally turns on. Now I understand why everyone is so reluctant to explain anything about being a shadowgazer. Apparently, in our tribe, we can only learn through direct experience or through the teachings of someone with the same ancestry.

"For now, you just need to have one thing clear, Elisse," Tared says. "Even though we have different functions in our tribe, or we are born with specific characteristics, everyone, without exception, has the obligation to fight. Not doing so is a sign of cowardice and an act of high treason to our race, because everyone who enters under the protection of a tribe of wanderers must be willing to die for them if necessary. That protection, that loyalty, that bond between our people is what we call the *Dreamcatcher.*"

Dreamcatcher. The word, despite the oath it represents, makes me feel less alien to this hunt.

When we arrive at the cabins, we meet Julien in the reserve's huge kitchen. It's a complete barracks with three exclusive meat freezers attached to a wall, a set of stoves, a large refrigerator, and plenty of shelves and pantries crammed with pasta, cans, condiments, and various boxes.

Tared drops the deer on the huge table, and he, Julien, and I begin cutting, gutting and cleaning the animal. It's the first creature I've butchered, but the blood and guts don't really disgust me. I mean, for years I've seen beings that look and smell much worse than a deer's insides.

Nashua enters the kitchen to grab a few things from the cupboard. He looks at me uncomfortably long and then leaves without saying a word.

"What's wrong with him?" I ask.

"Don't take it personally," the wolf says with a shrug. "He's just getting used to seeing you. Grandfather Muata was about a thousand years old when Nashua was born, so he never met the old man at his most splendid state."

"What do you mean?"

"If there's one bloodline that's rare in our race, it's the shadowgazer, and males are even rarer. They say those of your ancestry gave rise to the myth of the elves, so it's not easy to look at you without being a little shocked."

His words have a negative effect on me. In India, I always had to take care of myself, and on more than one occasion, flee for my dignity—not only from people who found my appearance repulsive but also from those who, worse yet, found it fascinating.

"I'd prefer to be stronger and less flashy," I say bluntly.

Tared narrows his blue eyes on mine, and suddenly, I'm forced to look down, afraid he might read my thoughts.

"Because of your age, the manmimicker part is probably already awakening," he says. "You can't match the strength of a skineater, but you'll become more powerful, move faster, and you'll begin to eat three times as much to support the energy expenditure needed for the whole transformation process."

"And for the record, this year we're dieting with this little animal." Julien laughs and points to the carcass with a knife.

Hours later, during dinner, I understand what he meant.

Before my astonished eyes, Johanna eats seven pounds of meat, and the skineaters gobble up at least twelve pounds each.

Too self-conscious by this amazing world even to take a drink, I just watch what's going on around me from my little tree stump by the bonfire. I still can't believe that these people who listen to loud music and drink like sailors are half animal. There's nothing about them that shows it.

I remain almost invisible until the touch of New Year's, at which point, Tared pulls me from the seat where I planted myself and drags me to the fire. Everyone, even Father Thunder and Nashua, squeezes me one after another in a powerful embrace that marks my bones and my memory.

On this night when a new cycle begins, in the middle of a huge swamp in Louisiana, I begin to cast the first roots of my new life.

✦✦✦✦

A COUPLE OF MONTHS HAVE PASSED since our New Year's dinner, and since then, my visits to the tribe have become fairly regular. The money in the Buddhist center is still disappearing, so I negotiated with Geshe to stay at the shop in the mornings, and then I can escape to the reserve for the rest of the day—all in order to avoid the glowering eyes of Carlton and the rest of the members of the center.

I've started to give a small part of my measly salary to help with the upkeep of the village. Johanna and Julien have their own jobs, and Nashua serves as a ranger on the reserve a couple of days a week. These jobs, together with the money from Tared's blacksmith shop and the rent for land owned by Father Thunder, help bring food to the table, so in a short time, I've become a part of this place. Each time I'm here, I grow more fascinated, not only by our world but also by the deepening closeness with my new family.

As we get closer to the reserve, colorful beaded necklaces gradually appear in the trees. Tared drives the jeep slowly as he tells me about the problems that have plagued the tribe for several months now.

Apparently, a few months ago, before the hurricane arrived, there was an attack on the reserve. A moose wanderer burst into one of the cabins during the early morning, catching everyone by surprise. Tared says Father Thunder tried to reason with it, but the creature was out of its mind. It snapped Julien's finger off in one bite and ran into the swamp. Luckily, Johanna and Nashua killed it before anyone else discovered what was happening.

Tared says they would have considered that a lone incident, but one dawn, he ran into another crazed wanderer—the deer he hunted to Audubon Park—hanging around the backyard of his blacksmith shop. After those incidences and the attack of the alligator wanderer, it's clear to everyone in Comus Bayou that someone or something is trying to mess with us.

I glance at the wolf, who finally parks the jeep.

Despite the intense relationships I've been building with the others, I think I've grown closest to Tared. I don't know if it's because everything started with him or because we've faced death together, but there's something about the way he speaks and moves that fills me with an overflowing confidence. It's like he understands me perfectly.

He's the type of person who inspires respect in a natural way, rather than imposing it, and although practically everything about him is intimidating, I feel like I don't want to be anywhere else other than by his side. I suppose that's what a good leader is supposed to do.

Tared gets out of the vehicle at the call of Father Thunder, who waits for him at the shore of the lake along with Johanna and Nashua. Immediately, the wolf greets the old man with a show of respect. In spite of everything, I'm still surprised by Tared's loyalty to Father Thunder and the duty with which he obeys his orders.

As a matter of hierarchy, the only ones with some authority in the tribe are Father Thunder and Tared. The wolf, from what Julien told me, is like a second-in-command. I don't know how he got to that level, but I have no problem with it. The werewolf has shown more than once that he can handle a pack of fools like us, so he's the only person I'd trust with my life.

"Little guy, come here!" Julien calls from the entrance to the kitchen.

I get out of the jeep and hurry over. The fool pats the crown of my head and earns a playful kick in the shin.

"Hey, I'm going out with the others and Father Thunder. Can you help Mama Tallulah in the kitchen?"

"Uh, yeah, sure," I say. "Where are you going?"

"To train for a while in the forest, let's— Hey, don't look at me like that. You know Father Thunder won't let you come to these things until you have an ancestor."

I tighten my lips and nod slightly. Julien, appearing somewhat distressed, heads out.

In the kitchen, Mama Tallulah boils a large pot of broth. I give her a hug and then lose myself in the mosaic of wild turkeys and maple leaves on the wall.

"Why does Muata hate me?" I ask in a low voice.

Mama Tallulah drops the ladle and looks at me.

"Oh, honey, why do you say that?"

"He never speaks to me unless it's to tell me he doesn't have the energy to answer my questions. He dismisses me all the time, and I don't understand why."

She laughs without mockery, and the sound is so sweet that, suddenly, I'm a little embarrassed. I feel like a brat complaining about nonsense.

"Don't take it personally, my boy. Muata is going through difficult times because he's still getting used to his blindness and the absence of his ancestor."

"Mama Tallulah," I say in a trembling voice. "Since the day of the hunt, something in me desperately wants me to go through my first change, something... instinctive that wants me to look for an ancestor. It's like I finally realized that I'm incomplete. How will I ever be able to manipulate spirits if I don't know anything about them or the middle plane? Then there's the bone monster, isn't that something we should take care of?"

"Oh, dear," she says. "I can only tell you that the middle plane is not the final death, so when a soul stays there too long it forgets what it is and what it was. It reaches a point where it rots and deforms in horrible ways."

"Ah... I guess that explains why my nightmares always look and smell so bad."

"Not just that. They tend to torment shadowgazers and people with magic. They chase them, cause nightmares, and draw them to the middle plane because they need their help to cross over to the human plane. Without a shadowgazer, there is no way a family of wanderers can control them, so your arrival was a blessing for all of us. You shouldn't worry right now about the spirit that haunts you, because as long as you don't have your ancestor, there isn't much you can do."

"Muata couldn't do something like that so we can kill it?"

"Ah, if it were only as easy as saying it. There's a difference between a shadowgazer with an ancestor and a shadowgazer without one. With an ancestor, you have the ability to do magic. Without one, an oracle can only come and go between the middle and human plane. So, without magic and blind as a mole, Muata isn't able to do anything useful there. But be assured that when he believes it wise, he'll teach you everything he knows. For the moment, you have to leave him and the middle plane in peace."

"I'm sorry," I say softly. "I know you're not supposed to tell me about these things, but I feel completely useless. I look at all of you, so strong, so capable, and I … I can't help you with anything. I couldn't even if I wanted to, and I feel like I don't deserve to be part of Comus Bayou."

Mama Tallulah smiles at me with infinite tenderness and walks over with little feather steps. She wraps her hands, as light as air, in a warm grip around mine.

"Elisse, even though we needed a shadowgazer, our care for you isn't based on what you can do for us, but on the happiness that your simple existence brings to our lives. We don't want muscles or abilities or great powers. What we want is your affection and loyalty, because those things are what really make a family strong. And you, my dear, with or without magic, make us very, very strong. Never forget that."

The old owl releases me. I feel what she said so powerfully that even the ground shakes beneath my feet. The feeling reminds me of the first night I spent at the reserve. I was sitting by the fire looking at my father's picture when Mama Tallulah saw me and asked me to tell her about him. When I finished my story, she asked if I ever thought about my mother. I was embarrassed to say no. Since the only evidence I had of a relative was the image of my father, I never embraced another parental figure. Mama Tallulah just hugged me and told me there was no lonelier creature than one who didn't know the love of a mother, so she was happy that I was no longer alone.

That night, and for the first time, I hugged her back.

Words can't describe the kindness of Mama Tallulah, the affection her cloudy gaze awakens in me, or the happiness her squeeze fills me with when she greets me at the village. I imagine her and Louisa as day and night, so different from each other but both full of a light that fills the loneliness inside me. I grew up without a mother, but here in New Orleans, I have won two without knowing if I really deserve them.

Being suddenly involved in this world, so human and extraordinary, has made me pause the search for my father. I haven't forgotten about him. In fact, every night his image and the undeniable desire to find him come to mind, but it's best to adapt myself first to all these amazing changes and then continue with my purpose. Maybe my skills as a shadowgazer will help me.

"My child." Mama Tallulah draws me out of my thoughts. "Can you go build the fire? Something tells me the boys will bring something good to eat today."

I thank all the divine that her attention is placed on the pot, since my eyes have filled with tears. I clean my cheeks with the sleeve of my jacket and leave the kitchen.

At the fire pit, I become entranced with the ashes. Tibet, India, the United States ... I'd always believed the key to fitting into the world was to try to look like everybody else, so I never imagined that I would find my true home in the midst of beings infinitely different from one another. And since discovering that I'm a wanderer, my nightmares—as I keep calling the spirits—haven't bothered me again, and that includes the bone monster.

Beyond that, I admit, the longer I spend here, the more I feel like I'm in the right place. The days I stay overnight on the reserve, housed in one of the cabins where I share a room with Nashua, Julien, and Johanna, add another page to the album of beautiful memories I've been building in my mind—some of which only Louisa and the wanderers enter.

In the heat of the bonfire at sunset and the amazing stories I hear before it, I think I'm really beginning to understand the meaning of family.

Chapter 21
A Cry Divided

The line of salt drawn along the window's edge forces me to hang from a pair of nails to spy through a tiny hole in the black plastic covering the glass.

A puff from your cold lips extinguishes the candle on your altar, and your profile fades in a dim glow. The smoke rises in strange shapes and disperses into the darkness. You look over the objects in front of you to make sure nothing has suddenly disappeared: skulls, flowers, horns, candle wax, herbs, and a small bowl of blood.

You devoted yourself to Voodoo as a child, a time in which I watched in amazement as your skills progressed. But over the years, your fascination with those objects mutated into a deep horror each time you returned to the rituals you had struggled for years to master.

Poor Laurele. In the glass of an old picture frame, you catch the reflection of a tiny wrinkle at the corner of your lips—the first line I've seen on your face. You lift the photo from the middle of the altar and touch the image of a young man, barely twenty years old, whose face shines with a broad smile. A woman whose eyes have stolen the heart of the world embraces him with a shrill joy palpable even through such an old portrait.

To behold that image steeps you in adrenaline. Your tight chest heaves and falls until you rise from your chair and pace the room to calm the fury.

You look warily at me and then into the daylight sneaking through the holes. You take duct tape from your cabinet and, one by one, cover the holes with several thick layers to block the view of your infernal little world. You stop abruptly with a piece of sticky tape trembling between your fingers.

A soft trickle of light from the last hole strikes the wall of the oval room. Panting, you peek through the hole to look outside for a few seconds, surely to calm your need to scream.

You want to escape. You want to stop seeing bones. You want to burn all those shrunken heads, throw the candles and skulls in the trash, and start from scratch, like a new woman. I know. I've watched you for years. I've watched you crash your head against the walls of this house countless times to silence the voices of guilt. I've seen you close your legs to the pain, the price you paid for your power. And each time you look at the boy in that photograph, what's left of your heart is overcome by a grim and grotesque desire, the reason I'm here observing your slow death among the shadows of your regret.

As if you heard me, you take another piece of tape, and in a fit of therapeutic madness, cover the entire window with every inch of that material. You are about to cover the hole through which I spy when you sense a quiet call warn you that you are no longer alone.

Chapter 22
Witch Doctor

It's two o'clock in the morning, and my eyelids grow heavy but not enough to close them completely. I've stared at the book in my hands for so long that now it feels like the pages are reading me. I throw the thing to the side of the bed.

Reading has always helped me fall asleep, but I don't think I'll be able to close my eyes for the rest of the night. Whenever I'm at the Buddhist center, I find it hard to sleep—maybe because I don't feel as safe as when I'm on the reserve, or maybe I'm simply not used to being alone anymore.

A cough catches my throat, and I get up for a glass of water from the kitchen. I cross the darkened hallway and pass the shop without any interest in looking. I want to ask Muata why my nightmares don't follow me more than once to the same place, and what happens to the portals those creatures come from. I don't even know why or how they appear, but I'm sure the old man doesn't give a shit about my concerns.

I flip on the light and fill a glass with water from the tap. Before I take a sip, my gaze drifts through the window to the neighbor's porch and meets a floating white face. I rub my eyes. Maybe my fatigue is making me hallucinate. But when I look again, there's a body under that face. A slender man with skin as dark as the night wears a top hat and a suit. He leans against a post and watches me. His feet are bare, and the white part of his face is nothing but paint.

Stay calm. Maybe he's here for Mardi Gras. The parades started weeks ago, and Louisa told me people dress up and wear strange masks.

I glance at the phone on the wall behind me and consider calling the police. I'm pretty sure that guy isn't one of my neighbors. When I look through the window again, I jump back.

"Fuck!"

The man now stands a few feet from the window and stares at me with black, hollow eye sockets. He sticks a cigar in his mouth and turns toward the backyard. An alarm rings inside me.

Follow him.

I drop the glass in the sink and bolt out of the emergency exit to see if he's reached the garden. I scan the yard. The glaring light from the house barely touches the night.

Nothing. He's vanished.

A faint burning smell rises behind me, and I turn around to see a thick cloud of smoke billowing from the emergency door. My pulse quickens. I run back into the center and inhale to scream "fire!" but I stop.

"What the hell is going on?"

I race into the living room where an enormous cloud of smoke swirls from a burning cigar on a wooden plate. I crush the tip of the cigar with my sleeve, leaving a black hole in the fabric.

I switch on the ceiling fan and, over the whirl of the blades, hear a metallic clink. My skin chills. On the table rests a pair of gleaming gold coins and a small straw doll with its entire body pierced by black needles.

✦ ✦ ✦ ✦

My boots crack against the asphalt as I head for the French Quarter and wind through the crowds that have multiplied with the arrival of the carnival. It took me all night to decide to come here. In the end, I realized I had to go to the first person I could think of who might tell me why that straw doll was at the center. I just hope Louisa never finds out. I couldn't bear to disappoint her, but it seems I'm already doing everything possible to achieve that.

To my surprise, from a half block away, I can see mobs of people swirl inside Laurele's shop and jam together as they stumble to enter and exit as if she were giving away trinkets.

I toss my hair back. It won't be easy to enter, let alone get her attention with so many clients, but I'm determined not to leave without answers. I take one of the gold coins from my pocket. The word "Gourde" appears in relief along with what looks like palm trees and a faded 1815 date.

"Elisse," someone whispers behind me.

I curl my fists and plant my feet on the cement.

"Eliiissse, I'm the spirit of your past meals," the unknown voice wails once more, and I turn around.

I raise an eyebrow at the giant hot dog dancing and waving its mustard arms like a ghost.

"What the fuck?" I say.

The hot dog stops dancing and crosses its arms.

"You don't recognize me? It's me, Julien."

"Oh," I say and relax. I turn around and walk away from him quickly.

"Hey, hey. Where are you going?" The huge sausage passes me in clumsy jumps and blocks my steps like a wall. He opens the grate covering his face. "See? It's me," the idiot says with a flushed face and shows that damn smile, which right now I'm tempted to knock out with a punch.

"You imbecile, you scared me."

"Ah, don't be a crybaby." He distorts his face with a pout that makes me laugh. "What are you doing here, little guy?"

"I came to see someone. And you?"

He flaps a "two sausages for the price of one" sign on his belly. "Working overtime."

"As a clown? Don't you have food carts?"

"Yeah, but none of my employees like the idea of a costume for promotion, so I have to do the dirty work myself."

"You don't seem that sad about it."

"Not at all. I get some exercise, and by the way, I make the girls laugh with my jokes. What else could I ask for?"

I hold back a laugh at the great confidence of my brother. Johanna says this fool compensates for his lack of brains with handsomeness, which in her words, nearly rivals Tared's. I squeeze the corners of my mouth. Her situation with Tared concerns me now that I know what could happen if two wanderers mated.

My attention returns to the voodoo shop, and I remain unreasonably silent. Julien follows my gaze and questions me through his brown eyes.

"Everything okay?" he asks.

"Of course," I reply so unconvincingly that even I'm suspect. My brother's face transforms and gives way to his obvious concern.

"Elisse, be careful, please," he says and grips my shoulder with his hand that's missing a finger. "Remember, you still don't have an ancestor, so you're not protected against an attack. Don't think of doing anything crazy on your own."

Julien sometimes surprises me. Most of the time he's childish and carefree—not to mention a fool —but his head is cool enough to understand things more clearly than I do.

"I just came to ask someone a few questions. Nothing serious. As soon as I finish, I'll go straight to the reservation. Promise."

"What time is Tared coming for you?"

"He's not. I'm having lunch with Louisa, so I'll go on my own as soon as I'm finished."

"Ah, now I know why he looked somewhat upset this morning, before telling me to go to hell when I asked him to try on the mascot."

"What?"

Julien closes the grate of his suit. "Anyway. We'll see each other later. And for God's sake, at least get a knife or something to defend yourself." He waves and enters the crowd while calling out offers of hot dogs.

I gather my courage and head to Laurele's shop. I stumble through the entrance and push my way through tourists, who seem to loot the shop left and right. Behind the counter, Laurele stuffs money into the cash register and maintains an extraordinary tranquility in the presence of everyone talking to her. My eyes meets hers, and her eyes shine.

"Ladies and gentlemen," she shouts. An icy stillness settles over the place, and every head turns toward her. The witch closes the cash register in one smack. "Get out!"

Everyone leaves the shop in an orderly fashion, one by one, until it is empty. Silence stands between my stupefied face and the smile of the half-crazy woman, Laurele. She draws near, and instinctively, I take a step back.

"What a pleasure to see you, boy," she says. "You've been slow to come see me."

"How did you do that?"

"How nice that you were dying to get your eyes on me again." She says and ignores my question.

I reach into the bottom of my bag, and something pricks my fingertips. I take out the voodoo doll and look at my fingers now freckled with blood. I toss the figure on the counter.

"What's that?" she asks.

"That's what I want to know. Yesterday, it appeared at my house, and after what I just saw, I'm sure you can tell me why."

She inspects the doll and then removes a cigar from her shirt pocket. She places the cigar in her mouth, and it lights by itself.

"How lucky, little one. It seems you've received a visit from a Loa."

"A what?"

"In Voodoo we have different levels of spirits," she replies. "The Loas are intermediaries between us and the supreme god, oracles of the spiritual world that serve to communicate with him. When a Loa wants something from you, it leaves gifts to let you know. I bet it has given you gold coins too."

I hold back my surprise, but truthfully, I *am* surprised. I immediately think of those coins at the bottom of my pocket.

"What does a Loa want from me?"

"It depends on what kind of Loa it is. It could be a favor, a sacrifice, or even that you offer your body for lustful ends. They are awfully capricious beings."

"Who in their right mind would do something like that?"

"Oh, my boy, the Loas love deals. I assure you that if you give them your service, they'll reward you with something valuable, something you really want, however impossible it may be. In fact, you should feel lucky. People are the ones who usually seek the favors of a Loa, but apparently, it's a Loa who wants a favor of you."

I'd like to appeal to my logic, tell myself none of this can be true, but I've discovered that I'm a supernatural being, there are spiritual planes, and monstrous creatures live invisibly around us. So, what's the likelihood that this is false?

A strange glow surrounds Laurele—not light, but a blackish aura, a rotten essence unraveling. This woman is strange, and I'm sure she's not a wanderer, but she has more mystical influence than I would like to admit. I'm tempted to tell her what I saw last night, but the words don't come out of my mouth.

"By the way, have you seen my book lately?"

Her question startles me.

"No. Actually, no." I say mechanically. "But thanks, uh, I have to go."

I race out of her shop and don't look back. Luckily, she doesn't hold me this time.

A mystery walks on my back. Will this have any connection to the crazy wanderers who appeared on the reserve?

Voodoo, Loas, favors. Everything is so alluring that it's nearly impossible to ignore the tingling of my fingers wanting that red book in my hands again. The meeting with the wanderers was so sudden, and I've been so busy on the reserve, that I'd completely forgotten about the book. Now my desire to know more about these mysteries erases time beneath my feet, and in a flash, I've reached the Buddhist center.

The first thing I do is pick up the kitchen phone. The line whistles, but I don't dial the reservation number. Muata's silence makes me consider the possibility that he doesn't even care what I have to say, so I go with my gut and hang up.

In my room, I pull the red book from the bottom of my dresser and give myself all the time in the world to sit on the bed and devour the pages. Symbols, recipes, and rituals dance in front of my eyes. I realize I possess within me not only a bestial instinct, a side called by nature and my animal blood, but also a darker, deeper echo that pulls at every string of my sanity.

The blood of the shadowgazer calls me with such a devastating force that I'm almost certain little or nothing will remain of that fragile little boy who couldn't stand in the darkness of a hallway.

Chapter 23
Scarlet Stars

IN THE PASSENGER SEAT of Louisa's car sits the knife I bought, as my brother Julien recommended. The owners of the hunting store didn't even seem interested in whether I was of age. The blade is small but sharp, and its leather handle makes it manageable. The cost of the knife along with what I spent on gas reduces my sad savings to zero.

It doesn't matter though. I have more things to worry about than money. When I called the reservation to tell them I'd be on my way as I promised my brother, I didn't even get a chance to say hello before Mama Tallulah told me to get there right away. She sounded nervous and said they'd wait for me at the entrance booth, so my only concern is to get there in one piece.

I switch on the radio and take in the passing landscape. A small space of mud and grass extends from the asphalt to the thickets of weeds and magnificent trees that border the periphery of the reserve. From time to time, animals peek through the foliage and nose the muddy ground for traces of food.

There's not a single house in sight, only miles of marshy nature and, fortunately, none of that fog which floods the city from time to time. There's just a clear sky and a bright sun that—

The car sputters and coughs through the exhaust pipe.

"Dammit. Now what?"

I crush the pedals and shift the gear, but in just a few yards, the bastard stalls completely and the engine smokes. I sprint out of the car to open the burning hood, and a blow of black smoke wafts over my face.

"Really, really?" I yell and step back, attacked by a raspy cough. "There wasn't a better place to break down than in the middle of nowhere?" I say to the purple car and resist the urge to kick the bumper. I may be the best driver in the world, but I have no fucking idea how to fix a car as old as this one.

I walk a few yards down the road, shielding my eyes from the intense sun with my hand. The last car passed by almost twenty minutes ago, and there's not even a cabin in sight.

Back at the car, I dig out a map. I flip it around a couple of times until I find my location. The nearest gas station is only three miles from here, so I hope I can find a mechanic or even a tow truck there. It doesn't make sense to stay stranded here waiting for another car to pass.

I shift the vehicle into neutral and, with some effort, push the car off the road and into the grass. I grab my bag, lock the doors, and start walking under the sun that slowly roasts me like a chicken.

It's a chilly day, but between the exercise and the sunlight striking my face, the walk becomes unbearable, so I stop to rest under a lonely, secluded tree on the side of the road and regret not having a bottle of water with me. A gentle breeze whispers through the grass and breaks the silence of the road. Just as I'm about to take off my poncho, something makes me look down the road from where I came.

An incessant, fleshy smacking sound grows louder, but I can't distinguish what it is. A head appears on the horizon, and then another joins it. Two people run, stamping their feet on the asphalt. A man and a woman, both with dark hair, appear about a hundred yards away from me. As they get closer, terror splits my spine when I see foam oozing from their mouths. Their faces begin to lengthen, their muscles expand through their clothes, and the skin of their bodies falls to shreds. They are wanderers.

"Shit!" In a split-second, I dart into the trees. The two wanderers roar like both human and beast as I slide through the thick undergrowth and mud. I don't make it far before the roots crack violently behind me, but I don't look back. Suddenly, the ground disappears beneath my feet.

I roll downhill, twisting through grass and mud, and crash into icy water. I splash about on my knees, desperately reaching for my bag floating a few feet away. I've fallen into a shallow stretch of one of the reserve's rivers where tall grasses grow in the water and mud pits that sink like quicksand surround the swamp. After I catch my bag, I have to slog across the river to get to the other side, but I don't even get more than five feet before the wanderers roar again. So, I pull the poncho over my head, squeeze my bag, and submerge myself up to my nose in the grassy water, hoping the mud will camouflage me.

A foul smell invades the air, and I breathe as little as possible to avoid the stench and to keep from being heard by the creatures who appear among the trees.

The first monster is enormous, even larger than the alligator wanderer. Hooves have replaced its hands and feet, but its torso and limbs, lined with brown fur, are still human. Its head, stuck in mid-transformation, sprouts a ram's muzzle below deformed human eyes, and a pair of thick horns coil around the sides of its head and grow larger as I blink.

The other wanderer is even more terrifying. A coarse beak protrudes from the middle of its misshapen face. But its slimy olive skin, webbed hands, and bulging hard shell tell me it's not a bird. Rather, it looks like one of those alligator snapping turtles that can split a small tree trunk in a single bite.

I push backward as slowly and quietly as possible, but something splashes at my back and pinches my calf. I have to grit my teeth to stifle a cry of pain.

A baby alligator clings stubbornly to my leg with its small sharp teeth. It twists my flesh and tears out streams of blood that redden the water. To my horror, the monsters raise their heads to sniff the air and then enter the muddy shore.

They can smell my blood.

I wring the critter until it lets go, and it takes a strip of flesh with it. Holding in a scream, I aim at the wall of trees on the hillside and then fling the little bastard as far as I can. Miraculously, the alligator soars up and over the trees. It writhes in the grass and makes enough noise for those monsters to bound toward it like maniacs.

As soon as they disappear behind the foliage, I spring up and run. Bearing the pain in my leg, I leap into the shallow part of the river, and in a few seconds, I reach the other side. But my luck ends when those demons realize my deception, and they charge down the slope in my direction. I head deeper into the bowels of the reserve and search for a low branch to climb, but the limbs are too frail or too high to reach.

"Fuck, fuck." I stop in my tracks.

The swamp forest ends abruptly and becomes a plain. The only thing in sight, about sixty yards away, is a small set of boulders I could climb.

The monsters' putrid smell reaches me along with their screams, and adrenaline floods my veins. Going back now would be suicide, so I inhale until my lungs might burst and throw myself into the arms of the meadow.

Because I run so fast and with so much power, everything around me moves in slow motion. The sunlight shining through the golden grass makes me feel like I'm running through a bonfire. When I reach the rocks, I scale the highest one, which is no less than five feet from the ground. Gasping for breath, I pull the knife from my bag and grip the weapon as my only hope against the monstrous creatures running toward me with the earth trembling in their path.

I'm going to die.

It's the last thought I have before an unstoppable reddish blur charges by my side. A giant man with the head of a bison launches toward the beasts. Its curly fur vibrates through the grass, and its enormous skull with horns rising like two black swords smashes into the forehead of the ram. The blow booms with the force of two comets crashing together.

The bison heaves the wanderer ram into the air with its horns and embeds it into the ground. The monster writhes and knocks against the body of the bison, who withstands the hit and releases a human fist into the ram's muzzle.

The beaked wanderer doesn't stop to help her companion but runs toward me. I raise the trembling knife in front of me. Using it against the creature will be like trying to stop an avalanche with a branch. My jaw quivers to the point of nearly cracking. Her strides draw closer at thirty yards, twenty yards, ten yards …

A new roar comes from the trees. It's another wanderer, a bear with human legs and arms covered in black fur. It smashes its giant paw against the beaked creature's face before she can reach me and claws out a gush of black blood.

The monster, in spite of the impact, stretches its neck at an astounding speed and closes its powerful jaws on the bear's forearm. The bear roars. In retaliation, it sinks its black claws into its opponent's shoulder and rips out a chunk of meat.

Behind them, the ram crashes its horns against the bison in such a powerful way that a shockwave vibrates through the air. Both struggle in an even-matched fight of muscle and bone as their foreheads bleed.

With chills on my back, I witness the roars, crashes, and blows of legend and reality colliding like titans. The meadow becomes a coliseum hosting a mythical battle. If I were not seeing it, I would never believe it. But, no one is yielding. Dammit.

I climb down the rock to find something, anything to offset the balance, even though I know that in the midst of those giants, I face imminent death. But above the fear that rattles my bones, instinct seizes my neck, and I look behind me. A ray of light blinds me for a few seconds. But it's not the light of the sun shining; it's the skin of the most amazing creature I've ever seen.

With firm steps that seem to stop time, the beast's enormous body, elegant and covered with silver fur, gleams like knives. On its shoulders glides a dense layer of fur, a dark cloud shot with lightning as if the wolf were the incarnation of a raging hurricane.

Tared walks toward me with eyes flashing like a beast drawn from humanity's oldest legends. His human build is strong and cut like marble, but his head, claws, and legs are so beautifully wolfish that I long to hear a howl from his black lips. In one of his hand-claws, he grips a thick spear that shines with an iron point so large it could be the size of my head.

"Tared?" I say to make sure I still have a tongue.

He passes by me and stops a couple of yards from the rocks with his back to me and locks his eyes on the battlefield.

"Nashua!" he shouts in a deep, powerful voice that reveals he can speak in his bestial form.

The bear man looks at us, and as if obeying an order, he drives his claw into the face of the beaked wanderer and jumps away. Tared raises the spear over his shoulder, squints his wolfish gaze, and then hurls the weapon with brutal force.

The spear whistles through the air and, seconds later, pierces the turtle woman's neck with such power that the point sheers off her head. Black blood spurts from the severed neck and spills in furious rivers at the feet of the animal.

In the midst of the carnage, a symbol shines on the thigh of the headless wanderer, but it disappears within seconds and denies me the opportunity to identify it.

"This … this happened before," I say. That glow, those markings. It's not the first time I've seen them. I lash my memory like a whip and vaguely recall the alligator wanderer.

Nashua and Tared rush toward the ram to help Julien.

My mind races to discern what I just saw. The symbol on that woman's thigh lasted just a second, but the alligator wanderer's displayed for longer. Why? Why was it still shining if the creature was … dying? It was dying.

"Stop! Tared, stop!" I yell at the top of my lungs. I close my hand tightly on the handle of my knife and jump from the rock. My ankles quake in pain at the landing.

"Stop, stop!" I scream again until I am out of breath. My torn calf throbs furiously as I run toward them.

My call distracts Nashua, and the damn ram heaves a powerful head-butt against his jaw. Blood from the bear's snout sprays into the wind and over the crazed wanderer. The bison then bashes the creature in its ribs and knocks it down as Tared pulls the spear from the ground.

Fuck! They're going to kill it if I don't do something.

Nashua and Julien lift the wanderer and hold it in front of Tared, who points his weapon at the heart of the creature. With expanding white eyes, the monster screams and throws foam from its muzzle.

I drive my knife into the black claw of my leader, barely hurting him, and the three turn to me.

"Don't kill him!" I shout. I'm close to vomiting from the exertion. "On your fucking life, do not kill him!"

"What the hell is wrong with you?" the wolf growls and throws me back. The power of his roar frightens me.

The ram wanderer goes mad. He writhes, shrieks, and struggles to get out of their grip to reach me, but Nashua and

Julien restrain him. I stare wild-eyed at the monster and use the last bit of oxygen in my lungs.

"Don't kill him for anything in the world, please!"

"Have you gone mad?" the bear roars with the nuance of Nashua's voice interwoven with a bestial growl.

The ram twists once more, so the wolf catches the creature's throat between his claws. Afraid he may kill it, I jump onto Tared's arm to pull him down with all my weight.

"No, no, Tared. Just hold him. Please, trust me. I beg you."

At my words, Tared flashes his furious fangs, and I want to let go. He could tear my head off this instant, but I don't give up despite the fear this angry wolf stirs in me. He waves his arm violently and shakes loose my grip, but to my surprise, he stands behind the ram and pulls its neck back. I don't give myself time to thank him. Immediately, I pick up my knife from the ground and grip it with force.

"For God's sake, don't let go," I order.

The monster, hungry for my skin, wiggles among the sea of arms. It's too strong, too resistant, and too alive for the symbol to appear. I wrinkle my nose at the disgusting smell and drive my knife into its hard stomach. I bury it so deep that even the handle pierces its skin.

But nothing. Not a single glow.

I stab him again in the same place and again as he cries out. Blood sprays my face as the hole opens wider with each stab of the knife, but the son of a bitch resists. I feel the intense look of my brothers over my shoulders, but I don't give up my horrifying work, especially when the creature, twitch by twitch, stops moving.

A symbol shines between its collarbones. The monster is dying.

"Drop it to the ground," I command, and luckily, the three of them comply without hesitation and still restrain the ram with force. I jump on the monster's chest. With my knife, I carve the symbol that appears, lifting layers of skin and hair in my path. But suddenly, my knife slides on a fully human chest, and I leap off.

I stare in horror at a man still under the grip of my brothers. He drools bloody teeth from his split jaw.

"Elisse? What's happening?" Julien asks.

I blink, and the man is once again the monstrous wanderer. I press my lips together, feeling something inside me twist in horror as I realize what I did.

Did I just murder someone? I look at my bloodied and trembling hands and drop the knife to the ground, but it's too late to regret. Before my eyes, and in the chest of that wanderer, of that person, appears the symbol marked by scarlet lines:

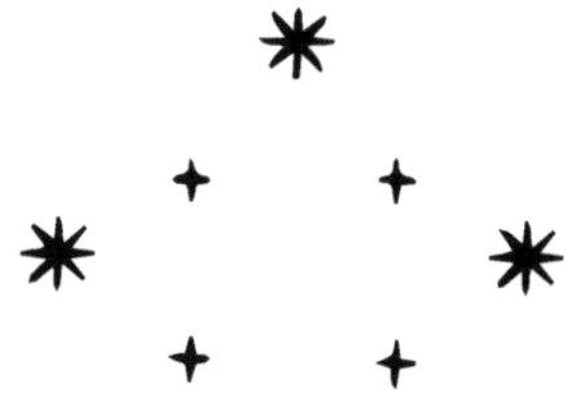

Chapter 24
Dust and Shadows

"My God," Johanna whispers when Julien throws the corpse of the colossal ram at her feet and a slight curtain of dust rises into the air. Afterward, she looks with special horror at my blood-soaked clothes while Father Thunder inspects the body.

Tared and Julien adjust the skins tied around their waists like sweaters. The sound of their flesh sticky with blood along with the musk of those coats stirs my stomach.

"What the hell happened?" Father Thunder asks.

"Two wanderers. Stronger than the previous ones," Julien answers between gasps. "Tared was right. Elisse was in danger."

I look at the wolf next to me. He crosses his arms and focuses his attention on the old man. From the depths of my being, I suppress the desire to cling to Tared's side, to hang on to his strength, so I don't fall through the hole that's opened beneath my feet.

By the gods. I've killed a man.

Mama Tallulah pushes Old Muata in his wheelchair. They stop in front of the body so the shadowgazer can lean over the corpse. He sinks his fingers into the rotted flesh, and as if perfectly able to see, he traces the lines I cut into the monster's skin.

"Do you want to tell us what happened, son?" Mama Tallulah asks. Her voice sounds so distant that I can hardly hear what she's saying.

A truck rumbles behind our backs. Nashua drives an old black suburban, dragging a trailer where the body of the turtle woman rests. He passes by us and goes behind the cabins to protect the vehicle for the moment under cover. Minutes later, he returns and takes a place beside me.

We have all arranged ourselves around the creature as if we were contemplating a bonfire.

"My car broke down in the middle of the road," I say softly, sick of myself. "I went to find a gas station, but these two wanderers appeared out of nowhere and—"

"No, boy," Muata says. "What we want to know is what you've done to this man's chest."

The sinister symbol is covered with dried blood, and the split flesh opens like pages of a book. I open and close my fists, still feeling the blood sticky between my fingers.

"When the turtle wanderer died, a symbol appeared on her thigh, one that only I could see. I remembered something like that happened to the alligator wanderer. A symbol appeared on his forehead and became clearer as he died."

I lean forward a little and contain my disgust as I recall my knife sinking into a human stomach.

“Why the fuck didn’t you say something until now?” Nashua asks.

“I didn’t remember,” I say in a thin voice. I’m so caught up in misery that I can’t even explode in anger at his provocation. “I was so stunned after the accident with the alligator that I—”

“Oh, how convenient,” he says. “And what about the deer wanderer they found in the park? Were you also too stunned?”

I squeeze my eyelids and lower my chin, unable to articulate with my silence what I’ve made evident.

“Hey, hey,” Tared takes a step toward me. He probably senses that I’m about to break. “Don’t worry. Okay? It’s not—”

“Don’t worry?” the bear man shouts. “Those things could have killed us out there. They’re not normal wanderers. They have no smell. There’s no way to know how many more there are. They could be on the verge of dropping on top of us, and you only care about shielding this damn kid.”

“Calm down, Nashua.”

“Don’t get in the fucking middle of this, Johanna.”

“Hey, don’t talk to her like that,” Julien says.

“Shut the hell up!” Tared roars with such force that the birds squawk and fly out of the trees. Everyone goes silent as if he cut out their tongues. “Arguing is only going to divide us, and I assure you that whoever is behind all this won’t hesitate to take advantage of that.”

“Elisse.” Father Thunder calls me. “Those of us who’ve lived in Louisiana long enough to be a part of these lands know what this is,” he says and points to the creature’s chest with his cane. “But you, future shadowgazer of Comus Bayou, show me that you are worthy of your ancestry, and tell me what it is.”

I stare at the scarlet lines, and a drop of cold sweat slides down the back of my neck. I recognize the type of archaic drawing. Laurele's book is full of them.

"It looks like part of a veve, a Voodoo symbol."

"Now we just need to find out what kind of veve it is, and who's behind all this," Mama Tallulah says with a sigh.

"Another shadowgazer?" Johanna asks.

"Maybe, maybe not," Muata says. "We're not the only ones who can manipulate magic. It could be a sorcerer who simply wants to erase us from the map."

"Or a Loa," I say in a low voice.

Mama Tallulah breaks down the harmony of her face. But she's not the only one. The others also look afraid.

"It... it could be a Loa, right?" I ask.

"What nonsense are you saying?" Muata says. "Do you even have any idea how the spiritual world works? Loas do not enter our plane."

"But—"

"You don't believe me? All right. Do things your way since you are so wise, boy."

I swallow the urge to yell at the old man and tell him about the visit I had last night, about the supposed favor a Loa wants from me. But I remember Nashua's accusations and realize it could bring more problems. I should find out more before I open my mouth.

Fine. If Muata wants me to do this on my own, that's how it'll be.

"How is it that these things found me?" I ask. "Isn't it assumed that since I don't have an ancestor, I don't smell like a wanderer?"

"We haven't the slightest idea," Tared says. "Somehow, they already knew where you were. We're lucky we found you in time even though we couldn't track them."

"But *you* could smell them, right?" Muata asks me, and my silence is sufficient for him. "I was afraid of that. Only a shadowgazer can perceive a spirit from the middle plane."

I'm so exhausted that I don't even bother to sigh anymore. If Muata gave me more information like this, I wouldn't be so immersed in ignorance, not so defenseless.

"We discovered something else, Grandfather," Nashua says and glances at me. "These creatures, including the alligator, seemed desperate to get only one thing."

Every head turns to me again, and this time, I can't hide my surprise either.

Muata beckons me to come to him. "Push my chair, boy. Take me to my cabin," he says with a rigid face.

I hurry and go to him. Everyone looks at me in a way I can't figure out.

"If we've asked you to come urgently, it's for a very important reason, Elisse." My skin prickles as if a cold wind entered my veins. It's the first time Muata has called me by my name. "Today, an ancestor has come to claim you."

MUATA'S CABIN IS LARGE, but it has so many things that the space in which to move is somewhat limited. It's like entering Laurele's shop but with a Native American feel. Feathers, necklaces, dreamcatchers, herbs, knives, fabrics—Everything is arranged on long shelves and tables made from logs. In the corner, skins and antlers are stacked in equal batches. Tared told me they pack and sell them to the people of the city and surrounding areas.

The sight of the skins makes me dizzy. There are pelts of wolf, bear, coyote, and bison, as well as several black horns. The reason for having them is simple but unnerving. When a wanderer wants to return to human form, they have to tear off their skin and horns—a dreadful method inherited from the skinwalkers.

When Tared, Nashua, and Julien shed their skins in front of my eyes, I almost vomited. At the moment of removing their furs, their bodies shrank, and the leftover skins transformed into a pieces of leather that they used to cover their nakedness.

Don't make that face, Elisse. When we get to the reserve, we'll tan these skins and get good money for them.

Julien was not kidding, and with that pair of huge black horns on his head, it wasn't hard to take him seriously. I asked him how on earth it was possible for someone to tolerate such a process. *With enough common sense*, he answered. He explained that if a wanderer doesn't remove their skin for a long period of time, their mind can't distinguish whether it's an animal or a person. They'll go mad, their body will deform in unspeakable ways, and they'll become violent, like the souls that remain too long in the middle plane.

"Everything is ready, boy."

Muata emerges from the threshold of a door at the back of the cabin. The man palpates the walls to move aside and show the mouth of darkness behind him.

Consumed by a mixture of fear and uncertainty, I cross the room. I reach the doorframe and contemplate the emptiness in front of me. When I step inside, a soft glow illuminates everything and reveals something that breaks my face in amazement.

The space would be empty if it weren't for a giant, magnificent deer with a coat as gray as ash. Its antlers are almost as large as its body and full of so many points that they resemble the branches of a tree. A blue sky covers its eyes in which, even at a distance, my image reflects like in the water of a pond. It's so sublime and so dark that I dare compare it with the shadow of nature itself. The wood walls of the room are incapable of overshadowing its imposing form.

Another miracle happens. Muata passes by me toward the deer and, step by step, grows younger in front of my awestruck eyes. His hair blackens, his skin stretches, his back straightens, and an extraordinary yet strange beauty paints his features, creating a bridge to the past where I can see this man in all his splendor. An androgynous being with dark skin and eyes as black as night, stands before me.

"This is *Deer Shadowskin*," he says in a very young voice while caressing the ancestor's cheek. "The ancient wanderers baptized him with that name because they said his fur was inherited from the ground of the middle plane."

The ancestor rubs his dark muzzle against Muata's hand, and a thin layer of smoke rises as if the animal were made of shadow dust.

"He's one of the oldest ancestors in the swamp," Muata says. "He's asked me to intercede to hand you over to him, so consider yourself lucky."

Attracted by an inevitable magnetism, I draw closer to the ancestor. I grow small before his magnificent presence and stand on tiptoe to touch his head. I caress him, and the coolness of his body transmits through my veins. We look at each other, and he speaks to me—not with a human voice but with the rhythm of his being.

He runs his snout through my hair, and an abyss expands inside me along with a kind of ache, like something opening my soul and widening my body inside.

I close my eyes to endure the pain, but almost immediately, the aroma of forest soil envelopes me and relieves the suffering. I merge with the drumming heart of this spirit. His skin covers me, his horns crown me, and his bones embed in mine.

When I open my eyes, the deer has disappeared. I find myself in a room as crammed with objects as the rest of the cabin while Muata, as old and blind as ever, stares blankly from the door.

"Shadowgazers have the task of delivering ancestors to wanderers who haven't been able to acquire one on their own," he says. "It's a pity that not everyone in this tribe appreciates the Indigenous transmission of teachings through the lineages. That ancient tradition is inspired by us."

"Where has he gone?" I ask.

Muata just turns around and walks away, touching the walls.

"Now, he is inside you."

Chapter 25
More Human Than Anything Else

TODAY IS THE THIRD TIME I've been born. I sense something has changed powerfully in me again. The shades of orange and rose painting the sky, the dark silhouettes of trees standing against the heavens, the thin moon hanging behind the clouds... I appreciate everything much more deeply as if this landscape were the memory of a home I left many lives ago and to which I have finally returned.

The scent of spices reaches my nose. For me, only a few minutes have passed, but seeing the others sit around the fire where skewers of huge pieces of meat and vegetables roast, I realize more time has gone by than I was able to perceive.

I push Muata's chair into the gathering and leave the old man with Father Thunder. My gaze travels to Tared's blue eyes, and he smiles and invites me to sit next to him.

He's wearing different clothes, and his hair is damp. His sleeveless shirt exposes the elaborate tattoos on his shoulders.

The ink is a little more discolored than I remember. I wonder if it's from pulling off his skin.

"You look cleaner than I left you a while ago," I say.

"I'd like to say the same about you," he says and looks me up and down.

I shrink a bit in my seat. I'm still as filthy as a pig.

"I think the dried blood makes me look badass," I reply.

He shakes his head, and a smile sneaks from the corner of his lips.

Truth be told, I'm glad he showered. I had no idea that besides wanderers looking like wild animals, they also smelled like them. Their fur issued a musky scent that competed against the two dead wanderers.

Also, I'm glad no one's naked. After the battle, there was something I couldn't help but notice. After Tared, Julien, and Nashua pulled off their skins, I tried not to look at them too much. Not just because they were covered in blood, but because, even transformed, wanderers still have sex organs, covered in hair if they want. But it's not like they can make them disappear by magic, ironically. I got so red that I earned giggles from the bear and the bison. I couldn't help it. I was raised by Tibetans, and in that culture, you're not a big fan of nudity.

Nashua said even Johanna has no problem being seen naked by her brothers once a battle is over and that I should get used to the idea that nakedness is something inherent in our world. We have to learn to live with a little less privacy in that sense, though we can still use our own skins to cover up.

"You did a great job over there in the plain," Tared says and pulls me away from my thoughts. "I'm sorry I freaked you out."

"Nah, you're scarier when you scold Julien." I make a bad and nervous joke. Luckily, he chuckles, maybe out of compassion, and gives me a playful punch on the arm.

I also try to laugh at my own joke, but truthfully, Tared is just as fascinating and intimidating as he is in his wolf form.

"How do you feel? With everything about your ancestor?" he asks.

"It's weird to have a deer inside my stomach without having eaten it, if that's what you want to know."

He laughs again, for real this time.

"Wow. You've turned out to be pretty special."

"Yep, telling bad jokes is just one of my many talents," I say and hike my shoulders.

He holds back a smile this time and fixes his blue eyes on me in a way that I perceive as curiosity. Unfortunately, I can't think of anything else stupid to say, but it seems that I don't need to.

The simple company of the wolf has been enough to take me far away from that body I mutilated with my own hands. It's strange. In general, the weak tend to feel even more vulnerable next to others who exceed us in strength and temperament. But Tared, he ...

It's probably just me who perceives it this way, but suddenly, the distance separating us feels like an empty space crying out to be occupied. But I don't dare fill it with myself. I feel so filthy with blood and dried mud all over me.

"Tared?" I feel sick because of what I'm about to ask him. "Those wanderers who we ... murdered out there were also people, right? Just like us. Do you think they have family? Someone who might be looking for them now?"

Tared looks surprised, so I bite my lip and look down.

"Come on, have a drink!" Julien falls on me like a sack of potatoes and offers me a frosty can. "Aww, don't look at me like that, Tared. If he can gut a wanderer, he can also have a beer."

Tared shakes his head. I don't know if it's in response to Julien's bluntness or because he couldn't say anything about what I asked him.

I accept the drink and notice that Julien's wound on his forehead is already white and scarred. I take a sip and swallow the delicious, bitter flavor down my throat. It's not the first time I've had a drink in my life, but now it feels more comforting than ever.

Nashua passes in front of us with a large bottle of liquor, and Julien immediately tackles him.

"Gimmeee some of what you have there, pleeeaase," he says, clinging to Nashua's shoulders.

"Get off me, stupid cow," Nashua shouts and moves in circles to get away from the grip of the redhead. Tared and I laugh.

"I'm a bison. Bi-son. Illiterate."

"Get away from my bourbon, child," Mama Tallulah cries from the other side of the campfire and lets out a loud laugh.

Johanna joins her, and in seconds, Nashua laughs too and gives Julien a playful blow to the head. We're all so relaxed that it seems like we didn't just kill two wanderers in such a bloody way, and I wonder if this nature, this brutality, is just another part of daily life for a family of wanderers.

A family.

Family.

Something inside me grows and throbs so hard that it nearly breaks my rib cage.

Father Thunder stands up and raises his arm in my direction. "Comus Bayou," he shouts. "We have a new warrior."

The rest of the tribe howl and cheer. Blood flushes my cheeks, but I still have the courage to lift my beer, grateful for their ovation.

"We celebrate, my children. Deer Shadowskin has claimed this boy as his oracle. Let's eat and drink. A blessing has fallen upon our lands."

A new wave of cries explodes around the campfire, and everyone rushes to take a skewer. Even Johanna has lost her shyness as she devours a piece of meat in a few bites. I, on the other hand, look at the food with hesitation.

"You're not hungry?" Tared asks me.

"Ah, it's not that. It's just … my ancestor is a deer. Won't he be offended if I eat another herbivore?"

"Maybe if you eat him," Julien says with his mouth full.

Tared laughs lightly as he leans over the fire and passes me a skewer. "Don't worry. The only way you can offend him is by failing to fulfill your duties to your tribe. So from now on, you are free to feed on nature like any other creature."

With shyness, I accept the meat and take a bite. The juicy flavor intoxicates my tongue with spices, and I moan in pure pleasure. I haven't eaten anything for hours. As I feast on the delicious meal, I look around the campfire circle. The flames are strong, but another kind of heat embraces me.

It's my proximity to Tared, the way my instincts guide me to him, and the way his presence warms me with barely a breath. It's Mama Tallulah's voice, like a whisper through the trees. And it's Johanna's eyes, which see places so far away that I get swept up in nostalgia. And even as I watch Julien, I feel his kindness, which makes me feel like he's a brother torn from my own cradle. It's the passion of Nashua, the strength of Father Thunder, and the silence of Muata, too. It's what each member of this tribe creates by my side—ties, loyalty, brotherhood, memories …

Here, under this sunset full of stars and the shadows of the trees behind the campfire, I realize that I would give anything for these people, for the love I have developed for them so quickly.

Comus Bayou, the forest, nature— Everything kills me with feelings of melancholy and joy.

After eating, Father Thunder, wearing his wolf skin, releases his speech about the stories by the fire, so Johanna takes out the Book of Generations and writes in it under my restless gaze.

Once I asked her if I could take a look, but she warned me that I would only find blank pages. Only bloodkeepers can see the words written in the mist of time. She said her eyes were not gray but covered with dusty memories.

Julien and Nashua stand up and retell the story of the battle in the meadow. With pride, both take off their shirts and show the marks of war that honor their ancestors. Their wounds have almost completely healed.

I look at the gash I have on my leg from the small alligator. It'll take weeks to heal on its own, so I make a mental note to ask Johanna to help me with it.

The demonstrations of my brothers impress the elders, especially Father Thunder, who seems to have a special affection for the skineaters.

I look down and sink into a puddle of envy. I feel like a son who, no matter what I do or say, can never make my father proud. The simple idea hurts and reminds me of my real father. Cruel thoughts attack my mind, thoughts I try to avoid when I think of him. Did he know I was a wanderer? Was it my strange nature that forced him to abandon me?

Nashua and Julien pay tribute to Tared by telling of his amazing feat with the spear, but he only smiles and keeps silent. Then, the moment comes when the werewolf puffs up his chest, and with a voice so deep and thick, tells about what I did on the field. Mama Tallulah and Johanna applaud my acts, while Father Thunder recognizes that my gifts as a shadowgazer serve the tribe with pride.

On the other hand, I'm still not sure how to feel about what I did to that ram wanderer. It should be easy just to say I'd killed a half-animal in self-defense, but it's not true. I can't think like that about creatures who are like my brothers, who are like me, who feel and reason, and whose lives are just as important as any human's.

Crazed or not, those wanderers we killed in the meadow were people. And by the gods, the alligator wanderer...

I look at my hands. Maybe they're bloodier than I thought, and if I keep thinking about this, I'll never be able to look at myself in the mirror again.

A weight presses on my head, and I lift my chin to catch the "look" of Muata. He fixes his blank eyes on me as if he were analyzing me through the shadows and not through the eyes. I'm not sure what this man thinks about me or why he doesn't want to teach me anything about my powers as a shadowgazer, but now that I have my ancestor, maybe I should learn about it on my own instead of waiting for him.

I finish another skewer and look around. I want this moment to last forever. I still have so many things to think about, and of which to regret, but the sky has been in full darkness awhile, so I know it's time to go. I touch Tared's arm. He turns to me and understands immediately.

"Father Thunder, I have to take Elisse back to the city."

The old man nods and dismisses the matter. I know it's probably selfish to say, but I feel a slight happiness at seeing my brothers show discontent, proof that they were enjoying my company.

Just as I stand up to leave for a much-needed shower and to see if Johanna can take a look at my leg, Muata's voice stops me.

"Elisse," he says. "Now that Deer Shadowskin is at your side, it's time to entrust you with your first mission."

My knees begin cramping, but I immediately nod to show some strength.

"If you are smart enough, you will know that nothing in this city is a coincidence. The smell of a corpse, the lack of will, the veves on their bodies … You'd have to be an idiot not to realize those wanderers are the stolen remains from the tombs of St. Louis."

"What?" I say.

"Have they been resurrected?" Johanna asks.

"No, my girl. No one can give life to something that's no longer alive. Those wanderers were only carcasses, beings without minds whose lives became extinct hundreds of years ago. They may have had a trace of their human soul that allowed them to speak and manifest as ghosts after they were killed again, but nothing more."

A ton of guilt rolls off my shoulders. They were not alive. They no longer had loved ones who could mourn them. That means … my hands are clean. I haven't killed anyone. I sigh in utter relief and notice Tared looking at me. He seems to know exactly what I'm thinking.

"But the situation isn't any less dangerous," Muata says. "Someone is playing the puppeteer, someone who has chosen dead wanderers from almost two centuries ago so even I could not recognize them."

"Is there anyone with such power?" Father Thunder asks. I never thought I'd see his stoic face so disturbed.

"The living dead are the proof, Lansa." The old man calls Father Thunder by his real name. "They are corpses. They no longer have ancestors, but being seized by spirits that inhabit the middle plane, they retain the scent that only shadowgazers can perceive. I imagine they could have pulled memories, bring back a little of what they were before they died."

"Wait, they can pull memories?" I ask the old man.

"Sometimes, beings with magic can materialize the memories of the dead, but it's a practice almost as uncommon as it is difficult," he replies with some reluctance. "That's how the corpses have been able to take the form of their ancestors without having one."

"That would also explain why, after killing them, they rotted so fast," Johanna says. "And then after their skin fell off, they shrank. They looked like humans again."

"We're facing a true necromancer," Father Thunder says with his face still troubled.

"Boy," Muata calls me. "The time has come to entrust you with your first mission, to give you the opportunity to prove that you are worthy of being the new shadowgazer of Comus Bayou."

Everyone's eyes fall on me and anguish stirs my stomach. The blind eyes of Muata pass through me along with a shiver, which gets worse when he pronounces his fateful commission.

"Human or wanderer, find whoever is behind all this, Elisse. When you do, your duty will be to kill him."

Chapter 26
Ashes and Bone

"Have they left?" you ask Father Thunder.

"Yes, and my boys have already gone to sleep," he replies and sits next to your wheelchair. "And after today, I wouldn't blame them if they didn't wake up for three days."

"Tared must be just as tired, but he still took the boy into town when it might have been better for him to stay and sleep. To tell you the truth, I'm surprised you're not pressuring the boy to move to the reserve. It's an expense of energy and money to make those trips almost daily."

Your words make Father Thunder's hands tremble, but something in your face shows that this is just what you were looking for, Muata.

The leader of Comus Bayou clears his throat. You lean forward in your metal chair to stir the fire's remains, which are no more than a handful of hot ashes. You trace patterns that, to my surprise, resemble small snakes.

"He insists it's no bother because they don't live that far from each other. And this time, he seemed happy to oblige," he says and squints. "Today… Elisse showed us he's very skilled, even more than he seems to understand."

"And apparently, each day your children grow more attached to him. Especially, Tared," you say.

"Bah. He can do whatever he wants if he insists on making himself responsible for that child."

"I've known you since you were a child too, Lansa. I'm sure your reasons for not bringing him to live in the village are more troubling than you dare to admit."

Father Thunder looks at you out of the corner of his eye. He raises his forehead to the sky, knowing he'll never be able to fool you, and sighs.

"They haven't realized, not even Tared, but I can't blame them since I hadn't sensed something like this before." He pauses and takes a breath. "You know well, the smell of a wanderer without an ancestor is unremarkable, but once they have one, they are imbued with the scent of the beast they carry, of the nature inside them. But… never in my life have I known a wanderer to smell of bones. And that smell hasn't faded. Not even now that Deer Shadowskin is inside him."

At his words, you don't move a single muscle, neither in shock nor in surprise. What you already suspected is apparent. Despite no longer being half the wanderer you were a few months ago, you're still an extraordinary creature, Muata.

You push your chair back and slowly move away from the dead fire. "I know," you say. "That's why there's something important you should know."

Chapter 27
An Inevitable Pain

No one likes a thief. No matter the motive or how small the theft, if you confess to someone that you used to steal, at a minimum you'll lose their trust, and over time, they'll squint when they see you and keep everything they own within reach. Afterward, hating you becomes easy.

As a child, I was part of a group of hungry kids from the refugee camp. We were not friends, just a score of orphans who met in the city from time to time to beg, dig in the garbage, and above all, steal.

As a Westerner, I could impersonate a lost boy who needed help finding my parents. After I had convinced my victim, usually someone alone, I would lead him to a remote corner or alley. There, among all of us, we would steal everything, even his shoes, but not before giving him a good trouncing by ten pairs of tiny bare feet. It was a form of survival that worked great for us, until the day we ran into a wall; the man we tried to attack was armed.

He fired at random and hit one of the children in our group. The rest of us fled into the alleys in fear for our lives. I have no idea if the boy survived, but sometimes, when I think about that scene from my past, I don't think he did, because the boy never returned to the refugee camp.

When that happened back then, I felt a tug in my stomach so hard that I thought my insides might open. And when I heard the mission Muata entrusted in me, I had a similar feeling.

How can he ask me to kill so casually? Wanderer or not, I was taught to value the life of all beings. Killing is wrong from any point of view. It's not that I can't do it. I don't want to. I couldn't stand the slick sensation of blood between my fingers again or the sound of air escaping from my victim's chest. How can I live like this? How can I go back to being the same person and look at myself in the mirror without seeing the reflection of the life that I've taken?

"Is that the car?"

I barely react when Tared points to the side of the road. I'm relieved when I see Louisa's car still parked where I left it.

The werewolf parks the black suburban in front of the vehicle, and we both get out to face the cold breath of the road. I make myself a cocoon with a layer of wool from Mama Tallulah and the flannel shirt Tared lent me. Almost all my clothes sit inside a plastic bag on the back seat, but some of the stuff inside my bag and pockets disappeared somewhere in the reserve—among them the voodoo doll and the little money I carried.

Tared grabs the hooks and chains from the truck to tow Louisa's car while I check the condition of the engine. When

I open the hood, I step back, coughing from a mouthful of dead smoke.

"Tared?" I call for him, and he immediately comes to my side.

"What's wrong?"

"Look," I say and point to the burned straw bundle on the engine.

He cocks his head and blinks. "Ah, come on, it doesn't look so bad."

"You don't see the straw?"

"The straw?"

That answers my question.

He leans closer to me with a look of fascination. "Got it. You're seeing things from the middle plane."

"What?"

"Your eyes."

Tared points to one of the car mirrors, so I walk over and look at my reflection. My pupils have dilated to the point of turning my green eyes black.

"Of what little I know, shadowgazers can sometimes see what happens in the middle plane without having to enter it," he says. "Do you remember what Grandfather Muata said? It's a place different from the human world, but it shares the same space."

"There's just so much I don't understand."

"And so much you're missing. You'd be surprised to know everything Grandfather could do."

Of course. I'll understand many things when the old bastard teaches me something. So far, everything I've learned has been from heart-stopping experiences.

I stare at the straw again, and the writings in the red book pop into my mind, as does Laurele.

"I know what happened to the car," I whisper, more to myself than to Tared. "Straw is one of the most common elements in Voodoo spells. It burns fast and facilitates the influence of spirits through fire, but regardless of what you use, for it to work, you need something that belongs to the person you want to charm. Clothes, waste, blood ... "

The wolf looks at me with a confused expression, and I find it hard to gather the words on my tongue.

"Whoever wants to kill us, ruined the car on purpose so those wanderers could reach me. And not only that. It's someone who has access to me and my things."

Tared's face tenses. He looks around and goes back to the job of connecting the car.

We already know that someone who practices Voodoo is plotting something against our tribe, and although Laurele is the first person who comes to mind, I have no proof beyond the deep aversion she provokes in me. Besides, she isn't the only Voodoo sorceress in the city. And there's no way that woman has an object of mine. Could it be someone in the Buddhist center? Carlton? No. Why would he do something like that? Also, the Comus Bayou tribe is quite old, so I don't know if we have more enemies.

With ideas spinning in my head, I go to the driver's door to help direct Louisa's car as we tow it, but Tared closes his hand on my forearm.

"Just put it in neutral. You'll ride in the truck with me."

"But—"

"Are you really going to argue with me?"

The wolf's face darkens with severity. Here's the authoritarian Tared against the disobedient Elisse. I can't really win against him, so I reluctantly climb into the suburban. With these two pieces of junk locked together and no one to steer the old Cadillac, it will take twice as long to get to the center.

I cross my arms and look at the clock on the dashboard. It's past eight at night, so surely another lecture from Louisa awaits me. I promised to call her as soon as I arrived at the reservation, but after everything that happened today, picking up the phone was the last thing that crossed my mind. She's going to kill me.

We start at a turtle's pace. Tared lights a cigarette to pretend we're not mired in an uncomfortable silence. I give him sideways glances from time to time but try to keep my face as close as possible to the window. About twenty minutes later, he sighs.

"Just tell them the car broke down," he suggests.

"Oh *sure*, and coincidentally you were passing by?"

He responds with a snort and doesn't say another word. The lights of the suburban's dashboard illuminate his face and give him a somber profile that reminds me of his wolf form.

I don't have to be a genius to guess that he didn't like my comment. Hell, I'm behaving like a child. He just wants to protect me, and it's not his fault I forgot to call Louisa.

I twist in my seat, somewhat uncomfortable with myself. I'm not used to disagreeing with him. It's rare that we have differences. The wolf is always patient with me, to the point that Nashua says he spoils me. Besides, he's my leader and has saved my skin several times, so the least I owe him is a little respect.

"I'm sorry. I shouldn't have snapped at you," I say.

The corners of his lips curl in the hint of a smile that, in the end, doesn't come out. He doesn't say anything, but he doesn't have to. I know he's much more relaxed because his presence weighs on me less. As we drive, the deer hoof swinging from the rearview mirror catches my attention. Tared brushes the hairs of my neck with his fingers, and I smile.

"Do you deal a lot with Voodoo?" I ask.

"No, not really," he replies. "We try not to mess with that. People with magic are perceptive, so Grandfather Muata always does his best to keep curious witches at bay. Besides, he's the only one who knows something about shamanism, Voodoo, or whatever. The rest of us don't understand or have any kind of magic."

"What about Johanna and Mama Tallulah? They can do peculiar things."

"They've inherited some qualities from the skinwalkers, like access to the Book of Generations, but their gifts don't come close to what a shadowgazer can do. Bloodkeepers are exceptional in their own way. They can't cure by magic, but they understand herbs and potions, how they work in relation to the body and the spirit. They have an innate ability to learn useful things. Even their own bodies possess extraordinary healing properties."

"Sounds unfair," I say. "The most convenient thing would be to have a few skills from each race, wouldn't it?"

Tared smiles. "Do you feel vulnerable?"

"Terribly. At least, physically."

"Nature works according to a balance few humans understand, much less imitate. Can you imagine if all species were predators? When a wanderer understands the delicate role they play within a tribe, however skillful they may be, they become just as important as the others. Here, there are no alphas, no chosen ones, no royalty. And no one deserves to be more or less protected than the rest of us. This isn't a pack, it's a family. The leadership Father Thunder and I have is a mere formality to make decisions, but we're not more important or more valuable than any of you, in any way. We're all part of the Dreamcatcher, Elisse. We all help to keep it closed, firm, and functional."

I just nod. His words are wonderfully reasonable, so I feel like the stupidest person in this truck.

"Anyway, I still don't know who's to blame for what's happening," he says. "I guess whoever's trying to kill us maybe thought you were easy prey as the newest member of the tribe. On top of that, you didn't have an ancestor."

"So, what *does* it feel like to change?" I ask with some hesitation. Until now, I always thought it was painless like in movies and fantasy books, but after what I saw today, I'm not so sure anymore.

"Change?"

"Yeah, to become your ancestor. Is it the same as when you tear off your wolf skin? Surely, after everything that happened this afternoon there's no reason for you not to answer me."

He takes his cigarette, gives it another puff, and smashes it in the ashtray. I tighten my lips. Whenever he does that, it's a sign he's going to say something I'm not going to like at all.

"Honestly? It's worse." He turns his face just enough to see me go pale. "When you tear your skin, it's just that, the skin. Instead, by taking the shape of your ancestor, every part of your being, however small, hurts like hell. Your flesh expands, you ache until the last hair comes out, your muscles stretch until they burst, and your bones grow so fast that they shatter your tendons. And not just the first time you transform. You feel it the same way, over and over again, because when the body changes so quickly, it'd be ridiculous if you couldn't feel anything, wouldn't it?"

Horror and curiosity silence me for minute.

"Not really, I don't understand why it hurts so much. I thought being a wanderer was more of a natural than a magical condition," I say.

"Birth is natural. Even then, it's tremendously painful. Pain is inherent in nature. It's present in all stages of life. But we are accustomed to seeing it as something harmful instead of a sign that something's changing. And maybe for our benefit."

"Yeah, I even remember as a child my bones hurt a lot when I was learning to walk."

"I imagine at four years old, right?"

I turn my head so fast that my neck cracks.

"Oh yeah. All wanderers begin more or less at that age. It's so hard to get away from our bestial nature that our bodies struggle for years to remain quadruped."

I try to speak, but I can't even move my lips.

"Surprised?" He smiles.

"You have no idea," I whisper as I look out the window.

On the side of the road, shapes that look like shadowy beings moving in a parallel world start to look less frightening and become more familiar.

Above, the shining stars have ceased to be white points and have become clouds of twinkling dust wrapped in darkness. The Milky Way overhead becomes a show so beautiful, so absolute, that only the vastness of the heavens could offer its immensity and mystery. I've never been able to appreciate its beauty until today on this cold road. And this extraordinary being by my side makes me feel and think things I've never experienced before.

I keep changing in ways that amaze me. Or maybe it's not that I'm changing. Maybe I'm just returning to my true nature.

✦ ✦ ✦ ✦

LOUISA RUNS FROM THE ENTRANCE as we arrive towing her car. "Now what happened?" she asks.

"Sorry, Louisa. I was halfway there when the car broke down."

"My God." She puts a hand to her chest. "Are you okay?"

"I'm fine. Tared saved my skin again," I say to reassure her. The werewolf just smiles and shrugs.

"For the Buddhas, Elisse. When are you going to get rid of that inconsiderate habit of not calling me when these things happen?"

"I'm sorry. It's just that—"

"Miss Fiquette, " Tared says, "I know something about mechanics, and I could take your car to my workshop and give it a look. I won't charge you for it or anything like that."

"Oh, dear, none of that. You've already done too much for this child. I should be rewarding you." Louisa pinches my arm, and I let out an "ouch."

Again, Tared tries to keep from laughing.

"I'll call Geshe to let him know you've arrived."

Louisa goes inside the center without giving me the opportunity to defend myself, and I release a punch to Tared's arm. He laughs, and I giggle too, relieved that it didn't go so badly.

"Are you going back to the reservation?" I ask.

He fiddles with his keys and looks to the side.

"I'm beat. I'd better get home."

"Yeah, I should get to bed too."

"But it's still early. Aren't you planning on going to the carnival? It's almost Mardi Gras, and the best parades are starting."

"I hadn't planned on it," I reply with a little heat in my cheeks. It's sad being in a city as beautiful as New Orleans and not going out to experience it, but my desire to walk as a tourist disappeared the night I encountered the bone monster in the French Quarter.

"Jeez, are you sure you're eighteen? You're missing the best carnival in the country."

"Maybe it's meant for the elderly like you," I joke. He laughs again and gives me a light shove on the shoulder.

"Seriously. No matter how much of a wanderer you are, you should also have some fun. If you want, we can take you out tomorrow to show you a bit of authentic New Orleans."

My cheeks would blush if the idea of returning to the French Quarter weren't so unpleasant. I scratch my neck, but when I see Tared's genuine interest, I have no choice but to nod. And to the misfortune of my tortured head, another question assails me.

"Tell me one thing. If you can't perceive the smell of the dead wanderers or me, how did you know that I … ?" I don't need to say more. He crosses his arms and strokes his beard.

"Instinct. I take care of what's important to me because of the bonds I have with my people. If something threatens my family, my instinct lets me know immediately."

After Tared leaves, I enter the building, still meditating on his words. Perhaps that's why Father Thunder has given some leadership to the wolf, because no matter what type of wanderer he is, I don't think everyone can have an instinct for protection as acute as Tared's.

Suddenly, I meet Louisa in the hallway. She looks at me with an eyebrow so arched it almost touches the top of her hair.

Chapter 28
The Honest Thief

I haven't been here five minutes—the place I said so many times that I would never step foot on again—but I'll admit it, I'm already in love. The French Quarter has gone from a place of nightmares to a dream I'm not sure I want to wake up from. The moon hangs high on Bourbon Street, and I go up to a bench to contemplate the scene from above.

Justice, faith, and power. Purple, green, and gold sparkle everywhere like colorful ghosts shimmering around people's heads, and scattered beads hang over every inch of this legendary street.

A rhythmic humming, sensual and alive, coats my ears with the caramel voices of saxophones and bass. Jazz flows from every corner with a beauty that gives me goosebumps and transports me to a vintage place painted in shades of gold.

The seductive fog of New Orleans enters each pore of my skin and intoxicates me with the city's mystique.

I grew up in India, one of the richest cultural sites on the planet, but this is even more extraordinary. I don't know if it's the beauty of its streets or the gloom of its culture and people, but the French Quarter that once terrified me, right now under the moon over Bourbon Street, feels truly magical.

The giant neon sign of Bar Louis Armstrong, just a block away, glows above the place where I'm supposed to meet Tared and the others. A woman sings from the bar. Her voice rises over a soft double bass and a drum that reverberates in my chest. I offer one last sigh to the moon and head there.

Even in my daydreams, I can't help but think of Laurele's shop, but I know it's not the time to tangle with that woman even though my tongue burns to ask her questions.

I don't see anyone from the tribe near the bar, but I know they're somewhere among the crowd. *Now*, I can feel them. It's like everyone else has the same flat, gray presence without a smell or anything to differentiate them, while the wanderers emit something I can sense through the environment when they are near—the scent of Johanna's hair, the rhythm of Julien's movement, the rigidity of Nashua's stillness, and the intensity of Tared's gaze ... which makes me turn around.

He stands right there with his arms crossed and leans on the same lamp post where I stood the first time I came to Bourbon Street. Our eyes meet. He smiles, and the world becomes tiny. I'm about to go up to him, but I change my mind when a couple of guys greet him first. Someone taps my shoulder, and I turn around to meet Johanna's gray eyes.

"Hi." She smiles and hugs me. "How are you feeling?"

Before I can answer, a thick arm imprisons my neck. Julien rubs his knuckles against my hair.

"Ten points for lighting Elisse's head on fire!"

"Let me go, sausage man."

"Oh hell, you've discovered my true ancestor." The redhead releases me and bites his nails in a ridiculous gesture.

Johanna laughs at our foolishness, and I can't help but join her.

"Stop making a fool of yourself, Julien. You look like an idiot," Nashua says as he emerges with a bitter face from the crowd.

"By God, somebody get this man a drink!" Julien says and gives his brother a loud slap on the arm. Nashua just rolls his eyes.

I shake my head without erasing the smile from my face. Now that I think about it, I've never met my brothers outside of the reserve. This is the first time I've seen them mingle with ordinary people. Ignoring the fact that I feel so small next to men the size of goalposts, and a girl who exceeds my sad five-foot-five height, I think they look pretty normal.

"Now what? Do we start the hazing?" Our leader arrives and puts his arm around my shoulders. He presses me against his side.

"Oh, don't start with your childishness," Johanna says.

"Party pooper," Nashua mumbles, and despite the hardness of his tone, a pleasant sensation twists in my stomach.

"Well," Julien says, "we'd start with a round of bourbon, but since Elisse is still a baby, we can't go into a bar without getting arrested."

"Excuse me for not having an ID, grandpa," I say.

The bison wanderer slaps his hand to his chest in mocking indignation.

"Let's just have a few drinks here on the street, then we'll see the parade on St. Charles," Tared says, and we all agree enthusiastically.

He and Nashua slip into the crowd to go to a nearby bar. They return several long minutes later with large disposable cups filled with frothy beer. I drink mine and find myself with a sad, non-alcoholic beverage, so I can't help but look at Tared with disappointment.

"Sorry. On the reserve have all you want, but in public, not until you're of legal age to drink."

"This sucks. I'd be old enough in India."

"Rules are rules," he says with seriousness, and the matter is settled.

We walk several blocks to the famous St. Charles Avenue, where we push our way to the sidewalk. On the road, a giant man with a fish tail leans over the people and raises a golden trident. A caravan of spectacular creatures follows him: a white-haired king with butterfly wings, the gigantic head of a woman covered in rose petals, undulating fairies with baskets of artificial flowers, and fantastic creatures with multicolored heads who throw necklaces to the crowds cheering from the sidewalks. The floats are made with such magnificent allegorical art that, suddenly, I feel like I've entered a fantasy world.

I've never seen a parade, even in my country, so the bath of lights, colors, and music compels me to push my way to see everything more closely without caring that my drink spills each time I bump into someone.

"Johanna, look," I say, but when I turn to her, she isn't there. I look around, but I don't see or feel my brothers anywhere. I'm an idiot.

I return to the sea of people and try to find them, but there are so many people that it's impossible for me to distinguish anyone in particular. I only get noise, crowd, and disorder until I sense a presence behind my back. When I turn around, the air expels from my lungs as if I were hit in the stomach with a mallet.

The bone monster, that creature who almost tore out my ribs, rises over the heads of the crowd a few feet away from me, glaring through empty sockets, with its cloak billowing between people's legs.

A sharp pain digs into the walls of my stomach so powerfully that I fold over. I hold back a scream while some sort of energy gathers its strength and crashes against my insides. After a couple more blows, it's clear to me that Deer Shadowskin is bashing his horns against the insides of my body to escape.

"What the hell are you doing?" I hiss at my ancestor. I close my eyes and try to contain the pain when several people begin gawking at me.

I open my eyes and stumble back. The bone monster is just steps away from me when I collide against something solid and spill my drink over my clothes. A scream pierces my back. I turn around and see a girl lying face down on the ground.

"I'm so sorry," I say with my voice in threads. I look around, and the bone monster has disappeared.

When I lean over to try to help her up, a strong hand closes on my wrist like the claw of an eagle and yanks me away from the girl.

"Hey, brat, are you causing problems?" A dark-haired man with olive skin looks at me with narrowed eyes.

"No, I . . . Ah, I didn't mean to . . . " I say, unable to spin the words because of the pain rattling my insides.

"I'm fine, officer. It was an accident," the girl says.

Officer? My eyes travel to the badge sticking out from the guy's jacket pocket.

He ignores the woman and wrenches me. He brings my face just a few centimeters from his and sniffs.

"Have you been drinking?" he asks.

Panic sends the pain in my stomach into the background.

"What? I haven't. I . . . " I turn to the girl who recoils at the officer's glare.

"Sir, really—"

"Get out of here!" the man shouts at the girl, who gives me a glazed, apologetic look before fleeing.

"E-excuse, ah, me, this is a-a mistake," I say in an ineloquent babble that doesn't help my case at all.

"How old are you, little boy? Fifteen?"

"No, wait, I—"

"Detective Hoffman."

The man sneers and turns to see who called. The air comes back to my chest when I see Tared only a few steps away from us.

"Look at the hero we have here," the detective replies. "*The* Tared Miller. You hang with children now?"

"Is there a problem?" the wolf asks and looks at me in a way I can't decipher.

"Only if you've been letting him drink more than milk from his bottle."

"Excuse me?" I say and jerk free from the man's grip. "I haven't done anything for you to treat me like this."

"Boy, behave yourself, and don't talk to the detective like that," Tared orders me.

"But I didn't do anything!"

"Elisse! Come here right now."

Tared's voice resounds through the crowd, and people turn their heads toward the spectacle. My surprise turns into indignation, and my veins heat up.

"Elisse, huh?" the detective says and pulls a cigarette from his coat pocket. "I thought you looked familiar. You were the main topic at the station. Apparently, you like to cause a lot of problems."

I clench my fist at his words. What the hell is this guy talking about?

He nails his dark eyes to me as a nasty smile walks through his mouth.

"Tell me. Have you already spent the money you stole from the Buddhist center? You should be ashamed after they've provided you with food and a roof over your head."

I'm about to lunge at the guy with the intention of making a mold of my knuckles in his face, even if I have to spend the night in jail, but my ambition falls to pieces when Tared pulls me back.

"Let go!" I demand, but he drags me a few yards away from the guy. He traps my shoulders with his hands and forces me to look at him. His face reddens, and the veins in his neck stand out like roots of a tree.

"My orders are to be respected whether you like it or not," he says through clenched teeth in such a severe way that he sounds like a loudspeaker. "And if you're going to behave like an idiot every time I give you an order, you can say goodbye to the tribe and the damned reservation. You hear me?"

The wolf releases me and turns to the detective. I'm left petrified and wide-eyed.

In a blink, I disappear into the crowd and weave around the people. Tared yells for me, but I don't look back. I rush through arms and sides, following an imaginary zigzag two or three blocks down the street. After several minutes of flight, I reach the edge of the sidewalk just as more floats pass by.

I try to focus on them to calm myself. I press the bridge of my nose with my forefinger and thumb to see if I can release the stress, but it's useless. The lights are too bright, the crowd is too annoying, and with my heart running away, I can't think clearly.

Throw me out? Kick me out of Comus Bayou? I thought this was permanent. I thought once you entered the family there was no turning back. I thought—

My anger vanishes. A man dressed in a black suit and a top hat dances wildly in the street and throws necklaces into the crowd. He turns to me, and I stumble back at the sight of his face painted white like a skull. It's the same guy I saw at the Buddhist center. One after another, more men like him dance from one side of the street to the other and throw necklaces to the people screaming and jostling on the asphalt. I'm so stunned that I hardly feel when someone touches my arm.

"Elisse? Are you okay?"

I focus my eyes and meet Johanna's concerned face. I point to the men in suits.

"Can you see them?"

She frowns. "Yes, I can see them."

Now my mind's a mess. When I look again, there's a float with the giant figure of a man wearing a top hat, suit, and a mask like a skull.

"What is that?" I point to the display.

She blinks several times and looks at me as if I've gone crazy. "Well … It's the float of Baron Samedi, a Voodoo deity."

A chill runs down my spine. I know that name. I know that Loa. In Laurele's red book, there was a small section about him, but I didn't recognize him until now. The book didn't say anything about his physical appearance, only his qualities and gifts.

Sockets without eyes, white face, peeled skin … The pieces fit.

The one who wants to contact me is Baron Samedi, the Loa of Death. The Lord of the Sabbath.

Chapter 29
Complex Feelings

"Can you tell me why up until now you haven't spoken about this supposed visit? And how is it you go investigate without telling me anything you've been seeing?" Muata says.

"If you were willing to teach me something, I wouldn't have to make decisions on my own."

"And you dare speak to me like that, you stupid boy!"

"What does it matter? The bone monster, the corpses, the resurrected wanderers, the veves. Either the Lord of Death is trying to tell me something, or one of his followers is trying to kill us." My arm waves up and down to give strength to my argument even though I know Muata can only hear me over the phone.

"Why the hell aren't you searching for that person instead of doing silly things at the carnival? How do you expect me to introduce you to the world of shadowgazers if you can't exercise good judgment? Stop wasting time with ridiculousness and do your job."

The dead line whistles at me from the handset. I whip the innocent device against the booth and lean against the glass wall. Johanna waits for me outside with a shocked face and asks with gestures what happened. I just shake my head and, for a few moments, stay inside the tiny space to recover from my frustration. A night that was supposed to be incredible ended up being a disaster.

"What did he say?" she asks me once I step out.

"That I'm an idiot."

Johanna rolls her eyes. "He's not a very subtle man," she says.

"Are you saying he's right?"

"That's not what I meant."

I brush off her comment with a shrug. She plays with her fingers, and for a moment, she reminds me of Carlton and the time he tried to make up for mistaking me as a girl.

"The others are in a bar a block from here." She changes the subject. "Do you want to meet up with them?"

"Tared's there too?"

She nods, and I just snort.

"I should go home. It's getting late."

Johanna squints, and I want to kick myself for being so obvious.

"Let me take you. If you walk, you'll get home too late."

She's right. I'm angry, but I know it would be stupid to go on foot from here to the Buddhist center.

We start walking toward the parking lot. We pass the bar where the others are drinking. I wait outside while Johanna enters. She returns almost immediately.

We make it to her little silver car, the one that almost never sees the light of day because it sits under an awning at the reserve.

After twenty minutes of fighting through traffic, we get out of the French Quarter. Johanna's unrelenting glances stick needles in my seat and make me stir.

"What's wrong?" I ask more out of discomfort than the desire to talk.

"Did something bad happen between you and Tared?"

I tell her what happened with the detective. I keep my eyes on the window. The thought of that jerk accusing me of stealing makes my eyes well up with rage.

"I'm so sorry," she says. "Too bad you ran into Hoffman."

"You know him?"

"Everyone who lives in New Orleans knows him and his bad attitude. If they haven't thrown him out of the police, it's because, for better or worse, he's a good detective."

"Yeah, I already found that out."

"Well ... Hoffman had no right to accuse you like that, and maybe I understand why you acted the way you did. Maybe," she says as if she didn't entirely agree with me. Something tells me it's because of Tared, so I prefer not to respond.

We finally stop at the entrance of the Buddhist center. Just as I'm about to get out, Johanna locks the door.

"Don't be mad at Tared."

My eyes nearly roll away from the muscle.

"Look, I don't think he wanted to be so hard on you," she says. "It's just that ... Hoffman is a difficult subject for him."

"Why is that my fault? He should deal with him and not take it out on me."

"Listen to me." She grips my arm, forcing me to look at her. "Mama Tallulah says that wolves are the wisest ancestors on earth, and they'd never choose to be born into someone who wasn't suited to guide a tribe, so Father Thunder put Tared in charge of us. His methods aren't always gentle, but he knows what he's doing."

"Are you doing this for him?" I snap at her. Shame overcomes me for revealing my anger.

"I'm doing this for all of us. We're a family, and the last thing I want is us fighting with each other when we have so many enemies out there." She moves closer, still gripping my arm. "Tared would never push you away from him or us. If he sided with Hoffman, I'm sure it was because he thought it was best for you. You have to believe me."

Her lower lip trembles and despair dampens her eyes. I feel somewhat sorry for her, so I finally give in to my damn weakness.

"Fine. What do you want from me?"

"Just have patience. Trust him. That's all I'm asking."

By the gods. So much drama just to tell me to endure Tared's scolding.

I get out of the car, and Johanna waves goodbye. The headlights disappear into the blackness of the night, and I go inside the house without the desire to lock myself in my room again.

At the entrance, Louisa's voice comes from the back room. I cross the hall and open the door to find her seated in the armchair.

"Oh, you're finally here. This boy has been waiting for you for almost twenty minutes. You should be ashamed."

My heart drops to my feet when I see Tared sitting in front of her. "What the hell are you doing here?" I ask.

Louisa crashes her hand against the back of my neck, hard enough for me to wince in pain. "Don't be rude."

My face reddens like a chili pepper. I rub the blow from her heavy hand while she takes her bag and leaves as if nothing happened. I glare at Tared when he twists his mouth not to laugh, and he clears his throat. He stands up, and I step back.

"You shouldn't have left like that," he says in a rather soft tone.

I don't look at him. I'm afraid anger will dominate me again, and truth be told, I'm still not sure if that thing about throwing me out of the tribe was serious, so I tie my tongue in a knot.

The wolf sighs and scratches the back of his neck. "Look... with Hoffman you have to be careful. It's better to have him on your side."

"I also have to be on your side, right?" I say sharply.

What the fuck is wrong with me? I can't believe I'm acting like this after I promised Johanna I'd try to trust him.

Tared crosses his arms, and his eyes turn into icicles. "I came here to give you an explanation, but I don't know why I even bothered. You're bullheaded."

"What? I've endured too much shit my whole life to let you align with an abusive cop who accuses me of being a thief."

"Who is accusing you?"

"You took his side."

"Because you were behaving like a brat."

"He was accusing me of something I didn't do. You don't believe me? You don't trust me?"

"Why do you want me to trust you? Just do your damn job!" he roars.

My legs tremble as the words of Muata explode in my head like gunpowder.

"My job? Is that who I am to you? To Muata? Someone to do a job? You should have said that before making me believe that I was already part of this family." I take a step back and sink myself in the armchair with a thud.

Tared just looks at me and doesn't say a word.

I hide my face in my hands. My head and my heart twist in knots. It's not that I hate being called a thief or being accused of something I haven't done. I just don't want to be alone again, and that simple idea makes me fall apart.

"Hey, I'm sorry," he whispers and places his hands on my shoulders. "I didn't mean to say that stuff. I wasn't serious. I'd never exclude you from the tribe. I just didn't know what to say to calm you down. I was so tense that it was the first thing that came to me, and it was wrong. I admit it. But if you'd give me a chance to explain ... "

The touch of his fingers burn through my clothes, growing too hot to bear anymore, so I nod.

He lets go of me and sits on the loveseat. He points to the space beside him, but I'm still hurting, so I don't move from my place. Tared just accepts it as if he understood the space I've imposed between us.

"I think if I share about myself, you'll understand a little better why I do the things I do."

He looks at me with somewhat trembling eyes, and something in my stomach tumbles. I've never seen Tared's gaze waver, and he's not the kind of man you'd expect to show the slightest bit of vulnerability.

Decency tells me I shouldn't let him share about his past, but my curiosity usually wins against the rest of my emotions, so I let him begin.

He sweeps his hair back and takes a breath. "Eight years ago, I left my mother and brother in Minnesota to come to New Orleans to work in the blacksmith shop of my only living grandfather. For the old man, it was already difficult to do various jobs, his hands were nearly crippled. So he was grateful when I moved here," he says.

Either the space between our two seats shrank, or I slipped a few inches closer to hear him more clearly.

"Things were never easy for me. I've always had a somewhat complicated character, and my grandfather died a few months after I arrived—"

"I'm sorry." I interrupt almost unconsciously. I just couldn't bear the stitch in my heart after hearing about his loss.

Tared shrugs.

"In short, I had a bunch of debts in Minnesota, and the workshop didn't make as much as I wanted, especially because I didn't know enough. The bills piled up, and there came a point when the creditors didn't stop calling me, so I had to find another job to try to get out of trouble. A friend I made here suggested that I enter the police force.

"Getting into the academy was a piece of cake. I advanced so quickly in my police training that in just a few months they gave me a position in the streets, a patrol, and a more experienced partner to help me start my rounds. The salary was decent. I was paying my debts. Everything was going smoothly."

He pauses a moment and eyes me to make sure I'm following the thread of the story. It's evident that my anger has yielded to interest, so he stands up, takes a couple of short turns, and finally, walks toward the window facing the courtyard. He opens and closes his mouth repeatedly as if he's having trouble speaking, and then he sighs. He looks sorrowfully at the ceiling and ... trembles? Suddenly, I feel guilty.

"On a night watch," he says, "two subjects were reported wandering through one of the poorest neighborhoods in the city, bothering everyone and causing a commotion. We were confident that we could deal with them, so me and my partner went there around three in the morning. But when we got there, there weren't just two of them. There were too many to take on."

Too many sends chills up my spine. I walk over to Tared, who looks into the night through the glass. His face is still, and his eyes darken. Perhaps it's the movement of the clouds over the moon that gives him a painful aspect like he might break.

"In the midst of them brutally beating us, I had my first awakening," he says. "I lost control and—"

"Enough," I interrupt. Tared shares in equal surprise at how my fingers have lifted themselves to pull at his jacket. "You don't have to ... "

"I didn't leave anything in one piece. Not them. Not my partner," he says coldly.

I let go of his jacket to cover my mouth, and he fixes his eyes on me.

"Please, you don't have to—" I say.

"The others arrived faster than I could process. Between Father Thunder, Nashua, and Julien, they subdued me. They tore off my skin and did their best to cover up the scene, like they were used to doing that kind of work."

"But how… ?"

"Apparently, they had been watching me for a long time."

Instantly, I remember how effectively my brothers erased all traces of violence when I had that incident in the park, and the way they stalked me in the French Quarter after that.

"The hardest thing was what came later, when the rest of the police arrived at the scene. I had no rational explanation for what had happened. I ripped them into pieces, so I had to lie. I told them that I was knocked out from the blows, and that I didn't know who or what had committed such carnage. For years, I stood by that version in public, and there was no evidence to the contrary. They swallowed the story without question and stopped wondering what had happened. The case was closed, and they believed me. All except one person."

"Hoffman," I whisper. I've been an imbecile. It wasn't that Tared didn't believe me; it was that I didn't trust him.

"I'm sorry," I say a second time with my voice wrapped in shame. "I've been an idiot."

He looks at me for just a moment and turns his back. I become the tiniest creature in the world. Would it help if I tell him I'm sorry again? That I feel like scum for forcing him to relive something like that? And it's not because I'm afraid of what he did, but because of what his eyes showed me when he bared his soul. I don't dare take a step toward him, toward his closeness, toward the desperate desire to wrap my arms around him.

Tared goes home without saying a word, leaving only an absence in the room. It hurts and makes me feel more alone than ever. I just sit on the couch, lost in overwhelming nothingness. By the gods, how is it possible that he can make me feel this way?

Chapter 30
Atrocious Feelings (and Rooms)

It's barely past six in the morning when someone pounds on the door of the Buddhist center. I curse, nearly dropping my coffee. I haven't even had a chance to eat breakfast, and my stomach's roaring.

Through the peephole, I see Louisa flipping her head like a sprinkler. Immediately, I know something's wrong, and I open the door.

"Louisa. What's happened?" I place my hand on her shoulder, and her body trembles under my fingers.

"I have to talk to you."

Now I'm the nervous one.

Louisa leads me into the kitchen in complete silence and sits me at the table. She paces like a caged lioness.

"Look." She turns abruptly to me and removes her glasses. "You're already grown enough to know what you're doing, but I'm not going to stop worrying about you."

"Did I do something wrong?"

She exhales forcefully. "Laurele told me you went to see her."

Suddenly, I feel like a child who's kicked his mother.

"I-I . . . " I stammer and try to hide my shame. "I'm sorry. You told me not to go near her, but—"

She raises a stiff palm in front of me. "You have your reasons. I'm not your mother to tell you what to do." Her words come out like a sigh and hurt. Her eyes become glossy.

"But I came for something else. For something much more important." She searches her purse under my guilty look. I lean back when she retrieves a voodoo doll, the one that appeared the night of the Loa's visit.

"Where'd you get that?" My stomach sinks.

"My sister left it at my house last night and had the nerve to ask me to give it to you."

My heart rages furiously against my rib cage. I'm such an idiot. I didn't lose the doll in the swamp. I left it at Laurele's shop.

"And the needles?"

"What needles?"

"The doll had a bunch of needles stuck all over it. I even pricked my fingers and . . . "

I bled.

I try to keep my composure so I don't frighten Louisa, but I can't keep my soul from leaving through my feet. Louisa pales as if she read my mind.

"For all you love most, do not go near my sister," she says. "That woman is much more dangerous than you think. Whatever she wants from you, it's no good."

"What has she done?"

She lays her hand on her chest and takes a deep breath.

"Ever since we were young girls, Laurele was always fascinated with our Haitian roots. She read everything she could about Voodoo. Memorized it, rubbed shoulders with the healers and witches of our neighborhood. She dreamed of becoming the next Marie Laveau. I always tried to stay out of her things because there was something in my sister's face that made my hair stand on end. I felt like she was getting into a world she could never get out of."

Louisa goes to the window over the sink and opens the glass to take a deep breath. I want to hug her trembling back until the shaking stops, but like a frightened animal, I remain still and observant.

"Over time, she became quite famous, and at seventeen she was already an expert," she says. "People began to knock on our door asking to see my sister, and each time, she did bizarre things for them that required more ingredients, more gruesome than the previous ones. Her room became a cemetery of bones, and her face expressed nothing but contempt when she looked at my mother and me. She became so strange that we both feared her. And then one day she left."

"Did you stop talking to her?

"Yes, but more because soon after she left, I got married to a terrible, violent man. The worst choice of my life, but I had no other options."

I try not to imagine the worst, but when Louisa passes her hand over her cheek as if she were recalling the ghost of a bruise, my chest contracts with rage. How could someone be so rotten to put a finger on a woman like her?

"Son of a bitch."

"Oh Elisse, at that time, being Black was the same as being an animal. We had no rights, no equality. We didn't even have decent salaries. So, being Black, and above all, a single woman, was the quickest way to starve to death. I was alone, mostly because my mother died shortly after Laurele left home."

She says it as if she needed to justify herself, but I would never have the heart to judge her.

"What happened to your husband?" I say and sow contempt in each word.

"Look, he ... " She covers her eyes with her hands and lets out a soft choked noise.

Louisa sobs, and immediately I regret that I asked. And I regret it more deeply when she shows her eyes soaked in tears.

"Do you know what a miscarriage is?"

The tips of my ears redden, and I nod slowly. Louisa exhales in relief, I imagine, that she doesn't have to explain it.

"During the years that my marriage lasted, I could never have a child. I was pregnant several times, but none of my children survived. None, except ... "

Louisa pauses to weep, and I jump up to get close to her. A devastating sadness dims her maternal glow, and my heart shatters to pieces.

"Nobody could explain what was happening," she says between sobs and catches one of my hands between hers. "All I know is that when I noticed a strange smell, it meant I was about to lose my child."

"A strange smell?"

"Yes, the smell of... death when I opened things, like bottles and jars."

I inhale slowly and try not to show my horror at the description so appallingly familiar.

"The only time I ever went to my sister's house, I didn't bother to let her know beforehand. My husband had just left me for another woman, and I wanted to talk to someone. When I got to her door, that same disgusting smell hit my nose. At that point I knew, in some way, that Laurele … "

Louisa suffers a moan. She doesn't need to explain the rest. I close my eyes upon hearing about that nightmarish act, and my head fills with questions. How the hell could Laurele do something so atrocious to her own sister? What benefit could she gain from something so monstrous?

Louisa sobs, so I hold her tighter in my arms.

"I could have forgiven her, if only that weren't the worst of everything she did to me." She wipes away a tear and firms her gaze as if a fire of contempt devoured her from within. "Before leaving, my husband gave me a miracle. My first and only child was born months after he left me. That gave me the happiest twenty years of my life, before my son … died of a heart attack."

"A heart attack? So young?"

Louisa shifts her eyes to the window as if she were searching outside for some trace of that lost son. "Impossible, right? But it happened. Since then, it doesn't matter how many people are around me, I always feel alone."

I hug her again. It's not hard to imagine that a part of Louisa's attachment to me is related to the absence of her son, and the idea doesn't bother me. On the contrary, I understand perfectly. For a long time, I've been trying to make up for the absence of my father.

She smiles gently and wipes away her tears as if she had nothing left to hide from me.

"I never imagined that my older sister could be so horrible," she says.

I lean forward and look at Louisa without moving a single eyelash. "Your older sister?"

"Her magic is real, Elisse. She's fifty-nine years old, but ever since my son died, she hasn't aged a day."

✦ ✦ ✦ ✦

I SHOULD CONSIDER BUYING A CAR because, at this rate, Louisa's will end up falling apart. I'm grateful that Tared repaired the car so soon; otherwise, it would have taken years to reach the French Quarter by taxi or bus. And truthfully, time is the last thing I have.

I called the reserve thirty minutes ago, but when no one answered, it was clear that I had to do things on my own. Besides, with my head steaming about what that bitch did to Louisa, I didn't think much of it.

My mind spins as I repeat to myself how stupid it was to leave that doll at Laurele's shop. I bled. I pricked myself with those needles and gave that damn woman every weapon to bewitch me. Now, I'm certain she caused the car to break down in the middle of the road, and I'm more than certain she's the one who's reviving the wanderers. But why? What the hell does she gain by killing us?

I park as close as I can to the witch's neighborhood and lie low as if a demon were chasing me. If Laurele's not in her shop, I'll set fire to her damn nest of…

At just a few yards from her place, I can see the security gate drawn across the door. I approach the window, and my heart races when I see iron bars in front of the curtains. I'm sure the bars weren't there before. I run to the door and peek through the small spaces of the gate to find everything turned off and ... empty. The place is empty. That bitch left.

"Fuck." I release a kick.

To my surprise, the gate pops open with a squeak. I look to both sides of the street to make sure no one's seen me, and then I slide the gate, inch by inch, until I'm inside the shop. The wood floor creaks beneath my boots.

Now that the place is empty, it looks much bigger. The only thing the witch has left is the wood counter. On the other side of the shop, a staircase leads to the second floor, but behind the counter, a doorway leads into darkness. I take out the lighter I brought with me and flick on the flame. I step slowly, still driven by the rage bubbling beneath my skin.

Along the hallway, grimy spaces, where pictures must have hung, checker the yellowish walls. At times it looks like faces are still imprinted in the dust. Doors line both sides, but none call my attention as powerfully as the one in back, the one as black as oil. So, I inch toward it. A shiver moves through me. Are those scratches?

I twist the knob, and I'm not sure which frightens me more, the silence that's followed me throughout the shop or the emptiness of the room. My lighter's dim flame reveals emaciated walls with paint flaking off, and there's a window at the back. Strange. The room isn't square but oval, something peculiar for an old house in the French Quarter.

I search for a light switch, but there's not even a bulb on the ceiling. With courage, I walk to the window and try to open it, but nails seal it shut, and a thick layer of black plastic and duct tape blocks the sun from passing through the glass.

Five long slashes mark the frame of the window and nearly cross the length of the wood. I examine them more closely and turn white. It looks like they're from a giant hand.

When I hear footsteps echo behind me, I turn around. To my horror, the door shuts and makes a single click. I sprint to try to open it, but it's closed like a tomb, and I can hear something crawling by me.

I raise the lighter to the ceiling, but nothing.

Whispers begin rising around me, and I wave the lighter from one side and then to the other, but there's only darkness beyond the flame. I take a deep breath as the number of voices increase, but I realize it's just the same voice echoing throughout the room.

I move the lighter toward one of the peeling walls. My eyes open in astonishment when different symbols appear as if a knife carved them as the flame passes. Stars, crosses, crypts—strange markings unfold before me.

"Veves," I whisper. "Hundreds of them."

I walk closer to the wall, and the mural of symbols freezes my blood. I circle around to the window, and another footstep sounds behind me. I pivot.

Fum!

The flame of the lighter explodes like a torch and illuminates the entire room. I scream with such intensity that I nearly shatter my throat. Corpses of men, women, and animals, with monstrous faces, dangle from the ceiling. Their bodies are naked and mutilated. Some are so small, that I'm sure they're children.

"Shit, shit . . . " The fire burns my fingers and I drop the lighter. Darkness swallows the room.

"Help me! Help me, please!" I beg for Deer Shadowskin. With no sign of him, not even an ache inside me, I squat down and crawl through the darkness. I cling to the wall, afraid the feet of the corpses might brush my crown.

The room is so small that if I follow along the walls, I know I can find the door and get the hell out of here.

I crawl and keep crawling. Despair eats me away because I can't find the damn door. The room has become infinite. Cold sweat soaks my body, and my heart beats so fast that I get dizzy. I go around and around the oval wall as if I had suddenly fallen into a pit and found nothing but silence and darkness.

"What the hell?" I moan. "Where the hell is the door?"

Heavy steps land behind me and terror fires my feet. I slide my hand and drag my shoulder along the wall as I run. Several minutes pass, and I still can't find the fucking exit. I'm plunged in the deepest darkness. I pull my hair, shake, moan, sweat, and grit my teeth. Run. Keep running.

When the line between despair and schizophrenia thins, my foot kicks something that bounces and flies away from me. I open my eyes wide and follow the noise, but I'm so terrified and confused that I'm not sure if my senses are tricking me.

I leave the safety of the wall and crawl on the floor to search for the object. I feel something. A stupid smile crosses my lips when the lighter dances between my trembling fingers. I flick on the flame and find myself in infinite blackness.

I continue running, running through absolute darkness, and my heart stops when I realize the walls have disappeared.

"No, no, no."

Elisssse.

I stop in my tracks and cover my mouth to keep from screaming when my name is uttered in a hiss. I wheel the flame around, and in the gloom, a white tail glides into the shadows.

I hear my name again, and the sick idea of that thing calling me comes to mind. For everything sacred, is this Laurele's trap?

The shape of the thing fades into the darkness, so by pure instinct, I run after it. The tail moves a couple of yards ahead of me like a thread of light, and at last, I can make out the creature. It's a snake.

I follow it, and the white tail disappears under the door.

"Thank you, thank you, thank you!" I whisper over and over, on the verge of bursting into a nervous laugh.

When I catch the knob, the door opens from the other side and sends me flat to the floor.

"What the hell are you doing here?" a human voice says as a bright light assaults my eyes. Pointing a pocket flashlight, Detective Hoffman looks at me and frowns.

By the gods. I never thought I'd be so devilishly happy to see this jerk. I stand up, panting, and keep myself from jumping to embrace him.

"Ah, I . . . " I mumble like an idiot, unable to recover from the scare. I look behind my back.

Damn. Shadowgazers must have the highest death rate among the wanderers. At this rate, I'll end up dying of a heart attack.

"I asked you what the hell you're doing here, brat."

I wipe the sweat from my forehead and swallow hard. "I came to look for the lady who had a shop here. I—"

"The woman closed last night and left. I think it's obvious enough that breaking in here is a crime."

"Ah, it's just that, you know, she owes me something, and I thought . . . "

Hoffman's gaze is so heavy that it feels like a rock crushing my skull. He doesn't give a damn about what I'm saying, so I take a breath.

"Look, if what you want is—"

"Listen kid, how'd you meet Tared?"

His question dislodges me. I open and close my mouth a couple of times.

"Answers!" he shouts.

"Ah, I . . . Once he came to the Buddhist center. He seemed nice." An obvious lie.

He leans toward me until he's only inches from my face. "You heard someone's been playing with the dead at the St. Louis Cemetery, right?"

Once again, I break into a cold sweat.

"Everyone knows. But what about it?" I respond with agitation. I'm afraid my sanity might collapse at any moment, or worse, that something will pull me back into the oval room.

"Careful. You never know what you'll find under a bed," he says.

My hands tremble at the thickness of his voice, and I'm sure that amuses him even more.

"Now get out of here before I lock you in a damn cell for trespassing."

He doesn't have to say it twice. I bolt out of there like lightning and run for the nearest payphone.

Chapter 31
First Love

Inside Muata's cabin, the whole tribe surrounds my chair. Mama Tallulah sits beside me and caresses my back. She tries to calm my tremors by passing soothing herbs under my nose.

"The witch Fiquette. I knew she'd give us problems sooner or later," Mama Tallulah says and looks at Father Thunder with concern.

"Do you know her?" I ask.

"She used to be the most famous sorceress around," Father Thunder replies. "Everyone said she was the incarnation of Marie Laveau. Then, one day she retired. She stopped taking clients and opened a voodoo shop in the French Quarter."

"I say we go break her neck right now."

For the first time, I agree with Nashua.

"Grandfather, what did I see in that room?" I ask with a strange feeling on my tongue as if I only called him "grandfather" as a formality rather than an attempt at closeness.

The old man sighs and shakes his head.

"Those people, those bodies, were certainly victims of the sorceress Fiquette. The dead can become trapped in the human plane, creating what we call ghosts. Sometimes they stay here because the end of their days was sudden or confusing. It's difficult to know where to go if you haven't realized you're dead."

An icy drop falls on my neck at the thought of the babies in that room and some of them possibly being Louisa's.

"That bitch. She could have killed you," Tared says. His face looks so angry that for a moment it resembles the one from his wolf state.

"What about the room itself?" I ask the old man.

"That witch has placed a spell to confuse the mind, to drive anyone mad who dares enter that room. I assure you, boy, the entire time you circled right there in that room, your head made you believe it was an infinite space. Perhaps the serpent you saw was an ancestor guiding you through the darkness to find the way out. We're the only wanderers who can interact with other ancestors besides our own."

I feel a mixture of wonder and helplessness at his words. I'm sure that without the guidance of Muata I wouldn't understand a quarter of the world of spirits.

"What do we do now, Father Thunder?" Julien asks. For the first time since I've known him, he's taking things seriously.

"We? Isn't it Elisse's job to kill that woman?" Nashua asks.

"That doesn't mean he should do it alone," Johanna says. "Twelve tombs, remember? Who knows how many wanderers are guarding her."

"Nashua is right. You shouldn't if it's my duty," I say more out of anger than desire.

“No way.” Tared steps forward and plants himself in front of me. “You won’t be able to deal with her if she has wanderers by her side, so forget about it.”

“But—”

“Fuck it, Tared. Even Deer Shadowskin refused to help him, so there’s no reason for us to do it,” Nashua says.

“Do you dare turn your back on your family?” The wolf’s face flushes, and the veins of his neck swell.

“That brat isn’t from my family.”

Tared throws a bestial roar, and we all step back as he bounds across the cabin. Nashua rages back, and both rush against each other.

Johanna screams, and in front of a shocked Mama Tallulah, Julien and I launch in the middle of the two men before they hit each other. The bison wraps his forearm around Nashua’s neck and pulls him back while I wrap my arms around Tared’s waist and push him until his legs hit Muata’s bed.

“Enough already!”

Bottles crash to the ground and every piece of wood in the cabin rumbles for a moment. Father Thunder honors his name by shouting so loudly that the entire place quakes.

We go quiet like frightened rabbits. Only the panting of Nashua and Tared, who still look at each other as if they’re ready to tear each other’s heads off, disturbs the silence. Our leader, the most reasonable man of the two, is the first to yield. He puts his hand on my shoulder, and although his breathing is agitated, I know he’s already under control, so I let go.

“Nashua,” Father Thunder calls him with such an icy tone that it gives me chills. “Once again you disrespect your leader. I’ll make sure you receive the severest of punishments. I will not tolerate rebellion in my tribe. Do you hear me?”

"Yes, father," he answers through his teeth, and Julien releases him.

"Tared, what is your plan of action? Quickly." The old man asks, and the wolf turns his head toward me for a few seconds. His blood-red eyes seem to look for a solution in mine. He faces everyone again.

"Elisse, you said that Miss Louisa is that woman's sister. Does she know where to find her?"

"I don't think so. Louisa does her best to stay out of Laurele's business."

Tared growls.

"Nashua, Johanna," he calls them, and they both go to him quickly, even though the bear's face is still filled with resentment. "Go to the city and find out where she lives. Take the weapons you need, and don't dare come back without that information."

The two nod and leave without asking anything else.

"Weapons?" I ask.

"Remember, our priority will always be to keep our species a secret, and it's not a good idea to transform in the middle of the city, so we carry weapons and silencers in case desperate measures have to be taken," Julien replies.

The shotgun Tared had in his truck the day the alligator wanderer attacked us flashes through my head.

"Are we really going to kill her?" I ask, still tormented by the idea.

"Not us, Elisse," Father Thunder replies. "Your brothers will protect you enough to get to her, but as ordered by Grandfather Muata, you are the one who must kill Laurele Fiquette."

✦ ✦ ✦ ✦

"YES?" LOUISA'S VOICE on the other side of the phone baffles me. Her breathing is agitated as if she had to run to take the call.

"Louisa, it's Elisse."

"By the Buddhas," she whispers. "Where are you?"

"At the reservation. What's happened?"

"Something terrible. Money is missing again, another thousand dollars from the safe. Carlton went hysterical, entered your room a while ago, and turned everything on its head. He found a stack of bills behind the bookshelf and called the police. They're looking for you."

"What? No, no, Louisa. I haven't stolen anything. Someone is trying to frame me."

"I know, I know, my child, I believe you. Even Geshe tried to defend you, but he hasn't been able to do anything because everyone in the center is mad. For now, it's best you don't come back here until things calm down."

"By the gods ... "

"I have to go, sweetheart. I'm alone in the center now, but who knows when the others will return. Take care, please, and don't move from where you are. I'll call you if anything changes."

Without a chance to reply, the call drops. I press the bridge of my nose and try not to panic.

"Have you already told them you'll stay here today?"

I startle and look behind me. Mama Tallulah enters the kitchen with a smile, and then squints and tilts her head slightly.

"They're not back, yet?" I ask in a failed attempt to distract her from my face.

"No, but they just set out this afternoon, so there's still time."

I scratch the back of my neck as she takes little feather steps toward me.

"Better get out of here, boy. It won't be long before that Julien comes to prepare the food, and you won't want to be his assistant."

I step by Mama Tallulah's side, but she stops me with a hand on my chest. Her foggy eyes shine in a way I find hard to decipher.

"Elisse … You're my son. You're my child like all the other children of this tribe, and nothing hurts a mother more than to see her son unhappy. You don't have to tell me what's wrong, but if you need me, I'm here for you. Always."

Without waiting for me to reply, Mama Tallulah hugs me. At nearly my height, she manages to squeeze my entire being with her body and presence. Her warmth and softness emit that forest aroma that makes me feel so melancholy.

I reciprocate her embrace and hold her against my chest with enough force that she could never escape my arms. I want to cry, but I push the urge to the bottom of my stomach, where I bury any feeling that threatens to break me.

NIGHT FALLS, and my boots squeak on the wet dock as the sun dies behind the trees surrounding the lake. One by one, precious twinkling stars splash the pink sky and invite me to worship nature from the bottom of my being. Every emotion floods me, all at once, but disappointment overcomes because I can't appreciate this vast beauty the way I would like. I'm too—

"Nervous?" Tared says from behind my back.

He approaches and looks at me as if he could read my every thought. His hair is pulled back, and he's wearing military boots. From the belt of his jeans hangs a gleaming pistol. He looks like a soldier ready for battle, and now that I think about it, we have both prepared for precisely that.

"Extremely." I say and squeeze a bit of the leather jacket I'm wearing. "I don't even know if I can be useful."

"Why do you say that?"

"Nashua said it himself," I answer with irritation. "I felt Deer Shadowskin wanting to escape from my body when I saw the bone monster in the parade, but when I asked for help in the oval room, I couldn't transform myself." I crush my fingers inside my fists.

"Elisse … " The wolf moves closer and leaves only a few steps between us. "Your mistake was to ask Deer Shadowskin to do something for you. The ancestors are not independent of us. They *are* us, even if you're not born with them. Instead of asking them to do a favor for you, be smart, demand yourself to do something helpful. Think of solutions for what you're facing. Do you need strength? Demand it. Do you need a miracle? Demand it. They'll give you their help with wisdom."

I struggle to smile. His words make sense and sound even magical, but even so, I can't help being afraid of what awaits us.

I walk to the edge of the dock and watch the water lilies sway in the ripples of the lake. I feel as fragile as the surface of the water as if the smallest thing could shatter me right now.

"Are you afraid?" he asks.

"More than ever," I answer honestly.

"You appreciate your life too much."

"Of course I do. I don't want to die. But that's not what scares me."

"What then?"

"For me, family is not important. It's everything, and I don't want ... " I don't have to say the rest. Tared's blue eyes have widened.

I know wanderers are neither animal nor human. In fact, I know it's not right to think of Tared as a "werewolf," but that doesn't mean we're not as perceptive as our ancestors. I'm sure the foul smell of my fear must be crashing like a tidal wave into his nose.

"Sometimes it's inevitable," he says. "So far, the witch has only attacked us, but imagine if she decides to use the false wanderers for other purposes. She could hurt Louisa or reveal our existence. Laurele can't continue like this."

"What will happen if one of us dies?" I contemplate the frightful possibility. We both stare at the water, which reflects the remains of the sun.

"Our life is never going to be assured," he says. "But remember that we've agreed to die for our own, next to our own. Because if we don't see that beyond duty, it's an honor, none of our struggles would be justified."

My heart swells until it hurts. The Dreamcatcher always touches the tender fibers of my being.

"Tared," I say softly and take a step toward him under his watchful gaze. "I don't want to kill Laurele."

"I know."

"You know?"

"I haven't known you very long, but strangely, it's never been hard for me to understand you. I know you don't want to kill anyone. I know you feel it's wrong, and if you do it, that you'll change in a way that will never allow you to be the same again."

"You must think I'm a coward."

"On the contrary," he says and looks toward the lake, "I respect you a lot."

"Why?" I ask somewhat agitated, caught by surprise.

"The boys, Father Thunder, and me ... We have all resigned ourselves to the role that nature has given us as wanderers, as skineaters. Even Johanna wouldn't hesitate to kill anyone to honor our purpose. But you're different from everyone I've known. Something about you reminds me that there's a human part within all of us that should prevent us from making decisions so lightly about the lives of other creatures. You have no idea how much I admire that."

He turns to me and stares with his icy blue eyes, which have suddenly swallowed the moon. I look up to make sure it's still in the sky.

"Don't worry about Laurele," he says. "I'll take care of it."

I'm tempted to take a step back. I wasn't sure I wanted to end a person's life, but I'm not sure I want Tared to do it for me either. I know this isn't the first time my brothers have killed a creature from the middle plane. They're skineaters; they're made for it. But we're talking about a human being. There has to be another way.

"Just worry about not getting hurt, okay?" he says calmly as if he were trying to break the tension. "We need you as much as we love you."

Love.

It's the first time in my life someone has said they love me.

My tongue sticks to my palate, and my eyes get wet. I would like to tell him not to worry about me, but the words don't come out of my mouth. I look at the lake again. I don't want to lose this family and their love—the home I've finally found after being alone for so many years.

I look at the werewolf. Our eyes meet for the thousandth time, but our lips aren't able to say anything. It terrifies me to see the moons tremble. Am I seeing fear in my leader's eyes?

"Tared! Elisse!" Julien trots toward us. "We found her!"

Chapter 32
Bonecatcher

It's four in the morning, but my anxiety kept me from getting a wink of sleep. On the other hand, Johanna and Tared look relaxed, so I try to disguise my cowardice to keep from clashing with them. In the rearview mirror, the black suburban is a few yards behind us, and both Julien and Nashua wear such a calm face that they might as well be taking a casual drive.

The werewolf grips the gearshift but then, almost as if he could read my mind, places his hand on my shoulder and squeezes it.

"Everything will be fine," he says. "You'll come with us, remember?"

I can barely nod, and the cold object in my hands takes on considerable weight. *Just in case*, Johanna said to me and handed me this little pistol equipped with a silencer.

However resistant we are in our beast form, we are still made of flesh, so it never hurts to arm ourselves with weapons, even if it's difficult to shoot once transformed. Thick fingers covered with hair can barely fit around a trigger.

"Over there?" our leader asks.

Johanna climbs from the back seat and points to a deviation in the road. "Turn there. Enter the first dirt road you see and go straight. It's the only cabin in the area."

Tared crushes his cigarette in the ashtray and hits the gas.

We pass a long stretch of trees lit tearfully by the headlights of the vehicles, and the thundering gravel on the road beneath the tires makes me feel like we're heading into our own horror movie. We lost all traces of civilization many miles back.

Nashua and Johanna discovered that Laurele owns a cabin on the outskirts of New Orleans. They asked in bars and venues near the voodoo shop if anyone knew where the woman lived, but Laurele is so private that the locals didn't really exchange words with her. That's when my brothers asked the neighbors about the move, whether any of them knew how the witch had moved her trinkets. The neighbors remembered the name of the company well because the truck had caused such a commotion when it entered the narrow street.

Calling the company for the address where they had delivered Laurele's things was a simple task, but investigating the surroundings of the property was not. Still, Nashua and Johanna returned with enough information to be certain they had the right place. They even saw the witch loading boxes into the cabin. So, everything was ready to ambush her, and there was no time to lose. We left early to catch Laurele off guard, but we knew it wouldn't be as simple as surprising her.

We have no idea of the magnitude of her power, and we're not certain of how many false wanderers she's created so far. They could exceed us in number and force, but apparently, betting everything in a situation of risk is something we wanderers should get used to. And I'm not willing to back down even though I'm dying of fear.

"How far are we?" Tared asks Johanna once the gravel road turns into a muddy path.

"About a hundred yards."

"Then we'll stop here."

The jeep leaves the path and enters the forest, and the suburban follows. We stop in the middle of a small clearing. We all get out and leave the keys inside the vehicles in case we have to make a quick escape; as well, we try not to leave a single light on.

"The cabin is behind that mill," Nashua says and points to an old structure that rises in the distance.

"Okay. Let's do this."

As if following an order inherent in Tared's voice, my brothers begin to undress.

Almost by reflex, I divert my eyes even though I can only make out their shapes under the moonlight. When they finish removing their clothes and leave them folded inside the vehicles, I can't help but look sidelong knowing well what comes next. They transform. And the process is extraordinary.

Their bodies stretch and cover with hair in a blink. Their bones crack and lengthen. Their faces deform without an apex of beauty, invaded by fangs, horns, and eyes that shine in the night. As they change, I can sense the magic released from their cells, the violent nature that gives them life under the moon.

There's no blood. No human skin bursting. There's only pain endured with brutal intent. Not one of them screams or complains even once.

Soon, I'm in awe, surrounded by four beautiful, lethal creatures—four children of nature, so impressive that the forest pales before them.

They rise like giants around me. Even Johanna, the smallest of them, is a head taller than me. Her crimson claws more than compensate for her compact frame now populated with muscles and covered with thick sand-colored fur. A black tail swings at her back.

We gather in a circle.

"From now on, everyone will take a different path," our leader says to us. "The idea is to attack the cabin from various angles in case Laurele decides to escape. Above all, be discreet. If you meet an enemy on the road, kill it with as little noise as possible. Use your weapons as a first resource. That's what the silencers are for. If things get heated, shout, howl, roar. The point is we don't want to lose anyone tonight."

Suddenly, the faces of my brothers wash in the utmost seriousness, and I realize this is really going to happen. We're about to risk our lives in battle.

Tared extends his thick arms, and as if he were a magnet attracting our iron spirit, we all draw close to him. My brothers, in tenderness and protection, bend so I can reach them with my human limbs.

The five of us unite in an impenetrable embrace, and our arms form a dreamcatcher in which we weave the threads of our brotherhood. Even Nashua, who stands next to me, squeezes his arm around me and presses his paw against my shoulder.

The smell of their coats, their breath, and the heat that emanates from their bestial bodies floods me. It's a strong odor, and although unpleasant at first, it conveys a protective warmth over me. This circle is my family, and I'm terrified of losing them tonight.

When we separate, we leave a cold emptiness in the air, and almost instinctively, we take different paths among the trees and merge our shadows with the darkness.

To my luck, it's not as difficult to see as I thought it'd be. The branches creak beneath my steps as the forest looms overhead like a cage full of leaves. The fog covers the ground with a thick blanket high enough to swallow my ankles.

I keep an eye on the mill, whose blades turn slowly as the wind blows a little harder. I wedge the gun into my belt as I replay in my head the quick practice I had before coming here.

It was bad. I could barely get five shots out of fifteen. But I think I'll need more than perfect aim to finish off an enemy if it attacks me, so I charge my knife on the other side of my belt.

Although I can't see them, I can sense my brothers several yards away gliding silently like spirits.

At last, I distinguish the foot of the mill between the hollows of the undergrowth and, farther on, Laurele's place. From the mill hangs a lamp that illuminates the ground and cabin with a ghostly white light, which bounces between barrels, stacked logs, and an old broken boat.

The branches creak behind me. A foul stench hits me suddenly, and in the distance appears a shape whose features are barely distinguishable in the darkness. I hear insistent gasps like the gurgling of something crawling in the mud. Out of caution, I draw my weapon when I see something moving slowly toward me.

Raspy moans come from the shadow, which gradually looks more humanlike. I begin to sweat. I cock the gun and point it toward the head, but when moonlight falls on the figure, I'm speechless. Strange rot deforms a man's face. One cheek is blackened, and the other oozes green pus. His lips weep, and exposed skull appears where there was once a nose. Blackish tumors push through his torn clothes to reveal his swollen body. His arms, covered with wormy sores, rise in my direction. He moves toward me as if he could see, but his eyes are missing.

Without a second thought, I shoot. The bullet blasts through his skull, and the body falls backward. I approach, trembling, and part of the veve of Baron Samedi appears on his arm:

The figure fades. I look at the monster in mixture of horror and alarm. It stinks like one of my nightmares, and I don't have to be a genius to know what it is.

"A zombie," I whisper.

Within seconds, the corpse decomposes as if it were boiling broth, and nothing remains but a filthy foam. I quickly race toward the cabin.

From the edge of the forest, I spot Nashua several yards away hiding behind a couple of barrels and camouflaged by his black fur. Over the bushes, I see and hear movement behind the cabin, so the rest of my brothers must already be surrounding the area.

"By the gods ..." I can't scream to warn them about the zombies, and running to Nashua would be just as fatal. It would expose us.

Suddenly, the lamp of the mill explodes. Someone shot it, shattering the light, giving us the advantage of complete darkness. I stay quiet in my place.

Tared emerges from the shadows and heads straight toward the front door of the cabin, risking the first attack. Powerlessness warms my knuckles when I can't do anything to stop him, so I point my gun at the small house, expecting the worst.

Tared's footsteps crunch on the earth, and the moon makes his silver fur glow brighter. The wind stops blowing between the trees, and the crickets hush. Fear chokes my heart. I hear the door unlock and a creak ... and then another creak ... and another. Silence.

Blam!

An army of creatures fires from every opening of the cabin—from the doors, from the windows, and from under the porch. In a few seconds, I count almost a dozen beings rushing against Tared like a torrent of demons.

My brothers spring from the bushes and charge into battle with their pistols firing against the hurricane.

The bodies of three of the attackers tear apart to make way for a pack of identical black dogs. The bullets strike them but have no effect, so it's not long before the weapons plummet to the ground.

The rest of the monsters are simple zombies who can barely walk but crave to sink their gums into our flesh. Even though I demand it from the deepest part of my will, I still can't transform. Frustrated, and with my heart beating like crazy, I dart out of the brush and fire my gun repeatedly at the undead.

Our leader collides with the first wanderer. He stabs his steel claws into its face and rips out a cheekbone. The other beast howls, spits out a splash of teeth and blood, and then clamps its jaws on Tared's arm. The werewolf rages with brutal force. He tears the monster off him and throws it on the ground. They engage in a battle of claws and fangs with a violence that makes me cringe.

A moan explodes beside me. I turn to the left, and the rotted snout of a zombie launches at me.

"Shit!" I jump back and drive my trembling knife in the middle of its deformed face. I pull the metal from its skull and a shower of blackish blood splashes over me. The zombie falls to the ground and bubbles in seconds.

In front of me, Julien clears a herd of the dead by hurling them into the air. One of the monstrous dogs attacks, and my brother defends himself with a powerful bash of his horns and slams his head against the dog like a giant hammer.

I stride forward with the pistol in my hands, shooting at every head I see and wasting an awful number of bullets thanks to my crappy aim.

With a swipe, Nashua splits the skull of one of the living dead as a couple more zombies climb up his body and bite as if they were piranhas. More come from the forest, and almost twenty of them soon surround us.

"What the hell are these things?" Tared throws a canine wanderer against a pile of barrels.

"Zombies!" I cry as my pistol coughs up smoke. It's empty.

"Where are so many coming from?" Johanna screams behind me.

I wonder the same thing because these weren't taken from the cemetery.

"Shit, shit!" I shout and spot another weapon on the ground a few feet away from me.

I rush toward it, but an invisible stab of pain inserts directly into my stomach and knocks me to my knees just a couple of feet from the gun. I squeeze my stomach as my bowels contort in agony. Deer Shadowskin kicks and gouges to get out of me at the cost of shredding my insides.

"By the gods!" I scream.

Scattered figures gather around me, and Tared shouts my name. The zombies surround me like vultures. I grit my teeth and drag myself out of the circle of monsters to pick up the gun.

Without being able to transform myself, and with only a single bullet left, I'm less than dead weight. I try to think of a way to help. When I see the door of the cabin half open, I realize the only thing I can do is find Laurele and try to stop her.

A rush of adrenaline stands me upright, and I run toward the cabin with my stomach still racked with pain. I raise the weapon, fire a shot in the neck of a zombie blocking my path, and without any more obstacles, jump on the porch.

Something roars behind me. I turn around, and a canine wanderer pounces on the porch at full speed with green foam oozing from its muzzle. I slam myself against the cabin door as Johanna knocks the creature down in a single thrust. She sinks her fangs into the shoulder of the creature, clinging to it with crimson claws like hooks, and then tears away the flesh.

"Laurele!" I shout. I close the door behind me even though it won't hold if a wanderer attacks.

I don't hear anything inside the cabin. I know I've risked my skin, and there could be a zombie in here—or worse, a wanderer.

I grope for the switch on the wall. A sepia light illuminates the room, but to my shock, I find it empty in all sense of the word—the walls, the floor, everything is bare. There aren't even rooms. The cabin is just a square and hollow space with footprints in the dust. I thrust open the back door with a bang.

In the light of the moon smolders the remains of a bonfire. I race to it and discover bundles in the ashes. I knock them out with several kicks. Pieces of dolls, jars, bones, boxes, and other scorched objects fly out along with the air in my stomach. These are the things from Laurele's shop. She's not here.

The roars of my brothers rise over the cabin as the groans of the walking dead crawl behind the thicket of the forest and surround us.

"Damn it." If we'd known there'd be zombies, we would have brought—

My heart sinks. I look at the cabin behind me and imagine the three wanderers Tared and the others are fighting.

Three wanderers. Twelve graves.

"The reserve!" I scream with every chord in my throat. "The refuge is unprotected. It's a trap!"

Without making sure the others heard me, I bolt through the cabin and jump from the porch. I throw myself into the undergrowth to cross the battlefield with Tared's cry dragging behind me. I move at such great speed that I'm certain my wanderer's blood propels me.

I sweat profusely when the darkness of the forest wraps around me, and I can only guide myself by instinct to reach the vehicles. Everything in me quivers with adrenaline as zombies too slow and too stupid to reach me fill the air with terrifying moans.

I leap into the jeep, start the engine, and crush the accelerator. The mileage number flips each second as I speed down the road. In just a few minutes, I cross the guardhouse as if it were the mouth of hell and enter the swamp.

The light of dawn paints the horizon, and I get the horrifying feeling that time is running out. I recognize the wall of trees I crushed the alligator wanderer against, so I must be less than a mile from the village. Suddenly, the hood of the jeep buckles and spits a plume of smoke.

I'm at a dead stop with a curtain of black vapor rising from the vehicle.

"What the hell?" I get out and open the hood ... a pile of straw. "Shit, I don't have time for this!" I sprint for the reserve.

The sky turns gray as the thick fog covers the grass and blurs everything in my path. I take a shortcut through the trees and leave broken branches and parts of my sanity on the road. And then my instincts stop me in my tracks, and I nearly tumble to the ground.

Over my gasps, the grass rustles in the distance accompanied by a pasty sound, like someone regurgitating a mouth full of flesh.

It's another wanderer exactly like the ones who attacked us at Laurele's cabin. Fortunately, it hasn't noticed my presence.

I tell myself to ignore it, to keep running toward the village before it's too late, but I don't. The noise the monster is making is the sound of it devouring something.

My jaw trembles as I scan the ground. A trail of white feathers extends from the creature to a few yards from my feet, and I burst into tears. Mama Tallulah lies motionless and torn apart under the wanderer's jaws.

"No, no, no!" I scream. The monster raises its enormous head and looks in my direction.

It opens its jaws, red like the inside of a sarcophagus, and roars. In a split second, it charges toward me like a raging bull and tramples everything in its path.

With my heart out of control, I run toward the cabins with my tears casting into the mist. I know I can't face the wanderer, but the creature closes on my heels and inches its way to my side. It's about to catch me, but to my surprise, its white eyes expand, and its misshapen face grimaces. It cuts away from me with a sudden leap and flees toward the forest.

As I run, a presence explodes in one side of my body. Deer Shadowskin screams inside me.

And then, I see it.

The bone monster, with its fangs saturated with blood and its black cloak beating against the wind, gallops toward me on all fours like a frightful beast from the remotest region of my nightmares. My chest explodes with pure terror.

The black cloak flies off its enormous body and finally reveals what's underneath. It's a skeleton composed of thousands of bones. Hundreds of ribs form its rib cage, piles of pelvic bones converge to make its hips, and vertebral columns align to create its own spine—a monster so horrible, I could never have imagined it if I weren't seeing it now.

I run with all my might, but its long fingers reach my shoulder in a blink. It pulls with such brutal force that my bones thunder and break, and a scream escapes my throat as I roll to the ground and land on my back in the grass.

My hand trembles over my lacerated shoulder. I release another scream at the dreadful pain and the hard knot pressing through my flesh. I'm sure it's my bone. My shoulder is dislocated.

That demon settles on me. Its claws, the only thing on its body comprised of a single part, close against my throat as I feel the cry of Deer Shadowskin echo inside me. The monster brings its skull closer to my face and opens its jaws. The ice-cold blood from its fangs spills over my flesh.

"Elisse," it whispers and lifts me by the neck. A moan escapes from me as the weight of my arm pulls on my dislocated shoulder.

The monster walks on two legs and heads toward the cabins while swinging me by the throat as if I were a slaughter hen. I writhe and kick in the air, but I can't reach it, and I'm suffocating from its closed grip. Dizziness sets in. I'm about to lose consciousness when the demon suddenly throws me on the fire pit. The still-hot ashes singe my back.

Coughing uncontrollably, I look around at the desolate village. The creature leans over me and exhales a breath that stinks of fresh blood.

"Mine, Elisse … " it screeches in an awful whistle.

The demon digs its monstrous claws into my chest and drags my skin as if it were trying to tear away my flesh. I scream in pain to the point of tasting blood, and I scream even louder when my skin stretches like plastic film under the creature's claws. It's going to skin me.

My own cries nearly deafen me, but suddenly, I go mute despite the atrocious pain. The piece of flesh the monster is tearing from my body fills with dark hairs and takes a shape, like the back of something writhing.

I can't believe what I see. What the creature is tearing from my body isn't my flesh. It's Deer Shadowskin.

Defying all logic, the monster rips my ancestor out of my chest and throws him several yards in the distance. When Deer Shadowskin hits the ground, he stirs like any animal and tries to stand up, but the bone monster jumps on him. The defenseless deer moans and writhes on the ground as the demon sinks its fangs into his neck.

"No, no, stop!" I say with a spit of blood from my wounded throat.

To my horror, the bone monster dismembers Deer Shadowskin with terrifying ease. The creature tears skin, bones, and flesh, crushing it all between its gigantic jaws, and swallows everything into an invisible stomach. Everything the demon ingests disappears inside its snout.

I want to scream for help, but nothing comes out of my mouth. My throat is so damaged from screaming that each breath feels like asphalt. The metallic taste of blood fills my mouth, and I cough and gag.

I look around and see the door of Muata's cabin has been knocked down. Two streaks of blood spread across the walls of the entrance as if hands had been dragged across the wood, and although I don't see his body anywhere, it's evident what happened.

I look at the monster again, and when I think it couldn't be more terrifying, it transforms. As it eats my ancestor, the antlers of Deer Shadowskin grow from the demon's horrifying head, but the antlers are no longer gray, they're violent red as if painted with fresh blood. The dark eye sockets of that beast fix on me.

My heart jumps into my stomach when the bone monster throws itself back on top of my body. It grabs me by the waist and throws me against what little is left of Deer Shadowskin. A muted moan of pain erupts when my dislocated shoulder hits the ground. The creature places itself over me once more with that abominable smell of blood issuing from its muzzle.

"Mine," it whispers in a chorus of voices.

I squeeze my eyes and wait for the monster to sink its claws or fangs into my flesh.

But nothing.

I open my eyes, and I'm alone with the remains of Deer Shadowskin. The bone monster isn't anywhere in sight. It's disappeared.

There's no air left in me, but instead of gasping for oxygen, I vomit a pool of blood. Coughing again, I grab my shoulder with a trembling hand and crawl out of the pile of intestines and flesh of my ancestor. I gather my strength to sit on the floor, moaning in pain and unable to stand up.

"What have you done?" A voice says behind my back.

Father Thunder stands at the foot of the fire pit with his side bleeding heavily and a deep scratch on his face that has torn part of his lip.

"You killed Deer Shadowskin!" he roars.

I open my eyes wide.

"N-no," I say with a cold voice. "The bone monster—"

"Assassin!"

He rattles from head to toe. With wild eyes, he advances toward me in a limp while I stumble backward.

"Listen to me." I spit blood and grab my throat.

"Father Thunder, Father Thunder!" Johanna shouts behind my back.

She runs toward us with the rest of my brothers trailing. All of them are still in their beast forms and soaked with blood.

"They killed Grandfather Muata! They killed Mama Tallulah! They're dead, they're dead!" she cries desperately but goes silent when she sees me among the remains of Deer Shadowskin.

"What the hell happened here?" Nashua asks.

Father Thunder points to me.

"Elisse killed him! He's one of them! He's in league with Laurele!"

Everyone's eyes fall on me, but I just look for Tared's. He clamps his blue eyes on mine, and I shake my head in the middle of a terrifying silence.

"This has to be a mistake," Johanna whispers.

"It can't be true. Elisse couldn't do something like this," Julien says from behind my leader, who's as still as a rock.

"You fucking murderer!" Nashua cries.

"The bone monster . . . " I finally manage to stand up.

"Lies! Since you've arrived here, you've told nothing but lies. Muata knew it. He knew everything," the old man howls.

"No, no, I don't know how—"

"He told me, but I never believed him, and now they're dead."

"No, wait!" I say.

"Father, please, he didn't." Julien takes a trembling step toward him.

"Kill him! Kill Elisse before he and Laurele finish the rest of us."

My heart breaks. The indecision in the eyes of Julien and Johanna doesn't yield, but just a blink is enough for Nashua to launch at me.

He throws me several yards into the distance. I roll on the ground and try to scream, but my mouth just expels another pool of blood. Nashua lifts me into the air by my neck and begins strangling me with his claws. The little strength I have left doesn't even let me kick.

"No!" A shout pierces my ears.

Nashua is knocked to the ground and drops me. I moan from the pain in my shoulder. Tared stands between the bear wanderer and me and then rises up in a display of his massive size.

"Go!" he orders.

"They'll kill you!" I scream, but he doesn't move an inch.

"Tared! How dare you betray us," Father Thunder says. "I trusted you. I gave you your brothers. I entrusted our lives to you. And you do this to us?"

"I told you to fucking go!" the wolf roars.

I stumble into the forest, holding my shoulder, and look back before going into the undergrowth. Nashua attacksTared while the shouts of Father Thunder barely manage to make Johanna and Julien react. Moments later, they're in pursuit.

I glide surprisingly fast through the trees to get out of sight. The pain of my dislocated shoulder shatters me, but I don't have the luxury of stopping to take a breath. I hear them coming. Their gasps and choked voices tread on my heels, and fear scratches the skin on my back.

I reach the dirt road and fall against the wall of trees. Panting, I clutch my shoulder, unable to bear it much longer.

My vision blurs, but I can still see the brush stirring in the distance as a sign Johanna and Julien are about to reach me.

I grit my teeth and think of Tared. My life is disappearing in front of my nose for the thousandth time. I can see Julien's horns peek through the trees. He advances. He steps on the road. He's a breath away from reaching me.

Bam!

A car slams against him so hard that it throws his body several yards. Johanna screams as the driver's door of the vehicle opens wide.

To my astonishment, Detective Hoffman looks at me from the driver's seat.

"Get in!" he shouts.

Without thinking twice, I get in and collapse over the detective's lap. I don't even close the door.

Hoffman puts the car in reverse and smashes the accelerator. Together we leave the reserve at full speed.

PART THREE
A MONSTER INSIDE ME

Chapter 33
The World in Pieces

"BITE THIS," Hoffman says and holds out a rolled-up kitchen towel. I place the cloth between my teeth and clamp down.

The detective plants one hand firmly on my chest, and with the other hand, he yanks my arm toward him. I hear a crunch followed by a powerful shock of pain, and finally, my shoulder returns to place. The relief is immediate. Now I can breathe normally, and when my blurry vision clears, I find myself sitting on a bed surrounded by bare, white walls.

"Better?" the detective asks.

I nod slowly, still grimacing from the adjustment.

"Finish the syrup, and the bathroom's there," he says and points to a half-open door at the back of the room. He leaves with the bucket of reddish water he used to clean my wounds.

I glance first at the medication next to the bed and then to the clean towels draped over the chair where a change of clothes sits. I limp over, grab everything, and hobble to the bathroom.

Inside is white, spacious, and without décor. I pass the mirror but stare at the cold tiles beneath my feet until I reach the glass shower.

As I remove my shredded clothes, my wounds draw a map on my skin. I turn the first knob and grind my teeth when the ice-cold water sutures my raw skin. My knees soften, and I gather what little strength I have left to stay on my feet. I want to scream, but my throat is crushed, so I bash my fist on the wall. Pain shoots to my elbow followed by a pale pink line that slides across the white tiles.

I don't give a damn if I shatter my arm. Everything important to me died out there, so the physical pain is just an itch compared to how screwed up I am inside.

I'm bombarded by so many doubts, so much hurt and helplessness, that I want to cry. I want to slam my head against the wall until I black out. I want to gouge out my eyes and rip out my tongue. I want to throw myself out of the window… But I just limit myself to biting my lips.

Mama Tallulah, the woman I adored like a mother, is dead. Muata is dead. My ancestor is dead. And Hoffman, shit, if it weren't for him, Julien and Johanna would have smashed me to pieces. The thought of my brothers chasing me through the swamp makes me twist in agony, but not satisfied with that, my mind conjures up something even more painful.

"Tared," I whisper. Horror permeates his name.

At least I'm certain of what happened to Mama Tallulah and Muata, but I haven't the slightest idea about Tared, and if he was hurt. What if Nashua and Father Thunder killed him?

After my shower, I sit on the bed with my head buried in my hands, dressed in a white shirt and a pair of jeans a couple of sizes too large.

It's all my fault. If only I hadn't gone to the reserve alone and instead taken someone with me, this wouldn't have happened. But no, I had to be an impulsive idiot and ruin everything. And by the most sacred, how the hell did that monster kill Deer Shadowskin, an ancestor, a spirit of nature? I never imagined Laurele could create a demon with such incredible power. We didn't stand a chance against her.

And what Father Thunder said ... Why did Muata predict I would kill Deer Shadowskin? Maybe that's why he was so cold to me.

The door of the room opens. Hoffman tosses a black sweater on my lap. "Take it. It's the smallest I could find," he says.

"Why are you helping me?" I ignore the ache in my throat. I'm too tired to pretend pain and fear matter anymore.

He sneers. "I always knew Miller was something more than what he appeared. But even in my wildest dreams, I never thought he'd be such a monster."

My fists tighten until my palms sting. "Tared isn't a monster. He protected me out there in the swamp."

"That son of a bitch is a murderer." The detective steps closer to me. "He and everything on that reserve are monsters. They're ruthless, hungry creatures ... But you're the least evil of those things."

"You're wrong." I drop my chin. "I'm much worse."

Hoffman takes a cigarette from his pocket and lights up. He walks over to the window and throws a puff of smoke over the glass. The light of morning hits his face. It feels like an eternity has passed since we escaped from the reservation, but it hasn't even been a couple of hours.

"From the beginning, I knew you were trouble," he says. "After I found you at Fiquette's shop, I knew you were doing weird stuff. Then your friends in the French Quarter, asking about the move … Following you to the cabin was easy."

"So, you saw everything that happened, right?" I ask the obvious. "Then, why are you helping me?"

"Helping you?" He breaks the distance between us with brutal speed and grabs my shoulder, but he removes his hand instantly when I flinch. He paces the room and sweeps his hair back in a gesture that reminds me of Tared when he's nervous.

"I don't know if you're one of them, but out of that herd of freaks, I believe you're the only one who can help me," he says. "So, don't think I'm suddenly on your side. I'm not doing this to save you or those monsters you call brothers."

"That was my family that died out there," I shout.

"The only one I'd like to put a bullet between the eyes is Miller."

I swing my fist to plant a well-deserved punch, but he catches my wrist in the air and twists my arm, though not hard enough to hurt me.

"But … " he says and tightens his grip. "Fiquette and I have even bigger accounts to settle, and nothing would make me happier than to see her with her throat slit, even if it means I have to side with that monster." He lets go of my wrist.

"So, what do you want from me?"

"We agree that the heart of the matter here is Laurele Fiquette, right?" he says. "Something about that woman has unhinged you—"

"It's much worse than that."

"Then you're going to explain to me what the hell is going on." His face reddens. "And explain it well. In return, I'll help you catch her."

"Don't make me laugh. Do you really think you can do something? Didn't you see what we're facing?"

"Do we have a deal or not?"

"I should just go." I step past him toward the door. With his temperament and my mental instability, we won't get anywhere.

"Where will you go? To the center to be thrown in a cell? To the reserve to have your head ripped off? Don't be an idiot."

"What do you expect me to do?" Anger inflames my tongue as tears betray me. "I know I just lost everything that mattered to me. I don't need a bastard like you to remind me."

He grabs me by the arm he just fixed and pulls me close. "I'm telling you I'm going to protect you, and that means you can stay here, idiot. What part are you missing?"

We look at each other with narrowed eyes. I detest with all my strength his damn habit of breaking my personal space so violently.

"What assures me you won't hurt my brothers?"

"Your brothers who want to kill you?"

"That's none of your damn business. Just answer me."

To my surprise, he doesn't yell. His eyes dim, and he studies me in some twisted curiosity.

"Are they worth it to you?"

"What happened wasn't their fault." I lose my breath when the memory of Tared facing Nashua replays in my head. "I don't even know if Tared's still alive," I say, not embarrassed by my tears anymore.

"And you'll never know by staying here to whine. So, do we have a deal?"

I try to guess the intentions behind those dark eyes. I don't trust him, but he's the only hope I have left if I want to stop Laurele.

"Anything to save them," I whisper. Far from being moved, he looks at me rather disgusted. I'm afraid the tension will crush us if I speak again, so I pull back and sit on the bed.

Pain, like the blow of a hammer, hits my chest, and I squeeze my eyes closed, clutching my shirt at the collar and gritting my teeth to keep from groaning. Without Deer Shadowskin inside me, I feel as though an organ has been removed. Now there's just a hole my body doesn't know how to fill, so it sends me signals that something is wrong. Hoffman just looks at me as if he were witnessing a grotesque spectacle.

"Why are you doing this?" he asks. "Why are you trying to stop Laurele? You could run away from everything and avoid all these problems. Here, you face not only her but also the rest of the people on the reserve."

"Instinct," I answer immediately. "Family is not important. It's everything. My instinct is to protect them no matter the cost."

Hoffman frowns and shakes his head as if I just said the stupidest thing in the world. But it's the truth. If I learned anything from Tared, it was to let myself be guided by my instinct.

"I'm going to get us some breakfast," he says. "Stay here, and don't touch a thing." He grabs the knob to open the door and looks over his shoulder. "I repeat. No weird stuff. Do you hear me?"

I look at the ground and finally let the desperate sadness eat me. "Hoffman," I say almost unconsciously. My lips tremble with indecision. "Can I ask a favor?"

✦ ✦ ✦ ✦

THE TEAPOT WHISTLES me out of a trance, and I limp to the stove to carry the hot water to a ceramic tile on the table. After stirring powdered coffee into my steaming cup, I take a sip and wince at the pain in my throat, which is still sensitive despite the liter of pain medicine I downed to numb the physical and emotional pain. Making coffee is just an excuse to keep my head away from the body of Mama Tallulah, from the blood on the walls of Muata's cabin, and from Tared turning his back on the others to protect me.

I wanted to stay longer in the room to finish soaking the pillows in tears, but I couldn't stand lying on that mattress, exchanging pain for fear every time I heard a sound in the house.

I dance my fingers on the brim of the cup. My cheeks get wet again, and I whip my face to try to stop the torrent of pain and replace the sadness with anger. I long for revenge as soon as possible because time is the last thing I have.

I force myself to be strong and composed.

I'm dying to go to Louisa and curl up in the warmth of her arms. It's the only thing that could comfort me in this moment, but I know it's impossible. With all the fuss about the stolen money, the last thing I need at this point is to get Louisa and Hoffman in trouble.

Now that I think about it, there's something odd about Hoffman. His kitchen hardly has any dishes or frying pans.

There are no photos in the rooms and no decorations on the walls. There aren't even cushions in those flat, mayonnaise-colored chairs. Nothing. It's like being in a house ready to be sold—or in the lair of a psychopath.

Suddenly, the hairs on my neck bristle. I leap up and the chair crashes to the floor. The smell of coffee gives way to the smell of rot. I'm not alone anymore.

"Who's there?" I ask even though I haven't seen or heard anything, but I can sense a presence crawling as it leaves a trail of that disgusting smell. "A nightmare?"

I walk to the bathroom mirror, the only one on the lower floor. I tremble when I see that the pupils of my eyes have dilated. I'm looking through the middle plane.

A presence moves just above my head, and I look up, but there's nothing there. It must be on the floor above. A wave of disparate emotions floods me. I'm terrified but anxious to know what dwells in this house.

I climb upstairs in great leaps and ignore as best I can the pain of my injuries. My pulse quickens as I open each door. The bathroom . . . The guest room . . . Hoffman's bedroom . . . The . . . toy room?

The squeak of the door echoes throughout the house. I stand before a zoo of bright eyes. Stuffed animals along pale pink walls smile from inside the room. The soft color saturates every piece of furniture and every garment as if I stepped into a fairytale. It's a baby's room.

The presence stirs again.

Pushed up against one of the walls is a cradle covered by delicate, translucent veils. The smell of death mixed with talcum powder and flowers grows more disgusting, so I cover my mouth and nose with the sleeve of my sweater.

Terror gnaws at my guts as I take slow steps forward. Something's moving inside the cradle. With a trembling hand, I part the veils, and a bomb explodes inside my stomach.

A bundle writhes under a pastel blanket stained with fresh blood.

I tremble from head to foot, but my fingers move toward the blanket as if they had a will of their own. I lift the edge, the smell making me gag, and the cry of a baby erupts in my ears.

"What the hell are you doing?"

I jump when I hear Hoffman's voice behind me. He's scowling at me from the door.

"Hoffman, I . . . " I look back at the cradle and blink quickly to make sure my eyes aren't tricking me. The room is empty with bare white walls. Everything that was here—the stuffed animals, the cradle, the veils—has disappeared.

"Where the fuck did you get that?" he asks through his teeth.

Suddenly, I feel a weight in my hand. I'm at a loss for words when I see a baby blanket in my closed fist.

"Answer me!"

"I was looking through the middle plane," I say softly, unsure of my own words. "Hoffman . . . Did someone die here? A baby, maybe?"

The detective turns white and doesn't reply. He just turns his back on me and stomps down the stairs.

I look at the blanket again. The bloodstains are now dry, and the fabric is tattered as if years had passed over it in just a few seconds. Did I . . . pull a memory? How can I do something like that? I drop the blanket on the floor and begin breathing heavily.

"Damn it, Laurele. What have you done?"

I give myself a few minutes to calm before going downstairs to the kitchen, where Hoffman stares at the dripping sink. A box of cereal sits on the table along with a carton of milk, and I sit down.

"Hoffman, I—"

He takes the cereal box and crashes on the chair across from me. It's obvious he doesn't want to talk about this, so I don't press any further. I lift the cereal box but set it back on the table. In silence, I sip my coffee. The bitter taste goes down painfully.

Hoffman's baby... Laurele... I'm afraid to connect the pieces.

"Maybe I should leave," I say.

"What are you talking about?"

"Laurele's going to find me. If I stay, you'll be in danger too."

"I don't give a shit. Let her come. It's better for me."

"Don't you understand how stupid that is? There's no way you can deal with these things. She'll tear you to pieces before you can even help me."

"Do you think I have anything else to lose?" He whacks the mug out of my hands, and it shatters against the wall into hundreds of pieces.

"Do you think I'm doing this for you? Don't make me laugh. I just want Laurele, and neither you nor a bunch of monsters are going to stop me from wrapping my hands around that whore's neck. You hear me?"

His voice echoes throughout the house. Anger, despair, resentment. I can sense everything, and in a weird way, I understand him.

I stare at the splattered coffee and broken cup on the floor, and then I get up to look for a bowl and a spoon, trying to ignore this man's stormy emotions. At this point, I don't know if I can blame him for being this way and reacting with such violence to the pain hidden beneath his skin.

He returns to his world of silent resentment, so once I find the dishes, I sit down again at the table. My eyes are heavy and burn like hell, and I heave a sigh like the ones that escape after sobbing.

"Did you find the book?" I risk another one of his fits when I remember the favor I asked of him before he left the house.

"No, and don't ask me to look again. It took me long enough to search your room with that stupid Carlton Lone breathing down my neck," he says more calmly than I expected.

"If you were kinder, people would make things easier for you."

"To hell with people."

"Whatever," I say. I'm exhausted and don't want to argue or see another explosion of anger. I lean back on the chair and cross my arms.

Laurele's red book is like her personal diary. There are so many things in it I can't understand, even the parts written in English. It might have the secret identity of the bone monster, and a way to destroy it, or even how to make a deal with Baron Samedi. And, damn, she's even got fucking zombies. If I remember correctly, they originated from Haitian Voodoo legends and are a type of creature summoned by sorcerers protected by the powers of Baron Samedi. There has to be something in that book to help me send all those monsters back to hell, but now, it seems that I've lost it all.

I shake my head and frown at the milk. My stomach's upset, but if I turn down the food of this deranged man, he'll probably shoot me. So, I take the cereal box and shake it over my bowl. Laurele's red book falls from inside and lands on top of the flakes.

Chapter 34
My Children Never Return

THE MICROWAVE SQUEALS, so with your heart racing, you walk to your small kitchen to take the hot dish that awaits you. You open the muzzle and look with some frustration at the smoking noodles. You aren't really hungry, but eating is one of those things that calm your nerves. We both know it's not the healthiest habit, but for a lonely woman like you, Louisa, it's the only thing you have left.

Softened by this thought, I slide down to your ankle and snuggle along the instep of your foot to offer a bit of my closeness. Every hour you spend without a sign of Elisse tortures your heart. You haven't visited the Buddhist center since yesterday. I suppose you're afraid to go and see the boy caught by the police or discover something even more frightening.

I don't know which has been worse, watching you call the reservation every twenty minutes, knowing no one will answer, or hearing you sigh each time you dust that empty room in your tiny house with the hope of Elisse living there someday.

You walk to the sofa with the weight of your loneliness dragging behind you. You watch television for a few seconds in your living room, and then the shrill doorbell startles you. Taking a deep breath, you squeeze your eyelids.

"Who's there?" you scream.

Nobody answers.

You leave your food on the couch and walk just a few feet to the entrance, demonstrating once again the small space that constitutes your home.

"Who's there?" you ask again, but still, there's no answer.

The door has no peephole, so you remove the latches and unlock it, certain that the iron screen will protect you from any assailant.

"What are you doing here?" you say and take a step back.

"Hello! Hello!" Laurele says and smiles at you from the entrance.

Her clothes are disheveled, and makeup runs down her face as if something ran her over. She emits an intense burning smell that causes an unpleasant itch in your throat.

"Get out of here before I call the police," you say.

"No, no, Louisa, you have to listen to me." Laurele pounces on the metal gate. She clings to the bars and presses her face between two of the rods. "I have very good news. You won't believe it!" she says with bright eyes and bare eyelids.

"I don't want to hear anything from you. You've been toying with Elisse, doing who knows what to that poor boy. Leave him alone!" you shout from the bottom of your tired lungs.

"I want to talk about that. Listen to me." Laurele's face turns into a twisted, grotesque grimace as if she had been half smiling before letting out a scream. "Tell me. Do you want to see your little Devon again?"

Your face fills with confusion.

"Look, look, how precious your child was." She takes from her bag a photograph, the one she always kept on her altar, the one of you and your son, Devon. "Wouldn't you like to have him back?"

Horrified, you look at the photo you thought was lost many years ago.

"Tell me where Elisse is and I swear, I'll give your son back to you. I can bring him to life. But forgive me. Please forgive me!" Laurele yells as if a monster were devouring her.

You take a trembling step back and whip the door closed with a violent blow in your sister's face.

"Louisa, little sister, please!" she screams from the other side as you slide the latch and turn the locks.

You don't move from your place. You just stand there casting tears of helplessness.

"Louisa! Louisa! I miss you, please, please … "

Your sister's screams quicken the agitation of your exhausted chest. You cover your ears and press so hard that the cartilage turns red. You run to your room and slam the door closed to do anything to block out your sister's cries.

Laurele's voice transforms into a lonely echo in the middle of the night, and I hug your shoulders to try to calm the tremors of your tormented body.

Chapter 35
The Bonfire of Miracles

Mix blood with ashes of straw to draw misfortune… Tie nine knots until the fabric is the measure of a baby. Say the appropriate curse over each knot. Tie another three knots, and bury the garment beneath the enemy's door. When the woman has crossed the door nine times then…

Young or strong blood is the source of youth and long life. Draw a talisman on the floor that must be made of wood. Draw a sarcophagus, invoke…

But great sacrifices are also the demands of the Lord of Death, whose payment must be fulfilled to the letter. The Lord of the Sabbath, hidden in the shadows of agony and owner of the souls offered to him, can give life to inert bodies that…

Unable to bear it anymore, I close the book and throw it to the other side of the sofa. I bury my face in my hands. I can't believe the spells in the book are starting to make sense, beginning to fit together like a puzzle. I don't follow everything I've read, but the little I do understand is disturbing. Everything points to Laurele's desire to preserve her youth by obtaining young or strong blood—ours, the wanderers—like she did from Louisa's son. But what about the miscarriages? Why take innocent life? And Hoffman's baby? Hell, I'm not even going to ask how he got involved with that witch.

Worst of all, Laurele's been reviving those wanderers and making zombies with the powers of Baron Samedi. If she can do such awful things with his help, how the hell am I supposed to defeat the Lord of the Sabbath, the Loa who rules death? Do I stake him? Fill him with garlic? Damn it. I need more information.

"What are you looking for?" Hoffman asks from the kitchen entrance, where he sips a cup of coffee.

"Advanced Voodoo." I feel somewhat stupid to say it that way, but I can't describe it in any other way.

"Didn't you say it's Laurele's handbook?"

"Yes, but there's nothing in it I need. Besides, most of it's written in a language I don't understand."

The detective walks over and picks up the book from the sofa. He looks at it and frowns. "This is in French, but I have no fucking idea what it says."

"Damn it. I need to know how to revoke the favors of a Loa."

"Favors of a Loa? Have you gone mad?" He tosses the book on the table and sits next to me.

Since yesterday, I've been resting on this damn couch, recovering from my wounds, and memorizing each page, but I still can't find what I need. I could try to translate it with a dictionary, but it would take too long, and I doubt I'd be able to understand some ideas. Once again, time is running out.

I look at the red cover, now worn from handling it so much, and my face breaks down in disappointment. I get chills when I remember the way the book appeared. I have no idea how it keeps coming to me. It's as if someone were determined that I have it. Laurele? Impossible. She'd be giving me an advantage over her, and even she looked upset when I showed it to her at the shop. Although, Baron Samedi could have ordered her. The section about him says he's a being who delights in bets and deals, even more than the rest of the Loas, so maybe he's having fun with me to see how far he can go. But if not, who?

"Now what?" Hoffman drums his fingers against his arm and throws me a skeptical look.

"I need to go out and find more information on how to fight the powers of a Loa," I say. "Otherwise, she'll continue to look for ways to kill us."

"The only one who's going to die is you if Nashua finds you on the street."

"He's not dumb enough to hurt me in broad daylight. But, you could come with me, just in case."

"Of course, so the rest of the police in the city see us together and know we have something on our hands."

"Are you going to give me an excuse every time I ask something of you? If so, forget about our deal." I squeeze the bridge of my nose because, hell, I sound just like Tared.

I grind my teeth at the thought of the argument I had with Hoffman this morning—well, one of the many. I asked him to investigate the werewolf, to look in his shop, to check hospitals, to search anywhere for someone that might have seen him. He refused a good while but ended up doing it reluctantly. When he couldn't find anything, he berated me for almost an hour for the time he had wasted.

I exhale and seek out the reserve of patience I had before arriving in Louisiana. Finding only traces of it, I get up and go to the kitchen.

I look toward the living room window at the same moment I feel crazed by my voluntary confinement in this cell and the inability to find out for myself what's left of the reserve. Unable to go find Tared.

"Hoffman, are there more sorcerers like Laurele around here?"

"You're in New Orleans, Elisse. It's swarming with those rats."

"No, those are swindlers who make you believe they know about these things, but no one takes them seriously. I need to find someone who really knows about Voodoo."

"You're crazy. Who says those people haven't aligned with her?"

"If you have a better idea, I'm all ears."

He flicks his tongue and crosses his arms. He turns a few circles on the seat like an angry dog and finally bites his own tail. He knows I'm right.

"Fine, you win," he says. "I know where to go, but we need to wait a couple of hours. It's too early."

THE SUN DROWNS below the waters of the Mississippi and gives way to the night as I watch the transformation of the streets through Hoffman's car window. We are far from the visual richness of the French Quarter. Graffiti and meaningless signs dull any trace of beauty that the architecture of this part of the city may possess. Houses are old, blackish, gnawed, and full of mold as if moisture devoured them through the throats of hurricanes. Gardens of dry land spiked with weeds and surrounded by steel bars accentuate the somber atmosphere of the neighborhood.

But there's something else here, something far from poverty and crime, something that makes my heart fire with blood as if it were possessed.

We drive down a hill to a street with only a few houses, which are as dismal as the previous ones. Hardly any streetlights work, but on the porches I can see rocking chairs covered with animal skins, candles perched on windowsills, and bones hanging from roofs and railings. Hoffman makes a nasally sound much like a laugh. Surely, he's amused by my curious expression.

We park on a corner of the street and get out of the car. I breathe deeply in relief to have a broader escape from the foul cigarette smoke that's been stinking up the car the whole way. The only thing Tared and Hoffman have in common is that chimney syndrome.

I cough and pull over the hood of my sweatshirt to hide my blond hair. It's a simple disguise, but in darkness, it may cover me enough to avoid being recognized in case we run into one of Hoffman's colleagues.

"Follow me," the detective whispers, and I stay close to him.

The street appears empty, but as a lavender sea covers the sky, orange lights awaken in the windows. I see movement in them. Gradually, men, women, children, and entire families leave their homes and walk down the street, just like us.

After a few blocks, we arrive at a house, of a larger size compared to the rest in the neighborhood, with a white facade strewn with Mardi Gras necklaces. The procession heads toward the backyard, so Hoffman and I join them.

The green lawn probably disappeared years ago and now has become scratchy yellow grass. On the ground, at the center of a large circle of chalk, an altar sits upon a red blanket along with glass candles, blackened by use, that portray images of saints and the Virgin, which I recognize from the Catholic religion. Statues of tall black skeletal figures are adorned with scapulars and necklaces as if they'd been draped with offerings throughout time. Coins, bones, skulls, and bottles of liquor also decorate the space. In front of the altar, pigeons and hens thrash in their cages and shriek frantically.

My heart sinks when I see them. It's as if they know their presence here has a frightful purpose.

Several Black women dressed in white surround the altar and carry bouquets of flowers and herbs in their arms while other visitors circle around them.

Although most of the people gathered here are Black or Latino, no one seems bothered by our presence. In fact, several tourists, who desperately seek to capture such a strange ritual, create a sea of lights with their cameras.

Suddenly, from the back door of the house comes a woman whose presence imposes considerable silence. She is Black, robust, and adorned in infinite necklaces and ornaments of bone. She appears to be the highest priestess here because unlike the rest of the women, she is the only one wearing red.

She raises her hands and speaks in a language I don't understand, but the pronunciation, like a nasal snore, is familiar to me.

"What is she saying?" I whisper to Hoffman.

"No fucking idea. I already told you I don't speak French."

I open my eyes wide. She's just the person I need.

The woman walks to the altar, picks up a bundle of dry branches, and sets them on fire. She passes the smoke around the statues, and the women in white raise their hands and clap as their mouths shout a strange mix of unintelligible cry and song.

They move in swings born as soft as a tide and then become raging. Their bodies leap, contort, and writhe as the drums pounding from inside the house lead a clamorous and violent rhythm with a grand harmony torn from madness.

The voices of families converge and rise toward the night as if their throats were possessed by the same delirious spirits that ride the women in white.

One of the women collapses to the ground. The rest run and grab the bottles of liquor to soak the bouquets in their hands. They beat the woman as she rolls back and forth on the ground and screams in euphoria amid the congregation of voices.

They all convulse. Their eyes roll back, and their bodies undulate with a dance that merges their physical essence with the smoke of the torches the priestess lights around the circle of chalk.

The smoke thickens and the real show begins. At least for me. Black shadows seize the women and then shake them, throw them, and grind against them in erotic and jarring thrusts.

I realize that the women are not dancing hysterically, but the spirits are moving them like puppets.

Hoffman's hand rests on my shoulder, and his breath hits my ear. "Welcome to the Bonfire of Miracles," he whispers.

A wave of emotions possesses me like the ghosts of the exalted women, and I'm convinced my excitement around all this mysticism is because of my shaman's blood.

My fingers grasp Hoffman's coat. I gasp in drunken amazement when the spirits turn to me while their hands contort between the women's breasts and thighs.

They're watching me.

"How did you find out about this place?" I ask, and my stomach crawls up my throat.

"I've been a detective for a long time. You'd be surprised how much I know about this city," he says as if this whole thing were funny.

The priestess walks in front of the people, and to the delight of the cameras, a touch upon the heads of her followers elicits violent convulsions. And then she raises her eyes and digs into mine. Madness tinges her face, and her robust body bounds through the crowd, who opens a gap to let her pass. She points at me.

"Come. Now," she orders and turns around to walk straight into the white house.

I glare at Hoffman, but he just shrugs and leaves me adrift. I know the jerk won't take a single step for me, so I gather my nerves and follow the woman in front of the astonished tourists, who seem to twist with the desire to be in my place.

If only they knew.

I cross the threshold of the house and try to distinguish between the shadows of the hallway and the woman who goes before me. The smell of dampness and incense slowly envelopes me.

Several doors on either side of the hall bring chilling memories of Laurele's shop, and I wonder if I'm making a mistake. At the end of the hallway, the priestess opens one of the doors, and with a nod, she directs me to enter.

I take a few steps inside, and a slight orange glow welcomes me. It's a small room with two red armchairs in the middle. The place is filled with trinkets like those Laurele had in her shop but with more Catholic images. The Virgin and saints in golden frames hang from the wall and observe me as candles dance before them.

The priestess takes a seat and invites me to do the same.

"I'm not going to bite, Elisse. Relax."

"You know who I am?" I ask, but I'm really not that surprised.

"Everyone in this neighborhood knows, boy. Send my regards to Louisa, if you ever return to see her again."

I remove my hood and rub my hands together nervously, trying not to look like a fool. "Did you know I'd come here?"

She just stares at me.

By the gods. I need to stop asking stupid questions. "I suppose you know why I'm here then."

"Laurele?"

My face says it all, but hers darkens even more. I don't know if it's from the flickering candles or the contempt reflected in her eyes.

"Ah, the Fiquettes. Both Louisa and her ma were very sweet, unlike Laurele, who was always more withdrawn, more … ambitious."

The woman reaches into the pocket of her long skirt and pulls out a cigar. A spasm runs through me when it lights by itself like Laurele's did in her shop.

Suddenly, I sense something around me, and I turn my head to each dark corner of the room. It feels like a whisper—

or several. Confused by the number of signals bombarding me, I look again at the priestess, who seems increasingly more somber.

"She's trying to kill me," I say.

"I know, boy," she says without concern.

Lately, the value of life, especially mine, seems to be something people couldn't care less about.

"The Loas were very restless yesterday, foretelling terrifying things. In fact, last night they sent me a dream about you. You've had some difficult days."

"Do you know how I can stop her?" I ask cautiously, but she looks at me as if I spit on her ancestors.

"Stop her? Do you know who you're up against?" she says with the tone of her voice rising. "Elisse, do you know one of the most effective ways to increase a sorcerer's power?"

I shake my head, not sure if I should be ashamed of my ignorance.

"Consume the remains of a being more powerful than them. And do you know what they say about Laurele Fiquette? That she was chewing the ashes of Marie Laveau for ten years. Do you understand what I'm saying?"

As if I didn't already know Laurele is almost invincible. But, I can't give up.

"Maybe I'll have a chance," I say, thinking of the few possibilities that my lineage of shadowgazers could offer me. Even without my ancestor and without magic, if I ever had it, I must still have shaman's blood. There has to be something I can do.

"Do you realize what you're saying?"

"Ma'am, this woman could have an end beyond just killing me."

"You think I don't know?" she replies and inhales the cigar.

She throws her head back and expels a thick layer of smoke. I grip the armrest when a dark shadow is revealed behind her, just like the ones outside.

"And I'm sure by now, you know who's on her side."

"Baron Samedi," I say as if his name were burned on my tongue. "Can you communicate with him?" I remain composed when the specter behind the woman opens its eyes, and they're solid white.

"Do you think I've cut the heads off fifty chickens in a month for fun? No, boy. I've tried for almost twenty years to receive a response from Baron Samedi, but he's turned his back on us, and we've already exhausted our resources. All because of Laurele. We have no choice but to leave ourselves to the will of the gods."

Twenty years? I press the bridge of my nose.

"If the Loa of death refuses to talk to those who've been his servants for many centuries, I doubt he'll give in for you."

"Not if I force him to listen to me," I say.

"He'll tear you apart."

"So I'll kill him first."

"What nonsense do you speak of, child? He's a Loa. No one can kill a Loa."

"For a Loa, he's got quite human tendencies," I reply. I remember that Baron Samedi, besides being a sadist, has a hedonistic appetite for sex and alcohol. "And everything human ends sooner or later. Everything." I cross my arms.

She stares at me with her eyes almost popping out of their sockets, and then she laughs like a deranged woman. She takes one last nasally laugh and wipes a tear with her skirt.

"Ah, little one. Rightly, Louisa has taken care of you. You have an unbreakable spirit, but you're as stupid as a mule," she says, and I blush.

When she mentions Louisa, I think about everything that's happened because of Laurele's heartlessness, and I wonder if that wicked witch is planning to hurt her now that Comus Bayou is divided.

I take the hands of the priestess between mine. She seems indifferent to the gesture.

"I need your help, please," I say. "I have no one else to turn to."

"Elisse, not even your race has been able to do anything. How do you expect me to be able to help you?"

I jump up, and the sudden impulse knocks the chair back on the floor with a crash.

"Calm, boy. I'm sure you could do more harm to me than I to you."

"You know of our existence?"

She remains serene against my tense gaze and extinguishes the cigar on the wood floor.

"I'm the only one who knows, at least among the sorcerers of the city, and if this leaves you calmer, I'm not even sure I know what kind of creature you are. It's only been a few weeks since I've known about your race."

"How did you ... ?"

"What's the use of knowing? You'll probably be dead in a couple of days."

I open and close my fists as if I were trying to hold on to something to avoid falling into despair.

"I suppose you're not going to help me."

"If I could, I would. But how am I supposed to stop a woman who's already received the gift to revive the dead from ashes and dust?"

"And not only that," I say. "She invoked an awful demon who devoured one of our spirits and—"

"It's done what?" She widens her eyes. "Devour a spirit? Child, in my life I have heard something similar. You're crazy if you think there's a way to stop that woman if she can do what you just said."

"Can you at least tell me where to find her? We went to her cabin in the swamp, but she wasn't there."

"Cabin?" She frowns. "Laurele does not live in any cabin."

"What? But there was a move. They took her things there. I saw them burning in the yard."

"No, Elisse. Look, Laurele was very rich in the past, but there came a time when she no longer wanted to do spells or gris-gris. Nothing. So, she set about selling all her things. The cabin you're talking about is where she lived at the height of her fame, but she abandoned it almost twenty years ago to move to the city when she started to run out of money. She bought a place in the French Quarter or bewitched someone to give it to her. I don't know. But she has lived there ever since."

"Fuck." I pull my hair back and remember the staircase I passed at Laurele's shop. "She was right in front of my nose. I need to go there. I have to find her and figure out how to beat Samedi."

"Boy… " She sighs and lowers her eyes to the ground. "You can't beat Baron Samedi. You can't beat death unless you are death itself."

"Oh no? How is it that Laurele got so many favors from death?"

"Laurele is a powerful witch, Elisse. The deals she offered him, I assure you, were very generous and—"

"That's it! The Lord of the Sabbath is the Loa fondest of bartering. If I offer him a good enough deal, he might reverse his alliance," I say more to myself than to her.

The priestess gazes into the immensity of nothingness.

"I have to offer Samedi something he wants more than anything else," I say. "Something no one's offered him before, something ... greater than what Laurele offered him that will make him retract his deal with her."

Immediately, I realize how ridiculous it sounds, and apparently, she does too, because a laugh escapes her lips.

"Don't take it for granted, my child. Whatever you think to offer, I assure you there's nothing in this world that can equal the value of your family's life. Both you and Louisa know that quite well."

✦ ✦ ✦ ✦

The return to Hoffman's house is more quiet than uncomfortable. My attention drifts through the window to the few stars that adorn the mantle of the night. People wander down the street peacefully, so alien to the hell that could be unleashed at any time, and for a few seconds, I envy their quiet ignorance.

I feel so helpless under the night sky, like a lonely soul crossing a road that leads to the precipice of horror and uncertainty.

"What's the matter with you?" Hoffman asks.

I look at him sideways. He just sucks up that nasty drug with his eyes fixed on the road and complains about every passing car as if he were oblivious to the danger we're in.

"I already know what I have to do," I say.

"Isn't that a good thing?"

I don't know. I answer to myself. I have to make a deal with Baron Samedi, and in order to speak with him, I have to invoke him. But how is that possible if Laurele is the only person he listens to?

Maybe if I can enter the middle plane I could contact him. After all, he's an intermediate Loa between our world and the other, but I don't have the slightest idea of how to do it. Muata was supposed to teach me, but now it's impossible. On top of that, there's that damn bone monster. How the hell do I destroy it? I described the creature to the priestess, but she had no idea what it is and much less, how to kill it.

"Well?" Hoffman asks impatiently.

"The problem is, I don't know if I can do it," I say. "I'm not strong enough. I don't understand enough about this."

"It could be worse."

"Oh yeah? How?"

"You could be dead."

Seriously, this man should just shut up.

Once we're out of the concrete jungle, we have to cross the Mississippi and several minutes of road to get to Hoffman's house in the parish of Jefferson. The tall grass and thin trees passing by make me feel a little more at peace. The contact with nature, even if only by sight, has become a refuge for me that, at times, dampens the desire to put a final shot in my head.

I catch something move in the trees. I squint and turn my head to keep an eye on it. My pulse races when I see a silvery glow in the thick grass.

"Stop, stop, stop!" I shout, and Hoffman slams on the brakes.

"What the fuck is going on?"

I don't even bother to answer. I open the car door and dart at full speed into the swamp forest with Hoffman's cries behind me. A silver back runs several yards ahead of me, and my heart flushes with adrenaline.

"Tared, Tared!" I shout at the top of my lungs, but the creature doesn't stop. For a moment, I believe it's not real, that I'm imagining everything, but when the wolf stops for a few seconds and turns its head toward me, I see them. Blue eyes.

Thunder rumbles in the sky.

It's real! It has to be him!

He takes off again. My feet fly off the ground, and the grass whips my body as I make my way through the field and the trees, which grow closer together at each step.

"Why is he running away? Why?" I ask myself as I reach a meadow that extends far in front of me. We run through the field, and the moonlight piercing the clouds shines against Tared's mirror-like back. Thunder crashes.

I almost reach him, but he jumps and suddenly vanishes. My feet rise from the ground as a pair of powerful arms restrains me from behind and lifts me with a strength I can't break. I protest as my captor and I fall backward onto the grass.

"No, no, let go!" I scream and roll violently, but his grip becomes firmer.

"Elisse, pull yourself together!"

Hoffman's voice echoes in my ears. I open my eyes, and in front of me, less than a yard away, is a wide, deep ditch with a river crashing against the rocks and rumbling like thunder.

"By the gods," I whisper. My blood goes to my feet.

If I had fallen, the current would certainly have dragged and drowned me. Hoffman still holds me tightly as if he were afraid that at any moment, I would throw myself into the void. And that's what I was about to do.

My mind is thrown into nothingness, and I'm not aware when Hoffman drags me back to the car. I don't feel when he pushes me on the seat. I don't hear his screams. I'm not awake the moment we return to his house or when he violently throws me against the armchair in the living room.

I can only hear, through muffled ears, Hoffman walk away from me and whip his bedroom door closed. I don't know how long I contemplate nothing and struggle not to scream.

That wasn't Tared. It was only his ancestor.

Chapter 36
Loyalty

YOU LIFT YOUR HEAD when you sense his arrival. You know it's him. His essence, his indecipherable scent, and his quivering presence remain the same even though Deer Shadowskin was ripped from his body.

The red hairs on your neck bristle, and your eyes dilate. Your leather-gloved feet strike the ground like the ticking of a clock counting down before a bomb explodes in your face.

With the hood of his sweatshirt covering his head, your target enters the lonely alley and passes right below you. Your breathing transforms into a raspy hiss.

"Almost . . ." you whisper.

You slink with extreme stealth between the rooftops and balance on the thin edges of plaster. Your prey reaches the end of the alley and stops in his tracks. From your pocket, you withdraw the catalyst of your intent. A silenced pistol. One shot and the task is done.

You move closer and descend a fire escape without a creak from your shoes. You're only a few yards away, and you point the barrel of your gun toward the head of your victim. He stands still, examining the map in his hand, and then removes his hood to scratch his head.

You cock the gun, and your breathing stops. Your hand trembles in time with the fluttering of his blond hair.

Elisse catches a glimpse of your presence, but you steal into the shadows of the roofs to keep him from seeing you.

Confused, the boy gives up on the map. He leaves the alley toward the sidewalk and mingles with the crowd across the street. You rub your face with the palm of your hand as nervousness buzzes through your spine.

"Why did you let him go, Julien?" Johanna asks with an empty, lifeless expression. She looks with her gray eyes at the pistol held between your trembling fingers.

"I can't. I can't do it."

"Maybe that was our only chance," she says. "Father Thunder's going to go crazy if he finds out you let him go."

You look at her as if she just kicked you.

"Would you have done it? Would you have killed him?" You confront her with your chest heaving and your face distorted by frustration.

Your sister wakes up. She bites her lower lip to counteract the feeling of powerlessness with pain. She looks away, crosses her arms, and turns a few times before looking at you again with dampened eyes.

"I thought so." You tuck the gun into your belt. "Let's go back to the reserve. We'll come up with an excuse when we get there."

You both leap from the emergency ladder and fall twenty feet as if the jump were only a step. You walk in silence until you reach Johanna's silver car parked a couple of blocks away.

"How did you know we'd find him around here?" you ask as you open the car door for her.

"If there's one thing I assume, it's that Elisse knows almost nothing about his powers as a shadowgazer. And with Grandfather Muata … dead," she says in a broken voice, "he's going to try to find somewhere to learn about it."

"I don't think he'll find much of anything," you say as you get into the car.

Yet, my little girl Johanna is absolutely right. The alley where you found Elisse is only a couple of blocks from the library.

The car starts. You both leave for the reserve, submerged in thought, while I curl up on the gear stick. After a few minutes of silence, you give in to the sting of your tongue.

"We both know he's with Hoffman," you say. "We have to find that guy to find Elisse."

The spine of the young wanderer tenses.

"Don't you dare tell Nashua or Father Thunder that he was the one who rescued him from the reserve," Johanna says and goes silent, revealing her null desire to see Elisse dead.

"Calm down. If we didn't tell them then, there's no reason to do it now," you say. "Also … I think we were both relieved when we saw Hoffman take him away, right?"

She doesn't lift her chin because she can't deny your words. You know she's nervous and confused. She has been since the day of the attack, but it's the first time that both of you have talked about it.

"Do you think he really did that? Do you think Elisse is an ally of that woman?" you ask in a low voice as if you were afraid your words might reach the ears of Father Thunder.

Johanna sighs. "I don't want to believe it. Grandfather Muata interpreted an omen in which Deer Shadowskin died at the hands of a wanderer, and he assumed that wanderer was Elisse. Father Thunder never wanted to believe him, and I think deep down it was because we all became attached to Elisse rather quickly. We cared about him too much. I think even Nashua felt it, in his own way."

"And for that, Tared protected him?"

Johanna turns her gaze to the window. Her heart shrinks as she remembers the fight between the wolf and Nashua. "I don't know. Tared risked getting something worse than punishment. Not only was he more loyal to Elisse than to Father Thunder, he—"

"He put his neck out for him," you say in a trembling voice. "He turned his back on the Dreamcatcher for him."

Johanna succumbs to the uncertainty and bites her lips again. She squeezes her eyes until the lids redden and wonders who made the real mistake.

Chapter 37
Pain

I INSERT THE KEY into the lock, spin it, and a loud click lets me into the house. I push the door closed with my foot and stagger to the living room, where I drop a stack of papers on the filthy coffee table. With a little more care, I place Hoffman's ID on the glass and take a seat on the rug.

"Where the hell have you been?" the detective asks as he comes down the stairs.

"I told you I was going out."

"Three hours ago."

"I didn't say when I'd return."

He passes by me and into the kitchen, mumbling things like "punk-ass brat" and "disrespectful piece of shit." I just ignore him and pick up the first sheet of paper.

It's just an excerpt from a webpage about Native American legends. It was the only one I could find in the half hour I was in front of the library's computer. I also photocopied pages from books that might help me learn more about wanderers. I didn't know where to start, so I copied anything I could find about ancient cultures, supernatural legends, and myths.

The image of a wolf watches me from the bottom of an article about totemic animals, and I chew my lips in the torment of uncertainty. I need to know why Wolf Lightningskin was on the road yesterday and led me to a cliff where I could have died. Why was he out of Tared? Could that monster have ripped him out like it did with Deer Shadowskin? Or…

"No, no, please, no." I pull my hair back and squeeze my eyes. Tared can't be dead, and that thought isn't just for comfort. He's by far the strongest wanderer of us all. A man like him wouldn't succumb easily to anyone. He's alive. He has to be alive.

I want to search for him, but I know for now, my priority is to discover what kind of creature the bone monster is and see if there's any way to destroy it. If there's not, I at least have to find a way to enter the middle plane. And I know without an ancestor, learning magic may be impossible. Hopefully, something in this pile of information can help me.

✦ ✦ ✦ ✦

I've been sitting here for two hours, and I haven't found a damn thing. Some articles speak of men who transform into beasts, but they just mention legends far removed from the true story of the wanderers.

I haven't found the bone monster in any bestiary either, and even though I have clippings that describe ways to communicate with spirits, they don't say anything about how to enter the spirit plane physically without being killed on the spot.

I fling the pile of papers at the thought of the time I've lost. My brothers were right when they said the existence of our race is a well-kept secret. I was naive to think I could gain occult knowledge just by reading spells. I could go back to the library to look for more information, but what the hell would that achieve? It would take too long, and I can't learn magic that way, let alone Voodoo. I'd need experience, some birthright from my family or roots, and even luck, such as being the seventh child of seven brothers or being born on the ninth day of the ninth month and other things based on Voodoo numerology.

"Are you done with that?" Hoffman enters the room and sits in the armchair.

"No, it's useless."

"Now what are you looking for?"

"Look, I know I have to make a deal with Baron Samedi, but that doesn't mean he's going to accept it. If he decides to rip my head off, I need to know if I have any chance against him."

"Why don't you just take a damn gun?"

"Do you really think that's going to work? We're talking about a Loa."

"What difference does it make? If you can't confront him the way of the, uh, wanderers, you lose nothing by protecting yourself other ways." He extends his arm and places a gleaming gun on the table. "Get up. Raise your tiny body. Let's go outside to practice."

"Practice?"

"Yes, damn it I saw you shooting those zombies at Laurele's cabin, and you're shit."

Hoffman doesn't wait for a reply. He just crosses the room and goes through the door that leads into the backyard. I glance at the papers on the table. The letters dance on the sheets, and the symbols mock my efforts.

Why am I fooling myself? I've searched like an idiot again and again for the solution to all this when I already knew what to do as soon as the priestess told me only Laurele can communicate with Baron Samedi. I have to talk to her and force her to intercede on my behalf; otherwise, I'll never get a deal with the Lord of the Sabbath.

"Gods . . . " I cup my face in my hands. I need a guide, someone to teach me about the hell I'm walking through.

Damn Muata. All this time he knew Deer Shadowskin would die, and he thought I was going to kill him. Was that also an illusion caused by Laurele to pit him against me? How the hell can you kill something that's never been alive?

I look at the bare walls. The whiteness of the paint and its starkness make me think of Mama Tallulah. The horrible memory of that wanderer devouring her body punishes me like a whip and dampens my eyes instantly.

"Why did it have to be her?" I whisper. Would I have had a chance to save her? The sweetest woman on earth was caught under the claws of a heartless, mindless monster. They've taken my mother from me. They've made me feel that once again, I'm alone.

The weapon's mouth points toward me.

Shoot. Get this over once and for all, a strange voice whispers inside my head.

I raise the gun and feel its weight loaded with my remorse and the bullets that cry to enter my chest. Slow minutes become an eternity.

"No, these aren't for me." I engage the safety lock and return to the white wall and the memory of Mama Tallulah.

As a child, more than the Buddhist teachings, hunger and misery helped me bury negative emotions in the depths of my being because I vowed never to lose hope in people. I forced myself to believe gentleness existed in every human heart and goodness still filled the world. Because if people weren't compassionate, I wouldn't have earned enough sympathy to get food or money from them.

I couldn't afford to lose my faith in humanity. Not because of the purity of my heart, but because of my need to survive. Now those suppressed feelings resurface in me in such a brutal way that they overwhelm me. I feel hate, an awful hate so ravenous that it devours my insides and tears my spirit apart.

I think of Laurele, and wickedness fills my head. I long to blast a third eye in her head with the mouth of my gun.

I toss the weapon back to the table, horrified by the sinister thoughts I didn't know I possessed. I rub my temples with the palms of my hands to calm my mind. I repeat to myself that I don't intend to kill anyone. Killing isn't heroic or admirable. It's an obscene act, and it's not going to bring back those I've already lost because of Laurele's evilness.

I'm not a murderer. The only reason I'm willing to fight is to save my family, the people I cling to. I would give my own life for theirs. There has to be another way.

The voice in my head, the anger in my stomach, the sadness in my heart—everything is replaced with a fragile shield of courage. So, I steady my grip on the gun and go to the backyard where Hoffman waits.

Chapter 38
Mardi Gras, the Night of the Spirits

The gun Hoffman gave me yesterday rests on the desk next to the bed. I stare at the weapon as if it were someone I'd chosen to spend the rest of my life with. In my position, helpless in front of the unknown and ignorant of my own abilities, the gun seems to be my only strength.

I rise on my elbows with some effort. Since I couldn't sleep at all, my body feels heavy and hungover. I reach to take the sheet off, and my fingers tremble like branches stirred by the wind.

It's not hard for me to admit that I'm more afraid now than when we attacked the cabin—or rather when we were ambushed there. And last night, I realized that this is infinitely different. At the cabin, I was not alone. Beside me were four experienced wanderers who could lift a truck without breaking a sweat, but now there's only me and that nine-millimeter pistol, which will do little or nothing against Laurele.

Hoffman's footsteps march down the hall. He's already preparing for something that won't even begin within the next twelve hours. We agreed it has to be today, the day of Mardi Gras, and that tonight we have to stop all this madness, but I don't know if I'm ready for it.

I get out of bed and look out the window at the movement in the street. There's a lot of activity even though it's just shy of eight in the morning. We're quite far from the French Quarter, but it's easy for me to imagine the commotion that must be raging at this moment. I can hear the celebration in the laughter that touches my ears, see it in the neighbors dressed in shimmering outfits as they come out of their homes, and feel it in the swarms of multicolored necklaces that have covered the city.

I abandon the window for a hot shower and then go downstairs for breakfast.

I exhale over a plate of eggs and review the fateful conclusions I reached last night. We can't kill Laurele, and it's not just because of my ethical reasons. If we kill her, the contract she has with the Lord of the Sabbath will be severed, and he could lash out at us for interfering with his business. We can't risk something like that.

First, I have to force her to bargain for me to speak to Samedi; then, I can offer him a better deal. That will give us a chance to reverse this whole mess, send the dead back to their graves, and make the bone monster disappear.

All these thoughts turn my stomach, and I shove the plate aside.

"If you go on like this, you'll wither away," Hoffman says, referring to the weight I've lost.

"Let's talk about something else, okay?"

The detective has left behind his trench coat and badge to disguise himself as a civilian. We'll be able to pass unnoticed tonight.

"All right," he says. "You already know the part of the plan I came up with, to get into Laurele's house. What's yours? What's the plan once we get inside?"

"Just watch my back," I say. "I'm in charge of talking to Laurele and—"

"Talking?" His face flushes three shades of red, and I shrink in my seat. "You're an idiot. As soon as I see her, I'm going to put a shot between her eyes."

I lean back and look at him as if he stabbed a knife through my hand.

"What are you saying? If you kill her, I won't—"

Hoffman hammers his fist on the table.

"I thought it was clear to you, brat. If I didn't kill Laurele years ago, it's because I needed proof that I wasn't crazy, and if I don't kill her now, I'll never be able to face myself again." He storms out of the kitchen and whips the few objects in his path.

I jump up and run after him.

"Listen to me, Hoffman! Hoffman!" I chase him up the stairs to his room, but he slams the door in my face. I bang on the door. "Don't be a fool! Open the fucking door."

And he does, but with the mouthpiece of his pistol aimed at me. I recoil and raise my hands, mouthing like a fish. The detective steps forward and touches the tip of the gun to my forehead.

"Hoffman, calm down."

"Be a good boy and go back to your goddamn room before I blow your head off," he says and steps back before slamming the door.

I stare at the white door long enough for my brain to react. I turn around, and as he asked, I go into my room and lock the door. I sit on the bed and run my hands through my hair.

I've got a big problem. Hoffman's not in his right mind. All he wants is revenge, so he won't hesitate to shoot Laurele as soon as he sees her. But I can't let him kill her, not until she helps me talk to Baron Samedi. So, besides dealing with whatever awaits us in that house, I'll have to figure out a way to stop Hoffman if it becomes necessary.

Damn. As if I didn't have enough things to worry about.

✦ ✦ ✦ ✦

WE ARRIVE AT THE HEART of the French Quarter wrapped in a silent pact as if Hoffman hadn't threatened me with his pistol this morning. I hide my own weapon in my pants and look at the clock on the dashboard glowing eleven thirty at night. Perfect timing. We leave the car in a parking lot and throw each other nervous glances as we walk quickly to reach Bourbon Street.

The party is in full swing with everyone screaming and dancing in celebration. The revelers pack together in the street so closely that not even a needle could slip between them. And they're dressed so strangely that we could have shown up naked, and no one would have noticed us.

"Don't let go of me," Hoffman says. He wraps his arm around my shoulders to press me against his side, and we enter the crowd. The detective uses his strength to help me move forward, and I wonder why on earth we couldn't have entered another street.

I blush when I realize what's going on around me. I haven't even been in the street for ten minutes, and I've seen more genitals and breasts than in the other eighteen years of my life. Here, nudity seems to be a tradition.

Young people crowd under balconies and act in outlandish ways to receive necklaces and colorful gifts, which I'm sure will end up in the trash by the end of the night. People throw offerings, drench themselves in alcohol, and flash their naked bodies to music blasting from every corner. If Mardi Gras isn't a grand Voodoo ritual, I don't know what is.

"Elisse," Hoffman shouts in my ear, "the patrols."

He gestures with his head toward the end of Bourbon Street. The police assemble with cars, horses, and units on foot to close the festival with a noisy parade of police sirens, as dictated by tradition, so we have to hurry.

We escape from the chaos and reach the street adjacent to the witch's place. A couple of half-drunk boys stagger down the street, so to keep from raising suspicions, we walk more calmly until we reach Laurele's block.

The first siren sounds, and as if they were sucked up by a vacuum, the few people on the side street rush toward Bourbon Street to witness the last of the symbolic carnival parade, while we hurry toward the alley next to the voodoo shop. Luckily, the gate doesn't have Romeo spikes, so Hoffman helps me climb over it. I open the gate, and we both head down the walkway to the patio of Laurele's house.

When I see the only window on the first floor, I can't take another step. It's the window of the oval room. I look at the heavy black plastic, and that dreadful experience I had in there walks down my back. I repeat to myself a thousand times that I won't make the mistake of entering that room again, and we pass that dreadful window.

Luckily, just a few feet away, there's a door, but it's locked. The detective takes an ice pick from his coat pocket to crack the lock. The door opens, but three heavy chains prevent it from opening completely. He slips the ice pick through the gap and does his best to shake the mechanisms, but his efforts are useless.

"Fuck. What now? This won't even fall with a kick," he shouts at me over the noise of the patrols.

We both look up at a row of three windows on the second floor. Thick wooden planks block the middle and right windows, but the first one is clear and open.

Hoffman and I throw a look at each other. We must be thinking the same thing. Too convenient.

"You have to climb up," he says and looks around.

There's a large trash container behind us, so I give Hoffman a light tap on the arm and point to the bin with no need to explain further. Between the two of us, we push the bin to the wall of the house, just below the window. With both of us balancing on top of the lid, Hoffman places one palm on top of the other and, with a power that demonstrates the physical strength of this man, thrusts me into the air.

I catch the edge of the window.

"Don't let go!" Hoffman shouts and pushes me from below.

I plant my feet on the wall and climb my arms and head through the window. In one last effort, I push myself and fall inside the house.

The thunderous sound of the patrols muffles the thump when I hit the floor. I stand up immediately and find myself in a long hallway punctuated by the bluish light of the moon. The soft light allows me to see the peeling walls and a small table with a vase in the middle. Next to me is the staircase I saw before I got trapped in that evil room, but my eyes fix to the back of the hallway.

Facing me is a door of crimson so intense that it looks like it's been painted with blood. Something in my stomach attaches to the worn knob of that door, and I catch the curious scent of wax, herbs, and straw. Laurele is in there. I can feel her.

Temptation cries out for me to cross the threshold, but my instinct sends me down the stairs to the first floor instead.

The yellow lights from the streets pass through the wide windows of the shop, and I move past them as fast as I can. The hallway behind the counter leads to the oval room.

I stop just inside the frame and face the powerful shadow of that concrete stomach. I hesitate at the thought of entering there once more, but in the end, I step forward with courage. I feel along the walls, coming across doors on either side. I reach the last one, right next to the oval room, and open it. To my relief it's a small kitchen, and in the back is another door, slightly open, that leads to the backyard. I recognize Hoffman's profile.

I remove the chains, and he leans forward.

"Wait. Don't come in yet. We have to talk." I press my hand against his chest and push him back.

"Talk now? Are you crazy?"

"Hoffman, you have to let Laurele live. I need her."

"What? Again with that shit?"

"I need her to get to Baron Samedi. If you kill her, I can't make a deal with him."

"I don't give a shit. I told you clearly that I'm not doing this for you or for anyone." He looks at me with anger-shot eyes.

"But—"

"Fuck off."

He shoves me aside and enters the house like a typhoon. He draws his weapon and holds it tightly between his fingers.

I grit my teeth in pure anger, unable to believe how selfish he is. Sliding my hand to pull the weapon from my belt, I reach him in quick strides.

Before he can turn around, I strike a blow to his head with the pistol as hard as I can. I hold my breath until he falls and slams his face on the kitchen floor. For a few seconds, I stand still with my eyes fixed on Hoffman's motionless body.

"Dammit," I whisper, and my heart aches when I think I might have killed him.

Carefully, I roll him over and jump back. His chest rises and falls, and I'm relieved, but I don't risk it, so I kick him in the ribs. When he doesn't even grunt, I know he's unconscious.

I summon all my strength and drag the detective's heavy body out of the house. I gasp for breath a little, but I'm surprised it's not taking too much effort. Hoffman must weigh twice as much as me, and he's almost as tall as Julien, so I must be growing increasingly stronger.

I lay the man on the patio and cover him with bags of garbage to hide him from sight. Back inside the house, I secure the door with the three chains, just in case Hoffman wakes up.

With my fingers still on the last lock, I stop in my tracks. I'm about to face Laurele, the woman who summoned an army of creatures that almost annihilated Comus Bayou in just a couple of hours, and I'm going to do it alone, with fifteen bullets in the barrel of my little gun.

I remove the safety of my weapon and cross the kitchen with trembling steps. In the hallway, I glance toward the door of the oval room.

The sirens of the patrols grow louder, but even so, I hear that room screaming soundlessly, humming over my skin with powerful vibrations. It's not that I hear the voices, but I sense them … lots of them crying out for me from behind that door.

A chill charges down my back, but focused on what I have come to do, I ignore the ghostly calls and climb the stairs as fast as my guts allow until I reach the crimson door.

As soon as I touch the knob, I jerk my hand back because a pang of familiarity twists in my head. The black cracks, like roots buried in the red, hammer my memory.

I … I saw this door in the only dream I've ever had, that night I escaped to India. But it wasn't a dream. It was a premonition. I'm standing before the threshold of hell itself.

I place my trembling hand back on the knob and twist.

Inside the expansive room, the moon, huge and round like an eye, peeks through the circular skylight and creates a glowing ring on the floor with darkness outside of its perimeter. The place seems empty, but Laurele is here. I can feel her.

I step into the room, and its spectral nature crushes me. The sounds of the sirens go quiet, and an ominous silence takes hold as if I entered another dimension. My eyes dart around the room, and my footsteps echo on the walls.

The door whips closed.

I jump and look behind me, but nothing's there—at least not that I can see—so, I look forward again. Something appears in the dark. I squint my eyes and glimpse a tiny dot of red light issuing thick smoke. The dense fog billows as from the mouthpiece of a locomotive and covers the floor in a mist that rises up the walls and pours through the glass of the skylight as if that barrier were not there.

Another piece of the mystery unfolds before my eyes. The unusual fog in New Orleans originates from here.

A moan, a raspy whine, creeps along the floor. I place my finger gently on the trigger.

"Laurele, show yourself!" I shout.

"Shhhhh … "

The hairs on the back of my neck bristle. The tiny red light recedes into the darkness and then hurls toward me. It falls to the ground and bounces a couple of times until it rests below the skylight. It's a cigar.

Instinctively, I jump back.

The cigar bursts into a fire whirl. Flames cast into the air and transform into floating candles scattered at different points in the room. They shine with enough light to reveal what hides in the corners.

I'm tempted to flee in terror, but that same fear betrays me and locks my feet to the floor. Yellowish teeth appear from the other side of the room and quicken a terror in me more atrocious than anything I have ever felt.

A being wrapped in the flickering light of the flames sits on a filthy bed and looks at me through empty eye sockets. With black-oil skin, a top hat, and a white skull painted on his face, Baron Samedi, the Lord of the Sabbath himself, smiles at me.

"How did you—?"

"Pass into your plane?" he says with a crooked smile. "Oh, all the great spirits can manifest in some way on the human plane, Elisse. I'm just lucky enough to do it in my own flesh, so to speak. You know, Mardi Gras, unintentional rituals, things that increase my power," he says lightly. "Also, someone has been helping me for almost twenty long years."

The specter points behind himself, and my horror just begins when at last I see Laurele lying on the bed completely naked. Her skin shines with sweat, and she doesn't move or raise herself in my presence. A reddish stain spills from her crotch and soaks her thighs.

"By the gods!" My jaw trembles. "What have you done?"

"The poor woman can't help you now, but I'm sure it's not *her* you're looking for."

I shake hearing the Loa. His voice is velvety like the hiss of a snake and possesses a deepness torn from beyond the grave.

He takes a lit cigar from the pocket of his elegant suit, mouths a few puffs, and expels the smoke. He stands up and walks toward me. Unable to restrain myself, I step back and aim the gun.

"You can't be serious," he says in a voice accented by a laughter that mocks my obvious stupidity and my even more obvious fear.

How can I not be afraid? He's a Loa, an untouchable being, from whom no weapon can protect me.

He steps into the ring of light. The bluish glow of the moon highlights his abnormally wide mouth filled with countless teeth that exceed any human limit. I gather my willpower to steady my voice so it won't tremble like my hands do.

"What do you want from me?" I ask.

"Me? Oh, boy," he says in a soft, almost plaintive voice. "Aren't you the one who wants something from me?"

An invisible force snatches the gun from my hands, and the weapon flies to a corner of the room and whips against the wall. I'm stripped of my only defense.

He laughs. He's toying with me.

"You left some coins for me, and a doll . . ." I say.

"Oh, yes. The doll. Courtesy of Laurele." He points to the woman, who remains unmoving on the bed. "Humans have such strange ways of getting what they want, don't you think?"

The horror in my face must please him because he smiles even wider and shows me an appalling second row of teeth in his gums.

"Come on now. The coins were a gift, an exclusive courtesy from me. You don't have to thank me, although you haven't taken very good care of them."

He reaches into his pocket and takes out the gold coins, which I last saw on the desk next to my bed in the Buddhist center. They shimmer with a golden glow. An emptiness grows in my stomach as the Loa circles inside the ring of light. He passes in front of me, and I catch the revolting smell of alcohol mixed with rot.

"What do you want, Elisse?" the specter asks.

"A deal to offer you." My accent returns to my tongue as a sign of how little I can control myself in the face of fear.

The Loa stops right in front of me, a couple of feet away.

"A deal, huh? Interesting, tell me more."

"The life of my brothers, I want that . . ."

He bursts into laughter and arches forward with his skinny finger pointing at me.

"Are you pleading for their life? That's what you came here for?"

I tighten my fists with courage as my blood curdles with humiliation.

"Laurele tried to kill us, and you helped her. I want to reverse the agreement she made with you," I say.

His laughter slowly dies, and he stands tall. He looks at me without losing that deranged smile on his face.

"Oh, Elisse, Elisse, Elisse." The Loa pauses and contemplates me with empty sockets. "Did it not occur to you, even for a moment, that it's me who wants you dead?"

"W-what?"

"Oh, Elisse. Laurele is wickedly good at what she does, manipulating the mind. It seems that ever since she placed three fingers on you, it's been harder for you to remember important things."

Three fingers?

Let me explain something about Voodoo, child.

The ice of fear splits my spine as memories from the back of my mind hit me like waves: Laurele holding my chin in the voodoo shop… Baron Samedi and his doubles dancing around me as I burn in a bonfire… I didn't forget that "dream" or the symbol on the forehead of that alligator wanderer. And I didn't forget that voodoo doll in the shop. They've been playing me all along.

I turn and run to escape through the red door, but something entangles my legs, and I slam against the floor. Black hands emerging from the fog cling to me and then drag me into the ring of light.

Baron Samedi squats over my quivering body and blows a puff of smoke over my face.

"Your family of wanderers means nothing to me, Elisse," he says. "I just thought it'd be easier to get to you if I got them out of the way. Fortunately for me, no one noticed in time."

I twist to get away from the grip of the dark hands, but I only writhe on the ground like a worm. Samedi's bony hand grasps my jaw and forces me to look into those infinite pits he has for eyes. I swing my hands at him, but to my horror, they pass right through him as if he were made of smoke.

Samedi tilts his head slightly as if he were studying me. He smiles again with those endless rows of crooked teeth stacked like tombs.

"Why... ?" I barely manage to get the word out of my mouth.

"Tsk, tsk, but look at what a gorgeous face you have," he says and ignores my questions. His alcoholic breath crashes against my face.

I taste my own bile from that disgusting smell and his chilling words. My fear turns into rage.

"Let me go," I say when he tightens his grip on my chin and digs his nails into my skin.

"I must confess. I prefer women. If there's one thing I can't resist, it's to catch those delicious creatures, those whores who know what they must do," he says as he turns his head slightly toward the bed where Laurele lies.

She looks back at us with near-lifeless eyes.

Samedi raises his free hand and snaps his fingers. The mist swallows the woman, and she disappears completely.

"But," he eyeballs me, "you're such a beautiful creature that I'm tempted to make an exception."

I explode in anger. I slam my closed fist against his face, and my knuckles crunch against his skull. The Loa's jaw dislodges, and his top hat tumbles to the ground and vanishes into the mist. Samedi and the wraiths loosen their grips, and he staggers.

I crawl toward the crimson door, and a terrible pain seizes my hand as if my fingers had been ripped off. My soul goes to my feet when I see from the knuckles up, my hand's been stripped of its flesh, reduced to pale bones, and as if cauterized by fire, it doesn't bleed at all.

I look up at Baron Samedi, who appears as stunned as I am.

"Well, well. What a surprise!" he says.

Black arms sprout again from the fog, grab me by each limb, and slam my back against the red door with such force that the wood cracks behind me. My first instinct is to scream, but the wind's been knocked out of me, so I can barely breathe. The hands lift me a few inches off the floor, and I float among the shadows and candles to the center of the room.

The Loa returns to stand in front of me.

"You know, for a few seconds after you struck me, I considered your deal. You almost convinced me," the Lord of the Sabbath says and strokes his chin where I punched him. "Almost."

He wraps his hands around my neck and tightens, but only enough to suffocate me breath by breath. Driven by my survival instinct, I try to move, but my energy quickly dwindles in absence of air. The things around me lose their shapes, and my breathing becomes a pant.

"Well, boy," he whispers. "Once you are out of the way, the others will be easy."

On the threshold of unconsciousness, my arm gains strength, breaks the grip of the spectral limbs, and rises. My fleshless hand clings to Samedi's arm. He watches my movement with a curiosity that, even in the lethargy of death, insults me.

I grow weaker every second from the lack of oxygen, and I crawl my fingers up the Loa's arm, tearing at his suit. A strange moan issues from his lips as he follows my hand until my arm falls languidly to my side.

He smiles.

"Oh, if you want, let's make this more fun."

He releases my neck, and instantly, my lungs fill with air. I can't catch my breath before several hands grab my arm to prevent me from moving my skinned hand again.

"Do you know why I gave you those two coins, Elisse?"

I barely glance at him, still reeling near unconsciousness.

"Shadowgazers. When the veil of blindness covers their eyes, those extraordinary creatures lose their ancestors, their magic, and therefore, their usefulness. They become ... mmm ... how do you say it?" He thinks a moment. "Oh, yes. Human."

He retrieves the coins from his pocket again and places them over my eyes, which I close instinctively. He presses them against my eyelids gently. Fear eats away at me with a force I can't describe as he withdraws the coins and slips them into the pocket of my trousers.

"Wouldn't you like to know what you're capable of as a common and helpless human? To save your family? Sounds like an interesting bet, don't you think?"

He places his hands on my face and caresses my cheeks. And then he directs his thumbs over my eyes.

"And Elisse ... " he whispers in my ear. "You know I love bets."

I scream from the depths of my lungs as he brutally buries his thumbs into my eyes and whispers something I can't understand over the howl of my throat. I cry out to all that is divine to free me from such torture as I writhe, convulse, and swallow the blood pouring down my cheeks.

Suddenly, his fingers, like daggers, disengage from my sockets, and my skull burns like fire. I squeeze my eyelids hard to do anything to lessen the pain.

The wraiths let go, and I fall to the floor, flopping like a lump of flesh. I palm my face and howl in a black world. I can feel my hands bathed in blood, which saturates my clothes in the warmth of my life draining away.

"A shame. You had such pretty eyes." Samedi's voice fades into a distant echo.

The sirens of the patrols come crashing into the room like a storm.

The intense pain slowly sedates me. Weakness overtakes me, and I whimper, twitch, and gurgle in my own blood as time goes by. I don't know how long. Sounds become fainter, and reality becomes a distant dream. I feel, in my own flesh, the immense cold withdrawing the life from my body. I'm dying.

Baron Samedi ripped out everything that gave my life meaning, and I couldn't do anything about it. All for a reason I will never discover.

I feel eternity in a powerless, distant, and painful flicker.

Elisse.

My name reaches my ears in a whisper.

Elisse.

The whisper draws near and rises in the darkness of my unconsciousness. I'm delirious at the gates of death.

Elisse!

The voice becomes a scream that my ears perceive with an impossible clarity in my dying state. A light is lit, not in my eyes but in my broken spirit. I recognize Tared's voice.

"My god! No, no, no. Elisse!"

I can feel his strong arms lift me up in the darkness as if I weighed nothing and my shed blood erased my presence on this earth. I can feel him. Tared embraces me against his chest, and he moans. Or was it a scream?

Death beats me down, rips me from his arms, and buries me in this room abandoned by hope.

Chapter 39
Wolf Skin

MORE THAN ONCE, I found you looking sorrowfully at nothingness, lost in a mind that, far from healing its emotional wounds, had hidden all those painful things you had suffered throughout your life under layers of rigidity. You thought you had faced the worst thing that could have happened to you years ago, a victim of experiences few people could have passed without touching madness. Worst of all was knowing that you were an incomprehensible half-wolf creature, a being born from the most frightening of myths, a being whose brutality you could not control. You had committed atrocities, horrific acts that you'd never dare to confess, and buried them beneath layers of lies just so you could sleep at night.

But there were more frightening things to face than the true evil of your nature, and the worst was destined to happen the night you and your brothers attacked Laurele's cabin.

Comus Bayou, loyalty, brotherhood, the old man you had taken as a father—none of that mattered. The only thing that seized your will at that moment was the uncontrollable desire to protect Elisse, to keep him alive, even at the expense of your own life, because you didn't want to lose your home once more.

When Nashua wielded the first claw, everything became so violent and confusing that the blow tore apart more than the flesh of your chest. Even though you'd always had your differences, he was your brother, someone you had grown up with and learned from in many ways. You had even fought side by side against the same enemies. So, to fight so brutally against each other was something that undoubtedly left you heartbroken.

You launched at him and locked your jaws on the bear's skin. In return, he buried his claws in those arms that had once held him in battle. He tore out years of brotherhood, and that loss hurt you both so deeply that not even time would be able to heal it.

At first, the fight was uneven. Nashua's ancestor, *Night Fury*, a beast of indomitable power, could not match the might of Wolf Lightningskin. And then things changed when Father Thunder, who was still healing from his wounds, called his own ancestor. *Blue Cloaked Wolf* emerged, and you knew the wisest thing to do was retreat. You weren't afraid to face them both. You just didn't want another member of your tribe to die—neither of them nor you.

You were wounded and confused, and you knew you couldn't turn back, so you fled from the village. They cornered you in your own swamp, and you had no choice but to jump headlong into the reserve's river. The current dragged you so violently that the odds of survival were almost nil in the eyes of those left in Comus Bayou.

The water washed you into a basin of one of the necks of the Mississippi hydra, where you took your purest form of a wolf to pass relatively unnoticed and survive the harshness of hunger and uncertainty. You didn't know if your loved ones were still alive. The very idea was unbearable and painful.

You refused to accept that Comus Bayou, your tribe, the one you had cared for meticulously for seven years, had dissolved in just a few hours. That family had welcomed you and taught you that you were not a monster but a being rooted in the bosom of nature and that your place in the world of humans had been forgotten in mythology. That group of beings had showed you that you were still a creature worthy of the deepest compassion and whose role on this earth was as important as the cycles of life.

The tribe was strong. They were united. And they had offered all this to you.

Over time, you had realized that there was still a hole inside you, a wound that didn't want to close. What you had never imagined was that one day you would find your cure in the overwhelming loneliness of a boy, someone who woke you up from your lethargy and made you believe you were getting a second chance.

You embraced the opportunity because that creature looked at you as if you were a bonfire in the night, a nook in the snow, a place to go after traveling a lifetime. He saw you as neither a leader nor a storm. He saw you as a home. You wished with all your being and all your brutality that you deserved to be a home for him as Comus Bayou had been for you.

But sheltered in a nest of weeds like a complete beast and dejected in the midst of an uncertain destiny, you realized that everything had vanished in a blink.

Now you were a deserter, a wanderer who no longer had a place in the home of which you were once a part. That world, that family, those ties that had been strengthened through the cradle of time, had ended in the worst possible way—with you, their leader, turning away for a young man who had so recently entered your life, a boy who seemed to have conspired with the wicked Laurele to kill your people.

Because how could it not be possible? Once he set foot in New Orleans, the attacks on the reserve began. Muata never trusted him, and Father Thunder always had his doubts. Then, why? Why did you decide to defend him?

You were alone and poisoned by uncertainty. Had you made a mistake in protecting Elisse? You didn't want to believe it. You refused to accept that the boy, that wondrous fire, had betrayed you. And the answer was given to you during the thread of a dream infected by desperation.

That same night, against all mystical laws of the wanderers, Wolf Lightningskin abandoned you.

You awoke from your stupor when a terrible pain shook your bones and the flesh that covered them. Before your eyes, your ancestor extracted himself from your chest, fought to shake free of your body, and then ran toward the plain. He left you drenched in blood and aching to the core. You couldn't believe what you saw, because you knew perfectly well that what happened was not normal. An ancestor abandoning a skineater? It was unnatural.

Confused, you covered yourself with the traces of skin left over from your transformation. Unable to know how much of your wanderer nature you had lost now that your ancestor had abandoned you, you ran in terror after him.

The wolf ran to a ravine cut by the river below and, in one leap, dissolved into the wind. You stopped before the steep fall and looked forward with great amazement at your ancestor on the other side of the river. The creature fled from you and disappeared into the grass.

You paced on the edge of the cliff and growled in despair. Without the wolf inside your body, you felt naked and incomplete. You couldn't understand anything of what had happened or how you were still alive without your ancestor.

More dejected and terrified than ever, you readied a scream, and a scream came up, but not from your own throat. Your name howled in the distance, again and again, in a voice you recognized instantly. You hid yourself in the grass and watched in disbelief as Wolf Lightningskin returned to the river with Elisse following him. But the boy was not alone.

Hoffman emerged from the brush, hugged the boy from behind, and lifted him into the air before he could throw himself into the void, saving him from almost certain death.

Like an invisible ghost, Wolf Lightningskin crossed the river to return to your side. But your ancestor never detached his eyes from the boy. He watched intently as the detective dragged Elisse away and then faded into the distance.

At last, the creature returned to your body and lashed every cell to ground you.

Elisse was innocent. You no longer had any doubts because in addition to desperately searching for you, he was with Hoffman, and an alliance between the detective and Laurele was something that could never happen even in the most twisted dreams of humanity.

✦ ✦ ✦ ✦

NATURALLY, YOUR FIRST REACTION was to go to Hoffman's house in search of Elisse, but you were a leader, a creature whose nature encouraged you to think well enough and fast enough to know how to make the best decision, so you took the time to analyze everything thoroughly.

The boy was living under the roof of someone you considered dangerous and volatile, and with the history of hatred that man had for you, to approach his home would have been a bad idea. To avoid the risk of being seen by them, you preferred to watch until the fateful night of Mardi Gras.

Distant and discreet, you followed them through the alleys and witnessed the audacious young shadowgazer being devoured by the window of Laurele's house. Later, your nerves crashed against a wall when you watched him drag an unconscious Hoffman from the witch's nest to bury him in a pile of garbage.

The young man returned to the house, and you waited until the moment his silhouette crossed the window of the second floor. You decided it was time to go to him. After taking a quick glance at Hoffman, you tore open the door effortlessly and threw yourself into the darkness.

You couldn't take more than a few steps before an alarm triggered by your instinct made you look back. Johanna watched you from the yard, pale as if she had seen a ghost. You looked at each other for what felt like an eternity, and then the girl drew the outline of words on her lips.

"They're coming."

You couldn't think much about the warning because a powerful, silent call came to your senses and made you run like a deranged man into the house and up the stairs to the second floor. That call, that voice that clawed at your flesh, was your instinct. Elisse was in danger.

The crimson door appeared at the end of the hallway. You stopped in your tracks, unable to move your legs before an avalanche of sensations. The reek of corpses filled your nostrils, and the most unnerving loneliness came crashing through every pore.

It was Elisse—his fear. He was more terrified than ever, and you trembled because you were losing him.

Your legs thrust you toward the red door. The knob didn't budge, so you transformed without hesitation. You hammered the wood. You clawed it. You kicked it. You hit it with all your might until blood stained the silver fur of your knuckles, but the door didn't yield. It was as if you were trying to break through a rock wall. But you didn't step back. You kept clawing, even when Nashua and Julien appeared at your back, because the only thing you could think of was destroying the barrier that separated you from Elisse.

They, on the other hand, took possession of their ancestors and charged at you. Each one grabbed you by an arm, and together they threw you backward and across the hallway. You stood up and shook your head.

Far from worrying about their presence, you saw your brothers only as an obstacle, a barrier you didn't have time to deal with if you wanted to save the shadowgazer. You only wanted to get through the bright red door.

You reacted, as you hadn't done in years, with blind brutality. You pounced on the other two wanderers. Your claw fell first on Julien's head. With the base of his horns in your grip, you hurled him like a doll into Nashua. The wooden planks of the windows split from the shock, and the roars of both creatures rumbled through the hallway.

Johanna didn't blink. Petrified, she was unable to take sides, so from the edge of the staircase, she watched Nashua get up again to attack you.

"Tared, no!" she cried when your jaws received your brother's neck.

Nashua writhed under your fangs, and he tore your face with a claw, sending you backward. The bear held his throat as best he could, and the girl, carrier of Coyote Garrasrojas, unleashed a mournful howl when she saw blood gushing from his wound.

Before she could take a step, an arm pulled her back and threw her down the stairs. She tumbled, unable to raise her arms to stop the crashing fall.

Meanwhile, even with doubt on his face, Julien attacked you once again. More desperate to stop you than to hurt you, he crashed his solid forehead into your chest and buried you into the wall with a force that left you encased in concrete. Nashua, with his wound still gaping, got up to help Julien.

Both were about to throw themselves back on you, when the sound of a gunshot rumbled over their roars. A powerful shot burst the arm of the bison. He shouted and crashed against one of the windows of the hallway.

Hoffman pointed the smoldering muzzle of his gun at the bewildered wanderers.

"Miller!" he screamed. "Where's Elisse?"

"The door!" you roared and tore yourself from the wall.

You rammed Nashua and threw him next to Julien. After they recovered from the shock, the two looked at you and Hoffman with wide eyes. They were perplexed by the incomprehensible alliance that rose up in front of them. Even in the fury of battle and the pain of their wounds, it was evident to both of them that something didn't fit into all the madness.

They stood up to fight, but when the thunderous patrols began to distance, something more than the sound of your fists bashing against the door petrified the beasts who populated that gallery of horror—heartbreaking screams at the end of the corridor.

Elisse's voice broke the air as if he were suffering the most frightful of tortures. His cries became faint moans, and finally, the door gave way.

You entered untimely and found something that made you howl from deep in your throat as the white eye of the moon shined upon you through the glass of the skylight.

Chapter 40
Darkness

They say when you lose your sense of sight, the others become more acute. It's as if the body tries to compensate for being deprived of the most essential faculty a human possesses. So, why do I feel so disoriented in my own body?

I don't know how many hours and days I have lain here, immersed in darkness and unable to sleep due to pain. The opening and closing of a door tells me I'm in a room, and the warmth of a blanket makes it evident I'm in a bed. A bandage covers my eyes, and another wraps my boned hand, which still feels the exposed meat rub against the gauze. I'm also aware that no matter the time, there's always someone with me in this place, and that someone is usually Tared.

He comes, takes me by my hand, touches it against some part of his skin, maybe his forehead or cheek, and whispers things I can't make out clearly. Prayers, perhaps? He usually asks for forgiveness, but I'm not sure for what he wants me to forgive him.

None of this has been his fault. I blame myself. It was reckless of me to have gone to the reserve on my own during the attack on the cabin and to have wanted to confront Laurele without help. I was worse than an imbecile to think I could make a deal with Baron Samedi.

All of this is a consequence of only my stupidity. In my place, Muata would have been much smarter, Tared more cautious, and Nashua stronger. Now, I have to lie here and await my death. What else am I supposed to do? I'm no longer a shadowgazer. I'm just a body wrapped in helplessness, waiting for the day the Lord of the Sabbath decides it's time to finish me.

That's why I refuse to answer, to move, or even to make a gesture that indicates I'm aware of what's going on around me. I don't eat what they bring to my mouth even though my stomach burns from its own acid. I don't drink the water they spill over my lips even though my throat is as dry as a desert. Because in my condition, it's useless to try to find another way to kill myself other than by starvation or thirst.

Sometimes, I'm afraid of myself. Despite the stinging heat in my eye sockets and the constant burn of my raw hand, I don't moan, I don't scream, and I don't roll in pain. I just let Johanna do whatever she does to my wounds without giving her a sign of life. At times, I feel like crying, but I gather the scraps of will I have left and hold it all back.

So, I ruminate for hours about my own death and find spaces of relief in the few moments of loneliness, spaces crushed by the sound of steps on the wood floor, like the ones that come here now.

The door of the room opens once more, so I sink back into my voluntary stupor and wish with all my soul that they haven't brought me a plate of food to try to feed me again.

"Is he asleep?" a raspy and unkind voice asks. Hoffman.

"I hope so," Tared replies. I'd recognize his voice even if he were whispering.

His wanderer's presence overcomes me, and amazingly, I can perceive it even without Deer Shadowskin inside me.

"How is his hand?" the detective asks.

"Terrible. The flesh won't heal."

"You sure you don't want me to bring a doctor?"

"No," the werewolf answers in a tired voice. "It's not bleeding. It's just raw like a piece of meat from the freezer. Johanna tried to cure it, but . . . "

"Is it some esoteric shit?"

"I don't know. Anything inside that room could have happened."

"And his eyes? They can't regenerate?"

"Don't ask stupid questions. If we could do that, Julien would have his finger back."

I'm shocked. The only time I ever saw these two together, Tared was in a sea of submission, but apparently, he's already tired of that performance.

"You're an idiot," Hoffman says. "What do I know about this crap?"

"I'm going to change the bandages," the wolf says. "So get out."

"Go fuck yourself, Miller."

"I'm not going to tell you twice."

"Or what? Are you going to tear my head off like the animal you are?"

I groan loud enough to raise my voice above theirs, and they gasp. I have no desire to intervene in their quarrel, but at this point, I'd rather interrupt than put up with their absurd argument.

"Elisse! Are you awake?" Tared says, and the mattress dips toward my side. "How do you feel?"

He buries his fingers into my hair to comb it back, and although his touch comforts me, I hold onto my frustration and my words. In my blindness, things seem farther away than they actually are, so I can never anticipate when someone is going to touch me.

The werewolf moves the bandage on my head. The door slams, and I hear a few diffuse complaints from Hoffman. I imagine he left the room to leave us alone.

"Elisse?" he asks again, but I refuse to answer. "Can you hear me?"

He returns to sweeping the sides of my head.

"I'm almost done with this," he says in a tender voice as if he were caring for a child—or an imbecile. "Your wounds are fresh, so don't open your eyes while I clean everything."

"Isn't Johanna supposed to do stuff like this?" I ask, and he stops moving.

I haven't the slightest idea of his expression, but he must be surprised. I bet he really thought I was a vegetable.

"E-Elisse," he says. "Oh my God." The mattress springs up. "Did you just wake up? Could you hear me? Do you want me to bring you something, water or—"

"I want you to let me die in peace. Please."

A sudden silence takes over the room, cut only by Tared's breathing.

"What are you saying?"

"Don't make this more difficult."

"You're delirious. It's the trauma of what's happened," he says, and my fingers curl up like snakes on the edge of the blanket. "It's over now. Let us help you."

"Over?" My blood boils and my throat explodes. "Do you think it's over?"

"Elisse, calm down."

Anger throws the blanket off my body. I sit up and fumble the edge of the mattress with my weak hands.

"What are you doing?" Tared grabs me by the wrists and pushes me back to the pillows. Any illusion of fighting for what dignity I have left is destroyed. I don't know which makes me angrier, that I can't face his strength or that it doesn't take much to subdue me.

"Do you really think I have a damn chance, Tared?" I try to twist free from his grip.

"I'm not going to leave you. You're not going through this alone. You've lost your sight, but you're still alive, dammit!" he roars with that voice so beastly, yet so human, that it vibrates every pore of my skin.

Alive.

I'm alive.

Those words echo inside my head.

"Do you think it's enough for me to be alive? For how long, Tared? How long do you think you'll be able to keep me here in this damn bed? Until you arrive one fine day and find nothing but my damn corpse?"

His grip loosens. I have no idea if he's looking at me or facing elsewhere. I don't know. I don't care. I don't feel anything other than a deep rage mixed with a fear my body can't withstand. My tongue sharpens like a spear.

"Oh, no, no, no, Tared. Things didn't end in that room where you found what little was left of me," I say in a low voice.

The rise and fall of my chest stabilizes. His, on the other hand, I hear become much more erratic.

"Baron Samedi has not finished with me. He was just having fun. Do you want that, Tared? Keep me alive long enough for him to find me and finally tear me to pieces? He only wants me. Do you understand? He'll kill you if you try to stop him. Do you think you'll be able to handle him? If so, you're an idiot"

My words take effect. I listen to his footsteps go away and the door shut like the slab of a tomb. Again, the darkness within me looms along with a sickening resignation that refuses to depart from my head.

I curl up in the blanket. Something hot runs down my cheeks, bruising my spirit, and I can't tell if it's tears or if the wounds in my eyes have opened up.

Chapter 41
Pride

Two days have passed since the night of the spirits, and it's the first time you reunite with Tared and the child he protects so jealously. Even though you plant your eyes on the emptiness of the house as if nothing in this world could destroy your iron spirit, I know inside, you are nothing but the rubble of the man you once were. But, as with all the difficult things that have beset you during your life, you don't allow yourself to demonstrate a single bit of weakness.

How is it possible, Lansa? How can you sit straight like a tree trunk after witnessing your loved ones die in such atrocious ways?

In your black pupils, you've plowed the memory of Muata being pulled from his cabin and into the darkness by hungry jaws, and in your ears, you've sown the voice of Tallulah hooting in the fog as she succumbed to a creature that didn't even give her time to breathe. That carnage all happened before your eyes as you held your aging body against a horde of creatures that had sprung from the same dust.

At that point, the agony of your heart was overcome by rage because the last thing Muata shouted before dying inside his cabin—in a way I dare not speak—was the name of Elisse. And then everything made sense to you. That's why, night after night, you see Muata die in the shadows and hear Tallulah scream in the forest as your entire being begs, for once in your life, to break into tears.

Naturally, with grief on your back and the obvious guilt of the young man, you could not see anything other than a murderer in Elisse, a deceptive creature who had ruined your children, your family, and the refuge your ancestors had protected for so many generations. I didn't blame you for it, Lansa, nor did I blame you when you wanted to throw yourself into the swamp after your little girl Johanna called you yesterday at dawn to tell you, between screams and cries, everything that happened in Laurele's frightening nest.

Your boys managed to get Elisse out of the French Quarter. They took refuge in the detective's home, where Tared put the child in the guest room and reluctantly allowed your only bloodkeeper to heal him enough so he didn't bleed to death. The night was long, but as soon as the girl finished, the wolf almost threw her out of the room, and I curled up at the feet of my dying child, attentive to all the fuss that dominated the once lonely home of Hoffman.

Confusion dominates your spirit, as it seems you have no idea how to control the wave of emotions about to drown you. In all the years that you've been the guide of your tribe, you've never had to face such a harsh test: endure the painful mourning of your loved ones along with the shame of admitting you were wrong, all without breaking your image of strength. Because if a leader can't show integrity in the most difficult of situations, why have you accepted the role of leader of Comus Bayou? Worst of all, you know Elisse is just a victim, but you—

"Tared. What was that?" Johanna's voice takes you out of your thoughts. "We heard shouting and ... "

Your boy bounds down the stairs.

When she receives no answer, Johanna places her hand on his shoulder, but the wolf pushes her back with a violent growl from a purely human throat.

"If anyone goes up these stairs, I'll tear your damn head off," he says to the entire room. He stops and stares at you with that blue lightning in his eyes full of cold resentment, and something inside you dies.

The young man exits the house, nearly ripping out the door before slamming it closed on the spectacle of shocked faces he left behind.

"What the hell happened up there?" Nashua asks Julien, who slowly descends the stairs.

Although you would never admit it, the sight of the redhead with a broken arm in a sling causes you deep pain. After all, Johanna, Nashua, Julien, and Tared are all, in your eyes, your children, and you've always loved them more with actions than with words.

"From what I heard in the other room," Julien says and leans against the wall, "Elisse is having a hard time."

"How long has he been awake?" the bloodkeeper asks as she takes a seat next to Nashua, whose neck is covered by a thick white scar that extends in an imaginary line to your own chest.

"Maybe he was never unconscious. And apparently, the problem is personal," the redhead says. "Laurele wanted Elisse from the very beginning, and getting rid of us was a way to get to him more easily."

"I can't believe it." Johanna buries her face in her hands and exhales. You swallow her sorrowful breath.

"He yelled at Tared, but I don't blame him. Whatever happened in that room must have been horrible," Julien says and scratches the back of his neck.

"They destroyed his eyes. What do you expect, dumbass?" Hoffman says.

"What did you say?" The carrier of *Fireback* reacts with an unexpected aggressiveness toward the detective, who in turn rises from his seat.

"Do you want to swallow another bullet?"

"Enough!" Johanna stands between the two men. "Now isn't the time to fight. We're on the same side in this."

"I never said I was your ally," Hoffman says.

"That doesn't mean our causes are any different, detective!" Your voice thunders in the middle of the room, and everyone turns to you. With slow effort, you stand up and support yourself with that cane you set down as a symbol of mere authority and took up as an extension of your weakened body. "That woman is still on the loose and, apparently, with more power than ever. We have to find a way to keep her from killing us all."

"And how are we supposed to do that, old man?" Hoffman tosses his cigarette butt onto the table. "With Elisse blind, none of you even have a chance to know what we're up against."

"How the hell do you know that?" Nashua says.

"He told me enough to realize that without him, you're no more than a bunch of animals that can only defend themselves with brute force."

"What the fuck are you saying? How much did Elisse tell you? You don't know anything about us, so don't you dare underestimate us."

"Does it hurt to tell the truth, kid?"

You, on the other hand, are stupefied by the idea of Hoffman knowing about the sacred history you've been so intent on hiding for generations. The fact that a person like the detective knows of the existence of the wanderers is almost as serious of a problem as Laurele. In other circumstances, it would have been obvious what to do about Hoffman, but knowing that you are no longer in any position to question Elisse's decisions, your veins heat up until they ignite.

"Be that as it may, detective, we have to create an action plan. As soon as Tared finishes cooling his head, we'll sit down and think about our next step."

"I don't know if Elisse can do much in his condition, father. I heard that Baron Samedi himself did ... you know ... that ..." Julien points to his own eyes.

"I refuse to believe it. Muata made it very clear. Loas do not get into our plane nor we into theirs." You try to sound as convinced as possible, even to yourself. "Laurele is the one who's done all this, and it's her we should worry about."

"When will you stop being such a stubborn old bastard?" Hoffman says.

"How dare you talk to him like that, asshole? Take it back!" The roar of young Johanna shakes you with amazement. The girl breathes restlessly and looks at Nashua with an expression so fierce that she only needs to show her fangs to make a display of loyalty that, at times, you feel unworthy of.

"Take it back?" Anger mutates Hoffman's face into scarlet. "You all saw what happened that night. If everything is a trick of Laurele, where was she? I assure you that damned bitch had no way to escape that house without any of us noticing. She didn't do that to Elisse."

"Do you understand the seriousness of what you are saying, detective? If perhaps what you insinuate is true, that Baron Samedi is the one who did that to the boy, we have no chance to win this battle."

"So, you suggest that we sit here sipping coffee like assholes and do nothing?"

"I'm suggesting that we go into that room and question that boy whether he likes it or not."

At your words, something strange happens. Hoffman relaxes the muscles of his face, sweeps his hair back, and sighs as if all his anger vanished through his fingers.

"Listen to me, please." The detective looks at everyone with a calm but disturbed expression. "I can't tell you if Elisse is a wanderer or not. I don't know if he organized all this in some twisted way so that we walk right into some sick trap, but I can guarantee one thing ... If you take a step toward that staircase, I'll blow your brains out without thinking twice."

Hoffman throws his raincoat back, and the gun on his belt flashes enough to be seen by everyone and especially by you.

"And I'm not stupid. I know bullets feel just as good to you as they do to any human," the detective says.

Nashua exhales, expelling rage through his nose, while his brothers look at the detective with suspicion.

"Why are you so obsessed with protecting that child?" you say and remain as calm as Hoffman himself.

"Protect him? Don't be an idiot. Laurele and whoever is behind her will come for that boy, and if he dies beforehand, no one can assure me that I'll get a chance to wrap my hands around that witch's neck. And since I don't know your intentions, nobody sets foot in that fucking room until Miller comes back. Understood?"

The silence of the room, and especially of your lips, lets the detective know he's been quite clear.

✦ ✦ ✦ ✦

"No, ma'am, don't worry. He's fine," you say as calmly as possible.

"Are you sure? Don't be afraid to tell me, Tared, please." The voice of the woman on the other side of the device softens her tone, signaling that she is now calmer.

I slide down your shoulder and settle on the metal box in front of you to have a better view of those frozen lakes you have for eyes.

"Do you need me to bring him anything?" she asks.

"It's best if you don't know where we are. Someone might try to follow you here."

"Oh, that's right. Will they trace this call?"

"I don't think so, it's a public telephone."

"Thank heavens. Just let me know if you need any help or whatever. And tell Elisse, when he feels better, that I love him, and I'm praying he'll return home soon."

"Of course, Miss Fiquette. If there's anything else, I'll get in touch."

You say goodbye and hang up the receiver. You lean your forehead against the small telephone box to see if the cold of the metal can help you think with a little more clarity.

Under the circumstances, it's not all bad news. Apparently, the police are no longer engrossed in the pursuit of the shadowgazer. They have so much work after the ravages of the night of the spirits that they only call the Buddhist center occasionally to ask routine questions but nothing more.

You slip your hands into the pockets of your jacket and squeeze your eyelids to try to get some tension out. I stretch my neck to get closer to your face.

I'm sure Elisse's words have hurt you in a way you're not sure you can handle—not because of what he said to you, but because of the simple idea of losing him. That scares you. It's not just that he's become someone beloved by you. It's that you tremble at the thought that maybe there's nothing you can do to save him.

You bury your hands in your hair with enough force to make you clench your jaw, and then you walk down the street to catch the first taxi that crosses you.

Twenty minutes later, you stand in front of that grim house whose interior protects the people who matter most to you. With the courage that characterizes you so undeniably, you cross the threshold and enter the scene you predicted several blocks back.

The detective sits on the stairs, swinging his weapon as if it were a harmless toy, and the survivors of the Comus Bayou tribe have scattered around the living room. Father Thunder sits in one of the few chairs in the house.

Everyone looks at you. Your blue eyes meet each one, and the absence of Mama Tallulah and Grandfather Muata finally scratches at you. You rise tall as if shaking off the burden of their bodies. You walk toward the detective, who is the only one who doesn't give much importance to your presence.

"How is he?"

Hoffman shrugs with genuine disinterest and pulls a cigarette box and lighter from his pocket.

"You haven't gone up to see him?" you ask.

"I'm not his nanny."

Your impatience pounds in your chest. At this point, you don't know which is worse—being defensive with your tribe or dealing with a psychopath who's only helping you keep Elisse alive for selfish reasons.

Suddenly, the world turns on its head.

"Tared." Nashua's voice rises behind you. "We want you to come back with us."

Those words, more than tender, bristle the hairs of your body with pure hostility. You lock your eyes on Father Thunder.

"Don't you realize I'm a deserter? Don't you understand that I chose Elisse's life over my allegiance to Comus Bayou?" you say without repentance.

Johanna, on the other hand, throws a grieved look, but by no means does that soften you.

"There was no way we could've known what was going to happen, Tared," Father Thunder says. "Laurele set a trap for us all."

"A trap you fell into. Didn't you, father?"

You see a flash in Lansa's eyes. The old man throws his chair back and steps toward you like a lightning bolt, despite his limp.

"You weren't there. None of you saw what I saw," he says. "You can't complain that I tried to defend my family."

"And none of us saw what happened inside that room. How do you know what happened to Elisse isn't just another hoax? How do I know you're not going to find a way to kill him?"

"Because I would prefer to kneel a thousand times at Laurele's feet than to lose you." Lansa gasps and takes a step back as if there were no more strength left in his lungs. "Innocent or not, I will always see the blood of Tallulah and Muata on the hands of that child," he says and drops his chin. "Still, I cannot kill him, because I know what that would take away from me."

For a minute, you forget to breathe when you see crystal cover the eyes of Father Thunder. And then you look at the wanderers in front of you and think about the seven long years you've dedicated to Comus Bayou. Your legs get weak, and you ask yourself why things had to happen like this? Why should you, of all the people in the world, debate the loyalty of your people, of your family?

No. You can't bear to lose anyone else, and you're certain Father Thunder can't either.

"Have you thought of anything?" you say at last.

"The only reason Laurele tried to destroy us was because Elisse was under our protection. We were his shield. And if it's true what the child says, that the Lord of the Sabbath is the one behind all this, there is only one course of action if we want to save what is left of Comus Bayou."

"What do you mean?" You take a step back.

I crawl up the stairs to the room of the young shadowgazer. Now, it's my turn to help my little one. I hear, only as a distant echo, Father Thunder's declaration.

"We have to leave New Orleans, Tared. And you know well, in order to do that, we have to leave Elisse."

Chapter 42
A Family of One

The door of the room opens slowly. I hear a couple of steps, and then the door closes. Someone sighs, and I feel the edge of the mattress sink. The heat of a wolf rolls over my arm like a wave.

I feel Tared's fingers on my shoulder and clench my fists in pure frustration. It infuriates me not knowing when someone's going to place their hands on me, and each time it happens, I jump like a scared rabbit.

"Does it still hurt?" he asks about my eyes.

"No," I answer. And it's true. Johanna's cures have been pretty effective.

"I'm glad."

It's interesting. Pay close enough attention, and you can hear someone smile. Something in the tone of Tared's voice suggests his lips have curled.

"Let me see," he says, and I recoil immediately.

The bandage around my eyes no longer feels necessary, but even so, I'm overcome by a terrible shame at the thought of taking it off. I must look horrible, and these wounds are evidence of my failure.

He sighs, and his warm breath over my cheek is the first pleasant thing I've felt in days.

"Do you want dinner? You must be hungry, and it's getting late. I can bring you something."

"Why are you still here?" I ask.

The bed creaks, and the heat radiating from his body becomes diffuse. I can still feel his weight next to me, but now there's tension between us.

"What? Why?" His voice sounds genuinely puzzled.

"The walls are thin, you know?"

The resentment in my voice is all too obvious even though what they said downstairs hurt me less than I expected. Weeks ago, I would have been shattered, but at this point, I doubt anything could destroy me more than I already am.

"Elisse, please," he says with apparent calmness. "Don't pay attention to that nonsense. What Father Thunder said has nothing to do with what Johanna or Julien think, and much less with what I feel."

He sounds convinced, but his words can't bring me any kind of relief. Although my brothers didn't say they agreed with the old man, they didn't refute him either. Can I blame them? Who am I to have them question their loyalty to someone they see as their own father? What am I compared to what they feel for him?

"You should go. All of you."

"I'm not going to leave you." The firmness in his voice weighs me down like a tombstone.

"Do you really want to lose your whole tribe just for me?"

The weight of his body on the bed disappears.

"What are you talking about? I'm not going to lose anyone."

"Father Thunder is right. Baron Samedi only wants me, and the fact that I'm not guilty of what happened doesn't mean it's any less dangerous for them. For you."

"Enough," he says. "Nothing in the world will make me leave you here. Laurele, Samedi, whoever. They could come at any time and you—"

"Hoffman will be here, won't he?"

"Like that bastard could do anything against them."

"And you can?"

"Don't insist, Elisse. I don't care what it costs me. I won't let you die."

"You were a family long before I arrived, so it's more reasonable that you go with them and remain united."

For the first time, I'm relieved that I can't see anything. Whatever it is, I couldn't bear to see Tared's expression. His weight returns to the mattress, and the heat of his closeness becomes unbearable.

"No, it's not true," he whispers as he slides his fingers to my hand and traps it in the warmth of his palm. "You're also my family, and once a part of it, you'll always be a part of me."

The werewolf's touch moves me from the tips of my fingers to the pit of my stomach. I almost want to smile. His hand, so large and firm, clasping mine, so small and weak, urges me to intertwine my fingers with his in a squeeze full of all the things I want to tell him, about everything he makes me feel.

"There's not much left of me to rescue, Tared. Don't lose the people you still have. Please."

I pull my hand from his grip.

"Elisse..." he says in a voice that's brittle, weak, and so distant from the strength it has always possessed. It hurts me deeply to hear him speak my name that way.

"I need to sleep. Please," I say and turn my back. Minutes pass, and he just sits there. Surely, he's contemplating the trembling remains of who I once was.

At last, the weight of fatigue pulls me toward sleep and leaves me with one last thought, a question that hasn't left my head since I was pulled out of that macabre room. Why does Baron Samedi want to kill me?

Chapter 43
The Serpent and the Moon

I INHALE, SWELLING MY LUNGS with a hit of cold air, and open my… eyes. My eyes! I can see!

I'm standing in a multicolored flower field that resembles a wave of foam balanced by the wind. Comets and stars traverse the night overhead, but the clear, brilliant sky illuminates the earth as if the time were noon. Day and night exist together, here and now, in an impossible composition that gives birth to a vast landscape.

In the distance, a dark forest covered by a gray sky appears alien to the kingdom in which I stand now. Crypts with mouths that open into an abyss make my flesh crawl, and the twinkling of small metallic lights spreads out in front of the tombs as if the darkness vomited up lakes of gold. A familiar terror awakens in my stomach, so I move away from that dark place until it becomes a black spot behind my back.

My body feels so strange. I don't know if I'm running or floating. It's as though I'm without flesh, but I can still feel it attached to my bones.

Before me, endless paths of trees meander through hills covered by green grass, and flowers spread out in all directions. I caress a petal within reach, but a twinge of pain makes me retract my fingers—exposed bones and bloody flesh. My shattered hand has followed me here, to this dream.

Wow, a dream …

But this time I don't want to wake up. Here, I can see again. I can perceive colors, movement, and space. I know it's an imaginary, faraway world where nothing exists but what the nook of my imagination creates. Regardless, it's a place of beauty where I'm not disoriented or abandoned to the terror of darkness.

Elisssse.

The wind hisses behind me. The night sky dawns, and the daytime earth darkens as if time were accelerating. Day and night dance in a mixture of light and shadow until they adjust to the same hour as if their movement marked the start of a cycle. The afternoon floods the plain with an intense and warm light that permeates every stretch of this infinite land.

The flowers stir and a path opens toward me. White scales, shining under the light of the absent sun, cast a winding rainbow that moves in unison with the enormous body to which the scales belong. It's the skin of a snake. I stumble back.

Why am I so afraid? This is a dream.

But my logic loses against my instinct, so I move toward the forest of thick trees at the foot of the hills. I turn and look back. The creature is breaking through the flowers. My back crashes against one of the trees as my hands curl and rise in front of my chest.

From the flower field springs a gigantic white snake of impossible proportions gliding at an incredible speed. Its huge head balances on a body so thick and long that its tail fades in the distance like a stream. Its forked tongue flicks the color of coal, and its impressive green eyes shine as bright as jade stones. Despite the snake's incredible beauty, my breathing grows more agitated as the distance between us becomes shorter and shorter.

"Elisse."

I stand motionless in surprise. The snake spoke.

"Why are you afraid of me?"

My face unravels. Its lips parted so elegantly for words to spring from its throat in a deep, yet gentle, masculine voice. What is he? A wanderer? An ancestor?

"Who are you?" I open my eyes wide so I don't lose sight of the majestic snake.

"Do not fear me, Elisse. My name is Damballah."

✦ ✦ ✦ ✦

THE PEACEFUL SONG of a distant stream splashing against rocks kisses my eardrums. Everything around me is so incredible, so fantastic, and so vivid.

The grass opens at my side to form a path for the extraordinary creature whose presence causes a strange heat in my chest. I walk side by side with Damballah, one of the most revered Loas, and according to Laurele's book, a being whose place resides at the top of Voodoo altars. He is so important that even his eminence exceeds that of Baron Samedi himself. He's powerful, wise, and so … unlike how I imagined. Despite his daunting appearance, the Loa has turned out to be surprisingly sweet. His words are gentle, and he speaks to me with a tenderness I've only received from Louisa and Mama Tallulah.

The wind gusts, and I pause as countless leaves sail from the trees and tangle in my hair. I take a leaf, and it crackles between my fingers.

"This dream is so real."

The snake curves his head toward me and studies me with that beautiful gaze so outside of any dimension.

"You are not dreaming, Elisse. You can't dream. While you sleep, your mind can have visions or be invoked by beings like me. A curious condition of your nature."

"Then, you brought me here," I say. "Like Baron Samedi did in that vision where he set me on fire."

"That's right, little one. It's unusual I must tell you, because spiritual rulers do not usually bring the minds of the living to our moors. Consider yourself lucky."

Lucky.

I've heard that so many times, but I only go from misfortune to misfortune, and each one is worse than the previous.

"What is this place?"

"We are in Guinee, the kingdom of the Loas, the world of spirits, which precedes the end of everything."

"You mean the middle plane?"

"It's not that simple, my boy. Listen to me with attention because I'm going to explain how it works, what you call the middle plane," he says as we walk on the magnificent land. "The middle plane is not just a place of transit between life and death. This state of existence is composed of parts, like a puzzle, where each piece is governed by spirit families so numerous and diverse that you'd need hundreds of lifetimes in order to know them all. The Loas are an example of these families.

"Each of these groups of beings has origins, ideals, and a common language. When a civilization or human society encounters the manifestation of one of these families, the worlds of mortals and spirits coalesce to create what you call religion."

"Are you telling me all religions are real?" I say. I'm as amazed as I am skeptical.

"To a certain extent. Everything has its exceptions, but yes."

"So, does a God also exist?" The inevitable question arises from my tongue.

Damballah smiles mysteriously. "It is enough for you to know, my child, there is a here and a there, a beginning and an end, and beings of lesser or greater power are distributed in the middle of all that. What lies beyond is not incumbent upon mortals or the spirits of the middle plane."

"What part of the middle plane am I in when I have my nightmares, when everything becomes concrete?"

"The place to which you are brought when a lost spirit invokes you is called the *bardo* of the middle plane."

"The bardo ..." That word is familiar thanks to the Buddhist teachings.

"Yes, desolate areas where there is neither light nor darkness. They are mere places of confusion, similar to reality, without regent spirits, and where many lost souls, deformed by the weight of their own despair, reside. You don't have to believe in any spirit family to reach final death, but there will always be dead lost in the bardos. Without spirit families to manipulate the place, it's so ordinary that shadowgazers can enter of their own volition or be invoked there in the flesh. On the other hand, one cannot enter a place ruled by a spirit family without being invoked, because those places are too complex."

A map of the middle plane unveils before me at the words of Damballah. Slowly, not only pieces of my life but also aspects of humanity make sense.

I understand that nothing in this world is truly mystical—religions, myths, history, legends. Everything fits into a logic suitable to those who've had the privilege to understand from both magical and spiritual perspectives. And I can't let go of the fact that there are people who've dedicated their whole lives to unveiling many of these mysteries, to know the background of human existence, of this life, and the other. In just a blink, almost everything has been revealed to me. Maybe I'm lucky after all.

"So, each family has a section of the middle plane that transforms to their whims?" I ask, drunk with this new knowledge.

"Yes. In exchange for sacrifices, prayers, and faith, spirit families reward mortals by guiding them through our sections of the middle plane, under our rules, to the other side. They worship us, and we grant them miracles. Sometimes, they even call us gods."

"Can spirit families enter the territories of the others?" I imagine my face if at any moment a Buddha were to fly over my head.

"No. Spiritual laws are very clear. We don't get involved with other families. But humans don't seem to understand the same concept. You are now in my own wilderness of Guinee, and here, nothing and no one can hurt you, my child."

To hear this Loa call me that, my heart burns, and the fire transmits to my cheeks. I'm caught by déjà vu, but it's not that this experience is familiar; instead, something tells me it's not the first time we've seen each other.

"Have we met before?"

"Not in person. But I've been watching you ever since you came to New Orleans. You and all of Comus Bayou."

"Really?"

"Yes, I even took the opportunity to help Hoffman, a little, and Tared ... although, in the end, I regret I couldn't do more for you."

"It was you!" I open my eyes wide. "Y-you sent me Laurele's red book. And the snake, the one I saw in the oval room."

He nods his giant head slowly.

"Why did you help me?"

"What greater threat is there to the delicate balance of Guinee than a Loa who does not accept his place in it? And worse yet, a Loa whose task is of such importance. To bring the dead to the other side."

I'm speechless. Even if I had something to say, Damballah's explanation leaves no room for doubt. As we walk, I look around to calm my excitement. The sky of this dreamland has stopped at a wonderful sunset as if the presence of the Loa compelled it to grant him infinite light.

The snake stops and gently lowers his head. He curls up on himself, and I draw close to him as if an invisible force pulled me. I snuggle against the snake's neck, and a warm radiance emanates from him. He's so different from that horrifying

Baron Samedi and proves Loas can be gentle, loving beings who consider the life of mortals a precious treasure. They're not like that evil being who destroyed my body, my spirit, and my family.

"I don't want to go back," I whisper as he wraps his tail around me. "I want to stay here with you."

"The living who remain too long in the middle plane die before their time, little one, and I do not want that to happen to you." He warns me in such a paternal way that my chest stings.

"Muata should have taught me about these things," I whisper with a mixture of anger and sadness. I resent more than ever the rejection of the old man.

"Don't feel pained, little one. Elder Muata, like the excellent oracle he was, foresaw what would happen to the tribe and to Deer Shadowskin. His old age and the abandonment of his ancestor prevented him from discerning clearly what the future held. He didn't know what role you had in the horrible fate of Comus Bayou, and that's why he chose not to show you the capacity of your powers or the secrets of the middle plane until he knew who you really were. Not because he hated you, but because he loved his tribe and feared seeing it fall. I think anyone would have done the same in his place."

I'm not able to reply because, despite my pain, I know he's right. I caress the scales of the Loa to soothe myself. His skin is so different from that of a reptile. It feels more like I'm leaning against soft fur.

Damballah slides his head toward me, and in a natural reflex, I reach out my arm to hug his cheek.

"Are you tired of fighting?" he asks.

"I don't even know where I got the strength to stay alive."

I'm tormented by the things I just discovered and the things I have yet to understand. Why does Samedi want to kill me? Why is he stooping to mess with a simple mortal like me?

"There are things you need to know, right, Elisse?"

I widen my eyes in surprise. Can he read my mind?

"The Lord of Death was not born of the original nature of the first Loas. He is the fruit of the rites, passions, and human needs of the New World. So, his ambitions are also quite human. Power over the rest of the Loas and to convert New Orleans into an extension of his kingdom. That is what Baron Samedi seeks."

It takes only a few seconds for me to draw the conclusion that the unusual wave of cold and fog in New Orleans was undoubtedly a way to expand his kingdom.

"How does my death help him achieve such a thing?" I ask.

Damballah's breathing quickens as if deep concern assailed him. "It's not that your death accomplishes something like that, Elisse. How that being reaches his goal lies buried in his own consciousness, and unfortunately, I don't have the answer to that."

"So..."

"The only thing we, the rest of the Loas, know for sure is that Baron Samedi needs to kill you for a reason much greater than his ambition. He's afraid."

"Afraid?"

"Afraid of you, Elisse."

His words fall on me like a bucket of ice water. I don't know whether to laugh.

"Why is Baron Samedi afraid of me?" I ask. "I don't believe it. I've never been strong or special. I don't have an ancestor.

And I don't know anything about being a shadowgazer. It's a mistake."

"It's no mistake, boy. The other Loas can't fight against him, not when we are using all our power to maintain the balance he's broken with such brazenness. Instead, you can stop him. Prove that one of the mortals he despises so deeply can defeat even the Lord of the Sabbath. Baron Samedi needs you out of the way, and that's an obvious reflection of the threat you pose to him. If you, the only creature in this world who provokes so much fear in the Loa of Death himself, give up, what remains for us to do?"

I tremble from head to toe, and my eyes tear.

"Why should he fear someone who can't even defend his own life? I don't know how to face him. How can I beat death?"

"Why do you say that? You've already conquered death countless times. Didn't you survive a life of gloom and misery? Didn't you stay alive despite being tormented by nightmares since you were a child? Didn't you resist, hundreds of times, the temptation to end your life, for pure and simple love, for the idea of being with your father again? Isn't that beating death? Isn't that beating the Lord of the Sabbath himself?"

I do everything possible not to cry. The words of the Loa, so beautiful and poignant, prompt a shift in my heart. I lower my head and suddenly feel like a small child again.

"Are you afraid?" he asks.

"I'm a coward."

"A coward? Why weren't you afraid when you crossed the ocean to look for your father? Why weren't you afraid when you refused to live with Louisa so she wouldn't get hurt? Where did you get the courage to face Laurele, even when your family turned its back on you?"

The answers, to me, are obvious.

"I've always loved my father even without knowing him. I wanted to be with him. And I didn't care about dying, not if I could save Louisa, my brothers, and Tared … " I say.

"You do it for the people you love. You are braver than you think, Elisse. Even when you feel fear, your loyalty and your sense of sacrifice makes you take a step forward. Beating death isn't just about survival, it's also about deciding for yourself the reasons to face it."

My hand slips to my face again to clean both cheeks. I swallow, unable to understand how the words of the Loa can have such a powerful effect on me. Is it because of his divine origin? Or is it because I imagined my own father telling me these things?

"There is something in you, my child, that terrifies the Lord of the Sabbath and makes you capable of being, among all the creatures of the earth, the only one who can stop him. And I don't know about you, but I think that hand must mean something."

"This?" I brush the raw flesh. "Yes, I remember … I was able to hurt Baron Samedi with this hand. But why? And how did I get this wound?"

When I don't get an answer, I look and find Damballah with his head stretched behind me and his eyes darkening like turbulent water.

I look over my shoulder and jump to my feet. The snake uncoils the length of its being and stands in front of me like a barrier.

"How did it get here?" I ask.

Damballah stares at the creature that appears in the distance.

The slayer of Deer Shadowskin, the bone monster, watches us from the foot of the hills. Its frightful body covered by that black cloak billowing in the wind paints a macabre vision in contrast to the beauty of the landscape. Petals and leaves crash against the dark cloth, which absorbs them like a black hole. I can almost hear the demon panting.

"Get away, Elisse!" Damballah shouts.

"What about you?"

"Who he wants is you!" With those words, my body stretches without apparent direction, and every cell slowly tears from my body.

"Wait! No! What am I supposed to do now?" I cry as I dissolve.

"Go to Baron Samedi's wasteland and face him."

"What is the gift he wants to kill me for?"

"No, you didn't understand," he shouts at me. "It's not a gift. It's a curse! Get out!"

Suddenly, I'm thrown backward. Everything shrinks and darkness shrouds my periphery. An inhalation is born from my mouth, which opens to draw as much air as possible. I spring forward on the bed and cough uncontrollably. My awakening is more violent than just leaving my unconscious. It's as if I had been under water for several minutes.

Darkness reigns around me. I have returned to reality.

Gasping, I stir in the tangled sheets. I try to stand up, but my blindness prevents me from seeing the edge of the bed, and the weakness of my starving body causes me to collapse at the joints. I tumble to the ground with a thud and gasp again.

"Damballah! Damballah!" I cry. "Tared!"

Heavy and fast footsteps, more than a pair, pound the stairs to come up here. The door of the room bangs open.

"Elisse!" Tared's voice crashes against my eardrums. A second later, I hear him fall beside me. He grabs my back and pulls me up enough to sit on the floor. I frantically feel his body to find a point of support.

"Wh-what's wrong?" Johanna's voice rises along with unintelligible phrases from Julien and Nashua. I'm relieved. They haven't left the city yet.

"Damballah, he—" I gasp, aware of the little sense my words make. "Damballah told me everything. He . . . "

A deep silence follows my uncontrolled cries as if my words bewitched everyone's tongue. My head spins like a top.

"The woman was right," Father Thunder's voice rises in the distance.

"What?" I ask. "What woman?"

"Elisse . . . "

My name pounds in my ears like a drum, and a familiar voice, tense and shaded with something I distinguish as horror, sneaks into my brain. Seconds later, I recognize the voice at last. It's the priestess from the Bonfire of Miracles.

Chapter 44
Seven

If I had more energy, I'd concentrate on the presence of this woman in the room, but I barely have enough strength to bring this spoon to my mouth. Tared's hand rests firmly on my back to support my weakened body as I gulp down my bowl. From what I've been told, it's the first meal I've had in two days, since Tuesday.

I spill gumbo over the corners of my lips and furiously clean myself with a napkin. More than one person in this room has offered to feed me so I wouldn't have to deal with this, but I refuse to suffer that humiliation.

"Elisse," Father Thunder's voice rises beside me, though I'm not sure how close he is to me. "This woman arrived at the house minutes before you woke up and told us Damballah sent her to help you, and that you were talking to him right at that moment. We would have killed her on the spot if we hadn't heard you scream the name of the Loa."

I would turn my head toward the priestess, but I have no idea where she is in the room, so I just leave the spoon inside the bowl to let her know she has my full attention.

"My name is Zema, for those who don't know me." The sound of a lighter is followed by the smell of a cigar. The smoke hits me directly in the face, so I assume the woman is in front of me. "I must confess, since you showed up at my house that night, I haven't had a peaceful night's sleep."

"What do you want?"

"At this point, you are well aware that you need to enter the kingdom of Baron Samedi to face him."

"The middle plane?" Johanna asks.

"It's more complicated than that," I reply. "I have to enter the kingdom of the Lord of the Sabbath specifically, but I don't even know how to enter the regular middle plane."

"Not a clue?" Julien asks.

"Do any of you know how to do that?" Hoffman asks over all the voices, but the silence itself is enough of a response.

"Grandfather Muata was very cryptic. He always said it wasn't worth instructing us in something we'd never understand," Johanna says in a brittle voice.

Before, I would have judged Muata for that, but after everything Damballah revealed to me, I wouldn't be surprised if the old man had a strong motive for not telling the others about the middle plane and its structure.

"And that's why I'm here," the priestess says. "Do you know the legend of the Gates of Guinee?"

I shake my head.

"Well, you'd be the only one in this room who hasn't heard about it, right?"

Several voices mutter a yes.

"In New Orleans, we have a story about how to enter the kingdom of the Loas. The seven gates of Guinee allow you to transfer to the world of the dead, and these portals are scattered throughout the city."

"Bullshit," Hoffman says.

"Bullshit like men who turn into animals and detectives whose families are shattered by Voodoo spells."

"What did you say, old witch?"

"Hoffman, that's enough!" I shout, annoyed by his damn attitude. Silence prevails a few seconds and then is cut by a snort from the detective.

"Damn it, Elisse," he says quietly. I hear quick steps and a slam.

Wow, he left. I'm surprised he didn't start an argument with me.

"As I was saying, boy," the priestess continues, "these seven gates open with great power on sacred days like the New Year, All Saints' Day, and especially, Mardi Gras."

You know, Mardi Gras, unintentional rituals, things that increase my power.

"That's how Samedi physically crossed into our plane," I say, remembering what he himself told me on Mardi Gras night.

"Exactly," Zema says. "No Loa has broken the spiritual balance with such boldness until now. Damballah, on the other hand, only manifested because of the energy his followers raised with prayer and ritual. When I read the signs, I knew he was trying to help you. And look, all those poor chickens didn't die in vain."

"Why did it take so long? Why did he wait until this moment to take me to his plane and talk to me?"

"Loas also require powerful energy to take the souls of living beings to their kingdom. According to our Voodoo laws, there is a day of the week assigned for each Loa. Damballah is Thursday, today, so he had to wait until after Mardi Gras to accumulate enough spiritual energy to take you to his kingdom. On the other hand, Baron Samedi—"

"Became powerful enough to enter the world of the living before his time," I say.

"You're smart, child. Indeed, and if Samedi can do it, it's because for twenty years, Laurele's been preparing for his arrival."

My hands tremble, so I touch Tared's fingers in a gesture to hold the bowl. He understands me perfectly and removes the dish from my palms.

"How?"

"Sacrificial souls, Elisse. Innocent souls and even young ones. She offered their deaths to Samedi in exchange for youth and power."

My blood goes down to my feet. Louisa's children, the ghosts of the oval room, and the murder of Hoffman's baby take on full and total meaning. It was a stroke of luck that the detective left the room; otherwise, I'm sure he would have gone mad hearing this.

"So, the gates of Guinee can take me to Samedi."

"Only one of them, boy." She corrects me with a deeper tone in her voice. "The seven gates open successively, and although the Lord of the Sabbath can cross through any of them, you can only reach his kingdom through one."

"You can't be serious," Johanna says.

"He'll get killed if he goes in there." Tared chimes in and takes his hand off my back. My spine softens under my weight.

"Do you realize what you're saying?" Father Thunder's voice rises above our heads. "This boy, as he is, will not be able to do anything against Samedi."

I clench my fists. Am I the only one who doesn't know what this woman is talking about?

"Fools!" she shouts.

I hear a chair crawl, and the priestess's closeness crushes me like an avalanche.

"The doorway to the threshold of Baron Samedi is none other than the tomb marked with crosses, the grave of the Voodoo queen, Marie Laveau. Your duty is to enter the realm of the dead to appease the Lord of the Sabbath. Fate already rests on your shoulders, and if you fail, the weight of death will fall upon New Orleans, and you'll never be able to return to the world of the living. Are you willing to accept the task?"

"I'll do it," I answer without hesitation.

"Elisse!" Tared shouts.

"I have to do it," I say, raising my voice twice as loud as his. "I don't have an ancestor. I can't fight in a battle with you. The only fight I can have is the one forced on me by Baron Samedi, and because of that, I'll go to that tomb even if I have to drag myself there. And I swear on my damn life that I *will* return with the head of the Lord of the Sabbath in my arms."

A sudden silence takes over the room. I listen to everyone's breathing, and in an incredible way, I can distinguish the rhythm of each one.

"Then, I'm going with you." Tared breaks the tension at last.

"No way," Father Thunder says. "Your place is next to your family."

"Elisse is also my family. And if you consider me a part of yours, you'd understand!" he roars and ignites something in my chest as if I were struck by lightning.

I remain still after his show of loyalty, unsure of whether to tremble or sigh with relief.

"Not so fast, warriors," the priestess says. "You'll have to prepare for whatever awaits you in the cemetery, and for that, you'll need all the strength and the greatest luck in the world, so I suggest you choose Saturday to attack."

"Excuse me," I say. "Doesn't Lord of the *Sabbath* ring a bell? Are you asking us to venture into the cemetery and cross the threshold on the day granted to Baron Samedi?"

"The opening of the portals lasts seven days, and it peaks on Saturday, the day of the Lord of Death. And yes, it will be the time at which Baron Samedi has more power, but the same happens with the portal. You'll be more likely to reach his place in Guinee with your fare without losing yourself, as well as return here intact."

"Fare? What fare?" I ask.

"What fare? Damballah must have told you. One cannot go to the realm of the Loas without being invited."

"What the hell are you talking about?"

"Boy! How do you think you're going to get to the world of the dead without fare, without an invitation from the Loa whose plane you will cross? Did you plan to throw yourself into the crypt, and that's it?"

"I don't know what the hell—" The image of Baron Samedi pressing two shiny gold coins over my eyes flashes inside my head. "The coins! Tared, were there coins in my pants when they brought me here?"

"Oh, yeah, they're in the drawer next to the bed."

"There you go, boy," the priestess says. "When the time comes, those coins will allow you to pass through the portal, but not for long, so take care of things as fast as you can."

I grit my teeth until my gums ache. That bastard Samedi made fun of me until the end and gave me the means to go face him as if he were certain I would lose. I touch the bandaged fingers of my torn hand and convince myself that the Loa of Death is making a grave mistake in underestimating me.

"Father, please ... " Tared's pleading voice booms inside me violently.

After a long minute, the old man sighs, and I hear a thud. Maybe his cane crashed to the ground.

"We'll wait until Saturday before dawn to attack," he says. "We'll ask Detective Hoffman to see if the cemetery is free of surveillance that day. Elisse will also have time to recover his strength. We pray to the gods to give us their blessings, to make sure the Comus Bayou tribe doesn't disappear from the face of the earth beneath the shroud of the Lord of the Sabbath."

Chapter 45
Queen of Crosses

I can smell it on them, and I'm sure they can smell it on me. Fear. That vile and disgusting smell mixed with uncertainty fills the black suburban. All of us have decided to gamble our lives today.

It's three o'clock on Saturday morning, and I sit in the back seat next to Johanna. Nashua and Tared sit in front, and Hoffman follows us closely in his car with Julien and Father Thunder.

The old man ended up coming in spite of our efforts to change his mind. I'd like to say that after everything that's occurred, whatever happens to him matters little to me, but I'd be lying. A part of me will always want his acceptance and affection. And today's danger doesn't leave anyone's life secure.

The truck stops and seatbelts unbuckle. I grope for the door handle, but someone opens it before I can do it myself, and I snort.

"Sorry, Elisse, but we have to speed this up."

I don't reply to Tared. Deep down, I know he's right.

He places my hand on his shoulder, and I use it as support to get down from the truck. The steps of the others approach along with the metallic clicks of guns cocking, which makes my skin turn ice cold.

"Everyone ready now?" Tared asks with his arm around my shoulders.

His strength guides me through a sea of unknown sensations that threatens to drown me. I'm surprised that even without my ancestor and without my eyes, I can sense the presence of the others closing in like wolves covered by the secrecy of night. And that's not the only thing I can feel. I can sense in the cold against my skin and in my bones, the St. Louis Cemetery stands before us.

"Which area?" I ask.

"Behind the cemetery," Julien replies.

"We'll have to climb the wall," Hoffman says behind me. "After the remains were stolen, the guards have been testing a system of security cameras, but the idiots only placed them at the entrance."

"Seriously?" I say. Obviously, I can't climb a wall. "How am I supposed to—?"

Tared secures me with his arms. My stomach turns as my body launches at full speed in a jump, and then I land abruptly on the ground. I can't complain when I hear the others fall close to us in heavy trampling.

"Come on, there's no time to lose," Father Thunder says in a low voice.

I stagger, pulling away from Tared's grip, and fumble for the gold coins in my pocket. The ancient Greek myth of

Charon comes to mind. To pay the boatman to ferry the soul to the underworld, coins were placed in the mouth or over the eyes of the dead.

So, with my offering held firmly, I open my eyelids and shiver when the skin brushes against the bandage. Carefully, I slip the coins under the gauze and adjust them over my shattered sockets.

A few seconds pass before the metal radiates a strange heat. The pain is unavoidable and I hiss. For a few moments, I debate whether to remove the coins, afraid they'll grow hot enough to burn me severely, but my whole body stiffens when I see a faint glow in the middle of my darkness.

I gasp as the cemetery takes shape in front of me as if the coins became oracles between reality and me—even through the bandages.

"Elisse, what's wrong?"

My mouth drops open. I can see everyone.

Tared looks at me with deep concern. He carries a long shotgun behind his back and a small flashlight. Nashua also carries a shotgun, while Julien, Johanna, and Hoffman each carry a gun with a silencer. Father Thunder is the only one unarmed. They look the same as in the real world, but there's something different about them as if touch alone could pass right through them.

"I can see," I say, which draws a hint of amazement from the mouths of my brothers.

"Don't get attached, boy, you know it's temporary."

Father Thunder doesn't have to remind me. I'm well aware of it.

"Congratulations. Can we keep moving?" The arrogant voice of Hoffman mobilizes us.

"Elisse ..."

Tared takes a small silver pistol with a silencer from his belt and hands it to me along with a few extra bullets and a flashlight. I take everything as firmly as my nerves allow, inhale deeply, and confront, for the first time, the St. Louis Cemetery.

The place gives off an energy so abysmal that it twists and exalts every piece of magic inside me with its brutal darkness. The crypts are white, at least the well-preserved ones, and surrounded by metal fences. Some are so impressive that they look like chapels, and one stands out in the form of a pyramid. In contrast, the older tombs are so corroded that they look like a pile of stacked bricks. There's no grass, only dirt and concrete paths. It's as if I entered a miniature city—an authentic infernal necropolis, cold and wet with fog.

"Come on. Marie Laveau's grave is near the entrance to the cemetery," Johanna whispers.

We all advance with vigilance. I don't know if the others can sense it, but the increasing cold chills my bones as if each step were a degree less in temperature.

"What the hell happened here?" Nashua asks, and like him, the rest of us stare in dismay at an open crypt so old that the paint has already worn away.

"It's the same pattern," Hoffman says and points to the concrete pieces on the floor. "When the twelve remains were stolen a few months ago, I noticed the pieces of cement were scattered only on the outside and not inside the crypt. It was like they'd been smashed from within. And in one fell swoop."

"This doesn't look good at all," Julien whispers.

I couldn't agree more. Of the twelve stolen remains, we've only destroyed eight false wanderers because they could never find the one that devoured Mama Tallulah. In the best-case scenario, we may face at least four of them and who knows how many zombies. May the most divine of this world protect us.

Tared and Nashua point their flashlights toward the opening of the crypt, but there's nothing besides dust and intact drawers where remains are kept, so we continue our search.

"It's over there. The tomb of Marie Laveau." Johanna points.

I can make out the structure about thirty yards in the distance. To belong to the queen of Voodoo, the tomb is rather unimpressive. It's just a tall, upright rectangle without any remarkable decoration. In fact, something's not right. The walls of the tomb are smooth and white.

"Shouldn't it be covered with crosses?" I ask in a low voice.

"They painted the tomb a few years ago," Johanna says. "Followers use to come here and mark three crosses to ask Marie Laveau for favors, but over time, the authorities decided to forbid the practice to preserve the crypt."

We surround the entrance of the tomb, and my surprise grows considerably when crosses appear on the paint and issue an almost imperceptible violet glow. A wave of dizziness rises from my stomach when the concrete sheet at the entrance swirls into a black and infinite abyss.

"Are you seeing this?"

Everyone's concerned faces are a sufficient response.

"Now what?" Nashua asks me.

"I suppose I should go into the tomb," I answer with my voice wobbling.

Suddenly, Tared raises his fist, signaling us to shut up. "I heard something," he says and readies his shotgun. "Pay attention."

We all look around. I check around the tomb, and then a glow other than the crosses catches my attention. It comes from a wall of recessed crypts, one that I recognize almost immediately from the newspaper. It's the tomb from which the twelve remains were stolen. As I remember, they resealed the tomb, but now there's a hole in it the size of a plate.

The cement crunches beneath my feet as I move closer to see what's shining in the darkness. A pair of small yellowish orbs glistens and moves slightly. I squint at them. They twinkle and fade. They're eyes!

"Tared!" I yell.

A monstrous howl echoes in the darkness, and then the wall bursts. A huge creature explodes from the tomb and throws me against the wall of another crypt.

The blow sends my gun and flashlight flying and leaves me stunned for a few moments. The others scream, and I get up as fast as I can and run down the crypt corridor with the monster at my heels. I look back, and it's Mama Tallulah's killer, the canine wanderer.

Its claw reaches my ankle and jerks me to the ground. The wanderer hovers over me, but the blast of a shotgun strikes its back before it can bury its claws into me. The creature roars and tries to bite me. In reflex, I fling my bandaged hand to protect myself. As soon as the monster's fangs touch my bandaged fingers, the creature recoils and howls. It waves its muzzle as a thick vapor erupts from its jaws.

"Elisse, get up!" Nashua shouts in the distance.

Flooding with adrenaline, I jump up and circle the beast. My pistol is a few feet away, and I leap on top of it.

"We're surrounded, be careful!" Hoffman says as he fires a shot into the darkness.

From the bowels of the corridors, three huge wanderers emerge. One is some sort of reptile with a long neck, another is a boar, and the last is an elk or a deer. All three still have humanlike torsos, but fangs and horns have grotesquely skewered the creatures' faces.

My brothers howl, transforming swiftly to receive the wave of monsters. Their skins stretch, their muscles grow, and their clothes and shoes fly shredded in all directions.

The canine wanderer launches at me again, and I aim my gun and shoot right at its muzzle. An explosion of blood splatters my face. The impact throws the creature back, but it returns to the charge with its jawbone dangling to one side.

"Die, damn it!"

I shoot again and again, but the thing advances as if the bullets didn't even tickle it.

Out of nowhere, another creature tackles and crushes the false wanderer's neck with its enormous jaws. I open my mouth wide as I witness for the first time, the bestial form of Father Thunder, a wolf as gray as ash, move with a blue iridescence.

"Elisse!" he shouts while holding the giant rabid dog by the neck with his long silver claws. "The tomb!"

I don't even respond since my feet are already on the ground running toward the crypt of Marie Laveau.

Tared, in his imposing werewolf form, fires at the wanderer boar and then swings a claw at its muzzle. Julien and Nashua ram the reptile wanderer while Hoffman shoots a hail of bullets at the canine wanderer to help a weakened Father Thunder. Even in their warrior forms, everyone still uses their weapons, which are perhaps more effective than their own claws and teeth.

Johanna, even with her smaller build in comparison to a skineater, knocks down the elk wanderer without much effort and buries her jaws in its shoulder. She shreds the skin of the creature to pieces, and a fountain of blood bursts, soaking her fur. In an excess display of violence, she releases a pistol shot into the wound she opened.

I hear the muffled shots of the silencers, the shouts of Hoffman, and the howls of the wanderers at my back as the crosses of the tomb shine with greater intensity as I get closer. Suddenly, the markings dance and move over the concrete as if they were projections on a screen.

My bones tremble when the crosses unravel, grow, re-arrange, and connect to create the brilliant veve of Baron Samedi on the side of the tomb:

"Elisse, watch out!"

I turn around and find myself face-to-face with a zombie who pounces on me and opens its jaws of rotted teeth. I shoot, and its head bursts like a grotesque balloon. A pair of zombies appear in my periphery and stand in front of the tomb's entrance. I thank Hoffman for the practice and shoot each one down, and they become bubbling foam on the floor.

"I need help here!" I cry when more undead surge behind me. I shoot until I have to reload.

Julien runs to help me, but a group of zombies intercept him and block his path forward. The weapons empty, our forces weaken, and the injuries mount as the number of living dead increases. The resurrected wanderers persist despite the shots while the zombies multiply like parasites that jump out from the darkness.

"Where the hell are they all coming from?" I shout, and then I remember the open grave we left behind...

No, it can't be possible. They're coming from the middle plane!

"Tared! The other grave!" I shout and pistol-whip one of the corpses to get it away from me.

The wolf dislodges the boar, leaving the false wanderer stunned, and then he runs to attack the zombies surrounding me.

"Johanna! Hoffman! The other crypt!" Tared rumbles like thunder.

Moments later, the detective and the girl run by my side with that damn elk wanderer behind them.

Tared hammers the zombies that appear one after the other and swarm him like piranhas over bait. Behind me, Father Thunder struggles against the canine wanderer, and a zombie rushes on his calf and embeds its rotted teeth.

By the number of enemies, the chances of survival seem so low that I can't watch any longer. My blood boils, and I look at the black mouth of the grave waiting to engulf me. I rip the bandages off my fleshless hand, and a lacerating burn races across the exposed bones now in contact with the cold air.

I rush toward the entrance to Marie Laveau's crypt, but a zombie throws itself over my back and detains me. I elbow its torn chest with enough force to knock it down.

A moan rumbles by my side. Another zombie attacks and sinks its teeth into my shoulder.

"Aaagh, get the fuck off me!" I claw at the zombie with my fleshless hand, and the corpse boils on contact.

Horror replaces amazement when the coins of Samedi heat up and blur everything around me. Powerful howls, cries I can't distinguish, rise up behind me, before me, and beside me. I don't know if the shrieks of pain come from my tribe or the resurrected wanderers, because I'm focused on the zombie I knocked to the ground. With a swipe, my claw impales its neck, and that dreadful monster melts in an instant.

Everything gets worse in a flash. The metal coins ignite with such an intense heat that I scream, and within seconds, I'm blind once again. Drowning in adrenaline and pain, I drop to the ground and crawl desperately to find the edge of the tomb as the burning grows more intense, but a claw clamps around my ankle and drags me backward. I scratch my nails along the concrete and nearly rip them from the flesh to cling to the ground.

I recognize the howl of the wanderer canine at my back, so I whip around blindly to strike at him. Its matted fur brushes against my fleshless hand, and the creature screams and gives up at last. I crawl as fast as I can until I reach the threshold of the crypt. I grip the edges and, without a second thought, plunge myself headlong into the darkness.

Chapter 46
Let the Witches Burn!

SCREAMS, CRIES, GUNSHOTS...The battle suddenly plunges into deep silence. I plummet, and my stomach is swallowed by the most frightening vertigo. Eternal seconds pass as I keep falling and falling. The tomb of Marie Laveau has become a bottomless pit.

The emptiness begins to penetrate my body, passing through each cell as if they were holes of a sieve. Then, I begin rolling, over and over on a damp surface, with my eyes still immersed in complete darkness. How the hell have I gone from falling to rolling without even feeling the change? After a couple more somersaults, I stop.

I squeeze my eyelids and groan, more out of confusion than pain.

"Damn," I whisper.

I blink a couple of times to adjust to the white glow of the light surrounding me. Slowly, I begin to see again. The

bandage and coins have fallen off, and there's no trace of burns on my eyes. Has the fare already been paid?

Behind me rises the blurred shape of Marie Laveau's tomb, which is empty and marked with crosses. There's a gray sky above my head and damp grass beneath my feet. Crypts similar to those of the St. Louis Cemetery, but farther apart from each other, dot the landscape. Shining gold coins spill from their mouths like abandoned treasures. A dense, dark forest surrounds the grassland, and the crowns of the trees rise like a wall.

I'm in the same landscape as my dream with Baron Samedi—the part of Guinee ruled by the Lord of the Sabbath. The portal has worked.

I check my shoulder where the zombie bit me. My leather jacket is torn, and pieces of my shirt peek through the opening. Bloody tooth marks penetrate the skin, but there's no pain. It's as if I've been sedated, because the blows and scratches from the battle don't hurt either.

Something passes by the corner of my eye, and I look toward the tombs. Dark shadows throw themselves on top of each other, back away, and then collide again. Gradually they become solid until some take the form of specters dressed like Baron Samedi with bundles of straw and bones tied to their clothes. The rest of the shadows are …

"Comus Bayou."

It's the fight! It's a projection of the battle in the cemetery. The zombies and the resurrected wanderers are specters of the Lord of the Sabbath, possessed decoys, which explains why there are so many.

"Interesting way of seeing things, don't you think?" a voice says behind me.

Baron Samedi sits on a tomb while holding a long black cane and smoking a cigar that sends out dense fog. His appearance is different from when I saw him at Laurele's house. He's left the hat aside, and the black suit has transformed into sheets of skin that hang from his body. A fleshless skull replaces his painted face and makes him look even more terrifying than when he manifests in the plane of the living.

A moan cuts off my thoughts. At the foot of the grave lies Laurele, naked and pale, with a chilling stain of blood between her thighs. She uses her elbows to crawl to the side as if she were trying to escape from either of us, but a brown bag tied around her waist with a rope weighs her down.

"Look at her. She's taking your money. Shouldn't you stop her?" He points to the small sack.

My face distorts in a grimace.

"Oh, I never told you! Right ... right ... " he says.

The specter casts his cigar into the grass, and with a deranged smile, he descends in a slow, ghostly leap. He circles Laurele as she crawls and trails a reddish stain across the grass to take refuge behind a tomb. She clings to the concrete slab, and her teeth chatter as if she were dying of cold.

The Lord of the Sabbath laughs. A glass bottle materializes in his hand and swirls with amber liquid.

"You should have seen the face of that idiot Carlton Lone when he found the stolen money in your room. And you should see his face when he realizes the money disappeared again. Who would have thought it'd be so much fun to see you accused of crimes you didn't commit, to see your people turn their backs on you without giving you a chance to prove your innocence? Humans. Wanderers. They're all very cruel, don't you think?"

"Bastard!" My blood rages. He's the one who stole the money from the center to frame me. "You'll regret everything!"

"What are you going to do about it? Are you going to beat me to death?"

"I'm going to tear out your fucking throat!"

By instinct, I tighten my fist until my fingers dig into my palm. The Loa tilts his head slightly toward my hand.

"We'll see if you can even get close to me, boy."

Screams begin clawing at my eardrums. From the tombs rise several servants of the Loa dressed exactly like him. They stretch their black hands toward me. They're the same wraiths that kept me bound the night Baron Samedi crushed my eyes.

The first one launches straight at my chest and knocks me, but I manage to stay on my feet. Its long arms tangle around my neck, and when I try to free myself, my human hand passes right through as if the demon were smoke, but when my bone-claw catches it, a thick vapor erupts from its skin. The wraith drops to the floor and writhes in pain before the stunned look of the other specters and me. What the hell is happening with my hand?

I don't have time to think, because the monsters snap out of their trance and rush toward me in a torrent like a wave of oil. There are too many. I won't be able to handle them all at once.

I flee into the forest, but as I run, the trees disappear and more tombs emerge in their place as if the cemetery were expanding with my every step.

"Shit, shit!" The only way to save myself is to kill them one by one. How the hell am I going to do that? Fucking genius, Elisse. No plan B. If only I had an ancestor to—

I stop in my tracks. About twenty yards ahead, in what appears to be half of the cemetery, a thick wooden mast rises from the grass, and bundles of straw encircle the bottom.

My heart stops. It's a bonfire.

A powerful blow strikes my neck and knocks me face down on the ground. I'm stunned, and my vision blurs. I try to get up, but a sea of hands looms over my body. They grab my hair, my arms, my legs, and my clothes. The servants of the Lord of the Sabbath surround me and begin dragging me toward the pyre. I try to free myself, but the blow to my head was so strong that my movements are clumsy and weak.

The monsters' arms detach from their bodies and wrap around me like thick ropes. My back is whipped against the pole, and the bindings tighten until I can't breathe. An even greater force restrains the wrist of my fleshless hand and renders it as useless as the rest of my body.

"Son of a bitch, son of a bitch!" I stir, trying to free myself. My heart pumps desperately.

Samedi sashays toward me, smiling with that cemetery protruding from his gums. His henchmen, now armless, dance around me.

"Hell, Elisse," the Lord of the Sabbath says. "You disappoint me. I really thought killing you would be more complicated. Now, I guess killing your friends will be the fun thing to do, don't you think?" he says with a disgusting smile. "Although ... if your leader just died, I suppose it won't be so difficult to kill the rest."

He points behind his back with the cane. My gaze travels the distance at full speed to scrutinize the shadows of the battle in the human plane. I can see him—a large motionless body surrounded by a few others who look like they're protecting him.

"Damn you! Damn you!" I shout. By the gods, Tared, no! I refuse to believe this wretched man! Tared can't be dead!

My arm breaks through the hands of the monsters. Samedi backs away as I use my fleshless hand to cut away the knots of arms binding me.

"Not so fast," he says and points his long cane at my hand. A new vine of arms snatches my limb to the side of my body and squeezes. "This time, I won't give you a chance."

My jaw aches from grinding my teeth, from how visceral my anger and despair have become. I think of Tared, Louisa, and the others, and of the few possibilities hanging over New Orleans.

A miracle, by the gods, a miracle, please!

My chest swells, my throat knots, and my eyes crush until they hurt. I'm about to cry.

Elisse.

My thoughts die suddenly, and my attention turns from the Loa of Death. Behind him, just a few yards away, an equally monstrous specter looks at me through dark chasms. Its breathing expands and contracts the bones of its hundreds of ribs. Its black cloak whips against its skeletal body. And its colossal red antlers touch the sky.

The monster who devoured Deer Shadowskin gazes at me as a witness to my bonfire.

"Elisse ... " the voice inside the skull whispers.

I scream when I realize it's the monster who's calling my name. I knew he was a damn servant of Samedi! I knew it! I stir again, tormented by the presence of that horrifying being. Samedi laughs out loud with pleasure, but I go mute when I see something strange happen. The creature stirs along with me, imitating me.

I blink, confused. I move again, and the bone monster mirrors me and matches my breathing.

"Who are you?" I shout. "Who are you?"

Samedi tilts his head and looks back, and then he faces me again.

"How quickly you've gone mad, boy."

Samedi can't see him? What the hell is … ? My eyes lock onto one of the bone monster's claws. Bluish skin and violet muscles cover the tips of its fingers, over the same part where mine are torn as if its body were regenerating flesh. It's the same hand as my fleshless one.

"You're mine … " the bone monster says.

The words of Damballah sting my memory.

"It's not a gift," I whisper. "It's a curse…"

"Let them burn, let the witches burn!" Baron Samedi says, suddenly catching my attention.

He snaps his fingers, and in an instant, a powerful fire engulfs me. My screams echo into the sky as the infernal heat chars my skin. The fire rages about my body, along with the sickening smell of burnt hair and flesh, swallowing me in a whirlpool of agony. Through the orange flames, I can still make out the bone monster, who's twisting with my suffering.

"I accept!" I cry out, dragging my tongue as it melts in the flames. "I'm yours! I'm yours!"

Baron Samedi bursts into laughter.

The bone monster stops moving. It lowers its head with a smile and swallows me through its abysmal gaze.

In an instant, everything I'm feeling, the pain and the despair, transforms. The black arms around me explode when my flesh, my bones, my spirit, and each and every part of my being lengthens, breaks, and stretches into dimensions the word pain can no longer describe. Burning to death would be a paradise compared to this agony.

The cries of my throat transform into thick roars, and the burning from the flames becomes soft licks against my body. I grow in size and height, and the ground moves away from me every second. An unknown force, an inexplicable energy, combusts in each of my cells along with a growing anger. I rise from the flames, dragging remnants of fire behind me, and receive the shrieks of Baron Samedi's specters as chants that honor my resurrection.

My arms touch the earth, and I rise into the gray sky. The waning moon shines above my head like a crown. A brutal instinct, unfamiliar and wild, drives me to howl, and the earth, the sky, the tombs—everything trembles before me. I have become the very monster that's tortured me since I arrived in New Orleans. He, who's taken the place of my ancestor, gives me his strength and his appearance.

I'm powerful. I'm a titan. And I'm pissed.

"No, no. I-it's not possible!" The skull of Baron Samedi mouths in confusion. He retreats, and I advance in indescribable delight.

"Samedi!" I shout in a frightful chorus of voices that seems to come from the deepest pit of hell.

"Samedi!" I shout again. My elaborate legs of bones slowly propel me toward the Loa, who from here looks like a quivering, disgusting human.

The Lord of the Sabbath issues a delicious smell that reaches the holes of my snout, and I moan with desire. It's the cold smell of flesh and blood. It's the smell of fear.

The very Lord of Death, Baron Samedi, shakes before me, and that gives me unspeakable pleasure.

"Kill him!" he orders.

My jaw exhales a hollow laugh.

Instantly, the armless servants of Samedi, along with several more, rise like ghosts from the graves and run toward me. A simple nod of my antlers casts them into the air. I kneel on one of the demons, and my jagged snout rips off its head like a doll. My claws hover over the others, and in seconds, those vile specters reduce to corpses in my grip.

Corpses. I have murdered spirits, creatures that have never been alive. Is this my curse? My power?

I feel a great desire to slide my tongue across the blood dripping down my long fangs, but I am pure bone and no flesh, so my desire turns into anger.

Samedi raises his cane in front of his body to protect himself.

"Are you afraid?" I ask and feel a pang of grotesque pleasure at seeing him tremble. "Are you afraid? Are you afraid? Are you afraid?"

My words imitate the chatter of a possessed person and provoke a mixture of horror and pleasure. But, am I not possessed? Didn't a monstrous creature just possess me? Am I not perhaps, a monster?

I walk toward Samedi slowly and he recoils. He snaps his fingers, and a blaze of fire envelops me, but I don't feel a thing as the fire licks my bones. I cross the flames as if they were a simple curtain of smoke.

"F-fear…" I find it hard to express myself with words as if human language had suddenly become something distant and unknown to me.

I heave myself toward Samedi, who takes a step back and drinks from his glass bottle. Within seconds, he spews a black, stinking torrent as thick as oil. I try to evade it, but the filthy substance touches one of my arms, corroding my bones, and the sizzling pain sends me backward.

Samedi runs like a damn coward, but I'm faster, so in a couple of strides I swoop down on him.

The bastard threads his staff into my bones, and I howl in pain from the depths of my ribs as if he pierced my invisible flesh.

He takes advantage of my bewilderment and escapes my grip. I snatch his ankle, and he slams to the ground, sending the bottle rolling away from his hand, and I crush the glass with my antlers.

"Damn you!" he shouts, crawling on the floor like a worm.

I grab him by the back and tear the staff from his hands to throw it away. I turn him over so he can see my face, and then I clamp my jaws on his shoulder and tear out a bite. His blood, as black as oil, sprays over my skull, and again, the desire to lick my snout arises. The Loa under my claws makes me smile with invisible lips for lack of flesh. My claw closes around his neck, and I lift him before my eyes.

"Please, please ... " he pleads, squeezing my thick wrist with his hands.

My heart fills with hate, unable to forget the atrocities that have been committed. No, I don't feel a shred of pity.

"You will pay, Samedi." I dig my nails into his neck and feel him squish between my fingers.

Mortal. Samedi is now mortal, and he seems to understand clearly because he whimpers and scratches like a scared animal.

Pleasure twists my insides.

"No, no, listen, listen!" he shouts. "I wasn't the one who put a price on your head. I was just going to collect the reward for killing you. I'm not your real enemy."

"What?" I can barely speak. I feel like the wind has been knocked out of me. "Lies!"

The monstrous Loa writhes under my claws with a smile in his teeth.

"It's true, it's true! Why do you think Laurele was increasing my power and preparing for my arrival for twenty years? Because it was predicted that you'd come to New Orleans."

Horror shakes me from head to toe. He's trying to trick me! I twist his neck again until it swells between my bone fingers.

"P-please," he begs. "Think about it. How else would your death serve me if it wasn't to make a deal?"

I growl, still not wanting to believe him despite how reasonable the idea sounds.

"Who?" I loosen my grip a little.

"I can't tell you his name! I-if I do, my tongue will explode into pieces! That was our deal!"

Unconvinced by his senseless response, I twist again.

"A reason … not to kill you … " I say.

He tries to open his lips but barely extracts a gasp from them.

"The souls of those who Laurele killed for me … will disappear with me. The d-daughter of the detective, th-the children of Louisa Fiquette … "

My claws dig so deeply into the skin of his neck that my nails embed in his spine.

"You lie."

"They are still mine. Th-that was the deal," he says.

The pages of the red book mercilessly pound my head like a hammer. The souls offered to the Lord of Death will belong to him ... *until he delivers them to the other side.*

I growl with pure hatred at the creature in front of me. I don't want to give in to the reasons that parade before me. I want to let myself be overcome by my evilness. I want to tear him to pieces, rip off each of his limbs in the most frightful way possible, and make him suffer a thousand times worse than I have. I want revenge. I want him to pay for Tared. For Mama Tallulah. For Old Muata. For Louisa and ... her children?

Something starts beating inside of me when I remember Louisa soaked in tears and think of her empty arms. I remember the bloody blanket of Hoffman's baby. So much pain. So much suffering. So many empty cradles.

If I kill him, Baron Samedi wouldn't be the victim of my hatred. He'd only be paying for his crimes. They would be the victims—those children who never became. Why do they have to pay for my revenge? I can't do that to Louisa. Not even to Hoffman. I'm a monster. But that doesn't mean I want to be one.

Even though he made me look like a thief, destroyed Comus Bayou, crushed my eyes, and sold my life ... I can't kill Baron Samedi.

"A ... deal?" I say.

"Yes, yes, let's make a deal!" he shouts, desperate to save himself.

Anger rages again, but instead of surrendering to it, I use all my will to spin the words inside my snout.

"You will live, Samedi," I say. "But if you can't give me a name, you will never say anything more."

I don't give him time to protest. My claw opens his mouth, and from it, I stretch the viscous muscle that's as black as oil. I close my jaws on the tongue of the Lord of the Sabbath, snap it off in one bite, and swallow it.

The moans of the Loa's pain become silent to my ears as that cold, black tongue wiggles and settles in the back of my throat. It becomes a part of my being, materializing what was there only in spirit. My mouth opens, and from the tip of my new muscle spouts a deluge of a thousand languages. Now, I can speak the language of the dead, that of men, and that of beasts.

Just as Deer Shadowskin's antlers are now my crown, the tongue of the Lord of Death becomes my own.

My claw releases the neck of the Loa, and he falls in a heap on the grass and cups his bleeding mouth. I bow my head to him, delighted by his painful agony.

"Your time as a god is over, Baron Samedi." Now, I speak with extreme fluency—not in the language of humans or beasts but that of the Loas. "Without your tongue, you will never be able to communicate again with humans or with spirits. You will dwell in the middle plane, staggering like a mute monster, only moving beings from one side to the other until the end of your existence. It sounds quite merciful compared to everything you've done. Don't you think?"

The specter looks at me with blood running down the corners of his mouth like any mortal. I release a delicious laugh that echoes throughout the cemetery. The Loa gets smaller as I rise before him and display my gallery of bones in all its splendor.

"You've made your last bargain, Lord of the Sabbath. I have spared your life in exchange for your tongue, so I hope you take advantage of it. It's your last chance," I say and revel in the whimpers of the Loa, who now is unable to scream.

Now that I know the great Lord of Death is nothing more than a mere mortal under my clutches, I'm not afraid of him anymore.

The desire to kill him in cold blood struggles to dominate me, but instead, I move away in the direction of the grave through which I entered and leave him to writhe like a maggot. I'm intimately pleased with my new tongue, to which I finally give the pleasure of smacking my snout.

Next to the crypt, I spot one last matter to solve. Laurele crawls toward the portal. Her now pale body shakes in spasms as she hauls on her hips that heavy bag of money. I reach her, and she looks at me with the deepest of horrors.

"Where do you think you're going?" I say.

Just before she can slide toward the grave, I grab one of her bare legs and drag her to me.

"No, no, please, please ... " she begs as I turn her face up. My enormous body stands over her, and my hands close on her throat like vines of bone.

"You've done unforgivable things, Laurele."

"No, please, Elisse, no!"

"You murdered innocent children."

"Please, let me explain!"

"I don't care about your lies."

"I just wanted to get my sister back!" she cries with tears running down her face. "I killed those people. I killed my sister's children! But when I realized what I had done, I was all alone ... Samedi promised to revive Devon if I killed you. But you wouldn't die. Despite everything I did, you wouldn't die! You're a monster! A monster!" she shouts, caught in her own madness and unable to realize her hypocrisy.

My jaw trembles with rage.

"You bitch," I whisper. "You didn't even do it out of love for Louisa. You did it for yourself because you didn't have the courage to face the consequences of your atrocities. You don't deserve her forgiveness."

"Elisse, no . . . "

I feel my bones. I feel my being. I feel my heart drenched in the blood of my sorrows and the deep contempt that infects each one of my cells. The woman lies below me, naked and helpless, in a position I'm sure she never could have imagined, even in her worst nightmares.

I tilt my snout toward her and whisper in her ear.

"Didn't you just say it yourself, Laurele? I'm a monster."

✦ ✦ ✦ ✦

My hands cling to the sides of the crypt to pull my body out with the little strength I have left. I crawl from the bowels of the earth as screams echo around me. The light of dawn breaks before me. I'm stunned . . . I've recovered my eyes.

My body, naked and human, collapses to the ground and curls up in a ball, free from the darkness of Marie Laveau's tomb. I'm so exhausted that I don't even gasp when I see that I still have a fleshless right hand with tips of bone as pale as the flesh covering my body, now almost as white as marble. It's as if I've been reborn, and the Indian sun had never kissed my skin. My head weighs mountains, so I tip it to rest with scarlet antlers still crowning it.

"Elisse!"

My name comes in screams, but I'm so weak and dazed that I can barely stay awake. Several pairs of feet surround me, and something warm covers my body. A silvery coat caresses me, and I shiver at its soft touch.

It's wolf skin.

Chapter 47
Far from Home

It's been five months since I first set foot in New Orleans. I came to this fog-devoured land embracing my bag and a dream—to be with my father again. Hope made me abandon everything—what I knew, what made me feel safe, and who I was. In return, I discovered the truth about my nightmares, my nature, and even humanity's mysteries.

I don't regret the fear and pain I endured, both physically and emotionally, because all that was overpowered by acts of love. That love—a painful, lacerating love—had failures, setbacks, and losses, and in the end, kept me alive at all costs. Maybe the only thing I regret is not knowing with certainty what awaits me or what I'm capable of doing now that I'm not a wanderer or a human. Now that I know I'm…

I lift the pen from the paper and use it to scratch the bandage on my head, to calm the itch of my wounds. Had I known it would be so annoying, I would rather have kept my antlers awhile longer before they sawed them off.

I toss aside Laurele's red book, whose blank pages I've been writing on, and I arrange myself a little better on the bed that once belonged to Muata.

Stroking my claw, which a leather glove now covers, I look at my severed antlers adorning the wall. As the only decoration in this cabin, it's a sure sign that I've started my own collection of oddities.

I sigh and try to stand, but my legs and hips hurt, so I lie back down. It's been almost a week, but I'm still suffering from the toll of the cemetery battle, so it's difficult to walk. Also, a part of me will never be able to accept everything that happened that day.

As soon as I left Marie Laveau's grave, Tared covered me with his skin. He carried me to the suburban and assured me that everything was over, that we had won. I was conscious only long enough to see, between whimpers and tears, Father Thunder, still in his bestial form, being brought to Hoffman's car. The old man, as I had predicted, didn't survive, and being the true leader of the tribe, he was the one who Samedi spoke about. One of the wanderers slashed his throat but not before receiving a fatal blow from Blue Cloaked Wolf.

The others barely survived. They reassured me that the fight had ended long before I left the grave, so I want to believe that as soon as I had Baron Samedi at my mercy, his spawns ceased to influence the earthly world. Still, the fact that they endured an endless army of zombies for so many hours is irrefutable proof of the power of my family of wanderers.

They piled the bodies of the false wanderers into the suburban and squashed them as best they could to fit. Hoffman accompanied us to the reserve and stayed until the afternoon of that day for the cremation ritual of Father Thunder, whose ashes were thrown into the swamp, just like they did with the ashes of Mama Tallulah and Muata. I didn't attend, because I was sleeping in one of the cabins, but Tared told me everything as soon as I woke up.

I'm always surprised by how slow time goes in the world of shadows.

The next day, they emptied Muata's home. With the exception of the bed, they burned everything that once belonged to him to make room for me, as is often done in the tradition of the shadowgazer. Each of us is different, and a unique essence imbues every object and acts as a mystical seal, so it's risky for another wanderer to use them.

"Welcome Home, Elisse" on a white cloth hung above the entrance of the cabin when I moved here. On the bed lay my old bag with my father's envelope and my knife. Somehow, they had recovered everything for me.

What shocks me most is that none of us has been brave enough to mourn and accept that nothing will ever be the same again. Since we returned to this swamp, to this village, things have changed in a way that will never make us feel at home again. Our parents are gone. Our grandfather is gone. A piece of ourselves is gone. And no one resents it—except Nashua.

He neither speaks to me nor looks at my cabin, but I don't blame him. I understand the pain he feels when he looks at me will never cease because in me, the indirect cause of his growing agony, he will only find the memory of the people he lost in the battle. Every day, he becomes thinner and more distant. In a matter of days, the three elders, the beings who loved him since he was a child, died. Hardly anyone recovers from something like that. I know because I'll never be able to get over the loss of Mama Tallulah, who I miss more and more every day.

Johanna and Julien have been less reserved. They come eat with me and try to start a conversation, but for days, I didn't say more than a couple of words. At first, they feared Samedi might have ripped out my tongue, but I am complete with all my senses, and now, it's too difficult to open myself to them for two reasons.

First of all, because of my guilt. When I see the girl, I cringe at the wound that marks her collarbones. I know that scar extends to below her navel—a wanderer almost split her in two that night. Julien lost a lot of blood in the battle and almost died too, but luckily, after a couple of days in Johanna's care, he was as good as new.

What surprised me was that Hoffman was unharmed. What's more, Julien assured me that the wanderers never intimidated the guy, and on top of that, he fired shots with deadly precision. Needless to say, he didn't need much help.

Tared and Nashua were able to endure more because of their tremendous strength, but still, they weren't spared from being seriously hurt.

Everyone could have died helping me reach Samedi, and I can't help but feel bad. I can't ignore the fact that Comus Bayou is now in tatters because they protected me, and it's that same demented shame that prevents me from looking them in the eyes.

I open Laurele's red book right to the page where I was just writing. I grip the pen and finish my sentence:

... a monster.

I close my eyes and try to keep my own darkness from devouring me. Luckily, the cabin door swings open. I set the book aside and exhale with relief to see the serene face of Tared.

"Good morning. How do you feel, American boy?" he says with a half smile.

They've given that nickname to me because after I left the middle plane, my accent completely vanished, and now it's impossible to distinguish me from any other Southerner.

"I'm better," I say in a low voice.

He smiles and sits on the edge of the bed. A pleasant tension grows in the air between us.

"Will you be able to walk soon?"

"Just give me a few days, and I'll be useful again."

"I didn't mean that," he says. "For me, you could do nothing but sit around and decorate the cabin. I don't want you to strain, that's all. You look somewhat tired."

"I haven't been sleeping well. I've been having nightmares."

It's half true. Since the battle, every night I relive the bloody and gruesome scenes that bombard my head and prevent me from resting. Worst of all, they're not dreams but memories. I never dream.

Tared wraps his arm around my shoulder. He holds me tight and rests his thick beard atop the crown of my head. Behind the scent of wood and tobacco on his clothes, I smell that peaceful essence of the cold forest that makes him so unique. My mind flies to the day I met Tared in his human form, and a sigh escapes my lips. Gods, how I wish I could bury my face in his shoulder. I want to catch the collar of his flannel shirt in my fists. But seeing the glove that covers my hand and remembering what's hidden under it, I don't.

Tared takes my gloved hand. Wow. Sometimes I forget, in some way, he can read my mind.

"Everything's over," he says to me as he does every day. "What happened that night in the middle plane… let it die there, in that memory. The only thing that matters is that you're here with us."

I cringe with shame because, once again, I had to lie to save my skin. When they asked me how I defeated Samedi, I told them that an ancestor had helped me transform at the last moment, but everything had happened so fast that I didn't know with certainty which one, and that the rebirth of my eyes may have been a gift bestowed for defeating the Loa of Death.

I didn't dare tell them that I let myself be possessed by the same monster that killed Deer Shadowskin or what I had to do to become, in a way, Elisse again. I say that because I feel after everything I've experienced, nothing remains of the boy who stepped foot in New Orleans for the first time, the boy who could hold his head high and say that he had never committed a horrific act. They believed me—and Tared more than anyone. So, remorse eats me every time he looks at me, every time he touches me, and every time his presence takes my breath away.

Suddenly, he wraps his arms around me in a tight squeeze. At first, I hesitate, but in the end, I hug his thick body between my slender limbs, which barely reach around him. The heat of my leader makes me feel like I'm in a burrow, a refuge from the most inclement storm. For me, everything outside the periphery of his arms—Loas, spirits, humans—brings only pain. There is fire inside this wolf, and this wolf is my home.

I wish I could stay like this forever, but Tared loosens his grip. I understand the signal, so I release him, and a pleasant warmth floods my cheeks with both happiness and shame.

"Hoffman is coming," he says quietly.

"Does he know about the money?" I glance at the drawer next to my desk, where I keep the bag I got from Laurele in the middle plane. Tared says the detective doesn't know, so I breathe a sigh of relief. I don't want to give up that money. Not before I know what the hell's going to happen with that warrant for my arrest.

"He wants to see you alone, so I came before him."

"To avoid crossing with him, right?"

He laughs. "You know me pretty well." His smile makes him appear younger for a moment. "I guess I won't see you until tomorrow. I have to stay late at the workshop today because I'm so behind from all the vacation time I've been taking."

Unable to stand it, I laugh at his sarcasm and nod in an attempt to make a sympathetic gesture. He gets up and glances at me one last time before closing the door after he leaves. I stare at the panel of wood for several long minutes, during which the second reason for my silence becomes clearer.

I can't reveal that beyond becoming a horrible monster, I am the target of a being even more terrible than Baron Samedi. The horrors we have seen may only be the tail of the lion, and if there's a being capable of paying the price of the Lord of the Sabbath, the hunt for my head has barely begun. And probably, none of us will make it out alive.

I can't disclose that frightening and magnificent powers have awakened in me because I ate the tongue of the Loa of Death. Or, that I've allowed the bone monster to possess me, and his damn voice whispers to me all the time, demanding that I perform terrible acts, like what I did to recover my own body.

I can't tell him that now, more than ever, I understand what Johanna feels, having to settle for just being—

Crack, crack, crack…

My spine stiffens at that sound.

Crack, crack, crack…

I look slowly toward the back door of the cabin.

Crack, crack, crack…

I open my eyes wide, but my lips remain pressed in a straight line.

Crack…

The cracking is over, and I breathe again. I lean back against the pillow and look up at the ceiling.

Most important of all, I can't tell Tared that I'm no longer alone. Because ever since I set foot in this cabin, in this realm of shadows, that cracking has pursued me from the darkness.

Something is there. And whatever it is, it's coming for me.

✦ ✦ ✦ ✦

HOFFMAN ENTERS MY CABIN with a smoking, stinking cigarette between his lips and frowns. He looks at me and smirks, and I imitate him.

"Son of a bitch, you're still alive?" He drowns a laugh in tobacco smoke.

"At this rate, you'll be the first to die." I point to his vice.

He bursts out laughing, throws the butt on the floor, and crushes it with the tip of his shoe. At least my comment didn't insult him, so I guess that's a good sign.

The detective sits in the chair next to the bed. It's the first time I've seen him since the battle in the cemetery, so I'm glad he's okay. After all, he helped us tremendously.

"How are you doing, kid?" he says in a way I want to believe is genuine interest.

"I'll be fine in a few more days. You know, I just sleep most of the time."

"Like every normal brat."

"Hell, Hoffman, I'm glad to see that you being an asshole wasn't affected by the fight."

The detective laughs, and I follow with a snort.

"It takes more than a pack of freaks to kill me," he says with conviction. "But I have to admit, at this point, I'm glad not to have you as an enemy. You're a tough kid. I almost admire you."

Hoffman's dark eyes stare into mine so intensely that I have to look to the window to escape his scrutiny. I clear my throat and prompt him to talk about irrelevant things for a while, and then finally, he asks the question I've been dreading.

"What happened to Laurele?"

"She stayed on the other side," I say calmly, almost with indifference. "She didn't manage to cross the portal, but I think she was close to dying anyway."

Hoffman leans back and stiffens like a tombstone. I can't help but wonder whether this man believes me or, regardless of the truth, if one day he'll be able to find some peace.

"You haven't had any problems with the police?" I change the subject. "For the damage we did to the cemetery."

"They didn't tell you? I was fired by those imbeciles."

"What? Seriously? I mean, yeah, it was a matter of time because you're such a bastard, but—ouch!"

Hoffman punches me on the shoulder and smiles as a sign he was not offended.

"We made some commotion that night, you know?" he says. "Luckily, there aren't many houses near the cemetery with curious neighbors. My superiors suspected that I had something to do with the destruction of the tombs and even with the theft of the corpses, but since they didn't have enough proof without cameras or witnesses, they couldn't do anything but throw me out."

"That sucks ... Do you know if they asked about my case with the Buddhist center?"

"I don't. But sometimes I call Ms. Fiquette to tell her you're fine."

"Louisa? How's she doing?" I ask in a thin voice.

"Not good," he answers. "She misses you a lot. It wouldn't be a bad idea to call her yourself."

My heart shatters because I miss her too, but my reasons for not having contact with her are much more significant than any hurt. And that's just one of many painful decisions I've had to make.

Even when destiny gave me a full family, completely different from the one I came looking for, nothing and no one will ever be able to fill the emptiness that my father left in my heart. That's why... letting him go is the hardest thing I have ever done in my life. I will never look for him again, because I discovered that whether you're a human, a witch, or a wanderer, being with me is dangerous.

Hoffman nudges my shoulder. "Come on, don't look like that. You shouldn't have any problems returning once it's clear you didn't steal anything. And what an idiot, that Carlton. Money disappears again, and even though you weren't even in the center, he still believed you were to blame."

"Thank you," I say, but he just dismisses it with a wave.

"I don't know any more about the case because I haven't been able to go there myself. My car broke down after loading Mr. Tantoo's weight."

"Tared could give you a hand with that," I say with my voice quivering at the thought of Father Thunder's body. "He's a good mechanic, you know?"

"No, thanks," he says and leans back. "I don't want that asshole, Miller, around my things."

His comment makes me sigh. I can't believe that after all that has happened, he remains on the defensive with Tared.

"Why do you hate him so much? You can't continue to blame him for what happened when he was a policeman. He didn't—"

"Do you really think you know Tared Miller? Has it ever occurred to you, even for a moment, maybe that man isn't who he says he is?"

"No. Tared would never be able to do something like that on purpose, and there's nothing in this world you can say or do to convince me otherwise." I cross my arms to make it clear that I won't discuss this point.

The man raises his hands briefly.

"Hell, his wife must have been crazier than you when she ... "

A beat stops in my heart as the world freezes.

"What?"

"Don't tell me you didn't know. Tared Miller has a wife."

Chapter 48
A Crack in the Middle of Darkness

THE LIGHT OF DAWN touches the reserve, and I unwind from the rearview mirror to let the sun caress my white scales. Gravel crunches beneath the jeep's tires as we enter the village of the Comus Bayou tribe. You park at the kitchen's entrance, where Johanna leaves with the small wooden box of healing potions she's been using on Elisse all week.

You remove the small dreamcatcher from the rearview mirror, and I take the opportunity to curl around your finger. You get out and inspect the soil and trees around the swamp with your lightning eyes. There's not a trace of fog. You smile.

"You're here early, Tared."

Julien approaches with a gesture of not having spent enough time with the moon. You tuck the dreamcatcher in your pocket, but your nervousness shows from miles away. The redhead furrows his brow. Clearly, he saw what you hid away.

"Ah, I ..." You scratch the scruff of your jaw and sigh. You take out the dreamcatcher and show it to the bison wanderer, who looks puzzled. "It's for Elisse."

"Is that the one from your truck? The one your mom gave you?"

"Yeah, I came to give it to him. He said he's been having nightmares, so—Why the fuck are you looking at me like that?"

"It's all right, I get it." Julien pats your shoulder and smiles. "Johanna just went to see him, didn't she?"

"I shouldn't have—"

"Tared! Julien!" The girl's scream cuts through the village.

You and your brother rush to Elisse's cabin. Johanna waits in front of the door. Her face is pale as if she just witnessed a massacre.

"What the hell's going on?" Julien says, and you pull the girl away to enter the cabin.

"Elisse isn't in there." She takes the redhead by the arm and enters the cabin to find you watching a thrilling show.

The boards have been torn from the floor and scattered throughout the room. The back door is stiff on the bed, and the curtains, in shreds, billow through the wide-open window.

Your heart freezes in your throat.

"How'd this happen? I was guarding last night, and I didn't hear a thing," the redhead says.

They look at you with broken eyes while yours remain rooted in the ground. You inspect each corner in your periphery until you capture everything in a single portrait.

I slip off your finger and radiate a warm trail for you to follow. I glide toward the dresser next to the bed, and you pitch your eyes to the half-open drawer where I wave the tip of my tail. A terrible fear climbs up your back. You slide the drawer out slowly and find not a single object in its belly. The money and the boy's belongings have disappeared without a trace.

Madness sows in your head. And I'm certain there's nothing left, in this world or the other, that can tell you what happened to Elisse.

END OF BOOK ONE

Acknowledgments

First, I want to thank the Atlanteans who have held up my world: my parents, the strongest people I know. Many thanks to my mom for being such an exemplary, self-sacrificing, and brave woman, and my dad for inspiring me to be a tenacious, intelligent, and persevering person. You are my role model, and despite the gap that separates our way of thinking, there's always been a bridge built with our love that keeps us close and united. Thank you very much for all your support and for the effort you've made over the years to understand my personal universe. I love you, from here to infinity.

I want to extend my thanks to: my brother Daniel, my best friend, the bravest saiyan of the universe and with whom I've grown in an enviable, extravagant, and fun way. I admire you for your strength and for your desire to get ahead despite the hardships you've faced. Great things await you. Never give up! Ana Redfield, who with her unconditional friendship and amazing talent for music, has been a part of this story in ways that cannot be measured. Thank you for your support, your patience, your care, and the twenty thousand reviews you did for this manuscript. Thank you for everything. I would not have gotten here without you and the family. You know how important that is to me.

Also, a huge thank you to my editor, Matthew Anderson, for having faith in this project, seeing its potential before anyone else and for all the love he has given to the story. This dream would not get very far if it were not for you. Thousands of thanks for the coffee!

Special thanks to all my Dreamcatchers: of Spain (my dear teachers Geshe Tsering Palden and Geshe Ngawang, Amparo Ruiz Cortés, Alberto, Ani-La and the entire family I met in Madrid, and the Tibetan Buddhist center, Thubten Dhargye Ling), the United States (the Moffat family: Elizabeth, María, Gayland, Hollie and Benjamin, for their love and for making my teenage years in Utah a dream come true.) And thanks to all my Dreamcatchers scattered throughout Latin America, and especially, my dear Venezuelan readers.

A special mention for Arturo Pulido, who passed us on the road.

Endless thanks to all the readers, booktubers and bloggers that supported the self-published Spanish edition (but especially, to Naytze and Montse, you have won the heavens).

It has been a long and amazing journey since that wonderful February 28, but we are finally here. Millions of thanks to all!

Lots of love to my #MexicanxInitiative family, especially John, who has been a hero for all of us. Thank you for all your love and support!

All my love and devotion to New Orleans for inspiring a love that can only be seen under the full moon on Bourbon Street.

And finally, but no less important, to you, reader, who has been given a sideways glance into this story from your chair, to delve into this adventure that is just beginning, and to do something invaluable: accompany Elisse. He's just a child, and the worst is yet to come, so thank you, thank you for not letting him go alone. I know he's in good hands.

Thank you all for being part of the Nation. See you in the next book.

About the Author

Mariana Palova (Jalisco, Mexico) is an enthusiastic alchemist who, from time to time, likes to practice a bit of magic. Her writing and art is strongly influenced by her love of nature, occultism, and folk music. Nowadays, her biggest dream is to live peacefully in a comfy cabin in Alaska and continue working as a writer and artist.

www.marianapalova.com

@marianapalova

@MarianaPalovaArtwork

@marianapalova